No Free Man

Graham Potts

EasyRead Large

Copyright Page from the Original Book

First published in 2016 by Pantera Press Pty Limited
www.PanteraPress.com

A Cataloguing-in-Publication entry for this book is available from the National Library of Australia.

Cover and internal design: Xou Creative www.xou.com.au
Typesetting: Kirby Jones
Printed and bound in Australia by Mcpherson's Printing Group
Author Photo by Cooper-Fox

Pantera Press policy is to use papers that are natural, renewable and recyclable products made from wood grown in sustainable forests. The logging and manufacturing processes are expected to conform to the environmental regulations of the country of origin.

SCAN HERE for more on our **GOOD BOOKS DOING GOOD THINGS** programs.

And drop in to **our website: PanteraPress.com** for news about **Graham Potts** and our **other talented authors,** as well as **sample chapters, author interviews** and much, **much more.**

To John Acutt
The English Teacher
The Modern Prometheus

No free man shall be seized or imprisoned, or stripped of his rights or possessions, or outlawed or exiled, or deprived of his standing in any other way, nor will we proceed with force against him, or send others to do so, except by the lawful judgement of his equals or by the law of the land.

Clause 39, Magna Carta
Runnymede, 1215

1

220 KILOMETRES NORTH OF SYDNEY, AUSTRALIA

MONDAY 12 SEPTEMBER

6:00PM AUSTRALIAN EASTERN STANDARD TIME (AEST)

A middle-aged couple sat at a table for two, barely speaking. The man slouched forward on his crossed arms and stared into his drink. The woman, hands in her lap, gazed through the window while fiddling with her wedding band.

No threat.

Three women gossiped loudly in the middle of the pub. Their lined faces were spattered with make-up and their clothes were stretched taut across their sagging skin. Cackling and snorting, their wild gestures threatened to knock over two empty wine bottles.

No threat.

There was a business meeting towards the rear. Five men in threadbare suits and gaudy ties howled at their own jokes and scored the waitresses out of ten. There were shaky hands, stained teeth, and greasy comb-overs lacquered with gel. The centre of mass was a stern man who had been ladled into his suit, a jumble of veins on his temples.

No threat.

Two newlyweds sat beside a window, huddled over uneaten meals. The woman talked and her tattooed husband stroked her hand tenderly. He was left-handed, muscular, his knuckles scarred and his skin tanned. His right leg shook as he tapped the heel of his work boot on the floor over and over again.

He was a potential but unlikely threat.

A young couple sat at the table beside them. The girl wore cheap clothes and expensive jewellery. Her companion was effeminate, his hair styled and his hands manicured. She smiled at him awkwardly, chewing her nails as he stared at her breasts.

No threat.

There was a birthday party in the corner. The guests chirped to each other and cooed at the birthday girl perched at the head of the table while taking photographs with their phones. Tokens of affection were placed before her and impatiently shredded in a shower of ribbon and wrapping paper. It was tedious to witness but it was innocent. None of them deserved to die.

A shadow crossed his table. "Would you like another drink, sir?" the waitress asked.

The ice cubes clinked in his empty glass as he looked at his watch. "No, thank you. Just the bill."

"Of course, but you'll have to pay at the bar." She cleared the table and sashayed away, promptly returning with a frayed leather wallet. He deposited some cash inside and placed it on the table.

Stepan Volkov glanced around the room again but he knew it was clean. Andrei hadn't arrived yet. Volkov could wait outside and finish the job away from the public, though it meant his preparations were largely useless.

He palmed the leather wallet and stood, shrugging his coat on to his shoulders as he walked to the bar. He hesitated, spotting a bright red coat out of the corner of his eye, and then he saw who was wearing it. The woman advanced, her hand raised like a pistol.

"You'd better be here to apologise," she said, stabbing him with her finger. She still looked like a porcelain figurine, he thought, as he paid the barman.

"Have we met?" he asked. The barman returned Volkov's change and retreated.

"Don't be cute," she scowled. A birthday cake emerged from the kitchen and the room paused to gawk. Everyone burst into song, including the staff behind the bar.

"Why would I apologise, anyway?" He leaned closer. "You left me, remember?"

She placed a hand on his chest. "Did you take a blow to the head?"

"More like a knife in the back."

"Will you give it a rest?"

"Relax, Slim," he said, brushing her hand away. "I had no idea you were here."

"Don't call me that, and you're lying."

"Am I?"

"I could always tell when you were lying."

"So you thought." Volkov peeped over her shoulder, and saw Andrei push through the door and study the room. His timing was good: everyone was distracted. Volkov rubbed his eyes. "Listen, I'd like to stand here and argue with you but I've got better things to do."

She took half a step back, her eyebrows arched. The birthday song was nearly finished. "Going home?" she said. "I can drive you to jail."

"Twin share or couple's rates?"

"Don't flatter yourself."

"You're the one who called me cute."

She scoffed, her cheeks glowing red.

Volkov made to move away—Andrei had started to cross the room, reaching into his jacket—but the woman grabbed his wrist.

"If you think—" Volkov ignored her and watched Andrei draw a pistol from his coat, "—I'm letting you out of this room…" Her voice trailed off as she realised Volkov had handcuffed her to the bar.

"Don't take it personally, Slim." Volkov pried her hand away.

The cake was laid before the birthday girl. Volkov moved into Andrei's path, palming a small remote control. Andrei's brow furrowed, his gun dangling uselessly by his side.

The candles were blown out, people cheered, and Volkov pushed the button. A signal sent, a signal received, and a strip of detcord cut the power with a sharp crack.

2

220 KILOMETRES NORTH OF SYDNEY, AUSTRALIA

MONDAY 12 SEPTEMBER

6:44PM AEST

Constable Leanne Waters sat numbly at the bar, rubbing the red welt on her wrist and staring at the victim's crumpled body. For a while his corpse had been arched backwards over the counter, his face contorted and a large knife jutting from his chest. He'd remained in that position for an uncomfortable period of time, until the clomping of police boots had caused the body to slither down the bar and on to the floor. A small onyx figurine, a black wolf, surveyed the body from its post on the bar.

"I thought I told you to go see the doctor." The police sergeant climbed on top of a stool with a groan. His stomach sagged over his belt buckle as he exhaled.

Waters wanted to pick up the wolf figurine and smash it to pieces. It just sat there, smugly watching the room and ignoring her. She was angry at the wolf but knew that she was really angry at herself for missing an opportunity.

"Are you listening to me?" her sergeant asked. "Leanne?"

"I'm fine," she said, finally looking at her boss.

"You've just been through a traumatic event," he said. "And your wrist looks sore."

"I said I'm fine," she snapped. "I don't need a doctor to grope me and tell me what I already know."

"Grope?" The sergeant sighed and raised his hands in surrender. "Right. I forgot. You don't like to be touched. How about you go home instead?"

"I'm waiting for someone to take my statement," Waters said. She was off duty, which left only two constables to interview the shaken diners. Cahill, the local detective, was on his way.

"Yeah, look, about that." He paused and cleared his throat.

"You don't believe me."

"This is a town of 2000 that is miles away from any major city," he said. "What the bloody hell would a man like that be doing here?"

It was a good question.

The pub was the town's attempt to capture the tourists who passed through on their way to Sydney. It was thought that candles on veneered tables, a sparse array of artificial plants, and garish art from a department store would lure people into town. People did stop by, but that had more to do with the good hamburgers and gourmet pies than the atmosphere.

The locals were friendly, though. Not now, of course. The diners were clustered around the uniformed constables, mumbling at their shoes. Even the haughty businessmen were short of words.

"I don't know what he was doing here yet," Waters admitted.

"If it was him, I'm going to have to pass it along to the federal authorities. I just don't want to cry wolf, you know?"

She glanced at the sergeant, but he didn't seem to realise what he had just said.

"Why did he cuff you, anyway?" the sergeant asked. "Did you threaten him?"

"No. I think he cased the town. He would've known who the cops were."

"You think?"

"Yeah. He would've checked for ways in and out, nearest medical aid, food, accommodation, vehicles, and even the weather."

"You're assuming he's your professional. He could've been an amateur who got lucky."

"Lucky people don't use detcord to sever power to the building. This was planned."

"Maybe."

Waters rocked back on her stool. "Are you serious?"

"This is a country town. Farmers have explosives."

"Detcord," she repeated.

"My brother uses it in the mines all the time."

Waters lowered her gaze to the body on the floor. "This killer stabbed the victim in the heart in the dark with a single blow without hitting the ribcage." She looked up at her boss. "Do you know any miners that can do that?"

"Like I said," the sergeant persisted, "lucky."

Waters let it go. The sergeant didn't know any better. She knew exactly who she was dealing with. Well, she did once.

The door wheezed open behind them and Detective Cahill strode in. The sergeant struggled off his stool to brief him.

Waters sighed and watched the two police officers saunter purposefully into the crowd. Cahill nodded thoughtfully, his head cocked to the side. He pointed at things, gestured at other things, and spoke with the authority of someone who knew exactly what had happened. He then casually approached the body on the floor, kicked it over with his boot, and crossed his arms.

"You see," he declared, "murdered."

"Thank God *you're* here." Waters suddenly wanted a cigarette and reached into her pocket for her bubblegum.

"Do you have something you wish to add, constable?" he asked.

"Don't start her," said the sergeant.

Waters tossed a piece of gum in her mouth and stood up, pulling a pair of latex gloves from her jeans. "Check his pockets." She handed over the gloves and retrieved a set for her own hands.

"Where'd you get those?" her sergeant asked as Cahill knelt beside the body.

"I snatched them from the first-aid kit behind the bar."

"Empty," Cahill said. "No, hang on." He found a cigarette case and held it in his hand. Waters snatched it before he could protest.

Inside were a dozen cigarettes, each one black with a gold filter. There was also a business card. "It's for a nightclub in Moscow called the King's Castle," she said, reading the card.

"How can you read that? It's in a weird language," the detective said.

"It's in Cyrillic. It's Russian."

"Why would he carry that?"

"I don't know yet. It's interesting, though. Our killer works out of the same nightclub." She removed a cigarette and sniffed the tobacco. "Sobranie. This is a Russian brand and fancy too."

"Russian," Cahill said to the sergeant. "I thought you were pulling my leg."

"I told you. Leanne thinks the killer is—what was it again?" he asked, clicking his fingers. "Step-and Ivano-something Vo-vo."

"Stepan Ivanovich Volkov," Waters said through clenched teeth. "They call him Volk, which is Russian for wolf, so most people call him the Wolf. That's why he leaves the trinket behind." She gestured to the stone figurine on the bar.

"Who calls him that? The agency?" Cahill snorted. "How would you know, anyway?"

"I watch a lot of television," she said. "What about a hotel key or something?"

"There's nothing else here." He picked up the pistol. "We probably won't get anything off this either. The serial number has been filed away." The detective carelessly tossed the pistol on the floor and tore off his gloves. "So, what evidence have you got that Mister Vo-vo was here?" he asked, standing up.

"We can get dabs off the handcuffs," Waters said.

"I see, and what about witnesses?" He swept his hand across the pub. "Nobody else seemed to notice the guy. The waitress couldn't even describe him, except to say that he was polite. You're the only person convinced of his identity."

Waters blew a bubble and it popped with a snap. Of all the places she and Volkov could run into each other, why this pub? The obvious conclusion: he was here to kill a man. More precisely, he was here to protect something—or someone—from the man he had killed. He didn't come here to see her. He seemed genuinely surprised that she'd been here. So, who else needed protecting?

The Russian girl must be here.

"They don't even have CCTV here, Leanne," Cahill pointed out.

"Why didn't he do this somewhere more private, anyway?" the sergeant asked. "He's taking a big risk, even without cameras."

"The explosives would've done the trick," Waters explained. "Sever the power, everyone's confused and they freeze. Then kill the guy and duck through the back door." She walked over to the people crowded into the corner of the pub and paced in front of them, inspecting each person in turn.

Waters stopped in front of a young woman from the birthday party, the only one not staring at the floor. Her straw-coloured hair was up and held in place with a long lead pencil. "I like what you've done with your hair," Waters said.

"Thank you," the girl said icily.

"What's your name?"

"Natalie," the girl replied. "Natalie Robinson."

"That's an interesting accent you have, Natalie. Where are you from, originally?"

"Geelong."

"Leave that girl alone," Cahill interrupted. "I already told you that nobody noticed the guy."

"Were any of you girls taking photos?" Waters asked, ignoring Cahill. "Did any of you accidentally get a photo of the man sitting at the table near the bar? Maybe a background shot, or something?"

Robinson crossed her arms while her friends salvaged mobile phones from their bags and started scrolling through images.

Waters turned to Cahill. "Since this town doesn't see the need for surveillance cameras, you'll have to rely on luck." One of the girls called out triumphantly and handed her phone to Waters. She smirked at Cahill. "Congratulations, you've probably got the first real photograph of Stepan Volkov."

"If it's really him," he sneered, squinting at the screen.

"Believe what you want," Waters said. "It's a blurry photo but the detcord, the Russian cigarettes, the business card, and the wolf figurine all add up." She held up the phone. "This photograph will be good for a promotion, I reckon."

"I'll make the call in the morning and see if the agency is interested," the sergeant said, rubbing the back of his neck.

"No," Cahill interjected, crossing his arms. "Make the call now. If we're wrong, then Constable Waters can talk to them."

3

CANBERRA, AUSTRALIA

TUESDAY 13 SEPTEMBER

4:32AM AEST

One hour and eight minutes.

Emily Hartigan tugged her sleeve to cover her watch and shifted uncomfortably in her seat. She crossed her legs and smoothed out her skirt, searching for a distraction. The VIP terminal had four rows of plastic chairs and each row had two lines clipped together in a chain. Each line was back-to-back and each chair was empty, except hers.

The terminal walls were adorned with military memorabilia and framed photographs, signed by politicians and diplomats who had passed through the room and desperately wished to be remembered. Their two-dimensional smiles and frozen handshakes were illuminated by pale fluorescent lights that buzzed loudly, accompanied by the groan of an old vending machine.

A small television was tucked into the corner just below the ceiling and cast a bright light over the terminal. A news program was on the screen, a reporter murmuring softly while showing the same pictures over and over again. A car bomb outside a

Moscow restaurant: twenty-four confirmed dead so far. Stepan Volkov had killed a Russian man in a pub in an Australian country town and escaped. Australia had discovered enough oil off the southern coast to supply the world for fifty years.

Hartigan stared unblinking at the images on the screen. There was vision of Parliament House in Canberra, men in suits beaming, and file footage of oil rigs clinging to the ocean floor. The graphic said "Oil Discovery in Australia" and had a subtitle: "China could be important customer". Hartigan looked away.

She'd been waiting for one hour and ten minutes.

She stood up and paced the private lounge, wringing her hands as she rehearsed her introduction. *It's an honour to meet you, Agent Singh. No, a privilege.* She scowled and turned on the spot, pacing towards the window. Privilege was too cliché. *I look forward to working with you.* She nodded at the carpet. That's better. Keep it simple.

Hartigan squinted through the window, trying to see the plane on the tarmac. Bright orange lights flashed in the dark and she could see the flickering silhouette of a jet but little else. The dim lights of the terminal washed out everything beyond the cold glass and she sighed, staring at her reflection.

There were creases in her blouse, she noticed, and she tried patting them down with her hand. It didn't help, so she buttoned her jacket and tugged on the lapels, trying to cover the wrinkles.

Not perfect, but better.

She untied her hair and it tumbled loose in blonde waves. She did her best to smooth it out before tying it tighter. Good enough, she thought, and she straightened her skirt and tugged at her sleeves.

Hartigan heard a man laugh behind her. She stared at the window and watched a pageant of plain-clothes police march across the glass. There were a dozen of them, some dragging trunks behind them and others manoeuvring trolleys laden with boxes and bags. They ignored her as they walked behind her, heading for the door at the end of the terminal, each one wearing a Gortex jacket emblazoned with bright yellow letters that said "FORENSICS".

"Are you Hartigan?"

She whirled around to see an Indian man with caramel skin and black hair. He spoke with a light Australian twang and his dark almond eyes looked her up and down. "Agent Singh," she sputtered. "I didn't see you there."

"You look like you just fell out of a tumble dryer," he said.

She wanted to point out his cheap suit and the polyester tie that hung loose in his collar but she deflated under his glare, her thoughts unspoken.

Levan Singh thrust his hands into his pockets and studied her curiously. She could hear him jingling keys. Finally, he grunted and said: "Grab your stuff and follow me. I want to be at headquarters before breakfast."

Hartigan collected her suitcase and laptop bag. Singh marched through the exit and she trotted after him, the door bouncing back into her shoulder. She stumbled outside, shivering when the wind swept past her. The sun was slowly clawing over the mountains and she saw an agency sedan idling in a parking space reserved for the disabled.

"Agent Singh," Hartigan began, squinting into the headlights. "I got a phone call from the deputy director at one in the morning and he told me to rush to the airport so—"

"Whoa, wait." Singh stopped abruptly, turning around, and Hartigan nearly walked into him. "The deputy director called you personally?"

"Of course," she replied, frowning. "But he didn't tell—"

"Stop talking, Hartigan." Singh held up his hand.

Hartigan could barely see him but she could still hear him jingling the keys in his pocket.

"You're an analyst."

Hartigan nodded. "I work the Russian desk."

Singh's tie snapped in the wind. "How long have you been with the agency?"

"Two years."

He slapped his tie away before tucking it between the buttons of his shirt. "Were you recruited out of school or did you apply?"

"They offered me a position when I was finishing my master's." She shivered again, peering at the car before looking back at the warm terminal they'd just left.

"What was your thesis about?" Singh asked.

"The potential influence of Eastern European transnational crime on global commerce."

"Eastern Europe. No Kidding."

"Why am I here, Agent Singh?" she asked in exasperation. "I mean, there are forensics guys and agents here, and the plane that dropped me off is still idling on the apron."

"Tell me more about your thesis," Singh said.

Hartigan sighed. "Well, I spent time researching the changing business practices of transnational criminal organisations. Over the years, they've been investing in legitimate businesses to launder money, and their investments are starting to make returns."

"Keep going."

"They have interests in mining, finance, even media, and they have a noticeable influence on international trade."

"How much of an influence?" Singh asked, crossing his arms.

"More than many people realise." She shivered again, hunching her shoulders and shuffling her feet. "The world is a small place and changes to domestic policy can have global effects, especially when it comes to trade. We spend most of our time and effort analysing other governments but we ignore criminal interests. I mean, there are huge criminal organisations that wield enormous economic power and we should consider engaging them in—"

"You said mining, finance, and media," Singh said, cutting her off. "What about energy?"

"Sure. They have investments in oil, gas, and coal," Hartigan said. "About seventy per cent of Russia's oil exports fund organised crime."

"Where does the oil go?" Singh asked.

"Mostly Europe."

"China?"

"The relationship is precarious and has been for years."

"What do you mean?"

"Russia isn't the most reliable supplier. The Eastern Siberia-Pacific Ocean oil pipeline is still under construction but there have been delays, and China needs oil. Africa isn't keeping up and the Middle East is falling out of favour. Russia is the only source left for China but there are some issues. Beijing is negotiating with the Kremlin at the moment."

"The Kremlin?"

"Energy companies are mostly state-owned. Criminal elements may have invested substantial amounts of money in the wells and the mines, but they don't have enough political influence to dictate trade policy." She shrugged. "Not in a boardroom, anyway."

"These negotiations with China..."

"The Russians made an offer to increase exports but they want China to pay more for transport," Hartigan said. "They won't budge on their price and Beijing has until noon Friday, our time, to announce their decision." She shrugged again. "But, if they want oil bad enough, I guess they'll pay the price."

The driver emerged from the parked sedan and tapped the face of his watch.

"Please, Agent Singh. What's all this about?" Hartigan asked.

"Call me Lee." He turned and walked towards the driver, jerking his thumb at Hartigan. The driver rushed over and snatched Hartigan's suitcase, dragging it to the back of the car and tossing it into the boot.

"I want you back on that plane," Singh said to Hartigan. "I need you to collect someone for me."

"Who?"

Singh opened the passenger door. "A police constable called Leanne Waters." He ducked into the car and emerged clutching a red folder. "Bring her back with you. Read this, and you'll understand why." He handed her the folder and climbed into the car.

She held the folder to her chest. "But Agent Singh—"

He slammed the door.

Emily Hartigan adjusted her laptop bag on her shoulder.

I look forward to working with you.

The sedan's tyres chirped as the car sped away from the kerb, winding its way towards the highway. Her shoulders slumped and she turned around, trudging back to the terminal.

4

JAKARTA, INDONESIA

TUESDAY 13 SEPTEMBER

4:06AM WESTERN INDONESIAN TIME (WIB)

The security guard opened the door and was startled to see a stranger standing in the alleyway.

"Sorry," Volkov said, smiling around the cigarette dangling from his lips. "I couldn't sleep and came out for a walk." He held up his hand to show a packet of smokes. The security guard's shoulders relaxed when Volkov offered him the packet.

"That's very kind of you," the guard said. He removed his jacket and placed it neatly on the concrete steps to use as a cushion. He sat down with a weary groan.

"Long night?" Volkov asked, lighting the guard's cigarette.

"Not too bad," the guard said, nodding gratefully. "Yours?"

"Worse than you know," Volkov grumbled, dragging deeply. He tilted his head back, noting that all the windows above them were dark, all the balconies empty.

"Have you been out here for a while?" the guard asked.

Volkov pointed to the security camera above the door. "You weren't watching me?"

The Indonesian smiled crookedly. "No, that's broken. You, ah—I felt." He paused and absently rubbed his ear. "*Keheranan*—in English."

Surprise. That's what the young man meant. Volkov had surprised him, but he feigned misunderstanding, forcing the Indonesian to reluctantly act out his reaction. The security guard made a face and Volkov smiled. "Oh, I surprised you," he said. "Sorry."

"That's okay." The tobacco crackled, flaring brightly as he sucked on the filter. "So, you can't sleep?"

Volkov shook his head. "I'd like to sleep," he said, rubbing a hand over his face. "I was here in Jakarta yesterday but I had to leave for Australia in a hurry and be back here before dawn."

"Well, it's just after four. You made it."

"Yes, but when my boss finds out why I left Jakarta, I could be in a bit of trouble." The alley was quiet. There were no cars on the street, and the fence that ran along the length of the lane hid them from the neighbouring buildings.

"I know what you mean," the guard snorted, pointing to the security camera above the door. "We disabled that camera because our boss wouldn't let us have smoke breaks. We sneak out when it's not busy and cover each other."

"You guys can't even have five minutes of peace to have a smoke?"

"It's worth it. We get paid okay."

"What about the people?" Volkov asked, waving his hand across the hotel grounds.

"The other security men are good. And then there are the tourists."

"Not so good?"

"They are bastards," he conceded, grinning. "They're all skinny white women and fat men with sunburn. They don't even have manners for the waiters and cooks."

"I don't get it myself," Volkov said. "It's not hard to be polite. We're guests in your country, after all."

The Indonesian smiled and butted out his smoke, tossing it in the ashtray by the steps.

"Is your shift nearly over?" Volkov asked, stamping out his cigarette.

"It finishes at dawn," the guard replied, standing up and stretching. "Will you be out here long?"

Volkov shook his head. "I was just about to go in."

The guard threw him a small salute and bowed his head. "Well, thank you for the smoke."

"You're welcome."

The Indonesian man turned away, scooping up his jacket and tossing it over his shoulder while drawing the swipe card from his pocket.

"Before you go," Volkov began, and the Indonesian turned around.

Volkov rapped his knuckles under the guard's chin, paralysing his voice. The young Indonesian dropped his swipe card and turned away, his fingers reaching for his throat. Volkov kicked the back of the man's legs and he fell to his knees, his face smacking into the brick wall. Volkov whipped a garrotte from his jacket and wrapped it around the guard's neck. He drove his knee into the Indonesian's back and rocked forward. The man reached for the garrotte with one hand while trying to push away from the wall with the other.

Volkov held the garrotte tight in his hands until the security guard's arms fell to his sides. The Indonesian's body flopped to the ground and Volkov crouched and collected the swipe card.

The Wolf silently studied the alleyway. Nobody else was there. There were no other sounds. The place was dead.

5

MOSCOW, RUSSIA

TUESDAY 13 SEPTEMBER

1:15AM MOSCOW STANDARD TIME (MSK)

Nikolay Korolev rolled a silver coin across the top of his fingers and watched the strip drift past his window. Neon signs poured light on to the street, brightening the darkest of corners, luring the bleary-eyed into artificial daylight. Prostitutes, drug pushers, thugs and addicts dotted the pavement. Some of the men huddled on concrete staircases or in the faded light of alleys, passing joints and pills and rubbing their hands together. The ladies were propped against the walls, their fur coats billowing like curtains.

He saw the parade of armoured luxury sedans squatting on the road, guarded by hefty men with guns under their vests. Meanwhile, the smugglers had parked their trucks in the alleyway beside his club, their illegal cargo vacuum-sealed in plastic and obscured by a load of horse manure.

Korolev's driver eased the car to a stop outside the King's Castle. It was his club, his place of business and, sometimes it seemed, his home. His bodyguards fell in beside him as he strode up the steps, the crowd parting before them as his boots pounded on the bare concrete. The door was held open for him and he shrugged off his coat, holding it in an outstretched hand. It was taken wordlessly as he walked.

The strip club was a fug of cigarette smoke, sweat and sex. The music throbbed and women shimmied against poles on stage, theatrically removing their clothes and dousing each other with soapy water and glitter. Other naked women sat on the laps of *boyeviks* and killers, smiling at them and stroking their stubbled hair while the men groped and sniggered.

Again, the crowd parted for Korolev and he walked through to a guarded doorway. The sentry whispered a message in his ear, and Korolev nodded curtly as he opened the door. Inside was the blacklit VIP room, where men with expensive jewellery and tattooed arms snorted lines off the stomachs of naked women who were already high. Hard men with bare chests sat on the edge of a plush sofa, chomping on cigars and cleaning weapons, while others wearing silk shirts played a game of high-stakes Poker under lamps at the rear of the room. All of them bowed their heads towards Korolev but he ignored them, shoving his coin into his pocket and plunging into his office. His bodyguards took up their positions on either side of the door, watching warily.

"You better have a good reason for being in here," Korolev said.

Maxim sat on the sofa, hunched over a computer tablet in his lap, an untouched glass of water on the coffee table in front of him. The screen cast an anaemic glow upon Maxim's strained expression, while his fingers scraped across the glass like the blades of a rake. He looked up at Korolev, his expression guarded. "You wanted a report," he said weakly.

Korolev grunted, tugging at the knot in his tie and unbuttoning his collar. "Be quick. I have work to do." He took off his jacket and tossed it over the arm of the sofa, noticing that the television was on but the sound was down. Ticker tape scrolled across the bottom of a news program while a blonde woman silently mouthed the headlines.

"Australia has announced their oil discovery," Maxim said, dipping his bald head towards the television.

"I don't pay you to parrot the news, Maxim."

"The announcement was earlier than expected."

"What is the reaction from the Kremlin?"

"Predictable."

Korolev ran his finger along the scar on his jaw and turned away, heading to the bar in the corner. "Do we have word from Australia?"

"The Bear reports that everything is on schedule."

Korolev poured a glass of vodka, strolled to his desk, and sat down in his leather chair. He peered over his glass at the television and saw footage of a car bomb that had exploded in Moscow. Twenty-four people were dead and many more were injured. It was the third bombing in two weeks.

"The president is starting to feel the pressure," Maxim said. "The people are tired of the bombings."

"Has she released a statement?" Korolev retrieved the coin from his pocket and studied it.

"She hasn't proposed any action, yet."

Korolev shrugged and rolled the coin across his hand.

"This is a big gamble, Nikolay," Maxim said.

"This is not a game of chance, Maxim." Korolev watched the coin tumble over his fingers. "This is chess. The moves are calculated."

"If the China deal goes through on Friday, we stand to make millions," Maxim said. "Perhaps billions." He cleared his throat. "Even if the deal fails, there are other countries in the world that will take Russian oil."

"This is not up for discussion." Korolev gulped down a mouthful of vodka. "Move on, Maxim."

Maxim shifted on the sofa and looked down at his tablet. "One of our assets informed me that an American operative is sniffing around. He's looking for Volkov."

"Have him picked up." The television caught Korolev's eye and he paused, snatching his coin and holding it in his fist.

"Do you want him interrogated?" Maxim looked up, his mouth falling open as he watched the news report. The footage showed uniformed police standing outside a bar in Australia, shrugging at each other. A body bag was wheeled past on a trolley and lifted into the back of a van. The graphic at the bottom of the screen was red and bold: Stepan Volkov had killed a man in Australia.

Korolev rose to his feet and pointed at the screen with his glass. "Where the fuck is he?" He slammed his fist down on the desk and turned to Maxim, his face red. "Where is Volkov?"

Maxim was already pawing at the screen of his tablet. "It can't be true, Nikolay," he said with a trembling voice. "Volkov is supposed to be in Jakarta carrying out a—"

"I know where he's *supposed* to be!" Korolev yelled. "Find him and find out what he was doing in Australia."

"I just have to—"

"Find him!" Korolev roared.

6

220 KILOMETRES NORTH OF SYDNEY, AUSTRALIA

TUESDAY 13 SEPTEMBER

8:08AM AEST

"So what did we learn today?" Leanne Waters asked.

One of the kids was attempting to tie his own shoelaces, his brow deeply lined as if he were solving an algebraic equation. Another boy with a runny nose was terrorising a spider in his palm, tearing its legs off one at a time, and a small girl with glasses was chewing her hair and staring vacantly at the wall. Waters hadn't exactly managed to hold their attention.

"Look both ways before crossing the street," she began, and the children joined in, droning in unison. "Avoid talking to strangers and always trust the police to help."

And don't pick fights with contract killers in bars.

She surveyed the children sitting cross-legged at her feet. "I hope you guys learned something this morning," she said, and they all applauded her. Jellybeans were given out and Waters ended the show with an outdoor demonstration of the police car's siren.

The teacher dismissed the children, who disappeared in a puff of dust to play cops and robbers, tumbling off the playground equipment and scraping their knees in scuffles over who was "arrested".

"Thanks for coming by," the teacher said. "It gives the boys something to interest them and the girls a positive role model."

"Well, it was fun to visit," Waters said, cramming equipment into the boot of the car. It wasn't really. Children made her uncomfortable. They could be too grabby. "It's much better than lecturing teenagers. I always end up in an argument with a pimply adolescent about whether the police are agents of oppression, funded by a government that is an instrument of corrupt capitalists who exploit workers and the environment." She slammed the boot shut.

The teacher sniffed and salvaged a ratty tissue from the sleeve of her cardigan. "Oh, yes. Some of those teenagers should be locked up. And their hair." She scoffed and blew her nose. "They should put them all in the army and teach them some manners."

"Right, and how to shoot people," Waters added, watching young boys make rat-a-tat sounds while pointing their fingers at the girls.

"They'd turn up on time and have respect. Mark my words."

"Anyway, I must be getting back," Waters said, tapping the face of her wristwatch.

"Of course. Thanks again." The teacher stuffed her tissue into her sleeve and crossed her arms, walking primly back to her classroom to prepare for the next lesson.

Waters shook her head, turning away just as Detective Cahill's sedan entered the car park, crunching over gravel and squealing to a stop near Waters' cruiser. Cahill climbed out of the car and hitched up his jeans before trotting to the passenger side and opening the door. A young blonde woman stepped out of the car and smiled gratefully at him. Waters rolled her eyes and leaned against the bonnet of the cruiser.

"Leanne," Cahill said, bowing his head slightly.

"What are you doing here? Shouldn't you be investigating the footy team's missing pie warmer?"

"Yes, well, that case is more complicated than you think." He stood aside with a sweep of his hand. "This is Agent Emily Hartigan." Hartigan was slender with delicate features and wore an unbuttoned woollen coat, a long pencil skirt, and a wrinkled long-sleeved blouse buttoned to the nape of her neck.

"Hi," Hartigan said, stepping cautiously through the gravel. She beamed brightly and extended a manicured hand.

Waters dismissed the offered hand. "I don't like to be touched, Agent Hartigan."

Hartigan pulled her hand away, hiding it behind her. "I'm sorry. I didn't know."

"Someone should've told you," Waters said, glaring at Cahill.

He coughed. "Emily's here to take you to Canberra."

"Why? Did I win the Lions Club raffle?"

He sighed impatiently.

"Can I see some ID?" Waters asked.

"Of course." Hartigan plunged her hand into the pocket of her coat and retrieved her badge and ID, handing them to Waters.

"Cute photo," Waters said, studying the ID. "Grade seven?"

"Waters!" Cahill cried.

"Well, she does look like she strayed from the playground," Waters observed, dipping her head towards the children running in circles on the grass.

"I'm sorry about this," Cahill said to Hartigan. "She's usually more cooperative."

Hartigan smiled awkwardly and looked at her feet.

Waters returned the ID and badge and drummed her fingers on the bonnet of the police car. "You're an analyst, not an agent."

Hartigan stepped back. "How did you—"

"You're not wearing," Waters said, gesturing to Hartigan's coat.

Cahill pointed a limp finger. "Hey, yeah."

"You just noticed that?" Waters asked in disbelief.

"I thought all agents had to wear pistols," Cahill said, ignoring Waters. "Since those attacks during the war, I mean. Didn't one of your guys get shot while dropping his kids off at football practice?"

"He was a field agent," Hartigan said. "Analysts aren't as recognisable because we don't venture outside much." She shrugged. "I've had the same training as a field agent but I don't have to carry a weapon. The risk is low."

"Should I come back when you two are done?" Waters asked.

Cahill looked away and cleared his throat. "Perhaps we should discuss the case," he said.

"Of course," Hartigan said, focusing her attention on Waters. "I'm here about the other night. In the pub. With Volkov."

"Oh, that." Waters plucked a packet of bubblegum from her pocket. "I'd already forgotten about that." She paused and eyed the detective. "You didn't even believe that it *was* Volkov."

"Read the statements: the guy didn't even have an accent," Cahill said defensively. "What the hell was I supposed to think?"

"If you need step-by-step instructions on how to use your brain," Waters said, pointing with her gum packet, "then you should consider a new profession."

Cahill exhaled through his nose, explaining through a clenched jaw: "Emily's going to take you into protective custody."

Waters tore the packet of gum in her hand. "I can look after myself."

"It's not negotiable."

"It rarely is." She tossed a piece of gum into her mouth.

Cahill groaned. "Jesus, Leanne. Could you act professional for more than a few minutes?"

"Volkov isn't interested in me," Waters said. "This was a hit on a stray *boyevik.*"

"A what?" Cahill asked.

"Boyevik," Hartigan interrupted. "It's Russian for warrior. It's what the *Organizatsiya* calls their gangsters." She swept the hair from her eyes and studied Waters curiously.

"The origami-what?" Cahill asked.

"The Russian Mafia," Waters explained.

He held up a finger. "Other than the card and some illegally imported cigarettes, we have no evidence tying the victim to—"

"Andrei Sorokin was a muscle-head who worked for an Australian energy company doing security," Waters said. "Titan Energy, the same company poised to suck our newly discovered oil out of the seabed. He assaulted his supervisor and got fired. Then he drifted through Russian nightclubs on the east coast looking for work." She shrugged. "It seems that Moscow didn't like his style and got rid of him."

Cahill shook his head. "How did you—"

"Google."

"But I never told you the victim's name."

"You should probably change your log-on password to something more complicated than 'password1'."

His face flushed. "You broke into my computer?"

"Could you give us a moment alone, Detective Cahill?" Hartigan asked with a kind smile.

"But she..." He cursed and threw his hands in the air, retreating to his car. "Fine."

"Was he getting on your nerves, too?" Waters asked.

"He seems nice," Hartigan said.

"Then why send him away?"

"Because I don't believe conflict is constructive."

Waters tilted her head. "I see."

"Our plane leaves in a couple of hours," Hartigan said.

"*Your* plane," Waters said. "You don't need me."

"But you might need us," Hartigan said.

Waters snapped her gum against the roof of her mouth. "Like I said, Volkov isn't coming to kill me. He'd have to kill everyone in that pub, too."

"You were the only one who recognised him," Hartigan said. "You were also the only one to report him to us. That kind of thing gets you noticed."

"Stop it," Waters said. "You're making me blush."

"It's not a joke, Leanne." Hartigan rubbed her forehead. "Look, you're right. This does look like a simple gang hit. Andrei Sorokin was a small-time thug who wanted to make it big, but he kept attracting too much unwanted attention. Russian operations in Australia are still fragile so they dispose of liabilities quickly." She dipped her head. "*You* are now giving the Russians *more* unwanted attention."

"I'm small potatoes, Agent Hartigan."

"Maybe, but it doesn't matter. That business card you found is for the King's Castle. It's a nightclub in Moscow owned by Nikolay Korolev, the leader of the biggest criminal syndicate in Eastern Europe."

"So?"

"A while ago, a drunken man relieved himself in an alleyway in Moscow. He didn't know he was urinating against the wall of Korolev's nightclub." Hartigan swept her hair from her eyes. "Korolev removed the man's bladder with an acetylene torch."

Waters cringed.

"Korolev believes that letting the small things slide makes him look weak."

"It's hard to piss on his nightclub from Australia," Waters pointed out.

"Living on the other side of the world won't save you," Hartigan said. "It didn't save Sorokin."

"Sorokin is different. He's Russian."

"Korolev has issued contracts against Australians before."

Waters snorted. "Bullshit."

Hartigan shook her head in exasperation. "The last Australian to cross Korolev was a thief named Simone Elliot."

"Who?"

"They called her the Serpent, and she decided to steal some of

Korolev's art while it was in transit through Europe."

"A gangster with art?" Waters rolled her eyes. "What was it, his collection of porn magazines?"

Hartigan snapped her fingers. "Listen to me, okay? This happened a few years ago. He sent a dozen assassins after her. Her fence, her contacts, and her friends were all butchered and the Serpent just disappeared."

"So she's slippery."

"Gone, Leanne," Hartigan said, cutting the air with her hand. "This was one of the world's best thieves, wanted for stealing millions of dollars in gold bullion, cash, art, and jewellery."

Waters shifted against the car. The volume of Hartigan's voice climbed higher.

"She didn't escape Korolev," Hartigan continued. "She didn't go underground or retire or hide. She disappeared. She vanished."

"Was it Volkov?"

"Maybe," Hartigan said. "We don't know. The killer or killers didn't stick around."

"Right," Waters mumbled. "Of course."

Hartigan pressed her lips together and looked up at the sky. "I'm sorry," she said. "I didn't mean to raise my voice."

"It's okay."

"No, it's not. It was unprofessional. I just..." She kicked at the gravel with her shoe.

"This is your first time in the field, isn't it?"

"Is it that obvious?" Hartigan didn't wait for an answer. "I've read about this stuff," she said. "I've read a lot, but the criminal world has always just been an abstract concept, you know? And now..."

"You're scared," Waters said.

"Yes," Hartigan confessed. "I am, and for good reason. Volkov has used long-range sniper shots, explosives, knives, poisons, garrottes, and, on one occasion, powdered uranium."

"Uranium?"

"It was sprinkled on the target's coat and he didn't notice anything until he developed symptoms of leukaemia. The authorities found an onyx wolf in the hospital room after the man died."

Waters looked down at her shoes, slowly chewing her gum.

"Most of the time he uses a pistol. He usually triple-taps: two to the chest and one to the head." Hartigan tapped the side of her head to illustrate the point.

"Jesus," Waters said.

"But what scares me most of all is that most of his victims die before they even realise he's in the room.

Imagine that," Hartigan said, gazing at the children. "Just watching television, or sleeping, or reading a book, or having a nice meal, and bam. No right of reply. No plea bargain. No second chance." She shrugged. "Just dead."

Waters frowned at the analyst.

"I can cuff you and make you come with me but I don't want to do that," Hartigan said. "You're a smart woman and you know Volkov might be coming for you. We can protect you."

"Look, I—"

"You mean nothing to him, Leanne. Come with me to Canberra."

Waters absently rubbed her ear and blew another bubble.

I mean nothing to him.

The bubble popped with a snap.

7

CANBERRA, AUSTRALIA

TUESDAY 13 SEPTEMBER

9:00AM AEST

Lee Singh checked the time on his wristwatch. He stood up and paced the deputy director's office, briefly studying the framed photographs and certificates before pausing in front of the fish tank.

Singh bent over, staring into the clear water. A small ceramic scuba diver was buried up to his chest in the pebbles at the bottom of the tank. He seemed welded to the floor, painfully unaware that he was out of air. Meanwhile, a large fish drifted in clumsy circles and a dozen small fish scurried meaninglessly from one side of the tank to the other.

Singh straightened up when he heard the door open.

"I didn't know you were waiting," the deputy director said, pausing in the doorway.

"You told me you wanted to see me," Singh said, returning to his chair.

"Of course, I just didn't expect you here this early." The deputy director marched behind his desk, dumping down an armful of paperwork and tossing his pen on top of the pile. "Coffee?"

"I'd like to get straight to it."

He frowned and sat down behind his desk. "Okay."

"A high-level hit man from Moscow kills a low-level thug in a town so small that you could sneeze and blow it off the map, and you call in an academic who read a couple of books and wrote a thesis, waking me up before dawn to meet her at the airport because you're worried about oil."

The deputy director removed his glasses and chewed the tips. "Your question?"

"What mistake are you trying to cover up?"

"No mistake." The deputy director reached into his drawer for a cleaning cloth. "We simply have a small trade issue."

"How high are the stakes?"

The deputy director puffed on the lenses of his glasses and gently cleaned them with the cloth. "Before our oil became public knowledge, the National Security Committee asked each intelligence agency to determine whether the discovery would have an adverse impact on foreign policy. Every asset in every embassy around the world tapped their contacts to gauge reactions and the analysis concluded that the effects would be positive, broadly speaking." The deputy director eyed Singh. "The prime minister personally asked for my assessment regarding the risk posed by transnational criminal elements."

Singh arched an eyebrow. "All of them?"

"He's particularly anxious about the Russians."

"Any assessment would be inconclusive," Singh said. "We don't have the sources."

"You underestimate me, Lee." The deputy director put his glasses on. "I told him that the *Organizatsiya* possessed neither the reach nor the resources to pose a threat." He folded his arms. "I went on to say that I found the possibility ludicrous."

"And then Volkov killed someone in our country."

"The prime minister hit the panic button and a representative will be here at ten."

Singh slouched in his chair. "So you want me to cram the worms back in the can."

"Discreetly, yes."

"Do you want to bring me up to speed?"

The deputy director drummed his fingers on the desk and took a deep breath. "Once our oil operations are up and running, China could become our largest customer. Sales hinge on the future of Sino-Russian oil trade, which will be determined—"

"—Friday." Singh tugged at the knot in his tie. "You're the second person to mention that to me today."

"Russia wants to increase their oil exports and has proposed a deal. Beijing will publicly announce their decision at ten o'clock in the morning on Friday, which will be noon here."

"Will China choose us?"

"We're not sure," the deputy director said. "Titan Energy won the rights to drill but their operations aren't fully developed. We can't produce enough oil to satisfy China's needs yet."

"So they're going to agree to Russia's proposal?"

"It depends on Beijing's strategic oil stocks. If China doesn't have enough oil to tide them over until we are up and running, they may not have a choice."

"If they reject the Kremlin's offer, the *Organizatsiya* will lose billions," Singh noted.

"The prime minister believes the *Organizatsiya* will act to prevent that loss," the deputy director said. "He believes they will attempt to force us out of the market with great violence. I can't convince him otherwise."

"Well, tell him we're safe until China makes a decision."

"Why's that?"

"The *Organizatsiya* won't act before then," Singh said. "If Beijing accepts Moscow's offer, then the *Organizatsiya'* s income is secure, and any action against us would be unnecessary." He shrugged. "Why start a war when you don't need to fire a shot to win?"

The deputy director stretched his lips into a smile. "Good point." He rose from his chair and started pacing the office. "Still, I'm inclined to stand by my original assessment." He traced out a large circle on his rug as he walked, his hands joined behind his back. "A pack of gold-toothed goons are hardly a threat to our security."

"I think they could surprise you if this deal goes the wrong way."

"For the prime minister's sake, I'm giving them the benefit of the doubt," he conceded. "I even ordered uniformed police to obtain information from persons of interest within the Russian immigrant community."

Singh rolled his eyes. "They'd be tight-lipped and they're too remote and low-level to know anything of significance."

"Yes, but it's worth a try." He turned around, retracing his steps. "Personally, I believe that Volkov is the key. He's intimately involved with the leadership of the *Organizatsiya* but he isn't bound by the same rules. His loyalty is bought. He gets paid well, which implies that his leadership worries about losing him."

Singh stroked his chin. "Do you want Volkov caught or killed?"

"I want to know what he was doing in Australia." He paused midstride. "Discreetly, Lee."

"You said that already." Singh crossed his legs, resting his foot on top of his knee. "Volkov's appearance probably isn't related to our oil trade."

"Tell me why."

"Volkov chose a strange target if his goal was to scare us."

"Discuss that with Agent Hartigan," the deputy director said. "See what she thinks. It might sound ridiculous, but she's the only person in government who knows anything about the *Organizatsiya* and their interests, so use her."

"I don't want her in the field."

"She's had the same training as the field agents. She's ready."

"She lacks experience."

"But is proficient at hand-to-hand combat—"

"In a controlled environment."

"—and outscored *you* in marksmanship."

Singh's jaw twitched.

The deputy director grunted with satisfaction. "You of all people know that—"

"She might freeze up," Singh said. "Training doesn't always help, and based on her academic history, I reckon she'll hesitate before pulling the trigger."

The deputy director eyed Singh. "You read her paper?"

Singh nodded, using his cuff to rub a mark off his shoe. "A couple of years ago. I had to get her to remind me what it was about." He paused, looking up at his supervisor. "Did you?"

The deputy director dismissed the question with a languid wave.

"She's too green for this," said Singh.

"She's all we have," the deputy director argued, sweeping his arm across the window. "Every other academic and analyst in this country dropped the ball on Russia. She picked it up and ran with it."

Singh muttered a curse, tugging at the hem of his trousers. "Look, bottom line: Volkov killed a scumbag in a small pub. This has nothing to do with oil."

"There was another hit last night."

Singh uncrossed his legs and put both feet on the floor. "Volkov?"

"It looks like he caught a flight to Jakarta as soon as he was finished with Andrei Sorokin." He brushed his sleeve with his hand. "There were no scheduled passenger flights between Sydney and Jakarta, so he probably chartered a private jet."

"That's not very inconspicuous."

"That crossed my mind."

"Who was the target?"

"Dr Marco Belo, a Timorese politician. Dr Belo was lobbying for a redrawing of the maritime border between East Timor and Australia," the deputy director explained. "Titan Energy has gas wells in the area."

"That doesn't look good, does it?"

"Which fuels the prime minister's anxiety," the deputy director said. "Everyone knows it's in our interest to stop a redrawing of the border. A UN ruling would force Titan to surrender Australian gas wells to the Timorese."

"So you had the man killed?"

"No, Lee," the deputy director replied impatiently. "Jesus Christ."

"Everyone will believe we had something to do with it."

The deputy director held up his finger. "It's just a coincidence and nothing more."

"Intelligence analysts don't believe in flukes." Singh hunched forward, his elbows on his knees, his fingers steepled. "Nobody expected the government to advertise that area of ocean as open for tender." He sat up straight. "And Titan Energy was a small company with the capital to match. They shouldn't have won the tender for exploration, let alone a licence for production. There are lots of bigger companies in a better financial position to exploit the reserves."

"The National Audit Office investigated the tender process," the deputy director countered. "They didn't find anything."

"That doesn't mean there was nothing to find," Singh observed. "And the calls for a Royal Commission died pretty quickly too." He smirked. "My bet is that Titan's CEO has something that greased the wheels. It wouldn't surprise me if *he* put a hit on this Timorese guy."

The deputy director held up his hands. "Or," he said impatiently, "it could be the *Organizatsiya'* s attempt to make Titan look dirty."

Singh nodded slowly and stood up, joining the deputy director at the window. The sky was grey, smothering every flicker of sunlight, and the earth was dark. The traffic was silently winding its way through the streets, a stream of white and red circles drifting through the city's roundabouts. "Look, even with the hit in Timor, this doesn't look like a prelude to an attack."

"I'm with you, Lee." The deputy director turned to his agent. "So let's prove it to the prime minister."

"I didn't say there *wouldn't* be an attack," Singh said. "I just said that Volkov's appearance is likely to be unrelated."

"Just make it all go away before noon Friday."

Singh checked his watch. "Seventy-five hours."

"Seventy-four hours and forty-two minutes, Lee. Don't forget it."

Singh shoved his hands into his pockets and jingled his keys.

"Hopefully, the young constable will be enough to lure Volkov out of hiding," the deputy director said.

"Lure?"

"You heard me, Lee," the deputy director said. "I won't be more explicit than that."

"I see."

"Volkov's words will convince the prime minister that we are safe to sell oil. I can't tell you how important it is that we capture this man."

"Making omelettes. Understood," Singh said, nodding. "Is there anything else?"

"Yes," the deputy director said. "I need Hartigan to prepare a brief."

"Who is she briefing?" Singh asked.

"She'll be delivering it at Military Headquarters tomorrow," he said, leaning against the windowsill. "Everyone is going to be there. Get her to pitch the information accordingly."

"You don't want me to fill her in, do you?"

The deputy director sucked in his lips and squinted.

"Good move," Singh said, turning to leave. "I don't think she'd like hearing this stuff, anyway."

"Speaking of which—" the deputy director began.

Singh stopped.

"—I need you to remember who the good guys are, Lee."

"Do you want to put that in writing?" he asked, turning his head.

"Your theories about Titan Energy and their business practices do not follow you out of this office. They are on *our* side and the Russians are working against us."

"This isn't my first day." Singh grinned. "I just wanted you to know that I know."

"Cut it out, Lee," the deputy director warned. "Ensure that Titan isn't the subject of this investigation or your career is over."

8

MOSCOW, RUSSIA

TUESDAY 13 SEPTEMBER

7:36AM MSK

Grigoriy took a deep breath when Korolev's office door slammed behind him. He walked quickly through the VIP room and out into the thrumming chaos of the club, suddenly feeling nauseous. The club was a dark forest of writhing bodies that flashed beneath blinding strobe lights and swayed to pounding music. Grigoriy threaded his way between towering men and giggling girls, assaulted by the stench of alcohol, tobacco smoke, and sweat. He thought he was heading to the exit but found himself standing at the bar.

"What will you have, Grigoriy?" the barman asked.

Grigoriy patted his unsettled stomach. "A glass of milk."

"What?" the barman shouted, cupping his hand to his ear.

"A glass of milk!" Grigoriy yelled.

The barman grinned and set about finding a carton of milk.

Grigoriy felt an arm wrap around his waist and his head snapped around to see who was behind him. "Anna?" The nineteen-year-old girl was wearing a schoolgirl's uniform with stockings and suspenders. Her skirt was short and her blouse was knotted over her breasts. She plucked a lollipop from her mouth and stood on the tips of her toes, putting her lips against his ear. One of her plaited pigtails tickled his nose.

"What are you doing here so early in the morning, Grigoriy?" Anna asked. "I thought you liked to sleep in."

"I had a meeting," he replied, nodding towards Korolev's office.

The barman interrupted them, setting a glass of milk on the countertop. He held up his hands in surrender. "No charge," he said.

Grigoriy mumbled his thanks and turned back to Anna. Her blue eyes were sparkling.

"Milk?" she asked.

"I have a stomach ache," he said.

Anna grabbed his glass with one hand and his arm with the other. She weaved through the crowd, dragging him along behind her until they reached a dark corner of the club. Anna parted a set of velvet curtains and led Grigoriy into one of the private rooms.

"Wait, Anna," he protested, but she pulled him through the doorway.

Even inside, the walls shuddered as the thunderous music played. The room was gloomy, the window shuttered. A plush sofa stretched along one wall, facing the queen-sized bed. The sheets had already been tousled and the throw cushions discarded on the floor along with empty glasses, bottles, and cigarette butts. A camera had been set up in the corner, along with lights and sound equipment. They were known to make movies here, Grigoriy remembered. Mostly for the internet, though some *boyeviks* liked to keep private collections.

"Sit down," Anna said, pointing to the sofa.

"I can't be in here, Anna. You're Stepan Volkov's girl."

"I know that, Grigoriy," she said, returning his glass of milk.

"That comes with certain obligations." He slurped from his glass.

"And freedoms, too," she said, untying her hair and kicking off her shoes. "I come here and perform on stage and make hundreds of dollars in tips. Nobody touches me, nobody says anything offensive to me, and nobody demands sexual favours. Even Dmitri and the other smugglers behave around me most of the time." She pushed him on to the sofa.

"Someone would have seen us," he said, shifting uncomfortably. "Volkov will find out."

"I'd rather they gossip about Volkov's girl giving Grigoriy a private show than see us talking."

"We've talked before."

"Not about this."

Anna took off her shirt and Grigoriy felt his face go red. He stared down at his glass of milk. "What are you doing?" he whispered.

"Taking my clothes off."

"Why?"

"In case somebody walks in." She took off her skirt. "Are you keeping up?"

"I don't think I am," he said, blinking. "I can see spots in front of my eyes."

"Nobody's going to tell Volkov I gave you a lap dance. They wouldn't dare." Anna slid her thumbs under the elastic of her underwear.

"Stop!" Grigoriy cried. "I think that's enough."

"You've seen women wear less than this, Grigoriy."

But not you, he thought. "Please. Tell me what's going on."

"Play along, okay." She straddled him. "Relax. We're just going to talk."

He looked down at his lap. "Can you at least cover up a little?"

She smiled and folded an arm across her chest. "What was your meeting about?"

"You first," he said.

She stole his glass and took a sip. "Nikolay wanted to know where Stepan was, didn't he?"

"How did you know?"

"I heard about it last night," she said. "I heard a lot of things last night, and I'm starting to get worried."

"What things?"

"You should see them, Grigoriy," she said. "You should see them like I see them. They're keeping a tally of the dead from the bombings in Moscow. They cheer whenever news of an attack comes on the television."

"Well, they're not very nice people."

"And Maxim is keeping a map of the bombs on his tablet," she whispered.

"You saw it?"

"I heard about it."

He slumped back into the sofa and scratched his head.

"They've also been talking about bears in Australia."

"Bears?" He frowned. "There are no bears in Australia." He raised a finger. "Unless they mean koalas, although they're not really bears."

Anna sighed heavily. "I don't think they were talking about wildlife, Grigoriy." She returned his glass of milk. "Does it mean anything to you?"

He shrugged. "I'll tell the boss. He might make more sense of it." He rolled his eyes. "You're worried Nikolay doesn't want Volkov to know about this stuff. That's why you dragged me in here."

"I'm glad you finally caught up."

"Take care of yourself," he said. "You're taking a big risk."

She ran her hand through his long curly hair. "I'll be fine, Grigoriy." She sat back. "Where *is* Stepan?"

"I can't tell you that."

She started caressing his hair. "Please?"

"Anna," he groaned.

"I'll take off the last of my clothes," she warned.

Grigoriy looked away. "I don't like it when you manipulate me."

"I'm only trying to help," she said innocently. "It's good to have people to talk to, to confide in."

"Stepan's on his way home." Grigoriy stared at his glass of milk before handing it to Anna. "He walked away in the middle of a job."

"What?" Anna asked in horror.

"His diversion made the news. That's why Nikolay was angry and wanted to know where he was."

"Why would he leave a job?"

"There was a contract out on Natalie Robinson, a girl he knows in Australia. I found out about it through some friends over there. Volkov was in Jakarta preparing for a job when I told him and he went to Australia to protect her."

"Who's Natalie? Why is she so special?"

"She's your predecessor."

Anna nodded slowly, smiling sadly. She took a sip of milk and placed the glass on the floor in front of the sofa.

"Are you okay?" Grigoriy asked.

"Da." She paused. "I guess I was just entertaining a fantasy about being the only one."

"I'm sorry," he said. "Um." He cupped her cheek in his hand.

"What?"

Grigoriy ran his thumb along her top lip. "You have a milk moustache." He lowered his hand. "It's gone now."

Anna blushed and smiled. "Did he save Natalie?"

"Yes. He killed the man sent to kill her."

"And he defaulted on the other contract?"

"No. He has already completed the contract in Jakarta."

"But that's not the point, is it?"

Grigoriy shook his head. "Nikolay is angry that Volkov abandoned the job for 'a personal dalliance'."

"You didn't tell Nikolay any of this, did you?"

"Yeah, I did."

"Grigoriy!" she cried, climbing off his lap.

"Volkov told me to protect myself."

"You can't betray him like that."

"I had to, or I would be dead."

Anna grabbed her clothes and started to get dressed. "That's the risk you take," she seethed.

"Why are you angry about this?" he asked, standing up.

She stopped dressing. "You have to be loyal to him, Grigoriy. You have to be brave. He will keep you safe.

He will look after you. Nikolay will not shed a tear for you." She threw her hands in the air in exasperation.

"We don't get to choose sides, Anna. We don't have any choices at all."

"You're wrong."

"I wish I was."

Anna finished dressing and placed her hands on her hips. "I have to get back to work," she said, glaring at Grigoriy.

He nodded and looked at his feet. He'd kicked over his glass of milk and it was soaking into the carpet. He raised his head in time to see the curtains close.

Anna was gone.

***

Maxim burst through Nikolay Korolev's door, a file folder tucked under his arm. "Stepan Volkov *was* in Australia. The bastard went off the reservation."

Korolev ignored him and continued typing on his laptop. His reading glasses reflected the iridescent glow of the screen, hiding his eyes behind two discs of white light.

Maxim's arms fell and he cleared his throat. "Nikolay?"

"I'm very busy, Maxim," he said, without looking up.

"But I have the information you wanted," Maxim said, holding his folder in the air.

Korolev grunted. "Bring it here, then."

"The news reports were right and Grigoriy told the truth," Maxim said, placing the folder on the desk. "Volkov was in Australia. Something must be done."

Korolev shut his laptop and picked up the folder, reclining in his chair. He placed the folder on his lap and adjusted his spectacles before opening the cover.

"He has gone too far, Nikolay," Maxim insisted.

Korolev licked the tip of his middle finger and turned the pages, skimming the articles.

"You can't let him make up his own rules," Maxim said.

"Is this all you could get?" Korolev didn't wait for an answer. "These are just news articles and blog posts."

"I'm still waiting to hear back from our sources in the region," Maxim said, flexing his fingers.

Korolev grunted again.

"There are images, too. They're from an online newspaper."

"Indeed," Korolev mumbled, flicking through the photographs. He stopped suddenly, running his finger down the length of a photograph. He snatched it out of the folder and held it up for Maxim to see. "Who is this?"

Maxim squinted. "That's Leanne Waters, a local police constable. She's a witness. The Australians are taking her back to their headquarters."

"She's bait." Korolev examined the photograph. "Waters, you said."

"That's right." Maxim ran his hand across his bald head.

"What do you know about her?" Korolev asked.

"This isn't about her," Maxim said. "This is about—"

"Maxim!" Korolev barked, pounding the desk. "I asked you a question."

Maxim's face flushed. "She's been in the police force for three years but her history is a bit thin. She's a nobody."

Korolev reached for his silver letter opener and smoothed the photograph out on his blotter. He pointed the tip of the blade at the throat of the constable. "This woman is no constable. This is Simone Elliot," Korolev said. "Do you know who that is?"

Maxim shook his head. "Should I?"

"Before your time, perhaps," Korolev said. "She is a thief, Maxim, and a very good one, too. Her peers call her the Serpent. She creates identities, slipping in and out of worlds, jobs, and friendships. She deceives, she manipulates, and she steals."

"Why does this matter?"

"She stole from me," Korolev said darkly.

Maxim snapped his fingers. "And Volkov betrayed you to her, right?"

"Enough," Korolev hissed. He took his glasses off and glared at Maxim. "*I* will deal with Volkov. Your problem is Elliot." He pushed back from his desk and stood up, twirling the letter opener around his fingers. "I want her dead."

"But the Australians have hidden her."

"Then you better find her," Korolev said impatiently.

"Just get Volkov to do it," Maxim snorted. "He—"

Korolev seized Maxim's arm and twisted it, locking his wrist. Maxim cried out as his face was slammed down on to the desk. He squirmed until Korolev placed the cold blade of the letter opener against his neck.

"Have Elliot killed," Korolev said. "Volkov is not to know about it."

Maxim closed his eyes. "I don't understand," he stammered.

"I don't expect you to understand," Korolev growled. "Do as you are told."

Maxim licked his lips and nodded slightly. "Yes, Nikolay." He held his breath. "But how will we fill the contract?"

Korolev released Maxim and stood up straight, retreating behind his desk. "I want eight men with no discernible connection to Volkov."

"Eight!"

"Don't interrupt." Korolev tapped the flat of the blade against his chin. "Each one will receive an equal share of a million-dollar bounty, so they are to work together. And I want capture protocols in place."

"But, Nikolay." Maxim took a step back, rubbing his arm. "Those protocols are rarely implemented. It'll be hard to get volunteers."

"Then it will be a good challenge for you."

Maxim opened his mouth, quickly closing it again and nodding in surrender.

"Make the preparations immediately."

"This could take up to seven days to arrange."

"You have three days."

Maxim nodded again.

"Once she's found, assign some men in Australia to watch her until the professionals arrive." Korolev paused. "Tell them not to approach her."

"She's just one girl."

"Maxim!"

"Yes, Nikolay. I'll start now," Maxim said, stepping back towards the door.

"Wait."

Maxim turned.

"Tell the men not to kill any cops during the job," Korolev said. "We don't need any Russian businesses raided by over-zealous police officers."

"Yes, Nikolay."

The door slammed closed and Korolev stared down at the photograph on his blotter.

Is Stepan looking for you? Or are you looking for him?

Korolev grunted. It didn't matter, anymore. He tossed his letter opener in the air and watched the blade plunge into the photograph, pinning Simone Elliot to the desk.

9

CANBERRA, AUSTRALIA

TUESDAY 13 SEPTEMBER

4:30PM AEST

Simone Elliot's face wrinkled as she felt a dull ache pound through her chest. She held her hand over her heart, closed her eyes, and took a deep breath.

Heartburn? Stress?

She *was* in pretty deep trouble and it was only a matter of time before somebody figured out who she really was. After that, Volkov would only be the start of her problems. Two days, tops, she thought, and then she could slip away, but first she had to give him a chance to find her again. She'd missed an opportunity and wasn't going to waste another one. All she had to do was answer to the name "Leanne Waters" for two more days and try to stay out of trouble.

Elliot glanced at Emily Hartigan, who was muttering while fiddling with the radio dial. Agent Hartigan frowned at the console and jabbed at the buttons in frustration.

"Brake, Emily. Brake!" Elliot cried, holding her hands up.

Hartigan stomped on the brake and the car shuddered, lurching to a halt behind a silver sedan idling at the traffic lights. "Sorry about that," Hartigan said sheepishly.

"Why don't you tell me what to look for on the radio so you can concentrate on the road?" Elliot asked, massaging her forehead with her fingertips.

"I'm looking for the news."

Elliot nodded and twiddled the knob. The radio hissed static and spat garbled conversations as radio stations faded in and out. "I'm not really getting anything here."

"Never mind," Hartigan said. "I need a new radio."

She needed a new car, Elliot thought. It looked like the car of a high school student. Its exterior was one tone of rust and two tones of faded paint, the chrome tarnished and the side panels dented and scratched. The upholstery was torn and bleeding blue foam while the carpet was fraying and breathing strange odours. The accessories only worked intermittently, and, even then, only when encouraged by an impatient fist pounding the dashboard.

Elliot noticed that the car was littered with traces of Hartigan's personality, too. The back seat was stacked with books, including a tome on body language that was bookmarked with a leaflet from a dating agency. There were three novels by Jane Austen that appeared well read, as well as a Russian–English dictionary.

Folded newspapers lay scattered on the seat, their puzzle pages exposed, the cryptic crosswords all solved. Academic papers about Soviet trade policies and Siberian mineral deposits poked out from under magazines with investigative pieces on organised crime. There were takeaway containers, empty coffee cups stained with lipstick, a faded can of body spray, and a pair of muddy running shoes.

"What were you hoping to hear on the radio?" Elliot asked. She saw a manuscript at her feet, the wrinkled pages wrapped in a rubber band, and she picked it up.

"Nothing specific." The light turned green and Hartigan shifted out of neutral. The clutch caught and jolted the car, the engine whining and the bearings squealing. The car started to shake when Hartigan put it into third and a tin of breath mints rattled in the ashtray.

"The media can't tell you much more about Volkov than we already know," Elliot said, ripping the rubber band from the manuscript and thumbing through the pages. "They usually get their information from you guys, anyway."

"I don't think the media's interested in Volkov anymore," Hartigan said. "The news is full of stories about our oil discovery."

"A press conference might stimulate some curiosity," Elliot said.

"Lee Singh is the agent in charge," Hartigan said. "He seems to believe that the public doesn't always have a right to know what's happening."

"Who wants to see how sausages are made, right?"

Hartigan glanced at Elliot. "That's very cynical for a police constable."

Elliot tapped a finger on the manuscript in her lap. "No free man shall be seized or imprisoned, or stripped of his rights or possessions," she quoted, reading from the page.

"The Magna Carta," Hartigan said, nodding.

"You wrote about due process in your thesis."

"It's important to remember, even when dealing with criminals outside our borders."

"Do you really believe that?" Elliot asked, turning the page.

"Yes, I do." A Mercedes sped past and zipped into their lane, cutting them off. Hartigan sighed and slowed the car. "Look, we all have rights, even the worst of us, even if we're not citizens of a democracy when we commit a crime against one."

"So Volkov deserves due process?"

"Of course."

Elliot clicked her tongue and closed the manuscript. "Do yourself a favour and don't mention this to your Agent Singh."

"I'm sure he agrees with the sentiment," Hartigan said.

"Is there anything I should know before I meet him?" Elliot asked, tossing the manuscript on the floor.

"He's a bit of a mystery, actually," Hartigan said, checking her mirror and merging into the next lane. "Apparently, he served in the military during the war but nobody seems to know what he did there. Some people think he's a burnout and others think he's the agency's best man."

"What do *you* think?"

"Well, he's not very popular and he's definitely not a team player," Hartigan said. "Everybody has been warning me to stay away from him." She shrugged.

"You didn't answer my question."

Hartigan pressed her lips together briefly, changing gears. "He's the new kind of agent, the one the media warned us about during the war. Our agents have new powers, carrying pistols whenever they feel like it, and they use dehumanising words like 'kinetic targeting'. Singh is one of those agents. His job is to kick down doors."

"You don't approve?"

"It's hard to explain."

"Try me."

Hartigan rolled her hands over the steering wheel and wriggled in her seat. "He's nothing like my dad."

Elliot clicked her fingers. "Hartigan. Of course."

"You worked with my dad?"

"I met him before he retired, and before I was a cop," Elliot said. "He was a good detective."

"He was." Hartigan nodded slowly. "I guess I can't help comparing every cop to him. He's a hero, after all."

Elliot shook her head. "There's no such thing, Emily."

"I honestly hope you're wrong about that." The car drifted to a stop outside a hotel. She dipped her head towards the building. "This is where you'll be staying. The booking is under my name and we've taken care of the bill for the next week."

Elliot peered through the window. Smooth white pebbles shimmered in a driveway that swept across the broad façade of the hotel, inviting guests to climb the stone stairs to the glassed entrance. The valets wore tailored suits and stood at the top of the stairs, flanked by neo-classical columns that held up a solid slab of stone carved with friezes. The palatial building climbed to a modest five storeys, though it was high enough to cast long shadows that stretched over the gardens. "Are you serious?" Elliot asked, looking back at Hartigan.

"Just don't touch the minibar."

"Why, what's in it, Belgian chocolates and cocaine?"

"European beer. It tastes terrible," Hartigan added, wrinkling her nose. "The food is pricey, but there's a good Thai restaurant around the corner."

"Right." Elliot opened the door.

"We have a team watching you from across the street in case anything goes wrong or Volkov reappears. They'll be there until nine in the morning. I'll pick you up at about eight-thirty."

"I'll keep an eye out for a gilded horse-drawn carriage," Elliot said dryly, stepping out of the car.

"Speaking of fancy," Hartigan said, clearing her throat. "Do you have any other clothes you can wear?"

Elliot looked down at her jeans and knitted top.

"You're at the dizzy end of policing, Leanne," Hartigan said. "It will pay to look professional."

"Good point," Elliot said. "I mean, I'd hate to embarrass you in front of your boss."

"Please, Leanne," Hartigan begged. "If you want, I can even bring you something."

"Don't bother," Elliot said, grabbing her duffel bag from the back seat. "I'll take care of it and I'll see you at eight-thirty." She closed the door and waved Hartigan away.

The car jerked forward and stopped. Elliot heard Hartigan wrench on the handbrake and turned around.

"One last thing," Hartigan called, emerging from the car. She popped the boot and plunged her arms inside. She rummaged through shoeboxes full of paper, eventually rescuing a thin folder from her mobile archive before slamming the boot shut. "I wanted to show you that even the best can lose when they play against the *Organizatsiya.*"

"You've already convinced me that I'm hip deep in shit, Emily."

"Still, it makes for interesting reading." Hartigan passed her the file. "And it's more entertaining than television."

"What is it?" Elliot asked, studying the cover.

"It's everything we have on Simone Elliot."

***

Simone Elliot plunged her hand into her duffel bag and pawed through her clothes. "Aha," she cried triumphantly. It was the only collared shirt she owned. She dragged it out of the bag and flapped it against her legs, suddenly wishing she'd been more meticulous while packing.

Elliot sighed and tossed the wrinkled shirt on the bed. The file was sitting on the bedside table. She wiped her palms on her jeans and sucked in her bottom lip before padding across the room. Her eyes closed, she used her thumb to lift the front cover. She took a deep breath and looked down, the tension bleeding from her shoulders when she saw that they still didn't have a good photograph.

Of course they don't.

Elliot shook her head and picked up the file, cradling it in her arm and scanning the pages. "Born in Australia," the first page said. "Notorious thief", "millions of dollars unaccounted for", "celebrity mansions, horse races, banks, gold depositories". She turned the page. "Descriptions of Elliot vary and witnesses are considered unreliable," she read. "Elliot alters hair colour, eye colour, make-up, language, and general appearance. However, witnesses all agree that she is attractive, athletic, and short."

Short? Elliot shut the file and tossed it away in frustration. "Short!" she spat, running her hand through her hair and turning to the linen cupboard. "I am *not* short," she muttered, opening the cupboard. "I'm..." Her voice trailed off. The iron was sitting on the top shelf. She stretched her arms into the air and stood on the tips of her toes but could barely get a finger to it.

Elliot groaned. You can't change what you are, she thought.

She used her foot to drag a chair towards her and climbed on top of it, reaching into the cupboard. The iron's electric cord had been severed. Elliot wearily rested her forehead on the open cupboard door, taking a deep breath.

I've been playing by the rules for too long.

He'd handcuffed her to the bar. He never would have managed to cuff her three years ago. Three years in hiding, living under a false identity as a police constable, fading into the background, and she'd lost the edge.

Elliot flopped on to the chair and pulled her duffel bag towards her, rummaging through her clothes. She pulled her satchel from the bottom of the bag, tipping its contents into her lap. There were forged passports, fake business cards and identification cards, a small roll of cash, a pistol, and two magazines of ammunition. She set aside the pistol and magazines and shuffled through her alternate identities.

Circumstances almost always forced her to be someone else but usually only for a little while. This time, however, it had been too long since she'd been herself. There was no pretending now. He was coming for her. She wanted him to come for her, and she would wait, but she had to be ready. It was time to think, to plan, to learn. She needed new clothes and a ready supply of disposable cash, at least until she could access her offshore accounts. And she couldn't waste any time.

She tossed her papers aside and heard the jingle of jewellery. Her forehead wrinkled, she rummaged through the pile, and her shoulders slumped when she found the necklace.

It was a small silver medallion on a matching chain. Etched on the medallion was a snake coiled around a sceptre that was crowned with wings. It was a caduceus, she remembered. The necklace had been a gift, one of the only presents anyone had ever given her. It had been a gift from *him.*

She wiped the medallion with her thumb.

It's time to see if I still have what it takes.

Elliot shoved the necklace into her pocket and grabbed her red coat.

***

A cold wind blew through the windows and the heavy curtains strained against their tethers. Across the bar, artificial leaves ruffled and napkins were swept to the floor. One of the oil paintings slipped on its hook and its corners clattered lightly on the rich maroon walls.

Simone Elliot's eyes scanned the room.

The waitress shivered and rubbed her bare arms but she didn't look up from her phone. She typed furiously with her thumb while balancing a silver tray on her hip. Her foot was propped on the leg of a stool and shook impatiently while she waited for the barman to finish mixing drinks.

The hotel's bar was nearly empty. A man and a woman were entertaining a Korean delegation in the centre of the room. They all sunk into soft leather sofas and discussed "organisational imperatives". The woman's face was flushed from alcohol and her head flopped around when she talked. The man beside her nodded thoughtfully while sipping from his glass, laughing and snorting when the woman made a joke. The Koreans watched with lined foreheads.

At the end of the counter, hunched on a stool, a silver-haired man in a rumpled Italian suit stared solemnly into his glass of pinot noir. A 700-dollar bottle of stomped grapes from the Côte-d'Or sat behind his glass but he only noticed it when he reached for a refill. He sighed heavily, using a chubby finger to nudge his wedding ring around an empty ashtray.

The barman cleared his throat. "Karen."

The waitress looked up lazily and blinked as the barman pointed to the drinks on the counter. She rolled her eyes, shoving her phone into her pocket and slapping the tray on the bar.

The barman placed a row of napkins on the tray, and then the glasses on the napkins, before watching his employee saunter towards the delegation. He muttered a curse before turning to his stock, ticking off quantities on a clipboard.

Elliot was the only other person in the bar. She sat on a stool with her back to the wall, spinning a packet of cigarettes on the timber countertop. The people in the bar were interesting but weren't what she needed. Elliot needed a specific type of bit-player to make her con work.

The perfect mark appeared just after dinner. Elliot was sitting in the lobby on a bulging sofa, her legs crossed and a folded newspaper on her lap. She had scribbled notes on the newspaper as potential marks checked in: 'bearded man in fedora hat'; 'woman with mole wearing snakeskin shoes'. All had been crossed out. None of them measured up to who entered the lobby next.

The woman sashayed into the hotel and posed in front of the check-in counter surrounded by an entourage of luggage. She flicked her honey-coloured hair over her shoulder as she slapped the call bell over and over again with a jewellery-laden hand.

"I'm Siobhán Miller," the woman declared loudly, and the concierge feigned patience while subtly placing the bell out of Miller's reach. She had an itemised list of petulant demands, including special care for her brand-new Mercedes, a massage in her room, and a bottle of gin.

Elliot had immediately opened an internet browser on her phone. Instagram, Twitter, and Facebook. She found images of Miller's husband posing in front of Montserrat and the Sagrada Familia, and Miller had added comments to the latest post: her tickets were booked and she was going to Spain to see him.

After checking in to room 314, Miller snapped her fingers to gain the attention of a hotel employee, sweeping her arm over her luggage. The employee scuttled over and scooped up the bags until he was teetering on his feet. Miller hissed at the employee to be careful before disappearing into the elevator, leaving the employee to trudge up the stairs.

Elliot migrated to the bar to continue the research. The more she read, the more she realised Miller was perfect.

Siobhán Miller had once been a fashion model, paid to look pretty and pout at the camera. She'd been lured away from her dead-end career by a man thirty years older. He'd drowned her in money, clothes and jewellery, and she had married him.

He was Alistair, the CEO of a regional airline. It was a small operation by international standards, but he wanted to change that. His trip to Spain was funded by a Spanish aerospace company desperate for investment. According to his Twitter, he was drunk in a bar in Barcelona. According to Google, the bar he'd named was actually a strip club and he was probably doing body shots off a belly dancer. At least that's what Elliot believed, though it didn't really matter.

Siobhán Miller was due to check out the next day so she could fly to Spain to meet her husband. In the meantime, her massage and gin would keep her occupied in her room for at least two hours, which was more than enough time for Elliot.

"What can I get you?" the barman asked.

Elliot looked up from her phone. "Scotch. A double, neat."

The barman nodded and fetched her drink.

Another couple entered the bar and Elliot placed her phone on the counter before turning around on her stool. He wore designer labels and twirled an Aston Martin key ring on his finger. His smile was flashy, his cheeks dimpled and his eyes deep. She was desperately pretty, with a light orange tan and bright gold jewellery. Her skirt was short, her top was low, and she thrust her chest forward and swayed her hips as she walked. She threaded her arm through his and laughed, running her hand through his thick hair. Elliot immediately named them John and Jane, stifling a laugh when they attempted to sit gracefully on the big leather marshmallows in the middle of the room.

"Here you go," the barman said, placing the glass of scotch on the counter.

Elliot nodded her thanks and turned back to John and Jane. The waitress, Karen, was hovering around their sofa and Jane scowled, wrapping her fingers tightly around John's arm when the young girl neared. John smiled readily and Jane's face flushed as she sneered at the waitress. The young girl took their orders and retreated back to the bar, leaving the couple to indulge in banal conversation. John talked about his car and Jane smiled and nodded vigorously.

Elliot gulped down her drink. "I'll have another," she said to the barman. "Plenty of ice, this time." He nodded and ladled ice cubes into a fresh glass before pouring in some scotch. "And I'd like to borrow your pen."

"Uh, sure," he said, handing her his ballpoint.

She took a napkin from the bar and flicked the lid off the pen with her thumb.

Jane and John finished their first round of drinks and he gestured to Karen. The young girl approached cautiously and John smiled warmly. Jane hissed their order and the waitress retreated again. Jane started to scold John, telling him to stop flirting with other women. He was dismissive and told her that she was overreacting.

Elliot scrawled a note on the napkin: "I want to pick up where we left off. Meet me at 11pm, same place. XX Karen." Elliot saw that the waitress was again preoccupied by her phone, but she had left the tray on the counter while the barman busied himself with the drinks.

Elliot placed the napkin on the tray, but the waitress didn't notice. The barman set the glasses down and waved her away. Elliot watched her reluctantly tuck her phone away and walk towards John and Jane.

Elliot gulped down her scotch.

"Who the fuck is Karen?" Jane shouted.

The waitress held the empty tray like a shield.

"I don't know," John replied with a shrug.

"Karen?" the barman asked the waitress loudly. "What's going on?"

"I don't know," the waitress protested.

"Are you Karen?" Jane shrieked. "You bitch!"

She jumped to her feet and tossed her drink into the waitress' face. The waitress burst into tears and ran away, hiding behind the counter. Jane waved her arms violently, shouting at John while he sat silently on the sofa. Jane tossed John's full glass against the wall. The barman grabbed the phone, dialling security.

Elliot was in the hallway before the barman had hung up and saw the two security guards tumble through the door of the security centre. They were in such a rush that they left the door of the security centre to close under its own weight.

Elliot stepped into the room and immediately sat down in front of a computer terminal, placing her glass on the desk. The computer was still logged on to the system and she navigated through the program easily. She initiated a reformat and the bank of security monitors went black. A dialogue box appeared on the screen, asking if she wanted to proceed and announcing the reformat and reboot would be completed in forty minutes. Elliot clicked "continue". As she stood, she noticed an open thermos of soup on the desk beside her. She tipped it over, spilling the soup across the keyboard.

A toolbox was stored on a low shelf and she unlatched it before rummaging through the tools. She grabbed a shifting spanner and a rusty bolt, shoving them into her back pocket before retrieving her glass.

Back outside, there was a lot of shouting coming from the bar, but the hall was empty. Elliot locked the door from the inside and closed it behind her before heading for the parking garage.

The guests' cars were parked in neat lines, bathed in fluorescent light. The hotel's plumbing crisscrossed the ceiling of the garage and the fire suppression system for the kitchen was tucked against the wall. The system consisted of two highly pressurised bottles of argon gas that were caged in an alcove. Flexible lines were connected to fittings in the brickwork, the gas pressurising the system in the kitchen, ready to extinguish a fire. Siobhán Miller's white Mercedes was parked right next to the alcove, isolated from the other cars by request.

Elliot unlatched the cage and allowed the door to fall open before turning off the valves on the gas bottles and using the spanner to disconnect one of the lines at the wall. She twisted the line and threaded it through the cage, aiming it directly at the windshield of Miller's car. Finally, she poked the rusty bolt into the hose before fishing an ice cube from her glass. The ice cube was too big for the line, but Elliot forced it in with her thumb until it was deep inside the hose. Satisfied, she opened the valve and the gas squealed as it pressurised against the ice, the hose resting against the bars of the cage, its aim true. She pocketed the spanner and latched the cage before retreating back up the stairs, knowing she had less than a minute before the ice cube melted.

Elliot left her glass on a side table and was at the elevator when the sound of a car alarm wailed through the lobby. The security guards dashed from the bar and trotted towards the parking garage to investigate. Elliot stepped into the elevator and pressed the button for the third floor.

By the time the doors opened, Miller was in the hallway wearing a complimentary robe and the masseuse was retreating towards the service elevator. Elliot could hear Miller talking on her mobile phone.

"No, I know," Miller said. "Look, I've got to go, baby. Something's happened to my car." She paused and giggled. "That sounds great. Look, I'll meet you in the bar tonight and you can buy me a drink. Then you can prove it to me in private." She giggled again. "Okay, baby. I'll see you tonight." She palmed her phone and closed the door, tucking her swipe card into her pocket.

Elliot pulled out her phone and marched along the hall, typing an imaginary text message. She crashed into Miller.

"Watch where you're going," Miller sneered.

"Sorry," Elliot mumbled.

Miller elbowed past and headed for the elevator while Elliot kept walking. The elevator arrived and Miller walked in. Elliot doubled back and used Miller's swipe card to get into the room.

A tower of luggage was stowed against the wall but one bag was on the bed, its contents spilling onto the quilt. There was also a suit bag hanging from the cupboard door with a charcoal Chanel suit inside. The jacket was a little long but it was good enough. Miller's purse was on the bedside table. Elliot grabbed it, rummaging through the contents. Cash, $1000. She paused.

Tonight? But her husband is in Spain.

Elliot left the cash in the purse and found Miller's computer tablet sitting on the bed. She skimmed through emails and images, taking some snaps with her phone before returning the tablet.

She grabbed the Chanel suit and left the room, dropping the swipe card on the floor in the hallway.

10

MOSCOW, RUSSIA

TUESDAY 13 SEPTEMBER

11:55PM MSK

Grigoriy slowed the car and craned his neck, scanning the crowd in front of the terminal, but he couldn't see Stepan Volkov. He pulled over into the pick-up zone and put the car in park, deciding to wait.

The car lurched and Grigoriy looked into the rear-view mirror, watching Stepan Volkov toss his luggage into the boot of the BMW. Volkov slammed the lid shut and opened the passenger door, pausing when he spotted Grigoriy's laptop on the seat.

"Open it, Boss," Grigoriy said. "I got what you needed."

Volkov placed the computer in his lap and rubbed his hands in front of the heater. "Any trouble?"

"No," Grigoriy replied. "The Australians need to update their firewall protection." He cleared his throat and tightened his hands on the steering wheel.

Volkov glanced around before studying his assistant. "Are we going, or what?"

"Anna gave me a lap dance," Grigoriy blurted out. He felt his face go red and sank into the seat.

"Okay," Volkov said slowly.

"I wanted you to hear it from me."

"No offence, Grigoriy, but why would she give you a lap dance?"

"She was worried," he said quickly. "I ran into her at the club and she took me into a private room. She took her clothes off and told me what she'd been hearing around the club."

Volkov nodded. "Clever girl."

"You're not mad?"

"What did she tell you?" he asked, gesturing for Grigoriy to start the car.

"Apparently, Maxim is keeping track of the bombings. He's been marking targets on a map that he keeps on his tablet." Grigoriy turned the key and the car roared. "The men get excited every time another bomb goes off."

"These guys get dogs to fight for fun," Volkov shrugged. "They get off on violence."

"I know, but—"

"Has she seen this map?"

Grigoriy shook his head. "It's just gossip."

"Anything else?"

"She mentioned koala bears." Grigoriy put the car in gear and pulled away from the kerb. "Does that mean anything to you?"

"I'd say she was just looking for someone to talk to."

"Speaking of which," Grigoriy said hastily. "I told Nikolay everything about your trip to Australia."

"Everything?"

"I didn't mention Simone."

"Risky."

"Maybe." He licked his lips. "Anna was angry with me. She thinks I ratted you out."

"In my experience, making women angry is easier than keeping them happy," Volkov said, staring through the window.

"Perhaps that rule applies to both genders," Grigoriy said, shifting into fourth gear. "Nikolay is pretty mad. He insists on a meeting. Our first stop is the club."

"Fine." Volkov drummed his fingers on the computer in his lap.

Grigoriy braked, the car gliding to a stop at a red light. "Aren't you going to open it?"

"Just give me a minute."

"I think you should pretend you didn't see her." Grigoriy cleared his throat. "Maybe it would be better if she didn't exist anymore."

"I'm not so sure." Volkov looked down at his lap and opened the computer.

"Apparently, Simone has been masquerading as a police officer for three years." The light turned green and Grigoriy steered the car through the intersection, weaving between the potholes.

Volkov skimmed through one of the documents on the screen. "According to this, she actually *is* a real police officer. The identity is false but the rest is genuine."

"Why would she join the police?" Grigoriy asked.

Volkov didn't answer.

"I heard from a contact overseas a few hours ago," Grigoriy said. "She's been picked up by the Australians and brought into their investigation, just like you predicted."

"Who's the lead agent?"

"A man named Levan Singh."

Volkov raised an eyebrow.

"You know him, don't you?"

"Forget it. What else?"

"Singh has been paired with an analyst, a young girl with no field experience. I think her name is Emily."

Volkov muttered an acknowledgement.

"Should we be worried? I mean, you said this would happen."

"No," he said, looking down at his lap. "The constable is the bait. They think I'll target her because she can identify me." Volkov continued scrolling through the documents.

"If Nikolay finds out, you might have to kill Simone."

"No, I won't."

Grigoriy stopped the car at another red light. "What if he makes you?"

"Stay out of it, Grigoriy." Volkov closed one of the windows and saw a document bearing the Great Seal of the United States. "What's the story here?"

"Oh, right," Grigoriy wriggled in his seat. "Nikolay wanted me to talk to you about that. The Americans placed a new operative inside the US Embassy. Apparently, his mission was to find you. The guys pulled him off the street last night and I did a social profile on him today. Nikolay wants you to interrogate. There's an envelope under your seat that has everything you need."

"Did the men rough him up?"

"A couple of slaps," Grigoriy said defensively. "Is that roughing up? What about a punch in the nose? Or a kick in the rear?"

"You don't have to defend them, Grigoriy."

"Yes, I do."

Grigoriy had two degrees, including honours in mathematics, and his hacking skills frequently frustrated the world's cyber-security experts, earning him notoriety in dark corners of the internet. He was living proof that the *Organizatsiya* knew how to mix intelligence with muscle to make their business work.

The muscles, the *boyeviks,* were the public face of the organisation. Tattoos, gym-weary bodies, large knives, and big guns were usually enough to deter journalists and law enforcement officers. Sometimes, however, the *boyeviks* were a little too keen to impress their superiors and their fists became loose. The *boyeviks* provided physical protection for thinkers like Grigoriy, but the thinkers protected them from their own stupidity, defending them to the bosses when things went wrong.

"Can he still talk, at least?" Volkov asked.

"*Da.* He can talk. And see. And hear as well, I think."

"I'll have a word to the men." Volkov closed the laptop.

"Does that mean you'll talk to them?" Grigoriy asked. "Or that you'll kill them?"

Volkov didn't reply and Grigoriy fell silent, returning his attention to the road ahead.

People always die when Volkov is in town.

***

Anna bent over and placed the bucket of glitter in the cupboard under the stage. She closed the door and felt a sweaty hand grasp the inside of her bare thigh.

"My, my, my," a gruff voice said. Even over the pounding music, the voice was clear in her ears.

Anna turned around and saw Dmitri, one of Korolev's smugglers and a man who liked being rough. He reclined in his seat, rubbing his hand on his t-shirt and removing a cigar from his mouth. She smiled the way she'd been taught, a fake smile designed to disarm a man's aggression. Dmitri smiled back and puffed a lungful of smoke into the air.

"You have one tight arse, *devotchka,*" he said. "What do you think?" he chuckled, turning to the men around the table. They leered at her with hungry eyes.

"Dmitri!" A man stood up from a stool nearby and bent over until his mouth was close to Dmitri's ear. "Don't you know who she is?"

"Bah!" Dmitri waved his hand dismissively. "I only care *what* she is, and what she can do with her tongue."

The men at the table chortled and one slapped Dmitri on the back.

"What's your name, *devotchka?*" Dmitri asked.

"Anna," she replied, still smiling.

"See," Dmitri said over his shoulder. "Only a first name. They're not people, they're cuts of meat."

The man behind Dmitri straightened up, his eyes darting around.

Dmitri chomped down on his cigar. He reached out and ran his hand up her thigh. "How about you and me go into a private room so you can make me smile, Anna?"

Anna wanted to slap his hand away but knew that she'd be punished for fighting back. "I'm sorry, I can't, but I can get one of the other girls for you." She felt his hand tug at her underwear and her mouth went dry.

"I don't want another girl," Dmitri said.

Anna continued to force a smile, wringing her hands behind her back.

Dmitri pulled her on to his lap. "I'm going to put something in your mouth and you're going to love it," he whispered in her ear.

"Hey!" a bouncer shouted.

Dmitri's bodyguard elbowed his way between his boss and the bouncer. "Mind your own business, buddy."

"Nobody touches that girl," the bouncer said, folding his muscular arms across his chest. "Understand?"

Dmitri pushed Anna off his lap and drew a pistol from his belt. "Sure, I get it." He nodded to his bodyguard.

Anna flinched when the gun went off and the bouncer fell to the ground. He clutched his hands to his chest and blood flowed between his fingers. The music stopped and everybody in the club turned and stared at Dmitri.

"Anyone else got something to say?" Dmitri asked through a cloud of cigar smoke. He turned the pistol on Anna. "We've got business to finish."

***

Grigoriy knew that the Chechens had named Stepan Volkov. It was easy to see why. Volkov was 100 kilograms of fibrous muscle and spring-loaded sinew, just like *volk,* the wolf. His movements were fluid, his eyes always hunting, his intentions simple.

Volkov had served Nikolay Korolev in Chechnya after being recruited into the *Organizatsiya.* Nobody knew where he'd come from or who he was. His sole purpose had been providing security for arms sales to the Chechen rebels, killing competitors and Russian soldiers. He'd never complained, never asked for reward and, in fact, had hardly ever uttered an unnecessary word the whole time he'd served in Grozny.

Uniformed soldiers and *boyeviks* liked to sit and drink and share stories about Stepan Volkov. Most were gross distortions but they had been potent enough to follow Volkov to Moscow.

Grigoriy knew that most of the stories were nonsense but it was easy to dismiss the Devil until you stood before him. Over time, he'd realised that Volkov wasn't a beast: he was a machine.

Passion prompted men to kill one another: jealousy, revenge, greed, fear, humiliation, and anger. Everyone felt them, but Grigoriy had his doubts about Volkov. The Wolf's kills were calculated, an exercise in pure mathematics.

Dmitri was taunting the crowd when they entered the club, his pistol aimed at Anna. Grigoriy felt angry, seeing Anna cowering against the stage, but he felt useless too. He jumped when Volkov tugged his sleeve.

"Stay here," Volkov said. There was no anger in his voice, no emotion at all.

Grigoriy nodded and watched the crowd part for Volkov, each *boyevik* wordlessly stepping aside as the Wolf stalked towards Dmitri.

But Volkov didn't care about Dmitri's name, Grigoriy thought. He and his men were objects, mathematical abstractions, a set of five elements occupying space that Volkov plotted as points on a plane. The Wolf's mind was calculating statistical likelihoods and probabilities, estimating outcomes through a series of sweeping arcs and intersecting lines. He would find the solution that provided the highest likelihood of success and follow a logical series of steps to obtain that solution. It was quick and simple, grotesque but elegant.

Opponent One was facing away from Anna, waving his pistol at the club to protect Dmitri. Volkov seized the man's outstretched arm and ripped the slide from the pistol. He grabbed the man by the hair and plunged the slide into the nape of his neck, the remaining pieces of the pistol clattering to the floor. All eyes turned to Volkov and the dying man gurgling at his feet.

But Volkov didn't pause. Opponent Two raised his pistol but Volkov slapped the man's hand away, pulled his knife, and plunged the blade into the man's chest. Volkov pivoted on one foot, withdrawing his knife from the dead man's body and severed Opponent Three's radial artery with one precise cut. Opponent Three dropped his weapon and clutched his wrist, falling to his knees as he tried to stem the bleeding.

Opponent Four was Dmitri and he was slow to shift his aim from Anna. Volkov slashed the back of Dmitri's hand and the pistol thudded on to the table. He grabbed Dmitri by the back of the head and smashed the smuggler's face into the empty beer bottles and dirty plates. Volkov's arm swept skyward and he plunged his knife into Dmitri's shoulder, pinning him to the table.

By this time, Opponent Five had navigated around the furniture and lunged towards Volkov. The Wolf turned quickly and threw the man to the floor. Volkov snatched Dmitri's pistol from the table and shot Opponent Three, who had managed to stagger to his feet. He then turned the pistol around in his hand and raised it above his head. The people in the club seemed to hold their breath as Volkov brought the butt of the pistol down like a hammer, crushing Opponent Five's windpipe. There was an audible crack and the man flailed his limbs, choking for air and slapping the floor with his hands. Volkov unloaded the pistol, tossing the weapon and the magazine away before turning his attention to Dmitri.

Dmitri was whimpering, pinned to the table with a broken cigar stuck in his teeth and broken glass jutting from his cheeks. He tried to grab the blade in his back but he couldn't reach it, and nobody was coming to help him.

Everybody in the club stood very still, Grigoriy saw. There was no music and the girls had stopped dancing. The only sound was the dying ring of a gunshot. Anna was propped against the stage, her fingernails digging into the timber surface. Her face was pale, her eyes wide, and her chest rose and fell rapidly. Her attention was fixed on Volkov. Everyone watched Volkov. He sat on a chair and drew his own pistol, the polished chrome flashing under the lights as he placed it on the table where Dmitri could see it.

"I'm sorry I interrupted you, Dmitri." Volkov casually lit a cigarette and raised his boots to the footrest of a neighbouring stool, inhaling deeply. He blew smoke at the ceiling and studied Dmitri. "Now, what were you saying to Anna?"

"Please, Volkov." Dmitri wept. "I didn't mean anything. It was just a joke."

"Well, I love jokes. How did it go?"

"Please," Dmitri sobbed.

Volkov glared at Anna while dragging on his cigarette. "What did he say?"

Anna was mute and Grigoriy willed her to speak. *Say something, anything.*

"Anna!" Volkov barked. Everyone jumped.

"He said he wanted to put something in my mouth," she stammered.

Volkov lowered his lips to Dmitri's ears. "Is that true, Dmitri?"

"Please, Volkov. I'm sorry."

Nikolay Korolev's bodyguards materialised from the crowd and Volkov waved them over. They hesitated briefly before they neared. Volkov whispered to them and one of the bodyguards reached into his jacket. He handed Volkov a small concussion grenade.

Volkov flicked his cigarette away and pointed to two girls standing on the stage. "Your stockings, now." The girls didn't hesitate, removing their stockings while Volkov ripped the knife out of Dmitri's back.

The bodyguards seized Dmitri and dragged him on to the stage. Dmitri tried to wriggle out of their grasp, screaming and kicking, his shoes squeaking across the polished timber as he was towed along.

Volkov tossed three stockings to the bodyguards and kept one for himself. The two bodyguards tied Dmitri to one of the poles on the stage, binding him at the ankles and tying his wrists behind his back. Dmitri writhed against his restraints, shouting for mercy. The third stocking was tied around his forehead to hold his head against the pole.

Volkov climbed the steps to the stage and dismissed the bodyguards. Dmitri's breaths were shallow and fast, and his eyes darted from side to side, desperately seeking help.

"Now, I want to put something in *your* mouth," Volkov said, holding the concussion grenade before Dmitri's eyes.

"No!" Dmitri cried. "Please, I'm sorry."

Volkov forced the grenade into Dmitri's mouth before gagging him with the last stocking. He pulled the pin and held it for Dmitri to see. "Swallow."

Grigoriy looked away but he could still hear Dmitri's muffled shrieks and sobs. In his mind, he could see himself tied to that pole. He imagined the whole club staring at him, the last thing he would ever see clouded by his tears as he pleaded with Volkov.

The grenade went off.

Grigoriy turned back to see Dmitri's headless body crumpled awkwardly against the pole, the stockings holding him in place. He looked like a discarded marionette dangling from frayed string.

Grigoriy's knuckles were white, his palms clammy. He was angry at Dmitri for taunting Anna and angry at himself for being afraid to help her.

Did Volkov feel that anger or fear?

He watched as Volkov descended the stairs and glared at Anna. She withered, staring at her shoes and bursting into tears.

No, Grigoriy thought.

The Wolf felt nothing.

11

MOSCOW, RUSSIA

WEDNESDAY 14 SEPTEMBER

12:33AM MSK

Stepan Volkov grabbed Anna by the arm and pulled her through the crowd, throwing her towards Grigoriy.

Anna turned to face Volkov. "Stepan, I'm sorry."

"I'll deal with you later," he said, poking her in the chest.

Nikolay Korolev appeared beside Volkov, a parade of his generals following him. "Are you quite finished?" he hissed. He turned to his generals. "I want everyone out of my club. Tell these dogs to go make me money and not to come back until tomorrow night."

The generals nodded and went to disperse the crowd.

"And find someone to clean up this fucking mess," Korolev shouted, pointing at the stage.

Buckets and mops were found in cupboards and men fell to their knees to scrub the blood out of the carpet. Others grabbed the bodies and dragged them away.

Korolev's eyes bored into Volkov. "My office. Now." He marched away, barking orders at his men.

Volkov turned to Grigoriy. "Get Anna some lemonade or something. It will help her feel better."

"Sure, Boss," Grigoriy replied, throwing his coat over Anna's shoulders. She smiled weakly at him.

"And stay out here," Volkov added. "I'll be back soon."

Volkov fell into step behind Korolev as he walked to the VIP room. They entered the office and Korolev immediately sat down in his leather chair, busying himself on his laptop. Volkov paused in the doorway and noticed a man sitting on the sofa.

"Hello, Maxim," Volkov said.

Maxim ran his hand over his bald head and bared his teeth in an attempt to smile, his eyes glaring at Volkov. "Stepan."

Volkov walked to the bar in the corner and uncorked the scotch. "I haven't seen you for a while," he said, grabbing a glass. "Last time we met was Hotel Africa in Monrovia, right?"

"I'm still spending time in Liberia," Maxim said. "Though I don't travel to Antwerp as much, these days."

"Is the hotel still a 300-room shithole?" Volkov asked, pouring a double.

"There's a casino and a nightclub now."

He corked the bottle. "So it's a 302-room shithole." He considered Maxim, noting his pale complexion. "Lots of time indoors?"

"Lots of sunscreen."

"That's enough," Korolev said, closing his laptop and standing up.

Volkov rested against the bar and sipped from his glass. "You wanted to talk."

"I just finalised payment for your job in Jakarta," Korolev said, gesturing to his laptop. "My share is eighty percent."

"Our standing agreement is sixty."

"You want to haggle?" Korolev said. "Let's haggle."

Maxim pulled his pistol from his jacket and slapped it on the coffee table.

"Why shouldn't I kill you?" Korolev asked Volkov, stepping closer. He was rolling his coin across the top of his hand, a US quarter, Volkov remembered. According to the stories, it was a trophy claimed from the first American operative Korolev had ever killed.

Volkov swirled his drink in his glass. "Why should you?"

"Because you are becoming increasingly difficult to manage," Korolev said. "You're insubordinate, unprofessional, volatile, and frustrating for business."

"The Jakarta job got done."

"You never leave your post," Korolev snarled. "Especially for a girl."

"Natalie Robinson was in trouble and I was in the area." Volkov shrugged. "Nobody will miss the guy."

"And what about Dmitri? Those trucks won't move from the alley beside my club until I can find another crew as dumb as his men."

"Dmitri was a pig. He raped two of your girls and beat another one so badly she ended up with brain damage."

"That is beside the point," Korolev seethed. "You do as I say. You wait for my orders. You are my instrument." He punctuated his words by stabbing his finger into Volkov's chest. "Do you understand?"

Volkov nodded once, staring vacantly at his glass of scotch.

"Your personal distractions have put you at unnecessary risk," Korolev continued, his voice more subdued. "You burned a cover identity when you hired that jet. You left a trail. The Australian authorities are now sniffing around."

"They won't get anywhere," Volkov said. "I took care of it."

"There would be nothing to take care of if it wasn't for your dalliances."

"I held up my end."

"That's not the deal. You owe me your life. I am generous with what I provide in return and if I find that you are not focused on your role, then I will demonstrate how powerless you really are."

"You wouldn't," Volkov said darkly.

"You know that I'm an avid vivisectionist," Korolev said. "Anna would make a fine candidate for study."

Volkov could hear his own heart pounding.

"Yes, that got your attention," Korolev said icily. "Don't forget your place again." He turned to Maxim. "Get out."

"But, Nikolay," Maxim protested. He looked to Volkov.

"You heard him," Volkov said, lifting his chin towards the door. "Go tell your yoga instructor I want my handcuffs back."

Maxim grabbed his pistol and scowled at Volkov before leaving the office, slamming the door behind him.

Korolev studied Volkov thoughtfully, rolling his coin across his hand. The coin tumbled over each one of his fingers but this time it toppled over the edge, falling towards the ground. Volkov's hand darted out, snatching the coin from the air. He held the US quarter in his fist.

Korolev's laugh rattled the ice cubes in Volkov's glass. "Do you know how many men I know with reflexes like yours, Stepan?"

Volkov opened his hand and Korolev retrieved the coin.

"None," Korolev said. "You are *that* good, and that's why I let you live. Just don't forget who owns you." He turned away. "Did Grigoriy make you aware of this American operative?"

"His cell is my next stop."

"I want him working for us. My American sources aren't what they used to be. I need new ones."

"That's up to him."

"No, Stepan," Korolev said, holding up a finger. "It's up to you."

***

"Volkov." Maxim was sitting on a sofa in the VIP room and stood up as Volkov closed Korolev's door.

"Haven't you left yet?" Volkov asked, heading to the exit.

Maxim blocked the doorway. "I told him he should kill you and cut his losses."

"I can tell he takes your advice seriously," Volkov said.

"I even suggested sending you to Monrovia."

"You haven't been to Africa in ages," Volkov said, tapping Maxim's bald head. "You'd be burnt to a crisp. So, where have you been and why aren't you still there?"

Maxim bared his teeth again. "You know, you'd do well in Africa."

"I wouldn't fit in," Volkov said. "I don't dress in drag and sing showtunes like the pussies you hang around with."

Maxim's toothy smile faded and his cheek twitched. "But you do put on quite a show. Five armed men, all dead, and all for a whore."

The *boyeviks'* coats were draped on hooks near the door. Volkov saw a holstered pistol poking out from under the folds of cloth. "Be careful what you say next, Maxim."

"Oh, please," Maxim snorted. "All women are the same." He noticed the unbuttoned holster too and stepped closer.

"Your aftershave stinks, Maxim," Volkov said, screwing up his nose.

"Take your police constable, for example," Maxim continued. "Waters, is it?"

Volkov tensed.

"She looks tasty, yes?"

The pistol was just within his reach, Volkov thought.

"I bet Anna tastes as sweet as honey." Maxim let out a low whistle. "But nothing beats a blowjob from a police constable, am I right?" His laugh rattled and he lunged for the pistol.

Volkov grabbed Maxim by the throat and lifted him off his feet, slamming his head into a table. Glasses and bottles rattled as the table shuddered and Maxim collapsed to the floor.

"I told you to be careful," Volkov said, stepping over him.

***

Grigoriy drank the last of his milk and placed the cloudy glass on the counter, peering shyly at Anna. She held a cigarette between her fingers and was watching the smoke curl up into the air.

"Are you okay?" Grigoriy asked.

She nodded silently.

"Do you want another glass of lemonade?"

She shook her head and slowly looked up from her burning cigarette. She smiled.

Grigoriy awkwardly returned the smile.

Anna reached out her hand and ran her thumb across his top lip. "Milk moustache," she said. "It's gone now."

He blushed and Anna laughed. Her smile quickly faded and Grigoriy sighed. "Look, he only got angry because you got into trouble," he said. "I think he was angrier at himself for leaving you unprotected."

"One day I'm going to get into trouble and he won't be here to help."

"Don't talk like that."

"It's true, Grigoriy," she said, slouching on her stool. "Some things are out of our control."

He reached for her hand. "Just do the best you can to stay alive," he said. "Do as he asks, follow his advice."

"Like you did?" Anna asked quietly, contemplating his hand on hers.

"What do you mean?"

"Telling Nikolay about—"

"Anna, I already told you." He pulled his hand away.

"I know." Her gaze settled upon the laptop bag propped against Grigoriy's stool. "I'm sorry I got upset."

"You don't need to apologise," he mumbled. "You weren't wrong."

"No, but I wasn't right, either."

Grigoriy followed her gaze, looking down at his laptop bag. It was lovingly cared for, and the computer's case was adorned with stickers of bikini-clad women and logos from surf-clothing companies. It gave him comfort. It was familiar, it was colourful, and it reminded him that there were places far away that were better and sunnier. He suddenly wanted to ask Anna if she dreamed of those places too.

"It's all about survival." Grigoriy shook his head. "Nice guys don't survive, Anna."

"Then how are you still here?"

He stared at his glass. "I wish you wouldn't say things like that. Every day, I wish I could be more like Volkov."

"You always said that we each have our part to play." She butted out her cigarette in the ashtray.

"Yes, but he walks through the club and the crowd parts to let him through. People don't make eye contact with him because they're afraid of him."

"Do you think he likes that?"

"Why wouldn't he?"

"Because he can never be happy. He may have people's fear but that's all he has."

"And that will keep him alive," Grigoriy observed. "We're judged for what we are and by what we do."

"Is that how you judge Stepan?"

"Of course."

"But you're his friend."

He snorted. "Nobody has any friends here."

Anna stared at the cigarette butt smouldering in the ashtray. "Perhaps that's true here, in this world, but what about the other world?"

Grigoriy tilted his head.

"What about if Stepan wanted to rejoin the human race?"

"I can't imagine him working as an accountant in a biscuit factory or a bricklayer on a building site," Grigoriy said.

"But he was a person once. He had family, friends, a job." She cleared her throat. "A lover."

"I guess," Grigoriy said slowly.

"Imagine being like Volkov," she said. "Could you bear it if a woman you loved hated you for what you were?"

"What are you trying to say?"

She took a deep breath. "Don't change, Grigoriy." She kissed him on the cheek.

Grigoriy stared at the table for several heartbeats before reaching up and touching his cheek. He started when he heard a loud bang, and he turned towards the VIP room to see Volkov march into the bar.

"Get your shit, Grigoriy," Volkov ordered. "It's time to go."

"What about Anna?"

"She's coming too."

12

MOSCOW, RUSSIA

WEDNESDAY 14 SEPTEMBER

1:18AM MSK

"Stop here, Grigoriy," Volkov ordered.

"Sure thing, Boss." Grigoriy pulled over, leaving the engine running.

Volkov shuffled forward in his seat and peered through the windscreen. The factory was two storeys of pale bricks that jutted out of the mud, the walls cracking as the foundation sank into the earth. The building stood in a puddle of faded light and shared a frayed wire fence with a scrap metal yard. The leaning lattice was crowned with rusted barbed wire that whipped around in the wind. A yellowed newspaper skipped along the potholed road, the scattered pages swirling into the fence and flapping restlessly.

Volkov turned around and saw Anna watching him. He faced Grigoriy. "Go ahead on foot. Leave the keys. I'll be there in a minute."

"But, Boss," Grigoriy protested.

"Just go," Volkov ordered. "Anna, give Grigoriy his coat."

Grigoriy retrieved his coat and grabbed the American's envelope from under the seat. He shouldered his laptop bag, wrapping his coat tight around his body before walking towards the factory, hunched into the wind.

Grigoriy faded out of sight and Volkov stepped out of the car. He shrugged out of his coat and opened Anna's door, helping her put the coat on as she climbed out.

"I need to talk to you," Volkov said and pointed to a huddle of trees that hung beside the road.

"Why?"

Volkov stopped in front of a tree and glanced towards the factory to see if they were out of sight. Satisfied, he retrieved a cigarette from his pocket and lit it. He squatted at the base of the tree, his back against the trunk, and dragged deeply on his smoke. "Why were you at the club?" he asked.

"I had to go, Stepan," she said, frowning. "I know you don't like it when I'm there but one of the girls was beaten the other night and ended up in hospital. They were short on numbers." Anna shrugged. "I just wanted to help my friends."

"You care too much. It's going to get you killed."

"Hopefully for a good cause."

"The cause never matters."

"I'd like to think—"

"I know, Anna," Volkov said firmly. "But they will take everything from you until there's nothing left. You have to look out for *you.*"

Anna nodded before kneeling in front of him. "Grigoriy has already told me."

"It's good advice."

"If Nikolay were to ask me—"

"Tell him everything you know," Volkov said. "If you don't, he'll kill you. What good is that?"

She pulled the collar of the coat higher and folded her arms across her body.

Volkov sucked on his cigarette. "It's up to you, but it might be a good idea to apologise to Grigoriy," he said quietly.

"I did," she murmured.

"Good. He was feeling really bad about it."

Anna's face fell. She cleared her throat and pulled at the grass in front of her, plucking it out by the roots. "You didn't bring me out here to talk about Grigoriy." She tossed a handful of grass into the breeze, watching the blades scatter across the darkened road.

"No, I didn't," Volkov said, flicking his cigarette away. He looked up as an old rusty bus rattled past, a late-shift express heading to the manufacturing district.

The passengers stared out with glassy eyes, the bus groaning and coughing black smoke. Volkov waited until he heard the wail of the bus fade away, its brake lights disappearing around a corner. "I need to ask you a favour," he said finally.

"What is it?"

"When was the last time you visited the cherry orchard?"

"At the Novodevichy Cemetery?"

Volkov nodded. "I know you're a fan of Anton Chekhov."

"He's one of my favourite writers," she admitted, smiling. "But I haven't been to his grave since..." Her smile faded. "I don't really remember anymore."

Volkov took his used plane ticket from his pocket. He grabbed a pen and scribbled some notes on the paper.

"Stepan, what is this about?" Anna asked.

He handed her the ticket.

"Directions?"

"Starting at Chekhov's grave. Follow those and you should end up standing in front of a tree that looks like it doesn't belong in the cemetery. Borrow a small spade and dig. About two feet down, you'll find a small wooden ammunition crate with Russian army markings. Take it, fill in the hole and cover your tracks. Take the box home and leave it under the bed in my room."

"Tonight? But what if—"

"Do it, Anna," he said. "I've made the arrangements, but you have to get there before dawn."

She nodded. "Okay."

"Take the car. Drive to Novodevichy and be home before the sun comes up."

She nodded again.

"One more thing," Volkov said, standing up.

He held out his hand, helping her up.

"Never set foot in that club again."

"But Nikolay—"

"Let me deal with him," he said. "Just promise me you'll never go back."

She gently squeezed his hand and his face softened. "That will be an easy promise to keep."

"Good." He pulled his hand away. "Now, what's this I hear about koala bears?"

She rolled her eyes. "Is that what Grigoriy told you? I told him they were talking about a bear in Australia, not koalas."

He tilted his head. "Did they say *a* bear or *the* bear?"

***

"Where's your coat?" Grigoriy asked. He stood at the entrance to the factory, rubbing his hands together and rocking from side to side.

"Never mind." Volkov dismissed Grigoriy's question with a wave. "Who are we waiting for?"

"Yuri," Grigoriy replied.

The *Organizatsiya* was full of men and women known only by first names or nicknames. A patronymic meant a family, a surname meant a past, and the *Organizatsiya* did not pay people to have either. People became what the organisation made them.

It was worse for the women, Grigoriy thought. Even Anna's name wasn't widely known. The men just called her "Volkov's girl". Nothing else mattered, not her identity, her past, her future, nothing. It made her vulnerable.

Grigoriy hated it. Someone should care about people like Anna. All of her, a random series of mistakes, good intentions, regrets, and hopes that had left her sitting cross-legged on the sofa in the hotel room, laughing at old British comedies while practising her English, her bright eyes searching for him while he hid behind his laptop.

"What are you smiling at?" Volkov asked.

Grigoriy cleared his throat. "This YouTube video I saw today. It had this cat and—"

"I'm sorry I asked," Volkov muttered.

"You didn't make Anna feel worse, did you?"

"She'll be fine, but she says you need to improve your listening skills."

"What do you mean?"

"Nikolay sent 'the Bear' to Australia."

"I don't understand."

"The Bear is a man, Grigoriy," Volkov explained, kicking a rock over with his boot. "He was a Chechen freedom fighter in the early days, but he lost faith in the cause when what he called 'foreign fighters' started to take over the insurgency. He joined the *Organizatsiya* because he saw it as a way to get back at the Russian government."

"You know him?"

"We worked together a couple of times. We haven't been allowed in the same room since."

"Meaning?"

Volkov's face darkened. "During an arms theft in Ukraine, he used a busload of high school students to clear a minefield as a diversion."

Grigoriy felt his stomach turn. "You didn't stop him?"

Volkov shrugged. "I tried." He kicked the rock away. "Principles only get you so far in this job, and then they get you killed."

"He sounds insane."

"Maybe, but he's no idiot," Volkov said. "He makes bombs. He lost a few fingers along the way but he was a fast learner. That was how he fought the Russians. That was why Nikolay bought him." He sighed. "And now he's in Australia."

"Maybe he's on holiday."

"I doubt it."

Grigoriy held up his hand. "Wait, you said he's from Chechnya. Is that why Maxim has been visiting the Caucasus?"

Volkov opened his mouth to ask a question but was interrupted by the screech of the factory door as it was wrenched open. A small man emerged. It was Yuri, and he beamed a diamond-encrusted smile. "Boss, sorry to keep you waiting."

"Don't keep me waiting longer, Yuri. Where are we going?" Volkov asked, turning away from Grigoriy.

Yuri gestured with a gloved hand.

Grigoriy and Volkov followed the diminutive Yuri into a large warehouse. Inside, ranks of men were assembling office furniture for export around Eastern Europe. Yuri led them to a loading dock where a different group of men were packing assault rifles, also for export into Eastern Europe, as well as Africa and the Middle East. They vacuum-sealed the weapons into plastic and stashed them in the bottom of tipper trucks. The weapons were then buried under horse manure and the tipper was covered in tarpaulin. Customs agents were reluctant to comb through the smelly cargo, especially when they were handed a wad of cash.

Yuri pointed to a large door on the inside of the dock. "It's an old meat freezer. It doesn't work anymore but it's still good, yes?"

Volkov saw that the door was guarded by a large tattooed man with no neck: Vlad. Beside him was a trolley laden with blood-stained tools, including hammers, saws, and an electric drill.

Volkov looked up from the trolley. "I hear you've been beating up the prisoner," he said.

"We thought that's what you wanted," Yuri said quickly. "He was poking around and—"

Volkov drew his pistol and worked the slide.

"No, Boss! Wait!" Yuri cried.

Volkov pointed the pistol at Vlad, who closed his eyes and cringed, holding his hands up in the air.

"It was me, Boss," Grigoriy said.

Silence hung over the dock. Vlad and Yuri held their breath and didn't dare move. Volkov slowly lowered his weapon and walked towards Grigoriy, his footsteps thudding loudly on the factory floor.

Volkov halted in front of his assistant.

Grigoriy swallowed and felt heat creep into his face. "I told them to beat the prisoner," he stammered. "It was me. It was my fault."

Volkov ran his hand along his stubbled jaw. "Well, Grigoriy. I'm going to have to come up with a special punishment for that."

Yuri and Vlad shifted on their feet.

"Yes, Boss," Grigoriy said.

"I hope you can type with one hand," Volkov added.

Grigoriy shuddered. "I'll do my best, Boss."

Volkov grunted and holstered his pistol. He snatched the envelope from Grigoriy's grasp. "Yuri," he said. "Don't beat the prisoners. I want to be able to talk to people before you cripple them. Sometimes, they want to work for us, remember?"

"Of course, Boss," Yuri said, nodding quickly.

"Recruiting new sources makes Nikolay happy," he added, offering Yuri a cigarette. "And that makes my life easier."

Yuri accepted the offered smoke. "Yes, Boss."

Volkov slapped him on the back. "Good." He walked towards the door and Vlad opened it for him. "But if you do it again," he said, looking up at the giant man before glaring at Yuri, "I *will* kill you."

Vlad fixed his eyes on an oil stain on the ground.

A man was tied at the wrists inside the disused freezer, his arms outstretched above his head and the knotted rope strung over a meat hook. His feet were manacled to a D-ring in the floor and a length of tape sealed his mouth. He was stripped of his warmer clothes, his face was mottled with bruises, and one of his eyes was swollen shut. A small part of his ear had been cut off.

Volkov closed the door behind him and the man raised his head slightly. A small steel chair had been left in the corner of the room and it screeched as Volkov dragged it across the concrete floor and placed it in front of the captive. He tore the tape from the man's face but he remained silent. The man's weight shifted and the meat hook creaked.

Volkov opened the envelope. "Gregory Bartholomew Lambert Junior." He flicked through the documents. "You're a West Point graduate who served in the United States Marine Corps and fought in the war. Did several tours, received some awards for bravery before being employed as an operative by your government. You did some low-level work before being sent out here on a big promotion."

No response.

"Easy, right? Anybody can find out that stuff." Volkov shuffled the pages. "It took us a bit of work, though. The Americans are pretty good with covert identities so we had to check through some fake names before we hit the real one. You see, what your employer is not so good at is stopping an operative's daughter from using Facebook."

Lambert winced as Volkov held a photograph in front of him. The chains rattled. "Tiffany Lambert, only sixteen years old. Pretty blonde with braces and a new boyfriend who Dad doesn't like because he's a bit too hipster. Dad works for the government and keeps guns in the house and it makes her uncomfortable. Standard Facebook whining." He let the photograph fall to the floor. "We found another one of her in her school uniform." He held up a photograph of a smiling girl with brown eyes. "It didn't take us long to learn which school it was." Another photograph. "This one was taken after we picked you up. That's your wife dropping your daughter off at school." Another photograph. "There's your wife pulling away from the kerb and waving to your daughter." Another photograph. "That's your daughter meeting her friends in front of the library." Another photograph. "That's your daughter behind the library, sneaking in a cigarette before class." Volkov clicked his tongue. "Peer pressure, I guess, though you've got to wonder how good your parenting really is."

Lambert was taking shallow breaths.

"We checked the phone book but you're not listed so we had to follow your wife home." He held up a photograph of Lambert's house. "That's from Google Streetview." He held up a photograph of a girl's bedroom. "That's from our guy on the ground. You recognise your own daughter's bedroom, right? She hides her diary behind her vanity mirror, in case you're interested. Did you know she tried pot last month?" Volkov lifted Lambert's chin so that he could look into his eyes. "Should I keep going?"

Lambert said nothing.

Volkov held up a screenshot of a Facebook page. "Tiffany's going on a date this Friday night. It's her first real date with the hipster guy. She's going to a concert with the hairy pinhead. Anything can happen in a crowd like that."

The chains rattled again and Lambert strained against his manacles.

"Do I have your attention?"

Lambert nodded slightly.

Volkov dumped the last of the pages on the chair and cleared his throat. "This is the fork in the road, Lambert. You have a decision to make." The Wolf's eyes shimmered as he glared at the American. "Would you prefer it if we raped your daughter in front of your wife or the other way around?"

Lambert started to sob.

"I know you've been looking for me," Volkov continued. "Your government has been looking for me for a while but what you need to understand is that the *Organizatsiya* has made a substantial investment in me. I'm worth a lot of money to them. You, though, are replaceable. There is no shortage of American men willing to sign up for the chance to have a star on the wall at Langley." Volkov picked up the papers and sat down on the chair. "It's not the end of the world, though. You can work for us, send your daughter to an Ivy League school, and have lots of money in an offshore tax haven. Nobody needs to know about it. Just a bit of information here and there and you become an investment worth protecting."

Lambert held his breath. His daughter's face stared up at him from the photographs scattered on the floor. "If I refuse?" he croaked.

"You live, but your employers will wonder if they can trust you. Especially after we drop some hints that you might be working for us. Your daughter and your wife?" Volkov shrugged and lit a cigarette. "That's not my decision but I can put in a good word for them when I talk to the boss."

Lambert's breathing was ragged. "I'm not a traitor," he rasped.

Volkov puffed on his cigarette. "Not yet."

"I'm not an assassin, either."

"My mistake. You guys call it 'targeted killing', right?"

Lambert shook his head. "I wasn't sent to kill you."

Volkov rocked back in the chair. "Well, if you wanted to talk, you could've just left a comment on my blog."

"I was sent to turn you."

Volkov frowned, scratching his forehead with his thumb. He cleared his throat. "Pardon?"

"Your boss is giving weapons to terrorists," Lambert said. "He's the mastermind behind the bombings in Moscow."

Volkov closed his eyes and shook his head. "How hard did Vlad hit you?" He dragged on his cigarette. "Nikolay doesn't sell to that crowd anymore. It's bad for business."

"Not selling," Lambert insisted. "I said he's *giving* them weapons and he's using Maxim as the broker."

"I see," Volkov said slowly.

"We've also lost eyes on the Bear," Lambert said. "You remember him, right?"

"The name rings a bell."

"He fell off the grid and it makes us nervous."

"So why come to me?"

"Our analysts believe that you're the one most likely to turn on the *Organizatsiya.* Nikolay is up to something and we have to stop him."

"By 'we', you mean?"

"We can do a deal," Lambert begged.

Volkov took one last drag of his cigarette before flicking it away. "Is this the part where I cut you loose and we hold hands and skip to the embassy?"

"I'm sure we can think of..."

Volkov shook his head slowly.

Lambert's face crumbled. "Nikolay knows I'm here."

"You have two options," Volkov said, holding up two fingers. "The best one for you is to work for us."

"I will never betray my country!" Lambert snarled, straining against the chains.

"Nikolay will go to work on your family next. He'll do whatever it takes."

"Go to hell," Lambert spat on the floor.

Volkov rose to his feet, pushing the chair away with his foot. "Option two will save your family."

"And what's option two?"

Volkov whipped his pistol out of his coat and fired. Lambert's head snapped back, his body sagging towards the ground, his hands limp. “Good choice,” Volkov muttered.

13

MOSCOW, RUSSIA

WEDNESDAY 14 SEPTEMBER

1:30AM MSK

Most of the soldiers had been slain and only the bravest or luckiest remained. The towering battlements had crumbled and the bishops had been killed while fleeing with armfuls of treasure from their vestries. One of the kingdom's knights had fallen, fighting valiantly until his last breath, while the other stood before the king. All seemed lost.

But the remaining knight was exactly where he should be: protecting his king.

Maxim groaned, shifting the ice pack on his head, and the chess board blurred out of focus. He took a deep breath and stared up at the ceiling. He'd worked for Nikolay Korolev for two years and, in that time, the chess pieces had never moved.

It was a timber board. The squares had been cut and joined and each of the pieces carved with a blunt tool. The light pieces were unfinished timber while the dark pieces had been charred by an open flame, the grain cracked where the fire had tortured the wood. There were small gaps in the joints and the edges of the pieces were rough and splintered. It was not perfect but it was still beautiful, patiently assembled from scraps and lovingly finished by a killer's hands.

Nikolay Korolev had made the chess board while serving a life sentence in prison. The reformers had thrown Korolev into a cell in an attempt to clean up the streets and rebuild Russia. The steel bars hadn't held Korolev, yet he'd still taken the time to build something. A kingdom, an army: an act of defiance and hope.

And Maxim was proud to be a part of it. The *Organizatsiya* had purpose. Everyone had their role and everyone knew their place, just like the pieces on a chess board.

So why does Korolev tolerate Volkov, a man who refuses to know his place?

"What are you doing in my home?" Korolev barked, slamming the door.

"Volkov knows I wasn't in Africa," Maxim said. He grimaced as he sat up, lifting the ice pack from the back of his head.

Korolev grunted. "Does he know where you were?"

"He didn't say."

"And then you fell over?" Korolev asked. He dropped his satchel on an armchair and walked behind his desk.

"Not quite. Turns out he's quicker than me."

Korolev stretched his lips into a smile and retrieved a cigar from his case. He sat heavily on his chair and reclined before resting his feet on the edge of his desk. "And yet you continue to claim that you're better than him." He cut the cigar.

"He killed five men without even drawing his own gun," Maxim said, tossing the ice pack on the coffee table.

Korolev struck a match, lighting his cigar and puffing contentedly. He eyed Maxim through the dense haze of smoke. "So?"

"Five men, Nikolay," Maxim said loudly, spreading his fingers in the air. "Volkov killed them just for touching his girl. They were his allies. What does he do to his enemies?"

"He's just a man, Maxim," Korolev said. He gestured to the bottle of vodka on his counter.

"You need to put him down," Maxim said. "He might ruin everything." He gingerly climbed to his feet and waited for the mist to lift from his eyes before staggering to the counter.

"He is paid to be loyal to me," Korolev said. "The risk is low."

"What do you have on him?"

"That's none of your business."

"Is it Simone Elliot?"

Korolev pounded the desk with a fist. "Enough."

Maxim nodded and filled two glasses with vodka.

"The plan will work," Korolev said. "Volkov won't interfere."

"I'm not sure if our army is enough."

"It's enough." A cloud of smoke drifted towards the ceiling. "I've been planning this for years."

"Planning and doing are different things."

Korolev puffed out his chest. "You don't think I can do it."

"Your changes will be brought about by force. Physics says that all forces are opposed."

"Nobody has the ability to oppose me." He paused. "Or the will."

"Perhaps the army or the people, or even the Australians?"

Korolev snorted. "What would you know of Australia?" He stood up and paced around his desk.

"A little," Maxim said. "I've seen what their soldiers are capable of."

"And?"

"They're not like our army or the US. They have fewer soldiers, fewer guns, and fewer bullets. When they shoot, they don't miss. They can't afford to miss."

"That's the view of a sentimental soldier," Korolev said. "You should widen your gaze."

Maxim handed Korolev a glass and sat on the sofa. "What would I see?"

He turned around and looked down upon his chess board, puffing thoughtfully on his cigar. "They're defined by what they sell. They're already China's coal bucket and, soon, they'll be a petrol bowser too."

"Are they likely to fight back?" Maxim asked.

"The war exhausted them," Korolev said. "To everyone else, it was just a fragmented insurgency that we each dealt with in our own way. For them, it was a battle that tore them apart, at home and abroad."

"Still, they know how to fight."

Korolev pointed to the chess board before gulping down his vodka. "I bet you I will have checkmate in three moves."

Maxim grinned. "No bet."

"Australia is not my concern. There are people in Moscow who are a greater threat."

"Like Volkov," Maxim murmured.

Korolev turned and narrowed his eyes, removing the cigar from his mouth and tapping the ash from its tip. It sprinkled to the carpet like poisonous snow. "You're like a whining schoolgirl, Maxim."

"I don't trust him."

"Volkov is a killer. He is my tool to use as I please. That is the end of the matter."

"But what if—"

"I said that is the end of the matter."

"Nikolay—"

Korolev whipped the back of his hand across Maxim's face. "Enough."

Maxim touched his lip and looked down at his hand. Blood glistened on his fingertips.

Korolev grunted with satisfaction and turned back to the chess board, dragging on his cigar. His phone rang and he reached into his pocket. *"Da?"* He listened for ten seconds, his jaw twitching as he walked behind his desk. "I wanted him alive." He puffed on his cigar. "I want his tongue cut out and mailed to the American Chief of Station. I want him tied to a billboard with his intestines at his feet. I want a fake money trail and I want his photograph in Europe's tabloid press." He hung up and tossed the phone onto his desk.

"The American?" Maxim asked.

"Dead," Korolev spat.

"I told you."

"I don't need reminding, Maxim." Korolev sucked on his cigar. "Tell the men in the US to stand down.

There's no reason to harass the American's wife and daughter now."

"And Volkov?"

"Kill Simone Elliot," Korolev shrouded the desk in smoke. "Then he will remember his place."

***

"What did he say, Boss?" Grigoriy asked.

Volkov pocketed his phone and jiggled his finger in his ear. "Wrap the body and put it in a coffin. Leave it outside the US Consulate." He handed Grigoriy a small stone statue of a wolf. "Put this on top of the coffin."

"This doesn't sound like Nikolay's idea," Grigoriy said, grabbing the wolf.

"Well, I just let off a shot in a confined space so I'm a little hard of hearing."

"But the wolf, Boss. Are you sure you want this attributed to—"

"It's another notch on my soul, no one else's."

Grigoriy hesitated, staring at the statue in his hand.

"What's wrong?" Volkov asked.

Grigoriy neared. "Boss, you know I can't do stuff like this," he whispered.

"I don't want *you* to do it," Volkov said. "Delegate and let others handle it. I've got other jobs I need you to do."

"Jobs? You have another one for me?"

"Are you sure Maxim has been spending time in the Caucasus?"

"Nikolay booked him an economy seat and Maxim ordered one of the hackers to get him an upgrade." Grigoriy shrugged. "I heard it from the geek who did the hack."

"Can you find out if his map of targets exists?"

"I can try."

"Then do it." He paused. "And another thing, Grigoriy." Volkov placed his hand on Grigoriy's shoulder. "That was very stupid, lying to protect the men like that."

Grigoriy swallowed. "I might have told them to beat up the American. It could be true."

"Be careful who you lie for. Others might kill you for it."

"Principles only get you so far?"

"Exactly."

"I don't know what's gotten into you, Boss, but you might want to consider taking your own advice."

"Feel free to get out of my sight, Grigoriy."

"Yes, Boss," he said, nodding quickly. Grigoriy straightened his jacket and clicked his fingers for Yuri and Vlad. They reluctantly came over and Grigoriy gave them their orders. When he finished and turned around, the Wolf was gone.

***

The latch was well-oiled and unlocked easily, the gate groaning open under its own weight. Anna sniffed and rubbed her nose, glancing around cautiously.

Nobody had followed her.

She pulled her coat tighter around her chest, closing the gate behind her and walking quickly, staying in the shadows. The paths were broad avenues haunted by ghostly trees. Branches stretched out above her like icy fingers, the leaves shivering in the cold, the boughs sheltering the dead. The headstones huddled in darkness, all of them sculpted monuments, each one unique and built to immortalise the person interred underground. She remembered visiting the cemetery as a child, wanting to see the graves of great Russians: Gogol, Eisenstein, Prokofiev, and, of course, Anton Chekhov.

Anna crossed her arms and held her hands under her armpits, shivering and studying Chekhov's headstone. The writer would always be remembered for his plays, translated and performed all over Europe and the US. The man, however, would only be remembered by a handful of letters, a name and date spelled out in

Cyrillic. The mourners were gone, and only half a dozen dying flowers were left, their limp stems teetering in a jam jar full of murky water. The petals were brown papery flakes, like the burned pages of unwanted books.

She shook her head to clear it, recalling Volkov's directions. She walked quickly, eventually finding the tree Volkov had described, unlike any other in the cemetery. The leaves of the other trees had already turned a golden yellow while the tree before her remained green. She looked around and was satisfied that nobody was watching.

Anna reached into her coat, pulled out a small gardening trowel, and fell to her knees. She burrowed into the soft earth, the cold air stinging her eyes. Eventually, her trowel hit something solid and she cleared the remaining earth away.

The box was heavy and the rope handles had frayed. Anna reached into the hole and wriggled her fingers underneath the ends of the box, heaving it out of the earth. She quickly filled in the hole and smoothed it over, standing up and clearing her tracks by brushing the ground with the leaves of a fallen branch. She removed her coat and wrapped the box, clutching it to her chest and carrying it to the car.

She didn't look at it again until she was safely inside the car. The box had a simple latch secured with a padlock, but the timber had rotted. She chewed the inside of her cheek and touched the latch with her fingers before tugging at the lock. The wood splintered and the latch pulled free.

Anna opened the box and peered inside. The contents were sealed in a plastic bag and she reached in and pulled the bag out, unsealing it and tipping it into her lap. There was a sand-coloured beret, two rows of mounted medals, several photographs, a passport, and a set of military dog tags. There was also an old wallet, with a driver's licence and a credit card that had expired seven years earlier.

Stephen Andrew Murphy.

"Stephen Murphy," she said aloud.

The passport, driver's licence, and credit card were in English, and all had the same name on them. The dog tags said "S.A. Murphy", along with "Australian Army".

Anna placed her hand over her open mouth and glanced around again. Nobody was watching her. She shuffled through the photographs. One was of Volkov—Murphy, she corrected—much younger, standing in a uniform. He was beaming proudly, as if he'd just achieved something great. There was a photograph of Murphy with another man, another soldier. They were both smiling, the other man propped against Murphy's shoulder. There was also a photograph of Murphy with a woman.

Anna turned the photograph over: "Stephen and Simone—Christmas Party" was written in English but the date was smudged. Murphy was sitting behind a table, smiling at the camera. He was wearing an open-necked shirt and trousers, and his arm was resting on the table. The woman, "Simone", wore a light summer dress, her dark hair shining and green eyes sparkling. Her hand was stretched out on the table too, her fingertips touching Murphy's hand.

The next photograph was stained with blood. It was "Simone" and another man, the man that had been leaning against Murphy's shoulder in the second photograph. They seemed sad and appeared to be standing in an airport. Anna turned the photograph over. "Simone and Darren—Deploying". There was no date.

Anna sniffed and placed everything back in the box. She looked up through the windscreen, her eyes glazing over as she stared into the darkness.

He's not a monster, he's a man, she thought. "Stephen Murphy," she said again, saying it slowly to breathe life into the words.

He's a man.

14

CANBERRA, AUSTRALIA

WEDNESDAY 14 SEPTEMBER

8:05AM AEST

"Can I help you?" Siobhán Miller asked, standing in the open doorway. The retired model flicked her honey-coloured hair over her shoulder and squinted. "Do I know you?"

"I'm from hotel management, Mrs Miller." Simone Elliot tapped a fingernail on the nametag pinned to her lapel. "I'm sorry to bother you, but we've identified a potential risk to your safety."

"Is this about my missing suit?" She neared, her voice a whisper. "I was right, wasn't I? I'm being stalked."

"I'm here to deal with another matter." Elliot forced her way into the room. "A factory recall was issued and we have to investigate our extension cords. They were all supposed to be inspected prior to check-in yesterday, but some rooms were missed."

Miller closed the door and stared at Elliot.

"It will just take one minute, Mrs Miller," Elliot assured her, kneeling next to the television. "We take the safety of our guests very seriously."

"I don't care about cords. I need to know about my suit. I have to leave for the airport soon and I want it back."

Elliot shook the sleeve of her blazer and felt the microchip slide into her hand. She stood up and showed it to Miller.

Miller screwed up her nose. "What's that?"

It was the chip from an air conditioner's remote control. Elliot had dissected her room's remote earlier that morning. "You've been bugged," Elliot explained.

"Oh, I hate creepy-crawlies." Miller shivered. "Can you spray or something?"

Elliot palmed the chip. "No, Mrs Miller. It's a listening device." She handed Miller a business card. "I'm sorry I lied to you but I had to get into your room to check for myself." Elliot drew a pistol from the small of her back and opened the door, checking the hallway.

"Private investigator?" Miller looked up from the card and saw the pistol, her eyes widening. "What the hell is going on?"

Elliot closed the door and crossed the room. She shifted the blinds with her finger and scowled at the window. "I was hired by your husband," she said. "It looks like you're under surveillance."

"Me? Why me?" Miller was breathing heavily. "Jesus, I *am* being stalked."

"There's a team across the street," Elliot said, tucking her pistol into the back of her skirt. "My guess is they've been watching you since you checked in." She tugged firmly on the tail of her blazer, hiding her weapon.

"Are they watching me now?" Miller asked.

"The blinds are closed and the room is dark," Elliot explained. "The human eye can only adjust to ambient light anyway, so they can't see us at the moment."

"Ambient. Like traffic lights?"

Elliot groaned and shook her head. "No, not like traffic lights. That's amber."

"That's what you said."

Elliot sighed and glared at Miller. "You're not the sharpest stiletto in the closet, are you?"

Miller put her hands on her hips. "Did you just call me a lesbian?"

Elliot gestured for Miller to sit on the bed. "Pay attention." She crouched in front of the young woman. "Your husband is in Spain negotiating a deal worth hundreds of millions of dollars. He believes he's at risk of corporate espionage and hired me to conduct a counterintelligence operation focused on you."

"Me?"

"He believed that the Spanish would use you to get information about him. It would put them in a good position to negotiate terms."

"I would never—"

"Carlos the language tutor planted this," Elliot said, holding up the microchip. "He's been using you."

Miller slowly raised her hand, taking the chip from Elliot. "But he was just teaching me Spanish."

"I've been watching you, Mrs Miller. You've been having an affair while your husband has been away."

Miller shot to her feet. "I have not!"

"I saw the photographs," Elliot said with a bored expression. "The phone calls, the messages, the late night meeting in the bar, and I've got a flash drive full of pictures of you two groping each other."

"How dare you!"

"I've done my job," Elliot said firmly. "Now, I have to report to your husband and tell him what I found." She turned to leave.

"Wait!" Miller cried, bounding in front of Elliot and grabbing her arm. "You can't tell him. Please."

"I have to tell him, Mrs Miller," Elliot said, shrugging off Miller's hand.

"No, he'll want a divorce," Miller sniffed. "And the prenup. I'll be ruined."

“Those are the consequences,” Elliot said, pushing past.

Miller threw herself against the door. “Wait, please. There must be something we can do.”

“I could lose my licence, Mrs Miller. I have a reputation to think about.”

“Haven’t you ever done something stupid like this?” Miller asked. “I mean, Carlos made me feel special. It’s like he loved me for me. Haven’t you ever felt that?”

Yes.

Elliot shook her head. “No.”

“What would you do if you did?”

Elliot stepped back. “You have to give me a reason not to tell him, Mrs Miller.”

“Tell him that Carlos tried to use me. Tell him he, um, b—”

“Bugged.”

“—buggered me, then.”

A raised finger. “Wait a minute.”

“But don’t tell him we slept together.”

“Jesus,” Elliot mumbled, running her hand through her hair. “Look, your husband paid me very well.”

"And I can pay you to do this for me," Miller said.

"No, I couldn't," Elliot said. "Besides, he paid me seven thousand. I couldn't—"

"I'll double it." Miller's face pinched. "So that's fifteen grand."

Elliot blinked slowly and her eyes narrowed. "Right."

Miller dashed across the room and plunged into her tower of luggage, rummaging through the bags. "I'm off to Spain today and my husband told me to put all my cash in a money belt, but I don't wear it because it makes me look chunky."

Miller emptied the belt on the bed and counted out the cash. Elliot thought it best to supervise the woman's arithmetic and watched over her shoulder. Miller laid out about 16,000 dollars.

Close enough, Elliot thought.

Miller handed over the cash and Elliot peeled off twenty notes, returning them to Miller.

"You should still do *some* shopping while you're in Spain," Elliot said.

Miller smiled. "Thank you."

Elliot tucked the rest of the cash inside her blazer. "I'll go back to your husband and say that you never even dreamed of cheating on him, even though Carlos tried."

"Thank you, thank you," Miller said, clasping her hands in front of her.

"You're welcome, Mrs Miller. And remember, I was never here."

Elliot returned to her room and changed into the Chanel suit before hanging the stolen hotel uniform in the suit bag. She shook out an A3 envelope, dumping the cash inside and tossing in her pistol and magazines, too. Her jeans were draped over a chair and she scrunched the pockets to make sure she wasn't forgetting anything. She stopped when she felt the necklace, dragging it out by the chain and placing it in her palm. The silver medallion felt like it was burning her hand and she touched it with her thumb before shoving it into the pocket of her pants.

The hallway was empty. Elliot left the suit bag hanging on a rack of dry-cleaning and took the elevator to the ground floor.

"And how are you this morning?" the concierge asked.

"I don't know," Elliot replied. "Is brain damage contagious?"

"Oh dear," he said, clicking his tongue. "You weren't watching one of those morning shows on the television, were you?"

Elliot grabbed the envelope from her satchel. "Can you please hold this for me until I return?"

"Of course," he said.

"Leanne?" Emily Hartigan approached the counter and looked Elliot up and down. "I barely recognised you," she said. "Is that Chanel?"

"It's a cheap knock-off." She pointed at Hartigan. "Is that coffee?"

Hartigan cleared her throat and pulled her jacket tighter around her chest. "Cola."

"You look terrible."

"Lee had me up all night writing a brief," Hartigan said. "I stole two hours sleep on the couch in the break room."

"Do you want me to drive?" Elliot tore the foil from her cigarette packet and tapped a smoke out of the pack. "You're bad enough when you're wide awake."

"Would you mind?" Hartigan asked. "I need to change my blouse before we get to Military Headquarters."

"Military Headquarters?"

"It's a long story," Hartigan said.

15

MOSCOW, RUSSIA

WEDNESDAY 14 SEPTEMBER

2:45AM MSK

Nikolay Korolev thought she hadn't aged a day, not in twenty years. He zoomed in and adjusted the focus.

Just as beautiful as the day we met.

She moved gracefully onto the terrace, her unbuttoned blouse fluttering in the breeze.

Using the cold air to sharpen her mind.

Her white tank top was tucked into her skirt, stretched tight across her flat stomach, her nipples outlined under thin fabric.

Korolev licked his lips.

She stretched out her arms before curling them towards her head, running her hands along her slender neck. Her fingers threaded through her hair, raising it skyward, and her breasts swelled as she inhaled. Her tank top pulled loose from her skirt, revealing her milky white skin. He could see the outline of her hips, the ridges vanishing beneath her skirt, inviting him to imagine, to remember.

Korolev rapidly snapped photographs.

She released her hair and it cascaded down her back. He adjusted the focus. She was wearing fake nails, or perhaps it was just a manicure. No, she was chewing her nails again. He knew it was true. The ashtray on the terrace had a dozen butts in it, all stained with cherry lipstick. She was smoking more, too.

As if to confirm his theory, she lit a cigarette before placing a hand on her hip. She dragged deeply, drawing the smoke into her mouth before pulling the cigarette away. The smoke lingered around her lips before she inhaled, her eyes closed. She exhaled, the smoke swirling away from the terrace, and raised the cigarette to her lips again.

Korolev lowered the camera and smirked, looking over his shoulder. The palace guard was watching Korolev and wringing his hands but he quickly looked down at his boots. He was a colonel, a commander of the elite soldiers whose duty was to protect the president. The soldiers were poorly paid and so Korolev had easily purchased access to the palace grounds.

Sweat beaded on the colonel's forehead and the bribe he'd accepted seemed to weigh heavily in his pocket. Korolev's bodyguards watched the soldier while Maxim remained in the shadows, studying the skyline.

Korolev raised the camera again. The woman was bent over now, running her delicate hand along her slender calf, stretching. He could see her naked skin at the small of her back.

He snapped more photographs.

Valentina Nevzorova flicked her cigarette away and sighed before pushing through the terrace doors and sitting down in an armchair beside the fireplace. She folded her legs underneath her body and placed a book on her lap. Her chin rested on an open palm and she weaved the fingers of her other hand between her toes.

Korolev checked his watch. Perhaps ten more minutes, he thought. He was poised to take more photographs when he noticed light glinting off metal. It came from the shadows of her study. No, behind the curtains. He adjusted the focus.

No. It can't be.

"Nikolay?"

"I'm busy, Maxim," Korolev said. "What is it?"

"Our time is up," Maxim said.

Korolev lowered the camera and looked away from the Kremlin's Presidential Palace. "Yes, of course. You're right." He turned. "You should arrange supper, Maxim. Stepan Volkov will be my guest."

***

President Valentina Nevzorova sat in the study of the Presidential Palace, her eyelids weighed down by the heavy glow of the crackling fire. A book lay open on her lap and the pages were blurry, but she didn't want to sleep yet. She wasn't ready for her solitude to end. She listened to the interminable ticking of the clock, clinging to the sound, her head heavy on her palm, her grasp slipping.

The flames flickered and startled Nevzorova. Her heart started to pound. She'd dismissed her security detail for the night. She was alone.

"I'm not here to kill you, Valentina," a voice murmured calmly.

The president blinked slowly. "'Ne'er the God made nature can be subdued by any tsars,'" Nevzorova quoted.

"Pushkin wasn't writing about me," Stephen Murphy said, emerging from the shadows behind the curtains. "I'm not here to challenge your authority. And I don't think you'd give up without a fight, anyway."

"Perhaps you should share your wisdom with Nikolay," Nevzorova said, looking into Murphy's eyes. "It might save the city." She stood up and placed the book on the chair's armrest, walking to the side table to pour a drink.

"I heard they gave you a medal for putting him in jail."

"It's true," she admitted, pouring some vodka. "And a promotion." She capped the bottle and started to feel around beneath the table as if searching for something.

"I disabled the alarm button. If you're looking for your cigarettes, they're in the breast pocket of your coat." He pointed to the hat rack by the door where the president's coat was draped on a hook. "You would've seen them when you took one to smoke on the terrace."

Nevzorova's shoulders drooped. "How long have you been in here?"

"Twenty-five minutes." He closed the curtains and noticed a framed black-and-white photograph on the side table. "I cut the alarm while you were powdering your nose."

"I should sack my palace guards." She returned to her chair. "Nikolay should not have sent his Wolf if his intention was to negotiate."

"Nikolay didn't send me." Murphy picked up the photograph. "Is this yours?" The image showed a young Soviet infantryman with a cigarette hanging out of his mouth. He had his arm around the shoulders of an American GI. "Your grandfather? Or did this just come with the palace?"

"It's my grandfather," she said, bowing her head. "That was taken in 1945 just before he helped take Berlin. The US and Soviet forces joined up on the Elbe River and greeted each other like brothers."

Murphy noticed that the GI had a US quarter and was rolling it across the top of his hand.

"Two days after that was taken," Nevzorova continued, "the Russian commander left his tent to inspect the lines. My grandfather went to collect some documents and found the GI taking photographs with a micro camera. He slit the American's throat."

Murphy placed the photograph on the side table. "I guess you can't trust anyone."

"Precisely," she said. "My grandfather gave me that photograph as a reminder. He always told me to trust my friends the least." She gulped down her vodka and placed her glass on the floor. "His advice got me this far."

"What happened to the coin?" he asked.

A smile crept across Nevzorova's lips. "He didn't send you after all, did he?"

"You think I'd lie to you about that?"

"What do you want, Stepan?"

"I want to know what you plan to do about the Australians. I want to know if you're going to fight to trade with the Chinese."

"Why would you want to know that?" Nevzorova asked, her cheek resting on her hand.

He shrugged. "My pension is tied up in energy."

The president curled her lip. "Is this a big joke to you?"

"I'm hoping it is, yes."

"Well, I don't think it's funny." She rose to her feet. "This country's direction is dictated by a small group of selfish people who feel that Russia owes them something." She stabbed the air with her finger. "Meanwhile we have people dying of tuberculosis and AIDS. We have bombs going off all over Moscow. We have coal miners who have barely been paid in decades and soldiers who are fighting wars with no equipment and no support if they are wounded or killed. We can't even afford to bury them in the proper manner," she seethed.

"Selling a lot more oil to the Chinese might help," Murphy pointed out.

"Many people believe that," she said. "So I did my duty. I made my final offer to Beijing. If I can maintain the flat-rate tariff, then I can upgrade our infrastructure and negotiate a reduction at a later date. If not..." She shrugged. "Well, China has enough oil in their strategic stocks to satisfy their needs for now."

"At least until Australia is ready to export, right?" Murphy shook his head. "You're not an idiot. You know Beijing won't accept your offer. You know that Australia is offering cheaper crude that can be pumped onto a tanker and floated to Beijing at a quarter of your transit cost."

Nevzorova grunted. "And when Beijing officially rejects our offer on Friday morning, I can finally show the dinosaurs in this government that people will not do business with us while we are stuck in the twentieth century."

"With all due respect, that is the most ridiculous thing I've heard in a long time."

"That's because you don't see what I see," she snapped. "We have burdensome tax laws and bloated bureaucracies, greedy kleptocrats and sticky-fingered gangsters. If we don't change, we will have no foreign investment."

"You're no different to every other nation."

"Did you know that if I initiated a campaign to dismantle organised crime in this country, it would precipitate the collapse of our financial system? You and your friends are a tumour that has spread and cannot be excised without risking the host's survival."

"No." Murphy held up his hand. "No, no, no. That's not it at all. You're lying to me." He pointed his finger. "If the trade deal succeeds, the *Organizatsiya* will end up with all the money and the people will get nothing."

She studied him warily.

"But if you let the market collapse, Nikolay loses millions, maybe billions. He won't be able to fund his bigger operations. He becomes someone you can actually defeat." He frowned. "You want to shrink the tumour before you cut it out."

Nevzorova didn't say a word.

"You aren't trying to make a political point," Murphy said. "This is a calculated move to destroy Nikolay."

She turned away. "You don't know what you're talking about."

"But Nikolay must know already," Murphy said. "I mean, I figured it out, and he knows you better than I do."

"He *thinks* he does."

"Is this why you can't sleep? Are you worried that Beijing may be desperate enough to accept your price?" He let out a low whistle. "That should backfire nicely and make Nikolay a billionaire."

She whirled around and roared: "Beijing's decision is out of

Nikolay's control." Her face glowed red.

"Is it? He can be pretty persuasive."

Nevzorova's eyes darkened and she marched up to Murphy. "If you want a war, that's what you'll get, even if I have to fight it myself," she said, poking Murphy in the chest. "I will freeze your assets and burn down your clubs. I will seize your drugs and take your weapons. Russia will survive."

"He won't be the only one to suffer. Millions will go down with him."

"What else is there to do other than start again? What is the *right* choice?"

Murphy sighed and shook his head. "I don't know."

"I thought so," she said. "Tell Nikolay I am willing to negotiate terms to secure his safe departure from the country. I don't care where he goes but he can't stay here. It's time for him to retire."

"You and I both know that he won't accept that offer." Murphy turned to leave.

"Where do you think you're going?" Nevzorova asked, falling into her armchair.

"I was thinking about doing some heavy drinking."

"I want information, Stepan." She flicked her hair behind her ear. "Tell me about the Bear."

"What about him?"

"I get briefings every morning about bombings in my city," Nevzorova said. "My intelligence chief believed the Bear was building the bombs and orchestrating the attacks. And then he found out the

Bear has been out of the country and has disappeared."

"He hasn't sent me a postcard either."

"You're being evasive."

"You've been lying to me."

"Is Nikolay using the Bear to make bombs or not?"

"I can't tell you what Nikolay is up to because I don't know."

She snorted. "I don't believe you."

Murphy gestured to her grandfather's photograph. "I don't expect you to."

Nevzorova's eyelids flickered and she stood up. "I will let you leave, but don't you dare enter this palace uninvited again unless you have information that will lead to the end of the *Organizatsiya.* If you ignore those terms, I will execute you in the middle of Red Square, and dress your corpse in a French maid's uniform and blonde wig before parading you around Moscow. Am I clear?"

He smirked. "Crystal clear."

Nevzorova opened the door to her study, allowing Murphy to lead them along the hallway. The president's shoes clicked on the palace tiles and Murphy couldn't help but recall another line of Pushkin: *"And all the night the madman, poor, where'er he might direct his pace, aft him the Bronze Horseman, for sure, keeps on the heavy-treading race."*

16

CANBERRA, AUSTRALIA

WEDNESDAY 14 SEPTEMBER

9:08AM AEST

Simone Elliot and Emily Hartigan climbed the steps of Military Headquarters and pushed through the doors, walking into the lobby. A naval officer with a crew cut was stationed at the front desk and provided them with visitors' passes and an armed escort: a young soldier with a broad chest and square jaw. A sidearm clung tightly to his hip, a green beret sat on his head, and his eyes never stopped searching. He made Elliot's skin crawl. The elevator arrived and the doors opened.

Elliot felt the escort place his hand on the small of her back, ushering her into the waiting elevator. She set her jaw, stepping into the elevator and shoving her hands into her pockets. The escort pressed the button for their floor and retreated to the rear of the elevator.

"I talked to my dad on the phone last night," Hartigan said. "I mentioned you."

Elliot arched an eyebrow.

"He said he doesn't remember you," Hartigan continued.

"Well, I remember him," Elliot said.

"He obviously left an impression."

"He certainly did." Big red welts, in fact, Elliot thought.

The elevator started to slow down and the escort shifted on his feet. He placed his hand on Elliot's shoulder.

"When did you say you met him?" Hartigan asked.

Elliot seized the escort's hand and whirled around. He yelped as she locked his wrist and slammed him face-first into the back of the elevator. She whipped his pistol from its holster and pushed it into the hollow of his cheek.

"Leanne!" Hartigan cried.

Elliot ignored her. "Listen carefully," she said to the soldier, her voice calm. "Your job is to escort us, not to feel us up. If you lay another finger on me, you will never eat solid food again, do you understand?"

The soldier nodded quickly.

"Say it," Elliot insisted, forcing the barrel deeper into the man's cheek.

"I understand," he squeaked.

The elevator came to a stop and Elliot released the soldier, returning his pistol. "Be sure to tell the other commandos that you lost to a girl," she said. He sheepishly accepted his sidearm and stared at the floor. Elliot straightened her jacket and glanced at Hartigan.

"Men," Elliot said, marching out of the elevator.

Hartigan trotted after her. "What just happened?"

"He touched me."

"I didn't think you hated to be touched *that* much."

"Now you know better."

"I guess so," Hartigan said. "Wait. How did you know he was a commando? I thought he was an MP."

"The beret. It's green."

"Right, but..." Hartigan reached out and grabbed Elliot's forearm. Elliot stiffened and Hartigan quickly let go, raising her hands. "I just wanted to ask one more question."

"What?"

"Where did you learn to do that arm-twisting thing?"

"The academy."

Hartigan shook her head. "I saw your file. You never did advanced self-defence training."

"Then how did I manage to do the arm-twisting thing?"

Hartigan's mouth opened but she didn't have anything else to say.

"You two are late," a man said, breezing past and gesturing for them to follow him.

"That's Agent Lee Singh," Hartigan said.

"It was a pleasure to meet him," Elliot mumbled. He walked with loping strides but his back was straight, his posture regimental. "He seems like a real sweetie-pie."

They followed Singh to a secure briefing room, where they were politely instructed to leave mobile phones and other electronic equipment in the lock boxes provided. Their escort sat on a chair outside, rubbing his cheek.

The room was full of people engaged in murmured conversations. Hartigan walked to the front of the room and Singh steered Elliot to a seat and placed a sheet of paper in front of her.

"This is a non-disclosure agreement that says you can be charged under the Crimes Act if you divulge any information you receive through this brief without prior authorisation." Singh held out a pen. "Sign."

"Or I could just leave you guys to it and go shopping."

"You're here to gain an appreciation for the people who want to kill you."

Elliot reached for the pen but Singh pulled it away before she could take it.

"Take this seriously," he said firmly, finally handing her the ballpoint. "Unauthorised disclosure is considered treason. The penalty is life imprisonment."

"Is that the best you can do?" Elliot swirled the pen across the bottom of the document and drew a smiley face next to her signature before holding up the page.

Singh took the document and passed it to an aide. "You'd prefer the death penalty?"

"You'd have to catch me first, sweetie-pie," she said. "I don't suppose you're going to ask me for my insight during the brief, are you?" She flicked the pen in the air and his hand darted out to snatch it.

"Opinions are like orgasms, constable."

"You mean you get yours from the internet?"

Singh's eyes darkened, his jaw twitching. "Mine are more important than yours." He turned and walked away.

Elliot watched after him and narrowed her eyes. She knew one other man with reflexes like that. Singh was not a cop, she thought. He had the suit, the scuffed shoes, the shiny badge, and the faded photograph ID, but his duty wasn't enforcing the law. He definitely wasn't assigned cases to make arrests. Singh was something else altogether.

Elliot folded her hands on the table in front of her.

I might be in deep trouble.

17

MOSCOW, RUSSIA

WEDNESDAY 14 SEPTEMBER

3:28AM MSK

Stephen Murphy paused in the shadows. The street was empty and the cars dozed silently by the kerb, glistening with dew. All of the streetlights were dead save one, which flickered maniacally. A cat squatted on a garbage can and eyed him curiously, its tail swaying back and forth. A Styrofoam cup scraped along the pavement, urged along by a frigid breeze. He heard a shoe scuff on the cobblestones behind him.

The Wolf sniffed the air.

Murphy whipped his pistol from his coat. He turned to his right, firing at a shadow next to the streetlight, and a man wailed. He crouched as he turned again, firing at another puddle of darkness. Another man staggered to the ground.

Murphy straightened up and pivoted, catching Maxim's wrist and stopping the knife before it drove into his side. The two men locked together, the barrel of Murphy's pistol pushing into Maxim's eye socket and Maxim's knife trembling near Murphy's ribcage.

"I told you your aftershave stinks, Maxim," Murphy said through his teeth.

"He just wants to talk, Stepan," Maxim breathed, the barrel of the pistol burning his flesh. "He said you would walk home this way. He prepared supper."

"I'm off the clock."

"Five minutes. I can take you to him." Maxim relaxed his grip on the knife. "And you can keep your gun."

Murphy slowly lowered his pistol and Maxim dipped his head in gratitude, his eye watering.

"This way," Maxim said.

Maxim led Murphy to a small restaurant, the doorway veiled in darkness, the dining room glowing warmly. The furniture was made of old timber, crafted by hand and softened by years of use. Red and white chequered tablecloths were spread across the tables, each of which had a simple centrepiece of candles and salt and pepper shakers. All of the chairs had been turned upside down and placed on the tables. All except three.

Nikolay Korolev pushed his empty plate away and dabbed at his lips with a napkin. "You have remarkable timing," he said to Murphy, gesturing to the chair opposite his. "Please, Stepan, take a seat."

The restaurant's manager was a stout man with a bald head wreathed with wiry hair. His feet were bare and his trousers held up by braces that left welts on his naked chest. He stood by the counter with his wife and daughter. They had been forced from their beds, roused to feed Korolev his supper, and they held each other while Korolev's bodyguards circled them.

Murphy sat down, glaring at Korolev.

"Would you like some wine?" Korolev asked casually, nodding to a bottle that sat on the table. He raised his hand and Maxim prodded the manager's daughter. She yelped and shuffled towards the table to clear away Korolev's empty plate.

"No," Murphy replied, peering up at the girl. She collected the plate and left.

"That's right," Korolev said. "You prefer scotch."

"I also prefer eating in the evening."

"I eat when I'm hungry." Korolev reclined in his chair and picked his teeth. "I bought this place some years ago," he said. "The manager is an exile from Italy. He has exquisite taste."

Murphy watched the manager hold his daughter and stroke her hair.

"He's spoiling me tonight," Korolev continued, reaching for the bottle of wine. "This is a bottle from Greve in Tuscany, a vineyard just south of Florence." He turned the bottle so that Murphy could read the label. "It's an excellent wine. There's a faint aroma of tobacco and the cherry is strong on the palate. It's playfully sweet but there is a smooth bitter finish."

Murphy lit a cigarette and heard Maxim sit on a chair behind him.

"It's made with Sangiovese grapes," Korolev said, sniffing his glass. "They appeal to me. It's the name, you see. It comes from the Latin *sanguis Jovis,* the blood of Jupiter." He held the glass by the stem and raised it up to the light. "It reminds me that men can do anything, even bleed the gods to make wine."

Murphy dragged deeply on his cigarette. "History is a mass grave full of soldiers buried by generals who thought themselves gods."

Korolev grinned, baring his teeth. "Not all men deserve to wear crowns," he said, topping up his glass. "The privilege is reserved for a gifted few. A true leader must understand power. He must be trained in its virtues, its use," he raised his glass, "its intoxicating effect."

The girl returned, placing a plastic chess board on the table before stepping away quietly.

"Chess, the game of kings," Korolev proclaimed. "I've always wondered if you play."

"I don't like playing games by another man's rules," Murphy said.

"I'm not surprised." Korolev grunted, hunching over the board. "Each of the pieces has its own role. They know their power, their limitations, their restrictions." He glanced up at Murphy. "And they know their place."

Murphy exhaled and shrouded the chess board with smoke.

"Some pieces are sacrificed and some are preserved," Korolev continued, "depending on their value and their utility, but all do as commanded to attain victory."

"Victory for the king, you mean," Murphy said.

"He's king for a reason," Korolev snorted. "Do you honestly believe a pawn deserves the same privileges?"

"You could throw the pawn a bone from time to time."

Korolev touched the scar on his jaw. "Tuscany isn't just known for its wine, you know. Many great men have called it home. One of them was born in Florence itself."

Murphy rolled his eyes. "You're going to lecture me?"

Korolev sipped from his glass. "Surely, you've heard of Niccolò Machiavelli, Stepan."

"Didn't he win the MotoGP World Championship last year?" Murphy said, tapping the ash from his cigarette.

Korolev's brow furrowed. "No, Stepan."

"No? I could've sworn it was him." Murphy clicked his fingers. "He raced for Ducati. He had a low-side crash in qualifying at Valencia and started twentieth on the grid."

"What the hell are you talking about?" Korolev asked, his nostrils flaring.

"He was paying $13.50 for a podium finish. I made eight grand."

Korolev leaned forward, his forearm pushing his pieces across the board. "Machiavelli was a writer, a philosopher and a statesman: a truly gifted man."

"He knows how to race a fucking bike, too."

"Enough!" Korolev shouted, cutting his hand through the air. "Machiavelli understood power. While others obsessed over using education and culture to enlighten a prince, he realised these were petty indulgences that led to decadence, and that a real prince knew what was truly important."

Murphy stubbed out his cigarette on the chess board. Korolev's eyes were expectant, his thumb tapping the edge of the table, waiting for Murphy to ask what was truly important. Murphy folded his arms and set them on the edge of the table. "Do you think Honda learned their lessons this season?" he asked.

Korolev slammed his hand on the table, causing it to shudder violently. The chess pieces jumped into the air and some toppled over. Korolev's king remained standing. "I know you went to see Valentina."

Murphy sat up. "Is that so?"

"I'd really like to know how you managed to get into the Kremlin undetected," Korolev said. "But I'll settle for knowing what you talked about."

"Oil."

Korolev grunted. "She's an idiot, and she'll sacrifice this country on the altar of her pride."

"I figured you'd say something like that," Murphy said. "So I started to ask myself: what would Nikolay do about it?"

"I have planned for all contingencies," Korolev said. "Except you."

"So you *are* willing to throw the pawn a bone. You could've just said that instead of going on and on."

Korolev placed his glass on the table and ran his finger along its rim. "Machiavelli wrote that a prince must be like a fox and a lion. A fox is sly enough to avoid traps and a lion keeps the wolves away. So, what must I do to achieve that?"

"You're concerned about my loyalty?"

"You have none left, Stepan. I know because I bought it all."

Murphy's eyes darkened and he snatched Korolev's queen from the board. "Machiavelli also wrote that 'fortune is a woman and if she is to be submissive it is necessary to beat and coerce her'." He touched the queen's crown. "But I never found fortune particularly submissive. Even the king of the gods couldn't overcome the Fates. Sometimes you lose, Nikolay, and Lady Luck is the one who decides."

Korolev stabbed the chess board with his finger. "You *will* win this war for me."

"What's in it for me?"

"It's not what I can offer but what I can take away that should concern you."

Murphy swept his pieces from the board and they clattered to the floor. The bodyguards reached into their jackets. Everyone in the room held their breath, watching Murphy dip his hand into his coat. He pulled out a small statuette of a wolf and placed it on the board, a lone figure facing Korolev's plastic army.

"How dare you?" Korolev hissed. "I swear to Christ I'm going to—"

"How did she catch you, Nikolay?" Murphy interrupted. "And why is it that the coin you carry was minted in 1942, three years before her grandfather claimed a coin as a trophy from an American GI?"

Korolev's face turned to stone. He picked up his glass and poured the wine into his mouth, his cheeks bulging, his bottom lip glistening. He swallowed loudly and sat back in his chair. "Maxim. Get everyone out and don't come back until I call you."

"But Nikolay—" Maxim protested.

"Out!" Korolev smashed his glass on the floor. "Now!"

The family was shuffled outside at gunpoint. Maxim was the last to leave, shrugging into his coat and looking over his shoulder before closing the door behind him.

The room was silent and the two men stared at each other over the chess board. A tap dripped somewhere and each drop clanged against the basin, the sound growing louder and louder.

Murphy lit another cigarette, puffing contentedly. "It was a honey trap, wasn't it?"

"She loved me," Korolev said. "They *made* her betray me. They lured her away with medals and promotions until they convinced her that I was the enemy."

"This is an obsession," Murphy warned. "Quoting Machiavelli doesn't make it a noble cause. It's all about her."

Korolev chuckled. "I feel nothing for her anymore. I learned my lesson." He held his hand like it was a pistol, aiming at Murphy. "You're the one who can't let go of a woman you haven't seen for over seven years, a woman who would sell you to the highest bidder."

Murphy tapped the ash from his cigarette. "You don't know her."

"You are my puppet because of her."

"You made me a guarantee."

"Exactly," Korolev spat. "She's like all the rest, Stepan." He held his hand to his chest. "Take my advice. Kill her, before she destroys you."

Murphy flicked his cigarette away and stood up, his chair scraping along the floor. "Do me a favour: keep your advice to yourself."

Maxim opened the door before Murphy could grab the handle.

Murphy paused, looking Maxim up and down before laying his hand on the Russian's shoulder. Maxim's eye was bloodshot and watery, his eyelid red and swollen. "How's the eye?" Murphy asked.

Maxim rubbed his eye with his knuckle. "Fine."

Murphy patted Maxim on the stomach and punched him in the face. Maxim fell back, sliding down the open door and coming to rest on the floor.

"How is it now?" Murphy asked, stepping through the door.

Korolev grunted at Murphy's retreating silhouette. "Two days, Stepan," Korolev whispered. "Two days and Simone will be dead." He scooped the stone wolf from the chess board and smiled.

18

CANBERRA, AUSTRALIA

WEDNESDAY 14 SEPTEMBER

10:06AM AEST

"That's the extent of our knowledge of their operations," Hartigan said, gesturing to the projected image on the wall.

Simone Elliot stifled a yawn, her eyes watering. Hartigan had just finished going through an itemised list of Nikolay Korolev's property, media, and oil holdings, which were extensive. It was all a bit of a blur for Elliot, and she couldn't help but study the room.

The others attending the briefing didn't dare look away from the presentation. A few of them occasionally interrupted with questions, but only to ensure that the interests of their organisations were adequately represented. The army had a commanding presence. A dozen uniformed officers sat in a row, wearing pressed khaki and strips of coloured ribbons on their chests. Their representative was a sandy-haired officer of middling rank who regularly rapped his knuckles on his armrest. His interjections convinced Elliot that the army had no idea what was going on.

Other agencies were equally oblivious but desperately tried not to show it. One analyst had asked a number of questions but he hardly paid attention to the answers. He wore a tailored suit and clutched a leather satchel embroidered with military patches. His slight paunch swelled against his belt, his currant-eyed gaze wavered each time Hartigan corrected him.

Another analyst seemed to interrupt for the sake of asserting his intelligence, though Elliot was convinced he didn't have much of that. He was a young man cultivating stubble on his chin. He wore a cardigan over a collared shirt and persistently swept his long floppy hair out of his face. Murmuring and nodding, he used the time it took for Hartigan to answer each of his questions as an opportunity to formulate more, rather than to listen to what she had to say.

There was one other analyst that made regular contributions, and she seemed reasonably insightful. She was a middle-aged woman who dressed conservatively and spoke quietly. Those around her had to lean close to hear her, and seemed desperate to catch every word. Those farther away couldn't hear her at all, so they chose not to listen.

The only other person of importance was the agency's deputy director, a man with dyed hair and glasses perched on his nose. Elliot had identified him as soon as she'd entered the room. He dressed like a bureaucrat, a man obsessed with appearances over results, and process over outcome. Men like him all looked the same to her. If she were an agent, she wouldn't even bother to learn their names.

"Which brings us to Monday night," Hartigan said, clicking the remote in her hand.

Elliot felt another yawn coming and clenched her jaw, looking down at the briefing document in front of her. She turned the pages until she found the photograph of Stepan Volkov taken by a teenage girl in a pub. The image had been blown up and was blurry and distorted. Like the briefing, it promised much more than it showed, and didn't teach her anything she didn't already know.

Volkov spoke eight languages and knew how to blend in. He had specialist military training, though nobody knew which country had provided it. Payments were impossible to track and skipped through accounts twenty times per second. Trace evidence hadn't helped determine who he was, only that he'd been in the room. He managed to sneak in and out of countries unnoticed because customs agents couldn't be everywhere and he knew where the holes were. It was a whole lot of nothing, which Elliot had expected, but that hadn't stopped her hoping for so much more.

A bloated photograph from a driver's licence appeared on the wall. "This is Andrei Sorokin," Hartigan said. "Stepan Volkov killed Sorokin in a country pub on Monday night." Hartigan outlined what they knew about Sorokin, including the business card for Korolev's nightclub that Elliot had found in his pocket.

"The state police say that Sorokin was not welcomed by the Russians," Hartigan said. "He stole the business card to flash it around, claiming he was a big-time gangster. The fancy cigarettes served the same purpose. In reality, he was a petty crook with a big mouth."

"Does that rule out the possibility that Sorokin was there to kill Volkov?" the middle-ranking soldier asked. "Perhaps one of Korolev's competitors put him up to it?"

Hartigan shook her head. "That's unlikely. A constable who witnessed the attack reported that Sorokin didn't recognise Volkov when he entered the pub. Even if we assume that the witness was mistaken, it still doesn't fit. All Russians know the stories."

"Stories?" the deputy director asked, peering over his glasses.

"The criminal syndicates in Russia are afraid of Volkov," Hartigan explained. "They say that if you shoot at him, be sure not to miss." She shook her head again. "Sorokin wasn't there for Volkov. They wouldn't have sent one man; they would have sent an army."

"So why was Sorokin in that pub?" the deputy director asked.

"We think he was running," Hartigan said. "He knew that the *Organizatsiya* didn't want him in Australia anymore. He was lying low, travelling with fake ID and paying all his bills in cash. We think he bought his pistol for protection. We found fingerprints on the bullets in the weapon and we know they don't belong to Sorokin. It looks like somebody else loaded the pistol so we think he bought it out of the boot of someone's car. The serial number was filed away and is unrecoverable." Hartigan referred to her notes. "State police seized Sorokin's personal effects yesterday. They're sending it all to us. Hopefully we'll learn more about Sorokin when his effects arrive."

"So what conclusions can we draw from the data, Agent Hartigan?" the deputy director asked, his hands knitted together under his chin.

"The evidence points to termination to preserve business interests in Australia," Hartigan said. "Sorokin didn't heed the warnings until it was too late. He was trying to stay mobile to evade detection but Volkov found him and killed him before his conduct brought the cops down on the local syndicates."

Nice theory, Elliot thought.

Clear, concise, well reasoned, and totally wrong.

The deputy director locked his eyes on Hartigan. "So, based on your analysis, it's unlikely that the *Organizatsiya* poses a threat to our oil interests. Do you agree?"

Hartigan's brow creased. "I'm sorry?"

"There's no threat," the paunchy bureaucrat interjected. "I don't think there is anything to be concerned about."

"That's not true," the floppy-haired analyst objected. "*This* hit was not related to our trade interests but the threat is still real."

"But you can't dismiss the tyranny of distance here," the soldier countered. "A small disorganised group can't project force halfway across the world."

"Force?" Hartigan's eyes darted between the speakers.

"This can't happen," the middle-aged woman said calmly. "Not here. Therefore, it *won't* happen."

"A cyber attack or a series of bombings would cripple us for low cost and high benefit," the floppy-haired analyst remarked.

"Wait a minute," Hartigan cried, attempting to regain control.

"But they won't act until they know for certain that Beijing will reject the Kremlin's offer," the soldier pointed out. "They have to wait for the deadline to expire."

"And we're just supposed to sit here and do nothing?" the floppy-haired analyst blurted.

"The agency needs to find Volkov," the middle-aged woman said.

Elliot sat up straight, her head snapping around.

"He's your best chance of learning the *Organizatsiya'* s intentions," the woman added.

"Then the agency better move quickly." The soldier tapped the face of his wristwatch. "We've only got about forty-nine hours," he said.

The room erupted in a heated discussion and the deputy director stood up, attempting to calm everyone. Elliot turned her head and saw that Lee Singh was staring at her. She slowly looked away.

"Thank you," the deputy director said. The chatter died and he cleared his throat. "All of these concerns will be covered in the next session."

"But, sir," Hartigan protested. "If you'll let me clarify—"

"No, that's fine, Emily," Singh said, standing up.

The deputy director glared at him before turning back to Hartigan. "Thank you. Your brief was very informative." He turned to the audience. "We'll take a break for ten minutes to chew on what we've heard, and then we'll reconvene to discuss possible courses of action," he said.

Spontaneous murmurs broke out across the room. Soldiers climbed out of their chairs and stretched while suited men huddled together and whispered insistently. Quiet conversations quickly turned to the topic of coffee, and words were punctuated by the shuffle of papers and the jingle of change in pockets.

Elliot watched Singh approach the lectern. She stood up, smoothing out her jacket and stepping closer.

"That's all we need from you, Emily," Singh said, propped against the lectern. "You won't be required for the next meeting."

"But you don't understand these people," Hartigan said, spreading her hands. "There's more. I believe—"

"Stop right there, Emily," Singh said, gently slapping the lectern. "You're paid for what you know, not what you believe. Keep it to yourself."

Hartigan's mouth fell open.

"Excuse me, Agent Singh." A young aide approached and produced a file folder. "From last night."

"Thanks." Singh opened the file and scanned the documents inside.

"So what now?" Hartigan mumbled.

Elliot saw Singh close the folder and look over his shoulder. Elliot winked at him and he frowned before turning back to Hartigan. "I need you to solve a puzzle, Emily."

19

MOSCOW, RUSSIA

WEDNESDAY 14 SEPTEMBER

4:08AM MSK

Stephen Murphy turned on the bedside lamp and the globe blinked into life, throwing a dim circle of light onto the ceiling. He ran his fingers along the edge of the box and grabbed the padlock, noticing that the latch had been forced. The lid squealed on its hinges when he opened it. He grabbed the plastic bag and emptied it on to the bed.

"Stephen Murphy," Anna whispered from the doorway.

"Nobody has called me that in a long time," he said, combing through his past.

"Can I call you that?" she asked.

"Maybe one day," he mumbled, picking up the photographs.

Anna watched him gaze at one of the photographs. It was of him and the woman, Simone. Murphy's finger hovered over the woman's face and his grey eyes softened.

"Did I wake you?" he asked absently.

"I was having trouble sleeping, anyway," Anna said, climbing on to the bed. "Who is she?" she asked, pointing to the photograph.

"I understand you're curious, but it's best if you pretend you never saw this stuff."

"Stepan," she protested.

"Anna, I'm serious." He swept his arm over the pile on the bed. "All of this was supposed to be left behind in Australia. I'm not supposed to have a past."

"I know," Anna said, crossing her legs. "Neither am I. I'm not even allowed to have a last name. I'm just a product."

"And I'm just a myth."

"But you are *also* a man," she said.

"And you do have a last name."

"I did once."

"In another world?"

"In another life." Anna picked up a pillow and held it to her chest. "Was Nikolay the one who took everything from you?"

"He got to me late. I was drawn and quartered before I got here."

"There must be something left."

Murphy studied the photograph again. Maybe, he thought. He tucked two photographs into his coat and shovelled his past into a duffel bag.

"Stephen?"

The dog tags were still on the bed. He picked them up and held them in his palm, the chain swaying beneath his hand. "I was in the army in Australia," he said, running his thumb along the stamped letters. "Until a young girl died." He cleared his throat. "My friend died, too."

"The man in the photograph?"

Murphy nodded. "Everyone blamed me for it. I lost everything and I went to jail. That's where Nikolay found me."

"And Simone?"

He cleared his throat again.

"Simone was close to your friend."

"He was her brother."

Anna's eyes fell. "Did she forgive you?"

"I don't know. I haven't seen her since."

"Why not?"

Murphy ran his hand down his face and sat down next to Anna. "You're a little like her, you know."

She cocked her head to the side. "In what way?"

"She was always worried that people would judge her for what she was, that they'd never care to know all of her." He wrapped his fingers around his dog tags.

"What was she?"

He hesitated. "A woman. Pretty. A little crazy."

"Did you judge her for those things?"

"There was so much more to her than that."

Anna shook her head. "But what she was..." She paused. "I mean, those things still mattered, right?"

"Not always."

"Did she find it hard to reach out to people?" She shifted on the bed. "Like maybe the risk of getting hurt was too high?"

He opened his hand and stared at the dog tags. "I can't believe you opened the box," he said.

Anna tossed the pillow away. "You knew I would."

"No, I thought Grigoriy probably would," Murphy said. "I hoped that *you* wouldn't."

"I had to know."

"Stop me if you've heard this one, but there was this girl called Pandora."

Anna reached for his hand. "What's going on, Stepan? Tell me, please."

"I'm not sure, yet."

"Is that why you asked me to fetch the box?"

He shook his head. "At the time, no."

"And now?"

"And now I can't think straight."

She nodded slowly and let go of his hand.

He stood up, picking up his pistol from the bedside table and checking it was loaded and safe before holstering it under his jacket.

"Do you know what my favourite line of Chekhov is?" she asked.

Murphy looked at her. "No, I don't."

"It was an entry in his notes. He wrote that being in love shows a man how he ought to be."

Murphy's shoulders sagged. He pushed his dog tags into her hand and folded her fingers around them. "Take this," he said. "One of the last pieces."

Anna nodded gratefully and accepted the gift. Murphy kicked the empty box under the bed. He picked up his duffel bag, heaving it over his shoulder, and walked to the door.

"You're going to live through this, Anna," he said, turning around. "I promise." He left, closing the door behind him.

Anna stared at the door and shivered. She draped the dog tags around her neck and they fell against her chest. They felt cold.

"I trust you, Stephen Murphy," she whispered.

20

CANBERRA, AUSTRALIA

WEDNESDAY 14 SEPTEMBER

10:15AM AEST

"This is getting frustrating." Hartigan retrieved her mobile phone from the lock box. She turned to see Elliot cast a withering glare at their escort. He stopped abruptly on the ball of his foot, his arms swimming backwards through the air as he fought to keep his balance. The commando retreated to his chair, wringing his beret in his hands.

"What is?" Elliot asked, hefting her satchel.

Hartigan exchanged a glance with the soldier but he looked away quickly. She shook her head. "What was I saying?"

"You were frustrated about something," Elliot said, heading towards the elevator.

"Oh, right." She followed Elliot. "I feel like I'm being made to sit at the kid's table."

"Maybe some fresh air will make you feel better," Elliot said, taking a cigarette out of her satchel.

"I don't smoke."

"Well, congratulations." Elliot placed her cigarette behind her ear and put her hands into her pockets.

"Do you think it's because I'm a woman?" Hartigan asked, pushing the button to call the elevator.

"Lots of women smoke."

Hartigan sighed. "Do you think—"

"Do you really need to be told that you're good at your job to be good at your job?"

"I guess not," Hartigan mumbled. "It just gives me a little bit of motivation. Purpose."

"Do you remember what you said about Volkov, the part that scared you the most?"

Hartigan nodded, stepping into the elevator. "I said that he could be in the room and you wouldn't know until it was too late."

"There's your motivation, right there, and you came up with it all by yourself."

"You're not much of a team player, are you?"

"I guess not," Elliot said. She pulled her hand from her pocket to push the button for the ground floor.

Hartigan heard something clatter on the tiles and looked down at her feet. It was a necklace. "What's this?" she asked, picking up the silver charm.

"It's a medallion," Elliot said, snatching it from Hartigan. She shoved it back into her pocket and looked at Hartigan apologetically. "It was a gift."

"From a man?" Hartigan asked, arching an eyebrow.

"It's nothing."

"It's a caduceus," Hartigan said, adjusting her jacket. "It's from Greek mythology."

Elliot didn't respond.

"You want me to stop talking, right?" Hartigan asked.

Elliot pressed her lips together and nodded.

"I'll stop talking." Hartigan heaved a sigh.

Elliot closed her eyes.

"You don't have many friends, do you?" Hartigan asked.

The doors opened and Elliot slipped through the crowd of people waiting to get in the elevator.

Hartigan trotted after her. "Have you ever had any friends at all?"

Elliot stopped and turned. "Why are you trying to paint me as some social mutant?"

"I was just curious." Hartigan hesitated. "About Angela James."

Elliot's eyes fell and she turned away.

Hartigan watched her leave the building and took a deep breath, briefly balling her hands into fists before walking towards the exit. She found Elliot outside, propped against a bollard and smoking a cigarette. The young analyst swallowed and stared at her shoes. "Lee wanted me to raise the topic discreetly."

"Do you want to try it again?"

"It's a little late for that."

Elliot tapped the ash from her cigarette. "You bugged my room."

"*I* didn't," Hartigan said defensively, her palm on her chest. "Lee arranged it. I didn't even know you talk in your sleep."

Elliot massaged the back of her neck with an open hand.

"Lee just received a report from the surveillance team," Hartigan explained. "Enclosed was a transcript of all that you said last night."

"It must be a short transcript."

"You kept telling a girl called Angela to wake up."

"You know who she is. I heard your father was the lead detective on her murder case."

"I want to hear what *you* have to say."

Elliot closed her eyes and rubbed her forehead. "She was a close friend." She puffed on her cigarette.

"I need more than that," Hartigan said, leaning against another bollard.

Elliot flicked her cigarette away and retrieved another one from her satchel. "I had known her since I was four years old," she said, lighting the cigarette. "We were at the same orphanage."

"Oh." Hartigan looked away.

"Everyone adored her," Elliot said. "I was the bad influence. I'd convince her to help me steal ice-cream from the kitchen or to sneak away and hide during mass. We always got caught and I'd get the strap. She used to get away with a warning. Not even the nuns could resist her smile."

"You grew up together?"

"She was adopted when we were twelve. It was a good family, a wealthy family with lots of influence. I think her new dad owned a newspaper."

"She was lucky."

"She went to all the best schools and was spoiled rotten," Elliot said. "I was in and out of the orphanage but we wrote letters and she visited me." Two soldiers in camouflage fatigues walked past and smiled at Elliot. Hartigan saw her frown.

"Do you know what happened?" Hartigan asked.

"She was murdered," Elliot said, puffing on her cigarette. "Her body was never found. Did your dad tell you about this case?"

"A little," Hartigan said. "Angela's dad started a big campaign in the papers. There was a suspect," she said. "They think she was murdered by a small-time drug dealer but he was killed in a pub brawl before the police could get answers." Her eyes glazed over. "Wrong place, wrong time, you know?"

"Are we still talking about Angela?" Elliot asked.

"That was my dad's last case."

"Really? Why?"

"A man escaped while being held for questioning." Hartigan wrung her hands. "He killed a lot of cops and beat up my dad on the way out the door. He broke his nose, fractured his cheek, damaged three ribs and," she took a deep breath, "broke his back."

Elliot flicked the ash from her cigarette.

"He was forced into early retirement," Hartigan said.

"Does he talk about it much?"

Hartigan shook her head. "I've always wanted to meet the guy, though, maybe in a dark alley with a loaded pistol."

Elliot dragged deeply on her cigarette and it flared brightly. "No free man, huh. I don't remember the Magna Carta mentioning dark alleys."

Hartigan glared at Elliot, her jaw clenched, but Elliot's eyes were empty. She took one last drag and stamped out her cigarette, exhaling a lungful of smoke through her nostrils. She reminded Hartigan of a dragon, a snort of sulphurous breath.

"You're a hypocrite, Emily," Elliot said.

"I didn't say he didn't deserve due process," Hartigan protested. "I was just saying..."

Elliot neared Hartigan. "You feel it, don't you?" she whispered.

"It burns inside you but it feels good."

"I don't want to talk about this anymore," Hartigan said weakly.

"Suit yourself."

Hartigan saw a coffee shop across the square. Picnic umbrellas jutted from the tables and suited men were walking through the glass doors, balancing towers of cups. "What would you do if you were me and you met the man that hurt your father?" she asked.

"I'm not you," Elliot said. She salvaged some change from her pocket and counted it in the palm of her hand. "And I never had a father."

"Yes, but—"

"I'd kill him," Elliot said. "And if I were him, I'd kill you." She nodded towards the coffee shop. "I want a hot chocolate. Do you have more questions or can I go?"

Hartigan shook her head and watched Elliot stroll casually towards the tight cluster of picnic umbrellas. A caduceus, she thought.

The caduceus is the staff of Hermes: the messenger god, the trickster, the gambler, the merchant, the killer, and the thief.

"Why didn't you call for help when he cuffed you to the bar?" Hartigan whispered.

21

CANBERRA, AUSTRALIA

WEDNESDAY 14 SEPTEMBER

12:52PM AEST

Lee Singh watched the deputy director shuffle his briefing papers into a neat pile on the lectern. The room was nearly empty, the last huddle of analysts murmuring to each other as they neared the exit.

Singh stood up and buttoned his jacket before approaching the lectern. "You're a smooth talker," he observed.

"They want to start selling oil to China." The deputy director handed his briefing papers to an aide, who obediently secured them in a briefcase. "They don't want to hear about problems."

Singh saw a junior agent bound through the door clutching a manila folder. "That doesn't make the problems go away," Singh said.

"No, but that's your job, not mine." The deputy director accepted the manila folder from the junior agent before dismissing him with a wave. The young man left as quickly as he came. "I can't recant on an assessment without good reason, Lee."

"Can't or won't," Singh said. "I mean, what *will* they say about you?"

"That's enough," the deputy director warned, opening the folder on the lectern. "I care about the country's security more than my career." He frowned. "Yesterday, you said this was all probably nothing, anyway."

"No, that's what *you* said." Singh thrust his hands into his pockets. "I just need to know that I have your support."

The deputy director adjusted his glasses and squinted at the file. "Just do your job, Lee," he said wearily. "You only have forty-seven hours left."

"I know, I know," Singh muttered. "What's in the file, anyway?"

He grunted and tapped his finger on the open folder. "Jakarta has graciously turned down our offer of personnel to help investigate the murder of Dr Marco Belo."

"They don't want our help?"

"This is a bad sign."

"They think we set up Volkov's hit," Singh said, jingling the keys in his pocket. "It's too bad. I wanted to see a proper scene."

"They attached the case file if you want to read it." The deputy director held out the folder. "My Indonesian is rusty."

Singh took the file and opened it. He paused and let out a low whistle. "Says here that Volkov was sharing a cigarette with a security guard behind a hotel. He killed the security guard, took his swipe card, and dumped the man's body in a skip bin. The security guard inside the hotel knew his friend was on a smoke break, so didn't look up when Volkov swiped in. Both men were strangled."

"Jesus."

"Volkov disabled the security system and went upstairs, avoiding the guard on roving patrol. He swiped into an empty room and used the balconies to reach his target's suite. The bodyguard on the door didn't even hear the shot."

"How did he escape?" the deputy director asked, adjusting his tie.

"He set a smoke bomb on a timer," Singh said. "The fire alarm tripped and he probably evacuated with the other guests."

"Volkov would've stood out in a crowd of Indonesians," the deputy director observed.

"The hotel caters to European and Australian tourists."

"Oh."

"You were right about the private charter, too. It was hired out of Jakarta at short notice, and all the paperwork was in order. His cover was good. Customs barely looked at him." He shut the folder. "Pretty thorough, don't you think?"

"Thorough?"

Singh handed the folder to the deputy director's aide, who added it to the other documents in the briefcase. "This hit took planning, research, and surveillance. He didn't arrange this on the flight out of Australia." Singh shook his head. "But he couldn't set up the job on Andrei Sorokin on the flight in, either."

"Where are you going with this?"

"The private charter was expensive and conspicuous, but it got him here quickly." Singh grew thoughtful. "Someone was keeping tabs on Sorokin and called Volkov out of Jakarta for the hit."

"Impossible," the deputy director said. "They'd have to predict where Sorokin was going to be before calling Volkov in. It's a long flight from Jakarta, plenty of time for Sorokin to relocate."

"Sorokin was an amateur," Singh said. "It would be pretty easy to drive him in a certain direction and flush him out when the time came."

The deputy director nodded slowly. "Does this mean Sorokin was more important than we thought?"

"I'm not sure," Singh confessed.

"Look into it." He pushed his glasses further up the bridge of his nose. "I'll call the embassy in Jakarta and tell them we're not coming."

Singh held up his hand. "Tell them to make arrangements for our arrival as planned."

"Why?"

"It'll put Waters on the grid."

"What do you mean?" the deputy director asked, checking his watch.

"Think about all the paperwork," Singh said. "We're talking rushed visas and plane tickets, and then there are visit protocols to implement through our embassy in Jakarta, and lots of phone chatter. Once we load up the system with all of that, there'll be a leak and Volkov will find out where Waters is."

"But that will only lure him to Indonesia."

"Not when we cancel the trip."

***

The elevator doors opened and Simone Elliot stepped into the corridor, pulling her red coat tighter around her waist. New check-ins had gathered in the lobby, brandishing brochures and backpacks and gawking at their phones while waiting for their turn at the front desk. Cars were queued up in the driveway and suited men wearing caps were carrying luggage through the glass entrance.

Elliot sidestepped stacked suitcases and an elderly couple perusing the restaurant's menu. She neared the exit and nearly collided with a man wearing a salmon-pink polo shirt and leather jacket, a black golf pencil tucked behind his ear. He mumbled an apology and joined his friend in the queue, a man wearing a green polo shirt and dark blazer.

She grunted her forgiveness and finally made it outside. She sighed at the sky. Sullen clouds had swooped over the city, dousing the light of the late-afternoon sun, and a swirling wind whipped her hair around her face. Still, she thought, there was space out here, room to breathe, room to think.

Her shoes squished through the watered lawn until she reached the pavement and turned towards town, searching for the Thai restaurant Hartigan had recommended.

Hartigan, she thought. Elliot had sat outside Hartigan's cubicle for most of the day. The young analyst had spent hours on hold with a Russian intelligence agency only to be told that they don't give out information about their own citizens to foreign interests. Customs, shipping, on-line hotel bookings, car hire, all contacted and none of them able to provide a unique insight on Stepan Volkov's movements.

And they still don't know who he really is.

Cars swished past her, racing to the next set of traffic lights, and she stepped carefully along the bulging pavement, the concrete cracked by tree roots snaking beneath her feet.

They're wasting their time, she thought, sweeping a low-hanging branch away with her hand. They couldn't see what was right in front of them, why Sorokin had been in that pub.

Natalie Robinson.

Two schoolgirls skipped past her, singing a song. One of them held a painting she'd done in class, the paper pincered between her fingers.

The agency believed that Robinson was just another bystander, but if they looked into her background, really looked, they would see that she was the girl with all the answers. A Russian girl, a prostitute, a stripper, a slave of the *Organizatsiya,* a survivor, she was the best kind of information source. Unnoticed and unthreatening, her head would be full of secrets, perhaps including the whereabouts of Stepan Volkov himself.

Natalie Robinson: the girl with that bloody pencil in her hair.

Elliot stopped at the traffic light and stabbed the button. A small group of people gathered around her, waiting for the little red man to turn green while cars raced through the intersection.

Elliot needed to talk to Robinson, needed to hear what she knew, but she couldn't contact the girl without arousing suspicion. She had to wait until the agents figured out that Robinson was worth interviewing. The waiting was the hardest part. It dulled her mind and made it hard to focus.

Pencil?

The traffic lights changed, the cars stopping. She wrinkled her forehead.

Behind his ear? A golf pencil?

A car stopped in front of her, inching deeper into the intersection, determined to jump the light. The car had tinted windows and Elliot could see the pedestrians reflected in the glass.

Uh-oh.

Behind her was a man wearing a salmon-pink polo shirt and leather jacket.

Shit! Idiot! Fuck!

It wasn't a golf pencil: it was a Sobranie cigarette, black with a gold filter, just like Sorokin had carried.

The Russians are here.

Elliot's heart thudded in her chest.

The light turned green and Elliot led the pedestrians across the intersection, noticing a red mailbox on the pavement ahead. A van was parked against the kerb, hazard lights flashing, and a man was emptying the mailbox into a sack. His task complete, he locked the mailbox. Elliot watched him open the rear door of the van, staring intently at the window in the door. She saw the street as it streaked across the glass.

A shimmering reflection: her tail was ten metres behind her and puffed on a cigarette. The wind whipped past and Elliot turned her head to flick the hair out of her eyes. The man in the green polo shirt was across the street and keeping pace. His blazer blew open and she saw a pistol holstered against his ribs. She patted her coat and remembered that her weapon was in an envelope in the custody of the concierge.

Her mouth went dry.

Cover was limited. There were buildings, some trees, parked cars, and so many people. She couldn't fight in public. And the agency would be tailing her too, which meant running was out. She couldn't turn back either.

There was only one option left.

She neared the Thai restaurant and stepped through a sliding door, a doorbell chiming to announce her entrance. She ducked under creeping vines and dodged a trickling fountain, frowning at the ornamental cat beckoning her to order.

"Yes, what would you like?" a young girl asked.

Elliot squinted at the laminated menu taped to the counter. "Uh, I guess I'll have a number seventeen.

And maybe a number eighty-nine." She popped her tongue against the roof of her mouth and the doorbell chimed. The floor creaked and she could hear her tail breathing behind her, the air whistling through his nose. "And I'll get a side of number six."

The girl tapped the keys on an old cash register.

Elliot handed the girl two small bills. "Do you have a bathroom I can use?" she asked.

"Down the hall on your left," she said, returning her change.

"Thank you."

"Your order will be ready in ten minutes," she said.

Elliot turned and walked along a narrow corridor. She opened the bathroom door and stepped inside, her eyes scanning the room. There were two cubicles, one sink, a cloudy mirror, a row of cracked tiles, and a frosted-glass window that was open, the security screen coated in dust. Two spare fluorescent light bulbs sat in cartons on the windowsill.

Elliot reached into her coat and found a coin. She shut a cubicle door and used the coin to lock it from the outside before kicking at a cracked tile. The ceramic pieces clattered to the floor and she picked up a long shard shaped like a hockey stick. Then, she reached up to the windowsill and retrieved a light bulb. She returned the empty box and slid the light bulb into her pocket.

The doorknob jiggled.

Elliot stood beside the door and pressed up against the wall, gripping the shard of tile. The door creaked open and a pistol hovered into the room followed by an arm clothed in leather, the weapon aimed at the locked cubicle.

She seized his wrist and slashed the back of his hand with the splinter of ceramic. The pistol fell to the floor and she stabbed him in the ribcage before yanking him into the room. The man stumbled, throwing his hands out. Elliot kicked the back of his leg and he fell to his knees. She reached over his head and shoved two fingers into his nostrils.

He cried out.

Elliot rammed the light bulb into his mouth and grabbed the back of his head before smashing his face into the sink. The man collapsed, spitting blood and glass on to the floor. He curled up into a ball, his fingers over his mouth.

Elliot rolled him away with her foot and squirted some soap into her hands. She washed up before towelling off and leaving the room.

"Your order is ready," the young girl called out to her, holding up a plastic bag.

"Thank you." Elliot claimed her order and walked outside, reaching into her pocket for a cigarette. She spotted the man in the green polo shirt leaning against a streetlight.

"Zazhigalka?" Elliot asked. "I need a light."

The man turned, his mouth falling open, but he reached into his blazer and retrieved a lighter.

"Tell Nikolay Korolev to send the Wolf." Elliot lit her cigarette, dragging deeply. "Anything less is a fucking insult." She tossed the lighter on to the roof of the restaurant and walked away.

22

CANBERRA, AUSTRALIA

THURSDAY 15 SEPTEMBER

10:14AM AEST

Hartigan clicked the mouse, maximising the window, and scrolled through the article, her eyes skimming the text. She twirled her pen around her thumb.

"Valentina Nevzorova," she mumbled.

Hartigan frowned and rummaged around her desk for a notebook, eventually finding a blank piece of lined paper. She scrawled a note on the page.

"You'd better not be reading the gossip column," Singh said from behind her.

Hartigan covered her note with her hand and swivelled on her chair. "It's research," she said. "I've been wondering about this trade deal. I was trying to see it from the Kremlin's perspective."

"What are you talking about?" he asked, tapping his fingers on the manila folder in his hand.

"Nevzorova." She turned back to the screen. "The conservatives in Moscow are criticising her handling of the trade negotiations. They believe the trade deal will collapse because a woman doesn't have the strength to dictate terms to the Chinese."

"Are they right?"

"No, they're pigs," Hartigan said. "But they have a point. She could do a lot more to secure the deal."

"Maybe she's incompetent."

Hartigan glared at Singh. "You don't become the first female president of a country like Russia by being incompetent."

"Do you have a theory?"

"No."

"Then let's talk about something else."

"I have a thought, though."

"Let's move on, anyway." He shifted on his feet. "Tell me about the latest bombings."

Hartigan rolled her eyes. "Two more in Russia." She folded her note and tucked it under her keyboard. "The first one went off in a Moscow department store. Eighty people are dead."

"How many bombings is that now?"

"Four in a fortnight. The Russian people are starting to panic. It was enough to get Nevzorova out of the Kremlin to tour a hospital ward and deliver a speech." She pushed away from her desk.

“Let me guess: resolute, firm, strong.”

“The second bomb was strange, though.”

“Oh?”

“The militants blew up a chunk of the Eastern Siberia–Pacific Ocean oil pipeline.” Hartigan twirled her pen around her thumb again. “They’ve never struck a target that far from Moscow before.”

“Many dead?”

“None, which was lucky. Can we talk about something relevant to the investigation now?” she asked. “Did you know that Andrei Sorokin was still getting paid by Titan Energy?”

Singh furrowed his brow and shoved his hand into his pocket.

“Didn’t know that one, huh?” Hartigan wheeled her chair closer to her desk and rifled through a pile of documents. She found what she was looking for and passed the papers to Singh. “Computer Forensics finally reviewed Sorokin’s financials. He was paid twenty grand by Titan Energy the day before he was murdered.”

Singh ran his finger along each line on the page, his lips moving as he read. “This says that the payment originated from Lime.”

"Right," Hartigan said. "Lime is a charity that raises money for cancer research. It's administered by the wife of Titan's CEO."

"Are you sure it wasn't severance?"

"I'm sure," Hartigan said. "And Sorokin didn't have cancer, either." She shrugged. "It's worth looking into."

"Leave it with me and I'll take care of it," Singh said, rolling up the documents and tucking them into his pocket. "I need you to arrange for another witness to be brought in, someone who was in the bar on Monday night."

"Who?"

Singh opened the folder and cleared his throat. "Natalie Robinson: inherited a substantial amount of money when her parents died in a car accident. She only tapped the money to buy a house. She works casual hours at a technical college teaching mathematics but dedicates most of her time to completing a physics degree. Her accounts are good, no criminal record, no affiliations with any clubs or societies, no churches, not even a fucking book club. Her internet traffic is straightforward. She buys shoes and clothes online but doesn't indulge in porn or online poker."

"Sounds like a solid citizen," Hartigan said, shifting in her seat.

"She is also Russian and conducting research into nuclear fusion." Singh closed the folder and tossed it on top of Hartigan's keyboard. "That makes three Russians in that bar. One is dead, one is Volkov, and one is this girl. I want to talk to her."

"Is this a sad attempt at profiling? I mean, being Russian doesn't make her guilty."

"Volkov carried out a hit in Jakarta after he killed Sorokin," Singh explained. "I think he had someone trailing Sorokin and Robinson fits the bill."

Hartigan stared at him blankly. "What are you talking about? What hit?"

Singh clicked his fingers. "That's right. I was meant to tell you."

"Jakarta?" Hartigan tilted her head. "He flew from here to Jakarta and killed someone? That means he was working two jobs simultaneously."

Singh tapped his finger against his nose and pointed at Hartigan.

Hartigan scowled. "Same amount of planning?" She reached for her mug. "I mean, was either job short notice?"

"Get the girl in," Singh said impatiently. "Put her in the same hotel as..." He raised his head and turned on the spot. "Where's Waters?"

"I don't care." Hartigan realised her coffee had gone cold. She sipped from her mug anyway.

"You were supposed to keep an eye on her," Singh scolded.

"She won't get far. I told security to make sure she didn't leave the building. I do care about protecting witnesses, Lee."

"I should've put her in the childcare centre."

"I'd just eat the children, sweetie-pie," Elliot said, wheeling her chair out of a neighbouring cubicle.

Singh narrowed his eyes. "You're going back to the hotel," he said. "Go down to the lobby and ask for Alan. He'll escort you back to your accommodation."

"You want me to twiddle my thumbs in my room?" Elliot asked.

"Get a massage," he said. "Order room service. Watch some movies. Read a book. There's nothing for you here."

"Still don't want my help, huh?" Elliot blew a bubble with her gum and it burst. "The clock is ticking and you're wasting time."

Singh gestured towards the exit. "I'm not going to tell you again."

"Have it your way, sweetie-pie," Elliot said with a sigh. "But I'm guessing your philosophy on orgasms hasn't worked out too well for you, so maybe you should reassess your regard for others' opinions." She took the gum out of her mouth and stuck it on the cubicle's partition before rising from her chair.

Hartigan watched Elliot walk towards the elevator. "You have a philosophy on orgasms?" she whispered.

"Do you have a plastic baggie?" Singh asked, examining the gum clinging to the partition.

Hartigan rummaged through her drawers and found a small bag. "Didn't you just say we should be watching her?"

"Yes, and you couldn't handle that." Singh snatched the bag and picked up Elliot's gum, sealing it inside. "The surveillance team will watch her closely while she's in the hotel. They'll be there when the fish takes the bait."

"Bait?" Hartigan shook her head. "She's a witness, not bait." She pointed to the plastic bag. "She's definitely not a criminal."

Singh tapped his finger against his nose and pointed at Hartigan. He turned and left her cubicle.

"I really want you to stop doing that," she said.

"Bring me Natalie Robinson, Emily," he called out over his shoulder.

Hartigan muttered a curse, rubbing her eyes before turning to her computer screen. She reset the page, highlighted the search bar, and typed "Volkov murder

Jakarta". News videos appeared and she clicked on the first one.

"Dr Marco Belo was murdered in his Jakarta hotel room by notorious contract killer Stepan Volkov, who escaped Indonesia undetected."

Hartigan tapped her pen on the edge of her desk.

"Born in East Timor, Dr Belo spent his life advocating for human rights and independence. Most recently, he was a tireless advocate for the redrawing of the maritime border between East Timor and Australia. A redrawing of the border would prevent Australian energy companies from taking the natural gas on the sea shelf."

The image on the video cut to file footage and Hartigan maximised the picture.

"One Australian energy company, Titan Energy, has spent millions stonewalling Belo's attempts at lobbying for UN involvement. CEO Geoffrey Geldenhuys—"

Hartigan paused the video and Geoffrey Geldenhuys froze on the screen. He was standing at a press conference, a cluster of microphones in front of him and his company's logo behind him. He was casually grasping the edge of the lectern, beaming an easy smile and winking at someone off-screen.

I don't think Lee is telling me everything.

She slouched in her chair. "Nobody is," she mumbled. She picked up her phone and dialled the extension for records. "This is Hartigan. I need a cross-reference. Do you have access to the foster care system database?"

***

A few hours later, Hartigan found Singh standing at a paper shredder, feeding documents into the chugging machine. "Lee?" she asked, her heels clicking on the tiled floor. "What are you doing?"

"Clearing my desk," Singh replied. "What do you want?"

"Robinson is on her way to Canberra," Hartigan reported. "Uniformed police are escorting her."

"Who?"

"Natalie Robinson. The girl who was in the pub when Sorokin was killed," Hartigan said. "You told me to bring her in."

"Oh, right." Singh dusted his hands. "Is that all?"

"Actually, I think I've got something."

"Make it quick. I haven't had lunch yet." He switched off the paper shredder and turned away.

Hartigan followed him, quickening her pace to catch up. "Volkov didn't have an accent," she said, walking hurriedly beside him.

"There's nothing in the witness statements about—"

"People don't report what they don't hear," Hartigan interrupted. "The investigating detective mentioned it when I met Waters."

"Okay, so one guy says—"

"Wait, I'm not finished. We know Volkov probably has military training of some kind, and we assumed that meant a foreign army, but he could be a former Australian soldier." She started rolling her hands. "I had the tech guys do a facial search on the military database using that image from the mobile phone but they got no hits, although they said the image was pretty poor quality and that Special Forces guys won't show up because their identities are classified for—"

"Jesus, Emily," Singh cried out, walking into the break room. "Will you make some kind of point?"

Hartigan ignored the interruption. "—national security reasons, right? Anyway, I started to think about Waters. Did you know she has a working knowledge of the military? Not to mention the *Organizatsiya.* I mean, while we were in Military Headquarters, she identified our escort's regiment by the colour of his beret."

Singh opened a cupboard and popped his lips. "When did we run out of bread?" He closed the door and opened another.

Hartigan started pacing behind him. "And the barman said that he thought Waters and Volkov spoke, almost like she knew him." She raised a finger. "We assumed that she just identified him and was challenging him, but then she didn't call out for help when he cuffed her to the bar, so I—"

"That's enough, Emily," Singh growled, walking up to the vending machine. "I'm bored, frustrated, and hungry. Go talk to somebody else."

"Agent Singh, I'm on this investigation because I—"

"—read a few books and wrote a paper," Singh interrupted, counting change in his palm. "You're here because the deputy director seems to believe in your potential, but it's not a belief I share." He looked up and groaned. "Fuck. When did the vending machines stop taking change?"

"So you're going to disregard everything I say?" Hartigan said, her voice trembling.

He gave up on the vending machine and opened the refrigerator. "That's likely, yes." He ducked his head into the refrigerator and shuffled the plastic containers on the shelves.

"Then why should I bother?"

"Give up and go home, if you want." Singh emerged from the refrigerator clutching a plastic container. A sticky note was glued to the lid bearing a name scrawled in ink.

"That's not yours," Hartigan pointed out.

"It is now." Singh peeled off the note and scrunched it up before tossing it in the bin. "Why are you still here, anyway?"

"Because you need to know that Leanne Waters was not at the same orphanage as Angela James," Hartigan said. "But Simone Elliot was."

"The Serpent?" Singh opened the microwave and cracked the lid on the plastic container. "You think Waters is the Serpent?"

"Simone Elliot disappeared the same year Leanne Waters joined the police force. It's a fake identity, a really good fake too."

"I thought so." He shut the door and set the timer.

Hartigan took a step back. "What?"

"We lifted fingerprints out of her room," Singh said, starting the microwave. "But so many people go through hotel rooms. That's why I picked up the gum. DNA evidence is much more believable."

"You know?"

"I suspected," Singh said. "At first, anyway. My suspicions were confirmed last night when she killed a Russian guy in a Thai restaurant's bathroom."

"Jesus."

"Wait until you hear how she did it."

"No! Lee." Hartigan groaned and paced the break room. "Our investigation has been compromised. A known felon has infiltrated our headquarters. We need to arrest her."

"Arrest her?" He snorted. "The Russian was from the *Organizatsiya,* which means Korolev has her under surveillance. And, if the stories about her stealing his art are even remotely true, there's a good chance Korolev will send Volkov to kill her."

"Which you're going to stop, right?"

"I haven't planned that far ahead," he said. "The mission is Volkov, Emily. We need to know what he knows. That's my priority."

"What he knows about what?"

"You know, you're not nearly as clever as everyone thinks you are."

"Oil?" she sputtered. "This is all about oil?"

"Bingo." The microwave beeped and Singh opened the door. "Elliot is perfect bait and she seems eager to wait this out to see what happens. I'm not going to do anything to spook her and make her run, not when we're this close." Singh retrieved a fork from a drawer and stirred the contents of the container.

"What if Volkov doesn't come for her?" Hartigan asked.

Singh shook his head and walked towards the door. "You know, I'm still not seeing what the deputy director sees." He left the room.

Hartigan took a deep breath and plunged into the hallway. "I ran a comparative search," she said to Singh's back, "cross-referencing military personnel with the foster care system."

Singh stopped walking and turned around. "Why?"

"Like I said, I wanted to see if I could tie Volkov to our military."

"I doubt it."

"I narrowed the search to include only Elliot's orphanage," Hartigan continued. "Elliot had a twin brother in the army. They were separated at birth but the cops didn't know about him until he was killed in the war. Simone Elliot's name was one of two on the guy's emergency contact list."

Singh dropped his fork into the container. "What was the other name?"

"That doesn't matter," Hartigan said. "What matters is the relationship. I think Elliot met Volkov through her brother while he was serving. I think Elliot and Volkov were lovers."

Singh shook his head. "Now you're just guessing."

"No, I'm—"

"—grasping at straws?"

"Look, Lee," Hartigan said impatiently. "Darren Harper is the key—"

"Whoa, wait a second," Singh said. "Say that name again."

"Elliot's brother's name was Darren Harper."

Singh suddenly seized her forearm, holding it tight. "Harper?" he asked desperately.

"Yes, Harper."

"The other guy's name, the emergency contact." He squeezed. "The one you found."

It felt like he was going to crush her arm. "Lee, let go."

"Think, Emily." He tossed the container into a nearby rubbish bin.

She closed her eyes and wrinkled her face. "Um, Murphy. It was some guy called—"

"Murphy." He let go of her arm and took a step back, his mouth falling open.

"Lee?"

"Come with me, Emily," Singh said quietly. "Right now."

23

CANBERRA, AUSTRALIA

THURSDAY 15 SEPTEMBER

4:17PM AEST

Emily Hartigan chewed a lock of her hair while Lee Singh paced furiously back and forth across the communications centre. The communications supervisor wrapped his hand around the mouthpiece of the telephone and looked up at Singh. "Sir, the governor says there might be some technical difficulties."

"Don't give me that shit," Singh snapped. "Murphy's still supposed to be in that cell. I want to see it for myself."

"She's just having trouble working the video teleconferencing facilities."

"Use a fucking laptop with a webcam," Singh growled. "Just make it happen."

Hartigan had already skimmed Stephen Murphy's army file. It was written by bureaucrats, not an analyst examining whether Murphy was a national security threat, forcing her to mentally take the file to pieces and reassemble it. The signs were there and they started at birth.

Murphy had been born into a loveless marriage and was the catalyst that kept his parents together. His father had been in the army, and the family frequently uprooted and moved from post to post at the whim of army headquarters. Murphy was twelve when his father was killed, and the untimely death was documented as a "training accident". His mother had remarried but died four years later from breast cancer.

Murphy had not been close to his father but reserved a special distaste for his stepfather. The man was a drunk and eventually turned on Murphy, assaulting him with a metal rod. Murphy retaliated, beating his stepfather ruthlessly and putting the man in a coma. The police had been forced to intervene and Murphy was sent to juvenile detention for three months before being turned over to the custody of his aunt. He stayed with her until he was old enough to join the army.

He had been an infantryman, a member of the elite Special Forces, and he had served in a fistful of wars, all of them before the age of twenty-four. Most of the battles he'd fought were still unofficial, and some would never be publicly acknowledged as ever occurring. However, Murphy's honourable service did not save him when Darren Harper and a family of three were killed due to his negligence. He'd been sentenced to serve twenty-five years in a federal jail.

Hartigan studied Murphy's photograph. The soldier's eyes were bright, his chin high, his face shaved and smooth. His very existence seemed so clear, so sharp, but the image of Stepan Volkov was murky, the edges blurred. Nevertheless, she couldn't deny the similarities: Murphy was Volkov.

"What makes you think he's not in his cell?" the communications supervisor asked.

Singh glared at him and continued pacing. "He escaped two federal jails before they tossed him into this one," he said. "I told them they should've thrown him into a bottomless pit."

"You *knew* him?" Hartigan asked, tossing Murphy's photograph onto the desk.

Singh didn't reply.

"Why didn't you recognise him from the phone photograph?"

"He's supposed to be in jail," Singh mumbled. "He's not supposed to exist anymore." He stopped pacing and jammed his hands into his pockets. "I didn't even think that—"

"We've got something," the supervisor said. He turned his monitor around.

Hartigan stood next to Singh and studied the screen. A thin woman with short grey hair and dark eyes peered at them through her webcam. "Agent Singh," her voice crackled, "I'm the—"

"I don't care," Singh said. "Show me Murphy."

"Agent Singh," the woman said patiently. "Everything is as it should be, I can assure you. Our paperwork all lines up. Stephen Murphy is definitely here. He's in the interview room with me now."

Singh leaned over the desk, his face nearly pressed up to the monitor. "Show me."

She shook her head in exasperation and turned her laptop around on the table. The camera focused on a man manacled to his chair, and his cratered face broke into a broad grin, showing his browned teeth. He chuckled and strained against his chains.

"Menya zovut Stiven Merfi." The man laughed. His body convulsed and he rocked excitedly against his restraints. *"Menya zovut Stiven Merfi!"* he shouted joyously.

"What's he saying?" the supervisor asked.

Singh picked up the computer monitor and heaved it to the floor. It crashed to pieces, spitting blue sparks and pouring glass across the carpet. He crouched on the ground, his head between his legs, and held his hands to his ears.

"Lee?" Hartigan laid her hand on his shoulder.

Singh swatted her hand away. He straightened up and stormed out, his shoulders hunched, his face fallen.

"What did that guy say?" the supervisor asked again, pointing to the remains of his computer. "What was that, Swedish?"

"He said 'I am Stephen Murphy'." Hartigan pawed through her pocket and retrieved her car keys. "He was speaking Russian."

***

Singh dropped a gold coin in the bucket. The man's eyes blinked slowly under his bushy eyebrows and he held out a paper poppy.

"God bless," the man said.

Singh grunted and took the poppy. He pushed silently through the bustling tourists and avoided the small groups of giggling schoolchildren, pausing at the edge of the courtyard. A dark pool stretched out before him, a torch mounted at its head. The flame flickered, tormented by the ghostly breeze that swept down from the sky. Singh smoothed out his tie and stared up at the green dome soaring above the memorial. Over 102,000 names were etched on the walls but he only needed to see one.

There were no tourists or family here, he noticed, pausing at the end of the roll. The war was too young for remembrance. It needed to be forgotten first. It would begin with the soldiers retiring and hanging up their uniforms in closets in spare rooms. Medals would be sealed in cases and stuffed in drawers, and photographs would be placed in frames and hidden on high shelves. Then the soldiers would grow old. A question might be asked by a son or daughter. The medals might be found by a spouse or friend. Stories would be told at funerals during eulogies for those claimed by car accidents and cancer instead of IEDs and small-arms fire. In the end, those that remained would each lose their final battle and the truth would be buried under heaped earth. That's when people would start to care, but not now, not yet. Soldiers only showed scars, never wounds. It's all people cared to see.

Darren Harper.

Singh ran his finger along the letters and placed the poppy in the wall next to Harper's name. His hand fell to his side and he closed his eyes. The war squalled through his mind, forgotten faces and stolen friends swirling on a gasp of red dust that choked his parched throat. He absently reached for his head, touching a Kevlar helmet that wasn't there. His hands trembled and he thrust them into his pockets.

A shoe scuffed on the pavement beside him. Singh turned abruptly. "Not now, Emily," he muttered.

"I'm sorry, I didn't mean to—"

"Yes, you did. You followed me."

Hartigan sighed and leaned against a stone pillar. "My dad brought me here once," she said, pretending to ignore him. "He told me some stories about his own time in the service. He always said that they never fought for a cause. None of that was important. The only thing that mattered was looking after the man next to you."

Singh jingled the keys in his pocket.

"Trust," she continued. "If you don't have that, what do you have?"

"Emily."

"Do you understand who these people are?" Hartigan asked. "I'm scared, okay."

"There's no—"

"Threat?" Hartigan shook her head. "I honestly thought this was about protecting a witness. And then there was that briefing, and then you said it's about oil."

"This is about noon Friday, Emily," Singh said. "The whole country is counting down because they're worried about what will happen if the Sino-Russian trade deal fails."

"This is ridiculous." Hartigan ran both hands through her hair. "You don't..." She groaned and folded her arms.

Singh studied her thoughtfully, jingling the keys in his pocket. "I didn't know your dad served. What was he? Army? Navy?"

She bit her lip and stared at the flickering torch. "He was infantry in the war before yours."

"Yours?"

"The war you served in."

"Not ours?"

Hartigan opened her mouth but didn't speak. Her gaze fell to the poppy in her hand and she twirled it between her fingers.

"All wars are ours, Emily," Singh said. "You can pretend to be an outsider, a spectator, but everyone has a stake."

"How much did you lose?"

Singh rubbed his eyes. The breeze tugged at his jacket and whistled in his ears. "Darren Harper and I were friends," he said. "We trained together before he joined the Special Forces."

"You knew him too?"

"The army can be a small world," he said. "Harper had friends at every base in the country. Everyone liked him." He glanced around warily. "I was working in intelligence during the war, and I came by some information that implicated Harper's squad. Murphy's name was mentioned. I set a trap."

"What happened?"

"Everything went wrong," he said. "People died. Harper died." He cleared his throat. "I thought it was my fault."

"Was it?"

He shook his head. "Murphy got him killed."

She nodded slowly and twirled her poppy, watching the red petals trace a blurry circle.

"The case was buried with Harper, and Murphy went to prison," Singh said.

"He has some surviving relatives," Hartigan said. "I was thinking we could call his aunt and uncle." She swept her hair from her eyes. "And his cousin is the same age, so they might have been close."

"No!" Singh cried, turning to face her.

"But Lee."

"They don't know where he is." He grabbed her arm. "Leave them alone, Emily," he whispered. "Promise me."

"You have to tell the deputy director about Murphy," Hartigan said, wriggling from his grip.

"Let me handle that," Singh said.

"You *are* going to tell him, right?"

"It doesn't matter who Volkov is," he said. "We still need to catch him. We still need to find out if Korolev has anything planned for us. The mission is still the same."

"Is it still the same to you?"

He glared at her and turned to leave.

"We have nineteen hours to go, Lee," she called after him. "It might not matter to you, but I need to know that I can trust you."

He paused and looked over his shoulder, tapping the face of his wristwatch. "You should stick around for *The Last Post.*"

Hartigan watched him weave around the tired tourists and plunge through the exit. She lifted her poppy and stared at the roll, unsure where to place her tribute.

A breeze whistled past her but it died suddenly, and she felt the cold creep across her skin. The trumpet called out and seemed to burst through her chest, the notes trembling past the etched names and swirling through the courtyard, the poppies quivering. Each blast battled the wind and clawed along the stone walls, searching for a place to sleep. The fight was short and the last note was snatched away.

Emily Hartigan realised she was holding her breath. She exhaled, shivering, her eyes settling on Darren Harper's name on the wall.

"This isn't just about oil anymore," she whispered.

24

CANBERRA, AUSTRALIA

THURSDAY 15 SEPTEMBER

4:58PM AEST

Simone Elliot stared at the silver medallion on the tabletop. She ran her finger along the chain, poking it in and out, making curvy shapes and zigzags.

"Here you are, Miss," the waiter said. He put a napkin on the table and gently placed the glass on top of it. He handed her a long spoon and a straw before turning on his heels and returning to the bar.

It was a towering glass of green soda with a scoop of vanilla icecream floating on the surface like an iceberg.

Angela's favourite.

Elliot picked up the spoon and sighed.

"The caduceus is the staff of Hermes," Natalie Robinson said. She sat down across from Elliot and placed her slender arms on the table. "God of merchants, travellers, gamblers." She clasped her hands. "And thieves."

Elliot crammed the medallion into her pocket and cast her eyes around the hotel's empty bar. The waiter and the barman were the only other people in the room and they weren't paying attention. "I didn't invite you to sit down," she said, pointing her spoon at Robinson.

"You should hurry up and drink that." She plucked a pencil from her straw-coloured hair. "The ice-cream is melting." She pulled her hair into a ponytail, tugging it tight and using the pencil to twist her hair into a knot.

"I told you to go."

"The agents insist I stay."

"Do they?"

"They've finally connected some dots. I was in the pub when Volkov killed Sorokin," Robinson said. "I also happen to be a little bit Russian. Therefore, the agency believes that I know something and have given me a room upstairs. Isn't that why *you're* here?"

Elliot pushed her chair away from the table and stood up. "I'm not, I'm leaving." The spoon clattered on the tabletop.

"You're a coward, Simone."

Elliot paused and turned, her nostrils flaring. "You want to shout my name a little louder?"

"I just wanted to make a point." Robinson picked up the straw and reached across the table, dragging the lime spider towards her. "Grigoriy fell asleep on the sofa one night and left his laptop unlocked. I know who you are. I know all about you." She stabbed the straw into the drink and sipped. "Wow. That's really good."

Elliot returned to her seat. She picked up the spoon and tapped it on the table. "Help yourself," she mumbled.

Robinson poked at the ice-cream with her straw. "Did Stepan give you that necklace?"

"That's none of your business."

"It seems like the kind of gift he'd give."

"How would you know?"

"I lived with him for nearly two years," Robinson said. "I know him *very* well, perhaps better than you."

Elliot's grip tightened around the handle of her spoon, her knuckles turning white.

"And you." Robinson took another sip through her straw. "I know that you're an orphan and spent your childhood in and out of foster homes, neglected, beaten, and probably worse."

Elliot lowered her head and screwed her eyes shut.

"I know that you stole to survive, to eat, and eventually ended up a thief."

She opened her eyes. "I never had the chance to be anything else."

"Until you found a family," Robinson said.

Elliot looked away.

"You had a brother."

Darren Harper had tracked her down. Not even the police could find her but he did. Elliot remembered that first meeting, standing awkwardly in a train station waiting for him. She still remembered that his train had been due at 12:15 in the afternoon. She had been so nervous she had checked her watch every thirty seconds. Three times, she had walked out of the train station but she had always turned around again.

What if he doesn't like me? What if he doesn't like who I am? What if it's all a mistake?

But it wasn't a mistake, and she knew the minute he stepped off the train that Harper was her brother. He looked right at her, in the middle of all those people crowding the platform, and he smiled at her. He *knew* that she was his sister.

Elliot moved in with Harper near the army base. She found steady work—legitimate work—and lived a "normal" life for a little while. He introduced her to his friends, beaming proudly as he showed off his newly discovered family. She enjoyed meeting the other soldiers in his platoon, including his best friend.

Stephen.

"Stepan was your lover, wasn't he?" Robinson asked quietly.

Elliot absently rubbed her arm.

"You knew him before he was the Wolf, but something happened, something that drove a wedge between you."

"What makes you think I'd tell you anything?"

"You don't have to," Robinson said. "I know there was a war, a promise, and a funeral." She shrugged. "You probably overreacted."

"He killed my brother," she seethed. "They went to war and Stephen promised to bring Darren home alive." Her chest started to ache. "Instead, my brother was carried home in a coffin."

"But that's not the whole story," Robinson observed. "Tell me the rest."

Elliot stared at her.

"You don't know?" Robinson asked in exasperation.

"I don't need to know anything else. He went to prison and then he disappeared."

"You don't *want* to know." Robinson pointed an accusing finger at Elliot. "It's much easier to just blame him. It must be someone's fault so it may as well be his."

"You don't know me," Elliot snapped.

"Yes, of course, you're special," she said. "I was fifteen when they kidnapped me while I was walking to school. My family was murdered so they'd never come looking for me." She took a deep breath and started stabbing the table with her finger. "I was bought by Nikolay Korolev and served as a slave in his club." Robinson pushed the lime spider away. "Stepan saved me. He gave me a second chance. And you judge him, the man who loved you, for something you never witnessed?"

"I never said—"

"Fuck you, Simone." Hot tears flowed down Robinson's cheeks. "He was the only one who treated me like a human being. He paid for my education, kept me fed and kept me safe and he never asked anything of me. Not once."

"Natalie, I—"

"He got me to this paradise," Robinson said, waving her arm. "He got me a passport, a driver's licence, full citizenship in Australia and fully paid tuition so I could finish a university degree. He also made sure I had plenty of money to make a start." She glared at Elliot. "He saved me."

Elliot slouched, running her hands down her face. "He's still a killer," she said coldly.

"You know he's more than that. You know he cares."

"Do I?"

"He was broken out of prison by the *Organizatsiya,*" Robinson said. "I'd say Nikolay arranged it. If it's true, Nikolay will enslave Stepan until he feels he has worked off his debt."

"What's your point?"

"Stepan wasn't a killer until he was brought to Moscow."

"You didn't know him before he went to Moscow," she said through clenched teeth.

"I was raped at gunpoint to make money for Nikolay. Do you think that's my fault for being beautiful?"

"No!"

"Do you think that I'm just a prostitute?"

"Of course not."

"Stepan kills to make money for Nikolay. It's what he knows, what he's good at, but it's not all he is."

"He could've stayed in prison."

"And you didn't have to steal things."

"I was trying to survive," Elliot shouted.

"And now it's all you know. It's what you became."

She looked up at the bar in time to see the waiter turn away and clear his throat. "I want you to stop talking now."

"None of us had a choice, Simone," Robinson said. "Choices are for people with options."

Elliot's hands were trembling. "Enough, Natalie. Stop it."

Robinson shook her head, her chair squeaking across the floor as she stood. She leaned towards Elliot, her hands flat on the table. "I don't pity you, I hate you. Not for what you stole, but for what you threw away."

Elliot looked down to see that her hands were balled fists. She unrolled her fingers and saw a bent spoon in her palm.

"I hate you, Simone," Robinson spat. "And I wish he did too."

Elliot raised her head, her eyes wide, and watched Robinson leave the bar. She lowered her gaze and stared at the lime spider, the icecream melting over the edge of the glass.

He still cares for me?

***

The elevator doors opened on the third floor and Lee Singh groaned. Emily Hartigan was waiting for him in the hallway. "What are you doing here?" he asked, brushing past her.

"Your DNA test results came back," she said, catching up to him. "She's definitely Simone Elliot."

"So?"

"I want to be there when you arrest her."

"I told you. I'm not going to arrest Elliot."

"But she's—"

"Not my problem," Singh finished. "Murphy is the man we want. Elliot is the bait."

"What if she escapes?"

"She had her chance. She's not going to run."

"What if we miss *our* chance?"

Singh stopped and turned around. "You know, you insisted I call Waters a witness but don't blink when I call Elliot bait. What's the difference?"

"I, uh." She cleared her throat. "I don't know what you're talking about."

"Is it because one was a constable and the other is a thief?"

"No!"

"Does it have anything to do with all the cops you called today?"

Hartigan laughed nervously. "You're—"

"The Angela James case, Emily." Singh rolled his eyes.

"Have you been tracking my calls?"

"Your dad was the detective in charge of the case, right?"

She pressed her lips together, her eyes darting around. "Elliot knows stuff about the case, stuff that was never made public. She must've been involved somehow."

"Maybe she stole the information."

"My dad never mentioned her involvement," Hartigan said. "It doesn't add up."

"Leave it alone, Agent Hartigan. Murphy is our target."

"Target?" Hartigan crossed her arms. "Do you want to pick another word?"

"Do you?" Singh opened the door to an office suite.

The room was supposed to be an executive's office but the desks had been pushed up against the windows and groaned under the weight of surveillance equipment. There were binoculars, a directional microphone, and a radio receiver and headset for the bugs in Elliot's room. Two laptop computers were humming on one of the desks, a printer and fax had been installed and the telephone lines had been activated. The suite had panoramic views of Elliot's hotel and had been manned since her arrival.

Hartigan wrinkled her nose and raised the back of her hand to her mouth. The smell of sweat and processed meat was so thick she thought she could taste it. Discarded takeaway containers and grease-stained pizza boxes were scattered around the equipment, while empty cans of energy drink had been stacked in a pyramid on the floor next to an overflowing rubbish bin. Two suitcases bursting with clothes were stashed in the corner and a cot had been set up at the rear of the room, the sheets tousled and the pillow stained with coffee.

An agent sat in the middle of it all and blinked slowly as he turned to face the new arrivals.

"I thought I told you pigs to clean this mess up," Singh said.

The agent immediately sprang to his feet, his back straight as if standing to attention. "Agent Singh, we weren't expecting you this early."

"Well, surprise," Singh said wryly. "Where's the other one?"

"Over at the hotel." The agent stared at Hartigan, his eyes clearing.

"Why?" Singh asked, squinting through the window.

"We watched her all afternoon, even while she napped." He coughed. "She 'napped' for six hours."

"You moron," Singh said, his hands on his hips.

"Sir, wait," he pleaded. "She left her room unnoticed but not the hotel. I went over there at about six o'clock and found her in the bar." The agent's eyes wandered, surveying Hartigan's body from head to toe. She pulled her coat tighter around her waist.

"And?" Singh asked.

"I stayed over there and read the newspaper cover to cover but she still didn't go to her room," the agent continued, smiling crookedly at Hartigan. "I had to leave before I got made so I checked that Natalie Robinson was settled and then I came back here and swapped out." He winked.

Hartigan realised the agent was undressing her in his mind. She averted her eyes.

The radio crackled on the desk. "She's on the move," a voice said.

"Is that him?" Singh asked.

The agent nodded. "He's been there for about ten minutes."

"She's talking to the concierge," the radio hissed. "She's picking up a package."

Hartigan frowned at the radio.

"Okay, she's in the elevator, going up."

"She's playing it cool," Hartigan said, eyeing off the cot.

"So far," Singh said. He turned to the agent and jabbed his thumb towards the door. "Get your friend and fuck off."

The agent nodded and grabbed his coat, winking at Hartigan again before leaving the room. She shuddered, kicking off her shoes and tossing her coat over the back of a chair.

Singh sat down on an office chair and looked through the window. A loud pop burst out of the headphones on the desk. "She's in her room."

Hartigan sat on the cot and massaged her calves, cringing each time her fingertips found a knot. She peered up at Singh, who sat as still as a statue, staring through the window. "You need to have a word to your agents. Did you see the way that guy was looking at me?"

"Makes you wonder if those sheets are clean, doesn't it?"

She screwed up her nose and stood, wiping her hands on her skirt. "Men are disgusting."

"And women are beacons of good behaviour," he said.

She sat on the chair and dragged her coat over her shoulder, spreading it over her chest like a blanket. "Are you talking about Elliot?"

He reached out, snatching the binoculars from the desk.

"Because I don't think she's representative of my gender," Hartigan continued. "I mean, have you read her file?"

The headset let out a muffled shriek.

"What was that?"

"She's destroying the listening devices," Singh said, putting his feet up on the desk. The headset shrieked again.

"How many are there?"

Another squeal. "Four."

"She knew about them when I asked her about Angela," Hartigan said. "Why wait until now to destroy them?" She reclined in the chair and closed her eyes.

"Exactly." The headset let out its last shriek. "Damn," Singh mumbled. "The fourth one was the tricky one." He nodded slowly. "She knows what she's doing."

"That's what I was saying," Hartigan said. "Did you know she stole about $30 million worth of stuff before she was twenty-five? Art was stolen from European galleries, jewellery was reported missing by fashion designers, and cash disappeared from the safes of bankers and media owners." She knitted her fingers together, placing them behind her head. "Documents disappeared from corporate offices and law firms. Diamonds and wine vanished from Sotheby's auctions."

Singh looked through the binoculars, cursing under his breath. "These are useless. We should have night-vision equipment." He tossed the binoculars away and reached under the desk, dragging a locked case towards him.

"And then she did that job on the Melbourne Cup," Hartigan continued. "She made off with about $2.5 million in a day. She did another job on a horse race in the UAE that netted her twice as much." She let out a low whistle. "Any wonder they call her the Serpent. Slippery and manipulative, that's her."

"When was the last time you fired a gun?" Singh asked. He kicked open the case and reached inside.

"Basic training."

"I heard you scored highly."

"Yes, but..."

Singh hefted a pistol and rammed a magazine into the weapon.

Hartigan sat up and placed her feet on the floor.

He handed her the pistol. "Safety is on," he said. "There's no round in the chamber."

She took the pistol with a trembling hand. "Do you know something that I don't?"

"Like I said, she's waiting. She's not scared of us but she wants us to stay out of it. She knows something's coming for her."

"Some*thing* or some*one?*"

He tapped his finger against his nose and pointed at Hartigan.

25

MOSCOW, RUSSIA

THURSDAY 15 SEPTEMBER

3:36PM MSK

"Still nothing?" Anna asked, stirring her tea.

Grigoriy shook his head and sat down, placing his mobile phone beside his coffee cup. "I left another message," he mumbled. "I don't know where he could be. Did he try calling you?"

"I already checked twice," she said. "Nothing."

"And you saw him leave your place yesterday?"

"I already told you," she said. "I saw him at four in the morning and he told me to get some sleep. Then he left. I haven't seen him since."

"I'm sorry. I'm just worried."

"It's not the first time he's disappeared on you."

"No, but thirty-six hours without contact is rare."

"I think he went to see her," she said, placing her teaspoon on her saucer.

"Her?" he asked.

She raised an eyebrow. "You know who I'm talking about."

He cleared his throat. "I don't, no."

"He has some photographs of her. He took them with him." Anna peered at him over the top of her cup. "He's in love with her."

"I thought you said he wasn't capable of love."

"I didn't say that," she said defensively. "I was just wondering if *she* could love him, even if she knew what he was." Anna glanced around the room curiously.

It was one of the fashionable cafés that catered to Russia's swelling upper class. Many of the people sitting at the tables were the children of wealthy media owners or bankers. Others were young lobbyists or politicians who worked at the Kremlin. All of them were desperate for places to spend their money, places where people would adore them for being wealthy and influential. Places where they could also forget about "everyone else". It seemed ambitious but they managed ignorance particularly well, even though the number of poor people in Moscow was growing faster than most of their share portfolios.

It was strange today, however, Anna thought. There was a quiet desperation, a restless insistence that was hidden between words and thinly veiled by the fragile hum of the café. People hunched over their plates and whispered, their faces stern, their gaze heavy. It was the bombings; life was no longer a promise others had an obligation to keep. At any moment, their bodies could burst in a cough of crimson ash and swirl away in the dust of a destroyed building. Their lives would be digits on a news bulletin and they would be forgotten by the time the commercials came on. Living was now more urgent, crying out for attention over the sounds of rattling cash registers and ringing mobile phones.

But it wasn't urgent enough, she thought.

Even on a day like this, each person was afraid to tell the truth to the one sitting across the table. They mumbled clumsy compliments, peeked shyly at one another from behind menus, and cleared their throats when they brushed hands reaching for the salt. It was always the same foolish dance, choreographed by romance novels and played to the irregular beat of cutlery clattering on plates. Anna glimpsed Grigoriy and realised she was stepping through the same dance.

And every day is urgent for me.

"I hope you're wrong," Grigoriy said. "If Nikolay found out Stepan was seeing..." He sighed. "Seeing *her,* we could all be in trouble." His eyes glazed over momentarily, and he shook his head. "But who could really love him, anyway?" he mused. "He doesn't seem to feel anything." The waiter hastily delivered two serves of chocolate cake before moving to another table.

"Do you really believe that?" Anna asked.

"I always thought of him as a computer," Grigoriy said. "No feelings or emotions, just inputs and outputs."

She shook her head and eyed off her chocolate cake. "He's like a painting, a portrait."

"I'm not sure I understand."

"The other day, when he killed Dmitri, he had this expression on his face. It took me a while to figure out where I'd seen it before."

"A painting?" Grigoriy asked sceptically.

"Not a specific painting," she said, sweeping the hair from her eyes.

Grigoriy picked up a fork and dragged his plate towards him.

"When I was a girl, my father used to take me to the Hermitage," Anna began. "I loved the paintings. I was amazed that something with no soul could hold eyes that seemed alive. I remember feeling insignificant because those eyes had looked upon thousands of people like me, and they seemed immortal for what they knew and what they'd seen." She shrugged. "Stepan can be like that, alive but dead, material but forever."

Grigoriy's mouth had fallen open and he poked his chocolate cake with his fork. "You know, in Slavic folklore, the wolf is a demon among the divine. He is the darkness at the edge of light, a murderous shadow that stalks the living."

"And in English, the wolf was always the destroyer. In Christianity, he was the Devil, preying on the flock while Jesus claimed to protect us."

"In Chechnya, the wolf is a symbol of national pride."

"We're still talking about a man, Grigoriy," Anna said.

"Perhaps." Grigoriy dropped his fork and stared at his cake. "But he could've killed Dmitri's men with his pistol. It would've been quick and painless but he wanted to make a point. He wanted to make an example of Dmitri."

"Computers don't do that," Anna observed.

"But a man?"

Anna blinked.

"Nikolay knows what he is," Grigoriy said.

"He doesn't know him."

"He knows what matters," he said. "Stepan came to his attention when he killed a man in an Australian prison. The man was a relative of Nikolay's who had been exiled in Australia. Nikolay wanted revenge but was so impressed by Stepan's skill that he broke him out and—" he paused, trying to find the right word. "Enslaved. Nikolay enslaved him." He stared down at his coffee. "Stepan served Nikolay in Chechnya. That's where he became the Wolf. That's all that matters here."

"It wouldn't matter to Simone," Anna said. "If she loved him."

He picked up his coffee cup. "That's much more complicated."

"How?"

"Simone lives in this world too," he said. "She's a thief, and a very good one." He sipped from his cup.

Anna sat up straight. "How do you know this?"

"Stepan has always used me to research stuff, including his targets," Grigoriy said. "I'd been working for him for two years when he asked me to search for Simone. I knew she wasn't a target so I kept it quiet. She was living in New Zealand at the time."

"Did he go see her?"

"No. He just asked for reports about where she was and any jobs she was doing. I gave him information every couple of weeks. He seemed happier when he knew she was okay."

"What happened?"

"She disappeared and I couldn't find her. Stepan changed after that. He seemed more distant, more committed to Nikolay's organisation."

"Where did she go?" Anna asked.

"She bought a new identity and fell off the grid for three years. She's been in the police force but we didn't know that until she suddenly turned up in an Australian pub at the same time as Stepan."

Anna folded her arms on the table. "Why the police force?"

"I don't know."

She waggled her finger. "But you know *something.* I can tell."

His face flushed. "You're manipulating me again."

"And you're evading me."

"Anna, you don't understand. People could die if I say these things aloud."

"I'll risk it."

"Anna, please." Grigoriy muttered a curse, running his hand through his curly hair and taking a deep breath. "Nikolay knew about Simone. He knew that she existed. Stepan made a deal. He would work for Nikolay as long as Simone remained untouched. In exchange, Stepan had to stay away from her."

"Why?"

"Korolev didn't want him to hope for another life," Grigoriy said. "Serving Nikolay is supposed to be Stepan's purpose."

"What happens if Nikolay finds out Stepan is seeing Simone?"

Grigoriy shook his head slowly. "Someone will die."

"Stepan?"

"Maybe, maybe not. See, you have to understand that..." Grigoriy paused. "There is a story. Simone knew nothing about the deal. She stole some paintings from a truck that was driving across Europe. They were being transported by Nikolay Korolev."

Anna's eyes went wide. "She ripped off Nikolay?"

Grigoriy raised his finger to his mouth. "Yes, but please." His eyes darted around. "It's a story, that's all. It was never reported in newspapers. The police never investigated. Nobody in the *Organizatsiya* mentions it. Even Nikolay's competitors believe it's just a rumour."

"Is it really *just* a story?" Anna whispered.

Grigoriy shook his head. "Nikolay was furious," he said. "He sent men to kill Simone but he kept it quiet. There are only three people alive who know the truth."

"But she's still alive."

"The men tried but they went for her fence first and she disappeared before they could reach her. Nikolay never breathed a word about it." He looked away. "Stepan depends on me for information, so I choose what to tell him about some things."

"You never told him?" she hissed.

He shook his head. "*Nyet,* no, never."

"Grigoriy," Anna scolded. "If Stepan finds out—"

"What should I have done?" he snapped, cutting her off. "Stepan killed five men because they were threatening you. If he loves Simone, if he really loves her, then what would he do to Nikolay?"

Anna nodded slowly. "And there are hundreds of syndicate leaders waiting to take his place. Stepan would be killed. We'd be killed."

"And what if you're right and she doesn't love him back?"

"I never meant—"

He held up his hand. "What if she hates him for what he is?" He let his hand fall to the table. "He's been hanging on to her for years. What if his hope is snatched away by Simone's hate?"

Anna stared down at her teacup.

"It's a mess," Grigoriy said.

"He told me that Simone's brother died in the war. Stepan blames himself." She looked up from her tea. "He's scared that she blames him too."

"Do you want to know what scares me?" Grigoriy stabbed the table with his finger. "It's that you're right, that he is a man. She's all he believes in.

There's nothing else, no hope, no reason to live. And if she turns him away..." He shuddered. "He would become exactly what Korolev needs him to be."

Anna realised that living was becoming more urgent by the hour. "If Nikolay asks, will you tell him that Stepan broke the deal, too?"

He crossed his arms and shrugged. "I don't know that he has, yet."

"Grigoriy, I know that you have no..." Her voice trailed off and she gazed through the window, biting her lip. "Don't you think Stepan deserves a chance?"

Grigoriy pushed his empty coffee cup away. "No," he said, shaking his head. "He is what he is. Who could see past that?"

Anna felt her heart sink and picked up her fork.

Who could see past that?

The question echoed inside her and she peered up at Grigoriy.

Could you, Grigoriy?

She took a bite of her cake but it tasted like ash in her mouth.

26

CANBERRA, AUSTRALIA

THURSDAY 15 SEPTEMBER

10:33PM AEST

Simone Elliot stared at the dark ceiling and listened to the rhythm of her breathing. She could hear the pop of the rafters settling, the hum of the refrigerator, and the swish of cars driving along the damp road beneath the balcony. The grip of her pistol felt cold in her hand but it still comforted her. She listened for creaking floorboards in the hall, or the scratch of tools at the front door, but there was nothing and her eyes grew heavy.

Angela!

Her eyes snapped open, her heart thudding in her chest. She rolled over and sat up, pressing the butt of her pistol against her forehead.

She wasn't going to sleep tonight.

I can't wait anymore.

Dawn was the time to run. The surveillance team across the road would be due to change shifts, their senses dulled and their thoughts on a warm bed and hot meal. She could sneak away easily, though her clothes would have to stay behind. A duffel bag would slow her down. She had to take only what she needed.

She placed her pistol on the dining table and thumbed through her passports, tossing them into her satchel. Siobhán Miller's cash went into the satchel next, along with the business cards, IDs, and cigarettes. She picked up her medallion and shoved it into her pocket, out of sight.

Feet shuffled in the hallway and Elliot froze. She grabbed her pistol, flattened herself against the wall beside the door, and listened carefully. There was a scraping sound, metal on metal. Someone was trying to hack the swipe-lock.

Her weight shifted and the floor creaked beneath her shoes.

She held her breath.

The power went out with a pop and the door burst open. Automatic fire ripped across the room and Elliot leaned away from the door, closing her eyes. The gunfire stopped and she heard a magazine clatter to the floor. The shooter waited.

Elliot leapt into the doorway and fired three rounds into the man's chest. He toppled backwards into the corridor and slid down the wall. Footsteps pounded on the carpet and she ran inside her room, snatching her satchel and draping the strap over her head. She vaulted over the balcony rail and climbed down to the next floor, huddling in the shadows of the terrace.

Boots clomped above her and she heard a Russian whisper harshly.

Elliot waited until the footsteps faded and vaulted the rail again, climbing down to the third floor. She yanked open the balcony door and stumbled into the room.

A man in pyjamas fell out of bed.

"Police!" Elliot bellowed. She waved her pistol in front of the man's face. "Stay in your room, do you understand? If you go outside, you die."

The man nodded quickly and hid under the covers while Elliot ran for the front door. She threw it open and sprinted down the darkened hallway towards the stairwell, skidding to a stop when she heard footsteps and voices echoing down the stairs.

***

"Emily!"

Hartigan jumped, the chair creaking beneath her, and a dull ache radiated through her leg. "Did you kick me?" she asked sleepily.

"Get up," Singh barked, working the slide on his pistol. "We've got a problem."

Hartigan scrambled to her feet.

Singh seized her wrist and dragged her to the window, thrusting the binoculars into her hands. "Take a look," he said.

"I thought these were useless," she said, peering through the eyepieces. "I can't see anything."

"Try the entrance."

Hartigan focused the binoculars. The concierge was gone but two men in business shirts and ties were standing at the front desk. One of them was rolling up his sleeves, baring his tattooed arms, while the other pointed at the ground. The bare-armed man bent over and dragged a body out from behind the desk.

"They slit the concierge's throat," Singh explained, snatching the binoculars away.

Hartigan's mouth went dry. "We should call for backup."

"There's no time," Singh said, handing Hartigan her pistol. "It's down to us."

"Us?"

"I counted six who ran past the entrance. They must've gotten in through the parking garage."

"That makes eight," Hartigan said.

"Two for Elliot's floor, two on the floor below to cut off escape, two rovers for support, and two at the entrance to prevent interference."

"Eight," Hartigan repeated, her voice cracking.

"They all have assault rifles."

Hartigan's feet felt heavy. "I can't."

"You have to, Emily," Singh said, opening the door. "There's nobody else."

***

The cleaner's storeroom contained shelves full of crisp sheets and cleaning fluids, as well as chocolates and bottles of spring water. Elliot placed her pistol on a shelf and grabbed a bottle, cracking the lid and emptying half of the water on to the floor. She studied the shelves and quickly found the ingredients she wanted, squeezing a generous amount into the water bottle.

She stopped working when she heard footsteps but they marched past her door. A voice called out in Russian: "Go back upstairs. I'll search this floor."

Elliot fumbled through her satchel and found her packet of cigarettes. She tore the packet open and found her last ingredient, adding it to her chemical soup. The man was searching the hallway by kicking down doors, and she could hear him nearing the storeroom.

Elliot capped the bottle, waiting for the man to get closer. A door smashed open and a woman screamed.

It was next door. Elliot shook the bottle, opened the door, and hurled the bomb down the hall.

There was a wet bang and the man shrieked. Elliot snatched her pistol from the shelf and ripped open the door. The man tumbled inside and collapsed at her feet, writhing on the floor. His face, hands and arms were burnt, his fingers and nose severed.

"How many?" Elliot said, pointing her pistol at him.

He was screaming in pain, rocking back and forth and clutching his face with blistered and bleeding hands.

"How many?" she asked again, standing over him.

He didn't answer.

Elliot shot him in the knee and he finally looked up at her, crying out silently, his mouth open wide. "How many?"

The man's head burst in front of her eyes and she froze.

"Now, there are six," a voice said from behind her.

***

"Wait on the third floor," Singh ordered Hartigan.

"What about you?"

"I'll go to Elliot's room on the fifth. You wait in the stairwell and stop anybody who runs down those stairs."

"But, Lee."

"Go!"

Hartigan nodded and pushed through the stairwell door.

Singh turned around when he heard voices and saw two Russians emerge from the security centre. They paused when they saw him. "Excuse me, gentlemen," Singh called out, leaning against the concierge's desk and holding up his badge. "Have you seen the concierge?"

"Actually," the man with the rolled sleeves began, "we just set off to look for him."

"No luck?"

The man shook his head. "I'm not sure where he went." He stopped in front of Singh and crossed his arms, but his friend kept his distance.

"Strange." Singh clipped his badge to his belt. "We got a call about a possible murder, something about Russian men with guns." He looked from one man to the other. "You haven't seen anyone suspicious creeping around here, have you?"

"I haven't seen anything," the man said. "Did you see anything?" he asked his friend.

The other man shook his head, holding his hands out and shrugging. His veined forearms were heavily tattooed. "I wouldn't know what a Russian looked like," he said, his accent thick.

Singh noticed that one of the tattoos was a cross, though it wasn't like the Christian crucifix. There were three bars on this cross: two straight and one lopsided. It was the symbol of the Russian Orthodox Church, tattooed in blurry blue ink. It was a prison job. "Okay, then. Not a problem," Singh said, turning to the first man. *"Spasiba za vashe vryemya."*

"Nichivo," the man replied, turning away. He stopped suddenly.

The Russian pulled a knife and pivoted on his toe, but Singh ducked, kicking out the man's feet. Singh fired at the second Russian, sending him staggering through the lobby's glass doors. The first Russian sprang to his feet and slapped the weapon from Singh's hands.

Singh stepped back as the Russian jabbed with his knife. Singh seized the man by the wrist and drove the palm of his hand into the attacker's elbow. He adjusted his grip, locking the Russian's wrist, and smashed his head into the counter. The Russian flopped on to the floor, unconscious.

Singh retrieved his pistol and dragged the Russian behind the counter, cuffing him to a foot rail. He crashed through the stairwell door and sprinted up the steps to the fifth floor.

***

Elliot turned around slowly. He was blond with a crew cut, his muscles bulging and his grip tight on his assault rifle. He was standing in the doorway, chomping on a toothpick and pointing his rifle at her chest.

Elliot kicked the door and it slammed on his hands. He yelped and pulled the trigger, spraying the room with bullets. She gritted her teeth while holding the door. He rammed the door and it jolted, her pistol dropping to the floor. He rammed the door again, sending her sprawling across the floor of the storeroom.

Elliot dived on top of her pistol and rolled over, raising her weapon as she climbed to a kneeling position.

The man was gone.

She heard two gunshots and a man gurgled and thudded to the floor. There was a grunt and a crash, three more gunshots, a groan, and then silence. Elliot crept slowly to the door. She raised her pistol and took a deep breath.

A hand seized her wrist and she was yanked out of the storeroom. She twirled through the hallway and slammed into the wall, her arm folded across her chest. She was trapped.

Grey eyes glared at her and she felt her face flush with anger. "Let me go so I can shoot you," she said, squirming against his grip.

"Thanks, it's great to be here," Stephen Murphy said.

"You expected me to bake a cake?"

He wrinkled his forehead. "You don't even know what goes into a cake."

"Eggs, milk, flour." She tried to twist free of his hands but he wouldn't let go. "Butter, bleach."

"Now I remember your cooking," Murphy said, nodding knowingly.

"You bastard," she hissed, writhing against the wall. "Just wait until you let me go. I'm going to—"

Murphy let her go and she slid down the wall, landing on her feet.

"You were saying?"

Elliot gripped the barrel of her pistol and swung at his face. Murphy blocked the punch and chopped her forearm. She cried out and dropped the pistol. She followed up by raising her knee at his crotch but he grabbed the back of her thigh and wrapped his hand around her neck. He lifted her up, sending her crashing into the wall again, and he held his body against hers.

He pulled her close and kissed her deeply, her legs coiling around his waist, his lips lingering on hers. His breath warmed her skin as their lips parted and she opened her eyes slowly. He gazed at her, clenching his jaw when she pressed the cold steel of his own knife to his throat.

"You son of a bitch," Elliot said breathlessly.

"You're upset," Murphy said. "I can tell."

"This is just one big joke to you, isn't it?"

"C'mon, Slim."

"Don't call me that!" She increased the pressure on the knife.

His face softened and he cleared his throat, the blade drawing blood. "You don't understand."

"You killed him," she said. "You promised to bring him home but he died and then you ran away."

His eyes darkened. "*I* ran away? Which face are you hiding behind today?"

"Shut up," she snapped.

"Who are you pretending to be? A cop? A cleaning lady?"

"I swear I'll put you on the ground with your friends."

"I don't have any friends," Murphy said.

"Don't lie to me," Elliot warned. "These are Nikolay's men."

Murphy's eyes narrowed. "How did you know that?"

Elliot's mouth fell open and she shrugged.

"Were you expecting these guys?"

She lowered the knife and her face fell.

Nikolay didn't send him.

"Freeze!" a woman shouted. "Don't move."

***

"I said don't move," the Russian growled.

Singh dropped his pistol and held his hands in the air. He'd made it to the fifth floor too late. A dead body was slumped in the hallway outside Elliot's room and she was gone. The only thing left was a duffel bag of clothes and a Chanel suit on a hanger.

"Where's the woman?" the Russian asked.

Singh turned around slowly and stepped towards the *boyevik,* stopping next to the television. "I was going to ask you the same question."

The Russian glared at him. He was athletic, with sinewy muscles that were hidden under a loose-fitting business shirt. He had a scar along the top of his bald head that made his skull look as though it had been assembled incorrectly, one half overlapping the other. The Russian pushed his slung rifle behind his back and pointed his pistol at Singh, his stance wide, his grip steady. "Open your jacket."

Singh obeyed and grabbed his lapel with a thumb and forefinger. He pulled his jacket aside and revealed the badge clipped to his belt.

"You're a policeman," the *boyevik* observed. He laughed without humour, stepping closer. "What were you planning to do, arrest me?"

"No."

"Kill me?" The *boyevik* clicked his tongue, taking another step. "You can't kill me. You have to obey the law."

Singh slapped the man's hand and the pistol went off. The television screen burst and the man dropped the pistol, turning away to cover his face. Singh grabbed the Russian's rifle sling, twisting it around his neck and yanking tight. He threw the Russian over his back and sent him crashing to the floor.

Singh collected the *boyevik'* s pistol and stood over him, aiming at his head. The Russian groaned and rolled on to his back. "There are laws," he wheezed.

"They don't matter to me."

Singh fired.

***

"Stay where you are." Hartigan aimed her pistol and tried to steady her trembling hands. They were silhouettes lurking in puddles of darkness ten metres away. She was eager to make the arrest but resisted the urge to run, stepping cautiously.

Remember your training.

"Turn around and face me," she demanded.

Murphy and Elliot obeyed, their hands hanging loosely by their sides.

"Hello, Emily," Murphy said calmly.

"How do you know my name?" She felt prickles on her back and her blouse was clinging to her skin. Her coat suddenly felt heavy.

"Yours is one of the names on my watchlist," Murphy said.

Hartigan's mouth went dry. The emergency lighting flickered to life, bathing the hallway in orange light. She saw his face. "You're Stephen Murphy," she croaked.

Murphy's eyes hardened. "Where did you learn that name?"

"Through her," Hartigan said, gesturing to Elliot. "She's been a big help."

Murphy glared at Elliot.

"This isn't a good time, Emily," Elliot said calmly, ignoring Murphy. "You should leave."

"Shut up," Hartigan cried. Three dead bodies were at their feet and she could see another man's legs sticking out through the doorway beside them. Her stomach turned.

"Take her advice," Murphy said, looking down at one of the bodies. "You don't belong in this hallway, Emily."

Sweat was pouring down Hartigan's face and she bit her sleeve with her teeth and shook off her coat. "Down on your knees." Nine metres to go.

"No," Murphy said. He crouched and lifted the dead man's shirt.

Hartigan tried to swallow. *What do you do when they say no?* "Please."

"Lee's going to get you killed, Emily," Murphy said.

"Stop calling me that!" Her voice cracked.

Murphy peered up at her, eyeing her curiously before turning his attention to the dead Russian. The man had gauze taped to his abdomen and Hartigan almost retched as Murphy massaged the bandages with his fingers.

Hartigan took three more small steps and licked her dry lips. Eight metres to go. "You're under arrest," she said.

"What are you doing?" Elliot asked Murphy.

"What does this look like to you?" Murphy asked, pointing at the gauze.

Elliot frowned. "Incisions from laparoscopic surgery."

"Radical nephrectomy?"

"Doesn't that require bigger cuts?"

Murphy shrugged, massaging the bandages again. "What am I, a doctor?"

Elliot rolled her eyes and crouched beside him, stabbing the knife into the floor.

"Hey!" Hartigan shouted, sweat stinging her eyes. "Are you two listening to me?"

Murphy grabbed Elliot's hand and pushed her fingers down on the man's side.

"What the hell is that?" Elliot asked, kneading the man's skin.

"Capture protocol." Murphy reached for the man's arm and held it so she could see his wristwatch.

Elliot's jaw fell open. "Oh, shit."

Murphy straightened up. "Emily, you have to get the people out of the hotel."

"Okay," she said, shuffling closer. "But you have to come with me."

"Emily, there's no time for this," Elliot said.

Hartigan shook her head and adjusted her grip on the pistol. Four metres. "We can help you. Lee can help you."

"You don't know anything about your partner at all," Murphy said.

Hartigan ran the back of her hand across her forehead. "Please, put your hands up. Get down on your knees."

"Listen to me, Emily," Murphy said. "Unlike Lee, I'm trying to save your life."

"You're trying to trick me."

"Why would I do that?"

"Because I've got the gun," she said, her voice shaking.

"You're not going to shoot me."

"How can you be so sure?"

"The safety catch is on."

She stopped breathing, her mind turning into molasses. Her thoughts became static and she couldn't remember where the safety catch was or how to turn it off.

"Like I said, Emily," Murphy said softly. "You don't belong in this hallway."

Hartigan's legs trembled and her chest tightened.

"Just put down the gun," Elliot said. "Turn around and walk away so we can evacuate the hotel."

"I can't," she whispered.

"Don't make us do this, Emily," Murphy said.

"Please," she whimpered.

Elliot moved quickly, ripping Hartigan's pistol out of her hands and lifting her from the ground. Hartigan tumbled over Elliot's back and crashed to the floor, the air wheezing out of her lungs. Elliot looked down upon her, holding the pistol in the air.

Hartigan closed her eyes.

I don't want to die.

There was a burst of pain and then nothing.

***

Murphy propped Hartigan against the wall and brushed the hair out of her eyes. He reached into his jacket and pulled out a stone wolf, pushing it into Hartigan's hand and rolling her fingers closed.

Elliot glanced towards the stairwell door. Singh would be close. "You need to go," she said, looking back at Murphy. "Now."

"You already made that pretty clear," he said, his face taut.

No! That's not what I meant. Elliot tried again. "You don't—"

"It's true, isn't it?" he said. "I thought it was another fake identity but you're really a cop."

"What?" she choked.

"You were helping the agency with the investigation." He retrieved his knife from the floor and sheathed it under his coat. "I thought you were joking at the pub, but you really want me back in jail."

Elliot took a step back. "What are you talking about?"

"My name," he growled.

"No!" she cried. "I wouldn't—"

"You already did, apparently," Murphy said. "I never told..." He growled a curse. "I don't even know why I..." He looked up at the ceiling and ran his hand down his face. "It doesn't matter, anyway."

She stared at him, her eyes wide.

Stay!

The word was trapped beneath the anger bubbling inside her. "I never even..." Her eyes hardened. "No. You know what? Fuck you."

"Right back at you, Slim." Murphy shook his head and brushed past her, placing his hand flat against the stairwell door. "I *am* sorry, Simone. For what it's worth, for everything."

“I don’t care,” she whispered. “I won’t forgive you. I can’t.”

“I never asked you to.” He pulled the fire alarm, and pushed through the stairwell door.

Elliot jumped when the door slammed shut.

27

CANBERRA, AUSTRALIA

THURSDAY 15 SEPTEMBER

11:12PM AEST

Singh finished cleaning the blood from Hartigan's forehead and tossed the washcloth into the bowl on the bedside table. He reached into his pocket and grabbed the stone wolf he'd found in her hand. He stood it on his palm and it seemed to tremble on his skin. That's when he realised his hand was shaking.

A uniformed policeman knocked on the door of the hotel room. "Excuse me, Agent Singh."

"What is it?" Singh stuffed the small statue back into his pocket.

"We've moved Natalie Robinson to a new hotel," the policeman reported. "She's fine. She was unharmed."

"Good."

"Also, one of your men wants your opinion on something in the storeroom."

"It can wait," Singh said.

"He said it was urgent." The policeman cleared his throat. "I can watch her, if you like."

"That won't be necessary," Singh said, buttoning his jacket. "Show me what the problem is."

The constable led Singh into the storeroom where a detective was crouched next to one of the bodies. The detective showed Singh the bandages on the victim's abdomen. "What do you make of these?" he asked.

"They're incisions made for laparoscopic surgery. It's usually done to remove a gallbladder, appendix, pancreas or kidney." Singh rocked back on his heels. "This looks like a kidney removal, a nephrectomy."

"Well, this guy and all his friends have the same incisions," the detective said.

Singh hunched over the victim and pushed his hand into the Russian's bandages, massaging his fingers along his side. "It feels rigid." He pulled on a pair of latex gloves. "Give me a scalpel or a knife."

"Um, I don't know if we can do that."

"Just do it," Singh ordered.

The detective handed Singh a pocketknife and watched the agent open the Russian's abdomen. Singh returned the knife and widened the incision with his fingers. "Oh, shit."

Inside was what looked like a lump of yellow plasticine. A small metal cube with a long cylindrical pin was stuck to the corner.

"What's that?" the detective asked.

"Plastic explosive," Singh said. He tore the gloves off and patted the victim's pockets. "Did he have anything on him?"

"No, his pockets were empty."

Singh noticed that the Russian was wearing a watch and ripped it from his wrist. It was counting down. There were forty-five seconds left.

"Everybody out, now!" Singh yelled.

***

Hartigan sat upright and grasped the side of the bed, her head swimming. She stood gingerly and shuffled to the bathroom. The light was already on and she ran the tap, cupping her hands. She splashed cold water on her face and squinted into the mirror. There was a bruise on the side of her head. It was just above her hairline and it was seeping blood.

She heard panicked yelling in the hall and went to investigate. Uniformed police and forensics officers burst out of the storeroom and scurried through the hallway, stumbling into each other. Singh emerged from the crowd.

He snatched her in his arms, sprinting back into the room and rolling over the sofa. Singh reached up as they tumbled, tipping the couch to cover them, holding her to his chest.

Thunder boomed and the wall burst open. The air around her seemed to squeeze down on her chest before it was sucked away. Shattered glass and plaster rained down from the ceiling and a wave of dust rolled over the room.

Hartigan opened her mouth and her ears popped. She looked up at Singh. His lips moved but his voice was muffled. All she could hear was ringing. She shook her head and sat up. "No," she whispered, wiping her eyes with the back of her hand. "I'm not okay."

***

"I need a room," Elliot said.

The man at the desk slowly looked up from his magazine. "It's the middle of the night, lady." He yawned.

Elliot dropped a thousand dollars on the desk. "You'll get another thousand if you wake me in four hours and make like you never saw me."

The man's eyes widened and he turned around on his stool, reaching for a key. "Room eleven," he said. "It's right near the back exit."

Elliot took the key and slid the wad of cash across the desk. "No questions."

"I wouldn't dream of it, Miss Smith," the man said, holding his hands up.

The floor creaked beneath her feet and the exit sign flickered at the end of the hall. Elliot rolled up the edge of the frayed carpet and wedged the exit open before retreating to her room.

The light inside buzzed and hummed, casting a pale glow over the room. She tossed her satchel on the bed and rummaged through the cupboards of the kitchenette. She found a drinking glass and wrapped it in a towel before crushing it under the heel of her boot, spreading the broken glass on the carpet in front of the door.

The springs on the bed squeaked under her weight. She retrieved the pistol from her satchel and placed it on her stomach before reclining on the pillow.

Nikolay didn't send him.

Dusty cobwebs clung to the corners of the ceiling, the sticky silk left to flail restlessly on a silent draught. She shivered and stared at the stained ceiling above her. The grey plaster sagged and seemed to bulge before her eyes, as if the night was threatening to burst into the room and drown her.

Nikolay didn't send him because he knows.

Elliot lifted her shirt and retrieved the photographs from the waistband of her jeans. She'd seen them in the pocket of Murphy's coat and had snatched them instinctively. There were two photographs.

The first picture made her chest ache. It was faded and smeared with blood but she could still see two people smiling back at her. One was her brother, Darren Harper, and the other person looked like her.

Is it me?

It felt like a picture of somebody else. She slowly remembered standing awkwardly in the departure lounge, her brother shouting at Murphy to take the damn photo so that he could carry his sister around with him. Harper was so proud of her, so proud of knowing that he had a twin sister when he'd thought that his brothers in the army were all he had. He wanted to show the photograph to everyone, to brag about how pretty she was, how smart and how funny.

Harper arrived back in Australia in a coffin, and Elliot greeted him at the airport. He was marched slowly off the back of a plane while faceless men in pressed uniforms and slouch hats stood and watched. She watched too but she could hardly stand. She saw a man in a pine box that wasn't big enough to hold his soul, his mortal remains draped in a flag. Men with medals spoke of his courage and bravery. He had believed. And he had believed in her. They had heaped earth upon her last chance to be a part of something, to be a person again. Then they all went home to their families and left her behind, alone again.

Nikolay knows something that I could never believe.

Two familiar faces peered out from the second photograph. It was a happy couple in shy embrace, her fingers just touching his hand. They were digitally frozen at a Christmas party, trapped in the past where they would always stay.

The photograph blurred and Elliot raised a finger to her eye. She wiped her cheek with the back of her hand before shoving the photographs into her pocket.

There was only one reason why Nikolay Korolev would not send Stepan Volkov to kill someone. It wasn't trust, it wasn't competence, it wasn't money and it wasn't risk.

Stephen still cares for me.

28

CANBERRA, AUSTRALIA

FRIDAY 16 SEPTEMBER

6:02AM AEST

Emily Hartigan closed her eyes and took a deep breath.

The debrief had been short. It had involved Lee Singh shouting at her while she was wrapped in a blanket in the back of an ambulance. She couldn't remember much of what was said, but he had thrust a pistol into her hand and told her to keep it with her at all times, adding "make sure you know how to work the fucking thing". Her stay at hospital was slightly longer than the debriefing. The paperwork was stamped DAMA—discharge against medical advice.

Hartigan had gone home and ended up erratically pacing her apartment. She had eventually forced herself to stand still, and spent two hours standing in the middle of her kitchen, staring into the sink. Sleep eluded her. Her mind was raw noise, thoughts crashing over each other like waves against a cliff. It was violent, unrelenting, and she couldn't escape. The waves kept coming and coming, higher, louder, hissing and booming.

"Your order?"

Who said that?

"Miss, your order?"

Hartigan's eyes sharpened, the world coming into focus. "Um, sorry." She glanced unsteadily at the barista. "Long black, please."

It was too early to go to work, she had reasoned, so she had stopped at her favourite coffee shop, a block away from headquarters.

I just need some personal time. Peace and quiet, and I can watch the sun rise.

Another wave crashed against the cliff.

Six hours to go.

To Hartigan, dawn was a time for those who enjoyed their solitude. The sun was dependable and eternal. Today, however, everything seemed different. The sky was bleeding, the colour pooling in the clouds and dripping to the earth. The sun seemed mortal, and she felt like the only person in the world who had noticed.

Hartigan jumped when the barista's coffee machine clunked and whirred. She closed her eyes and rubbed her forehead, flinching when the shop's door slammed.

She tried to concentrate but only sensed fragments: a tradesman in a fluorescent windbreaker with a weathered smile; the waitress cackling; a man chewing a muffin with his mouth open; a woman's bracelets clattering on her wrist; a curse and dabbing at spilled coffee with a napkin.

"Miss?"

Hartigan jumped again, her hand on her chest.

"Your long black."

She snatched her cup from the counter and grabbed a newspaper from the rack, retreating to a corner table. She immediately opened the newspaper to the puzzles, cracking the pages and folding the paper. Hartigan found a pen in her bag and studied the cryptic crossword.

Five across: Fool, one taken in by her dressmaker? Eight letters.

Hartigan tapped her pen against her lips.

Ten across: Forgotten old man on street. Four letters.

She sipped from her cup and it burned her mouth and throat, leaving her tongue feeling prickly, her chest aching.

Old man, like a father, like her father. Pa. And the abbreviation for street. The solution was "past". My father has a past. No, he has a history. He is legendary, a hero. He would never hesitate. He was never afraid. I will never be the cop that he was.

Hartigan shook her head and filled in the squares before gnawing on her pen.

Fifteen across. Understudy with good reputation. Eight letters.

Understudy. Like a replacement, a reserve, a stand-in.

A fraud, a fake, a liar, a...

She groaned in frustration. "Stand-in" followed by "g" for "good" gives "standing". She penned in the answer.

"Agent Hartigan?"

She started and felt for the pistol under her jacket, looking up from her crossword to see a man in a flannel suit. He was in his early thirties but his hair was silver around his temples, his shirt open at the collar.

"I'm David Frost," he said, placing his hands on the chair in front of him.

Her heart was pounding in her chest and she took a deep breath. "Frost?" she asked shakily.

"You called me about the Angela James case," he added.

"Oh." She narrowed her eyes. "How did you find me?"

He cleared his throat. "I called your office and they said you like to come here before work."

She shifted in her seat. "I see."

"I wanted to talk to you in private." He patted the backrest of the chair. "May I?"

She felt for her pistol again and nodded.

“That bruise on your head looks terrible,” Frost said, pulling his chair closer to the table. “Are you okay?”

She touched the bruise on her hairline and cringed. “I’m fine.”

“I’m glad.” He grinned crookedly, wringing his hands in front of him. “Before we begin, I have to ask—”

“He’s my father,” she said.

“Oh.” Frost became tense. “Then you might not like what I have to say.”

“Aren’t you supposed to be a constable?” Hartigan asked, reaching for her coffee.

“I left the police force after the James case.”

“Why?”

“Your order, sir?” a waiter asked, hovering near their table.

“Nothing, thank you,” he said, shooing the boy away.

Hartigan sipped from her cup and eyed Frost sceptically. “Mr Frost—”

“Professor.”

“I’m sorry?”

“It’s Professor Frost, now,” he said, beaming proudly. “I work at the university and lecture in criminology.”

"I see," she said slowly.

"I read your thesis," he added. "It was excellent."

Hartigan sighed impatiently. "Professor Frost."

"David, please."

"Enough!" she snapped. The other customers in the store glanced at her but quickly looked away. "I'm running out of patience, Professor David Frost."

Frost absently scratched the back of his hand. "I'll get to the point," he said.

Hartigan nodded. "Start by telling me about the case."

"I think I should start by telling you about Angela James," Frost said. "You'll understand why, once I'm done."

"Fine. Tell me about James."

"She was the adopted daughter of a media mogul. Her parents loved her but weren't always there for her. She was in a car accident a couple of years before her death and injured her shoulder. She suffered from chronic pain every day after that."

Hartigan scrawled a note beneath her crossword. "Go on."

"She tried codeine, and that worked for a while. When that wasn't enough, she moved on to morphine. When that stopped working..." He took a deep breath. "Heroin."

"Be serious."

"I am deadly serious, Agent Hartigan," Frost said. "After that, it was all downhill. She had a miscarriage, a broken marriage, hepatitis, and no job. Her parents abandoned her."

"Where does Simone Elliot fit in?"

"Elliot returned to the country after a job in the UAE and visited her old orphanage. It was abandoned but she found James huddled on the steps. She was homeless."

Hartigan leaned forward.

"Elliot bought her an apartment and helped her clean up.

Everything was going okay."

"And then James disappeared." Hartigan poured the last of her coffee past her lips.

"We found the apartment clean, no evidence of foul play, not even a fingerprint. Your father was convinced it was murder."

"I heard it was her dealer."

Frost shook his head. "That's just the story they used to cover it up."

Hartigan sat up and folded her arms across her chest. "What are you talking about?"

"Simone Elliot was the suspect."

Hartigan shook her head. "No, that's not right."

"She killed James' dealer and we caught her and dragged her back to the station." He cleared his throat. "She didn't say a word while she was in custody. Your dad was furious. He was convinced that she was the killer. Then she escaped during the night and killed just about every cop on shift. She's the one who put your dad in hospital." He stared at the table.

"This doesn't make any sense." Hartigan tried to scrawl another note on her newspaper but her hand was unsteady. "Why didn't this make the papers? Why did they sell the dealer to the press?"

He shook his head, finally finding the courage to look her in the eye. "Like I said, your dad was furious. When she was in custody, he bound her wrists and hung her from a rafter. He stripped her naked and doused her in ice-water."

"That's it," Hartigan said, standing up. "I've heard enough." She tossed some money on the table and shouldered her bag.

"Wait, Emily," Frost cried, blocking her path.

Hartigan bowled past him and rammed through the exit, her lungs aching as she inhaled the frigid morning air.

"Emily, wait," Frost called out. He was holding a DVD. "I knew you wouldn't believe me so I brought this."

"A snuff film?"

"It's evidence," he said slowly. "Look, you're not the first to pretend this didn't happen. Your dad was an old-fashioned cop. He got things done but times changed. Your dad didn't."

"You're telling me my father tortured a suspect," Hartigan hissed, her eyes burning.

"Yes, I am," he said, his voice trembling. "I was there. I tried to stop it. I wanted to stop it." He rubbed the back of his neck. "I used a hidden camera and took it to Internal Affairs. They hushed it up and retired your dad quietly."

"Why would they do that?"

"Because of James' adoptive father," Frost said. "He wanted this to happen to Elliot." Frost held the DVD up in the air. "He wanted justice."

Hartigan stared at the disc.

"Look, it was a mess. They tried to beat a confession out of Elliot but she escaped and then lashed out. A lot of cops died and the chief inspector wanted it tied off. The dealer was the best scapegoat because he was dead."

"Why didn't you take this to the media?" Hartigan asked, nodding at the disc. "Someone other than James' father."

"I was paid off," he said quietly.

Her nostrils flared. "You're as bad as the rest of them."

"I was finished as a constable. I needed to start over." He pushed the disc into her hand. "Watch it," he begged. "Do something."

Hartigan folded her fingers around the disc. "Were you there the night she escaped?"

"Yes."

"But she didn't kill you."

"I never laid a hand on her."

"So why didn't she kill my dad?"

Frost sunk his hands into his pockets. "I've always wondered that myself, Emily."

29

CANBERRA, AUSTRALIA

FRIDAY 16 SEPTEMBER

7:35AM AEST

"I'm not seeing any students today," Sharon Little said over her shoulder.

"I'm not a student, Ms Little. I've come to see you about something personal."

Little swivelled on her chair and faced the woman in her doorway. She looked the visitor up and down before taking her glasses off. "Who are you?"

"My name's Simone Elliot."

Little's jaw fell open and she rose slowly from her chair. "My God," she said. "How did you find me?"

"I found your name on one of my brother's things," Elliot said quickly. "I would've called but—"

Little swallowed Elliot with her heavy arms but quickly pulled back as Elliot squirmed. She put a hand to her mouth. "I'm sorry, I completely forgot. Darren told me years ago that you don't like being touched."

Elliot gave her a crooked smile. "Don't worry about it."

"No, I'm really sorry," she said. "I'm just so happy to meet you."

"So you know who I am?" Elliot asked, struggling to remember the woman in front of her.

Little nodded vigorously. "I saw your photograph every day while I was deployed with your brother. I'm surprised I didn't recognise you as soon as you walked through the door."

"I guess time changes people."

Little gestured for Elliot to sit. "I was looking forward to meeting you when I got back but I never got the chance."

Elliot picked up a stack of books from a chair and placed them on the floor before sitting down and surveying Little's office.

"I went into full-time study after the war and now I teach," Little explained.

"History and military strategy?" Hardcover tomes were stacked on dusty shelves, with wrinkled tags jutting from the pages. Paperbacks littered the floor, their spines broken and pages pasted in highlighter. Her desk was blanketed with essays and papers from her students.

"We try to understand the mistakes so we can prevent them from occurring again," she said wistfully. "Of course, it only helps if those in command of the military are interested."

"I imagine that doesn't happen very often." Elliot caught a glimpse of the photographs on her desk. "Little. Now I remember you," she said, pointing to a photograph.

A young woman in camouflage fatigues was propped against a signpost in a dusty town. Her sinewy arms had been baked by the sun and her curly caramel hair framed a delicate face, her eyes squinted at the camera. Her rifle was slung over her shoulder and her webbing was at her feet. Elliot remembered *that* young woman from the airport when she had waved her brother goodbye.

Little tilted her head, gauging Elliot's reaction. "Like you said, time changes people."

Once, the woman in front of her had been lean in body and wisdom, trudging through the desert to fight a war, but she'd left that behind. Little was no longer marching through mud to defend an idea, she was crawling through history to find one, any one, that would give her mind rest.

I understand.

Elliot cleared her throat. "I've wanted to talk to someone." She stopped and shifted in her seat. "Needed to, I guess. I, uh."

Little nodded slowly, pointing to the books on her shelves. "Sometimes it's hard to ask questions when you're afraid of the answers. Sometimes, we focus on the wrong questions so we get the answers we want."

Elliot wrung her hands. "I'm sorry. I shouldn't have come." She grabbed the arms of her chair and stood up.

"Stay."

Elliot cringed. The chair sighed when she sat down. "This is hard."

"I know," Little said softly.

"When his coffin came home, I left it all behind." Her shoulders sagged. "I don't think I was ready to hear it."

"I understand," Little said softly.

I need to know.

"I loved your brother," Little said. "I was just a baby and he looked out for me."

Elliot peered up at her.

"I was over there as a linguist," she began. "I sometimes went on patrol with the soldiers to translate. I was mostly there to talk with the women, to find out what they knew, and to keep our men from talking to them to keep the peace." She opened a desk drawer, burrowing down until she found what she was looking for. She handed Elliot a stack of photographs. "I usually went with the regular army patrols but I tagged along with your brother's specialist unit on a few different occasions."

Elliot thumbed through the photographs. Little was there, posing with bronzed men, all of them wearing dark sunglasses and dusty boots. She recognised her brother and she recognised Murphy. Both men were smiling and Harper's arm was around Murphy's shoulders.

"They usually did search and destroy missions," Little explained. "They used to hunt down the enemy and kill them where they slept. On one occasion, they attacked a camp and found three young girls who had been taken from their homes, so they returned them to their tribe." She shifted in her seat. "The militants used to marry into the tribes to gain a foothold. They would slowly take over a village and take advantage of their cultural hospitality. They'd take food, medicine, and sometimes women. The more they married, the more integrated they were into the tribe, the more they could get the locals to do what they wished.

"One chief, going against all traditional practice, refused to allow it and he kicked the militants out. One night, they came back and stole the young girls they believed they were entitled to marry. Darren's unit stumbled into the middle of it."

"The village would've been happy to see them back alive."

"Yes and no," Little said. "The traditionalists thought the chief was breaking the rules. They believed they were culturally obligated to provide the hospitality the chief had refused to give. The more superstitious believed they would be punished by God for not allowing the marriages."

"What happened?"

"The unit was often invited back to the village to eat and celebrate." She paused and started to scratch the armrest of her chair. "They went back a few times. The last time, there were some problems. We had a new rookie officer." Her face pinched and she drummed her fingers on the chair's armrest. "Damn, I can't remember his name," she said in frustration. "I told myself I'd never forget it, either."

"It's okay," Elliot said.

"Anyway, command figured the task was culturally oriented rather than combat intensive, so the rookie would be fine. The sergeant had come down with food poisoning and was stuck at the base. The young officer insisted on making the meeting without the sergeant, so Spud was appointed to lead the section."

"Spud?" Elliot closed her eyes. "God, I forgot they called him that."

Murphy—a name as common as potatoes.

Elliot opened her eyes and saw that Little was studying her with sparkling eyes. "So, uh, was everyone okay with that?" Elliot asked. "Spud, I mean, Stephen." She exhaled. "Was everyone happy having Murphy in charge?"

"Oh, yes," Little said, "everyone liked Stephen. You knew him," she added with a wink. "He was one of those people who made you feel that everything was going to be okay. The men would have followed him to hell and back."

"Really?"

"Nobody had a problem with it, except for the new officer. They didn't get along. I think the lieutenant was straight out of training and was on his first tour." She shrugged. "He confronted Stephen about his soldiers' haircuts and uniforms, all the trivial stuff that doesn't matter when you could die the next day. Stephen tried to reason with him but the officer kept yapping like a dog."

"He hit him, didn't he?"

"How'd you know?"

"Like you said, I know him."

"Put him on his back," Little said, grinning. "Anyway, Stephen took us back to the village and I tagged along. We got there and learned that the chief's daughter had been snatched the night before. The family were frantic and the villagers were baying for blood. I was busy talking to the mother, trying to get some sense out of her, and Stephen was talking to the father, the chief, trying to find out what had happened. The lieutenant was very jittery, pacing around the room, and Darren was keeping an eye on things.

"We heard cheering outside and suddenly this young girl was carried into the house. She was wearing this bright red hijab," Little said, gesturing with her hands. "I'll never forget that." She cleared her throat. "Not as long as I live."

Elliot hunched forward.

"The family went to hug her, to welcome her home, but she told them to get away from her. She was crying. Oh, God, I've never seen a young girl as frightened as that." She started scratching her armrest again. "Her mother knelt in front of her and opened her shawl and we could see she was strapped with a suicide vest. Everyone started to freak out, except for Spud and Darren. Stephen told me to talk to the mother and the girl and find out what had happened. He especially wanted to know if she had the trigger or if someone else was holding it. So, I was busy doing that. Meanwhile, the lieutenant was losing it, yelling that we needed to kill the girl before she killed all of us. Your brother was trying to cool him down but it didn't help. Eventually, the lieutenant pulled his weapon."

Elliot watched Little's eyes glaze over.

"He killed her," Little murmured. "Shot her in the head. I was right next to her when it happened." She crossed her legs. "Now her parents wanted us dead. Stephen broke the lieutenant's nose, arm, and collarbone in half a second. He dragged him outside while Darren was pushing me out the door. I was talking over his shoulder to calm the family down and then..."

The only sound in the room was Little scratching the armrest of her chair.

"Your brother saved my life," she whispered. "He pushed me through the door at the last second. He was standing up and the girl was lying on the floor. A table blocked most of the blast but not enough to save him. Stephen ran straight past me and into the house and I leapt up the steps. It was too late, though."

There was a long silence and Elliot could hear voices in the hallway. Two students chuckled, their shoes scuffing the carpet. The voices faded away.

Elliot felt her medallion burning through her pocket. "Did Darren say anything before he...?"

"He told Stephen not to feel bad, that he knew what he had to do. Then he handed him your photograph."

Elliot nodded slowly.

"Stephen got us out of there before the locals tore us to pieces. He carried your brother all the way to base on his shoulders."

"What happened when you got back?" Elliot croaked.

"The young lieutenant told command that Stephen had neglected his duty and allowed a suicide bomber to breach their security, leading to the death of a member of their team and three civilians."

"But that's not what really happened," Elliot protested.

"No, it wasn't. Technically, it was true though, and that was enough. None of the other soldiers were in the room except for your brother and I. Spud's men *wanted* to defend him but they couldn't, and command took the officer's word over mine."

"And then he went to jail."

"Well, yes, but there was no trial."

"What?" Elliot cried.

"The unit was top secret so it was all hushed up. We all signed non-disclosures and Stephen was dishonourably discharged and sent to a civilian prison."

"I don't fucking believe it." Elliot clutched her forehead. She took a deep breath and looked up at Little. "What about the girl?"

"She was forgotten. She was listed as collateral damage in the report, not as the bomber." Little shook her head. "I just wanted to scream at people for weeks after that, to tell them the truth about what happened, but I couldn't breathe a word about it. Murphy and your brother did everything they could and it was all ruined by a young officer who panicked."

Elliot slouched back in her chair and sucked in her bottom lip.

"That's the last I ever heard of Stephen," Little said. "As far as I know, he's still in jail. Most of his unit left the army soon after that tour. So did I. I have no idea what happened to the lieutenant. It's like he just disappeared into thin air." Little shook her head quickly, her shoulders drooping. "I have to confess, telling you all that doesn't make me feel any better. I had hoped it would."

"If it helps, I'm not sure it made me feel any better either."

Little shuffled her chair towards Elliot, reaching out her hand.

Elliot jerked her arm away.

"You're not an easy person to comfort." Little curled her fingers and sat up. "Your brother told me it took him months to earn your trust."

Elliot widened her eyes. "He told you that?"

"Confided, I suppose," Little said. "Not even a handshake, he said. You'd always squirm."

"He never said anything to me," Elliot murmured.

"Did you ever tell him why? I mean, there must be a reason for it."

Elliot shrugged.

"Is that a no?"

"My personal space, my rules."

"But those rules didn't apply to Stephen."

Elliot flinched.

"Stephen was different, right?" Little paused. "You were in love."

"It's complicated." Elliot's face fell. "We were young, you know?"

"So you haven't seen him lately?"

"No."

"You blamed him," Little said knowingly.

"It's not that simple."

"Did he try to reach you?"

"He might have but I don't think so. I've been hard to pin down."

"Running away?"

"Working."

"If he hasn't tried to reach you, then he probably feels guilty."

"He does. I know he does."

"It wasn't his fault."

"He promised me Darren would come back alive," Elliot mumbled.

"And you held him to that?"

Elliot stared down at her hands.

Little's chair creaked as she sat up and swept her arm across the bookcase. "You know, I've been hoping to find one book that tells us how we can stop all this. Someone must have figured it out and written it down. Somewhere there is a scrap of paper with that one piece of advice that we can use to save ourselves."

"I don't think there is."

"I like to hope there is." Little leaned forward. "What are *you* hoping for?"

Elliot shrugged and rubbed her chin. "I want to find him again."

"He was never lost. He's still in a cell."

"In a metaphorical sense," she added, curling her fingers over her lips.

"You didn't answer my question."

Elliot's hands fell heavily into her lap. "I hope I'm not too late," she said quietly.

"For what?"

"To tell him I understand; that I was wrong; that I was..." She choked. "I *am* afraid."

"What changed?"

Angela.

"Simone?"

"I really should go," Elliot said, standing up. "I've taken up enough of your time."

Little clicked her fingers. "Singh."

Elliot froze.

"That was the lieutenant's name," Little said. "Lee Singh. He was Indian but I think he spent his entire life in Australia."

Elliot looked down at Little. "Singh."

"You know him?"

Her mouth fell open. "The name rings a bell." She flexed her fingers and closed them into a fist.

30

CANBERRA, AUSTRALIA

FRIDAY 16 SEPTEMBER

8:46AM AEST

Lee Singh despised women like Natalie Robinson. She was *that* woman, the one who sat alone in cafés, nursing a cup of tea, her elbow on the table with her hand against her cheek. A closed book, Singh thought, but the story was always the same.

She would read a newspaper or a paperback, but she could never find the right words when she spoke. She had photographs on her refrigerator, pictures of her posing around the world, well-travelled but still lost. Of course, she had friends, all the company she could ever need, but she would always be lonely.

Singh had seen the men who pined for her, too. They would steal glances across the café and sigh longingly as they imagined saying something that would prompt her face to fracture into a smile. They would imagine a carton of skim milk in their refrigerator, one of their t-shirts fragranced with her scent and tossed carelessly over the foot of the bed, and lost strands of hair that clung stubbornly to the pillow. Then they would realise that she was empty, and to peel off her clothes was to see all of her. So they would leave, forgetting her forever, and she would still be alone. The only men left for her were those who would devour her whole while pushing her mind to the side of the plate.

"Make yourself at home, Agent Singh," Robinson said, sweeping her arm across the hotel suite.

Singh unbuttoned his jacket and sat on the sofa. The same old story, he thought. All her life spent writing out her soul word for word in a diary and, in the end, it was just a collection of tangled lines and blank spaces because she never bothered to find someone to help make sense of it—and was too afraid to do it herself.

Robinson sat on an armchair and poured a glass of water, peering at him with mournful eyes. Her movements were graceful and precise, barely creating a ripple in the universe, as if the laws consciously surrendered to her wishes.

"You're a physicist," Singh said.

"No," Robinson said. She left her glass on the coffee table and settled into the armchair.

Singh stroked his chin. "You study physics."

"Yes, but I'm not a physicist." She plucked a pencil from behind her head, her hair tumbling down in straw-coloured waves. "I haven't contributed to the field through research. I am only a student."

Precise. "It's a strange choice of career for a woman like you, isn't it?"

“What kind of woman am I, Agent Singh?”

The door opened behind him. He heard a rustle and turned his head to see Emily Hartigan take a chair against the wall. He slouched into the cushions before stretching his arm across the back of the sofa. “Your accent is barely noticeable,” he said to Robinson.

“My parents were Russian but I was raised in Geelong.” She pulled her hair taut and used the pencil to bundle it into a knot. “It’s difficult not to be influenced by Australia. You have a unique language.”

“English?”

“That’s too simplistic. Australian language has a distinct character.”

“I thought scientists were fond of simple explanations.”

“Sometimes.”

“Are you?”

“Fundamentally, the laws of the universe possess an elegant simplicity. That is their foundation.” She pushed a strand of hair behind her ear. “But the laws swirl around us and twist together, creating randomness, irrationality, and chaos. It is one thing to unweave the rainbow and quite another to understand the rainbow as a whole.”

“I see similarities in my work.”

Her eyes flashed but her voice was calm. “Your laws are a tangle, not a tapestry,” she said.

"A criminal's motives are often simple."

"But a person's nature is not."

"True. It can be random, irrational and chaotic," he said. "It can be ugly."

"I feel sorry for anybody who believes the world is ugly."

"I'm talking about people."

"Are you exempt?"

"Is Stepan Volkov?"

Robinson's expression remained disinterested. "So it's true," she said. "It was him."

Almost had her. "Yes, it was." Singh fiddled with the knot in his tie. "Stepan Volkov killed Andrei Sorokin on Monday night, in a pub that is over 200 kilometres away from where you live."

He paused, hoping that she would feel compelled to fill the silence but she was guarding her words. Her hands remained casually clasped on her lap and she stared at him, waiting for him to speak again.

"What were you doing in that pub?" Singh asked finally.

"I was attending a friend's birthday party," Robinson replied. "Her family lives in the town so we made it a long weekend."

"Do you know Stepan Volkov?"

"I read about him on the internet."

"You've never encountered him before? You *are* Russian."

"There are 143 million Russians on the planet. Technically, I'm not one of them. I certainly haven't met them all."

"Fair enough." Singh leaned forward, his elbows on his knees. "Let's talk about something else instead," he said. "Tell me about the CEO of Titan Energy, Geoffrey Geldenhuys."

"My professor's chair is funded by Titan Energy," Robinson explained. "He conducts research into renewable energy on behalf of Mr Geldenhuys' company."

"Are you involved?"

"Yes."

He folded his arms. "How?"

"I read an article one day and approached my professor to discuss the potential of using helium-3 for fusion power. He gave me some information and equations and invited me to help him with his research."

"Is that normal?"

"He's attempting to nurture my potential."

"Are you sure he's not sexually attracted to you?"

"I'm certain he's not." She answered the question without outrage or doubt.

"How do you know?" said Singh.

"Because I know when a man is attracted to me, or another woman for that matter. I'm a brain on a stick to him."

"Is Mr Geldenhuys happy with the direction of your research?"

"I have no reason to believe otherwise."

"Was he happy to see a young woman assist the professor?"

"He seemed grateful that the research could continue if my professor were to pursue retirement."

"How grateful?"

"He offered monetary bonuses to fund my research in exchange for sexual favours."

Singh sat up. "Are you serious?"

"No, I'm not. I'm just annoyed with your ridiculous questions. If you want to ask me if he wants to sleep with me, just ask."

Singh heard Hartigan stifle a giggle behind him and he frowned. "Do you think he wants to sleep with you?"

"Yes."

"Would you consider sleeping with him?"

"No."

"What if there was a fully funded chair in the physics department at stake?"

"I don't need his money."

"Has he propositioned you at all?"

"He satisfies himself by staring at my breasts."

"Are you comfortable with that?"

"I can live with looking. Men do it all the time. However, when he pinched me, I felt compelled to knock out one of his teeth."

"You hit him?"

She nodded. "He apologised afterwards and asked me not to tell his wife. He's been much more professional since then."

"Has his wife noticed his interest?"

"She started calling and emailing me threats, telling me to stay away from her husband."

"You didn't tell the police?"

"That a woman is jealous of me?"

"Do you still have her emails?"

"They're on my laptop." She pointed towards the desk in the corner of the hotel room.

"Did you tell the professor?"

"No. We often receive threats. Our close relationship with Titan Energy draws accusations of collaboration or conspiracy. Activists are perhaps the worst."

"Surely, you would call the police? It's against the law to use email and phone calls to make threats."

"Yes, I know. The Criminal Code Act 1995, Division 474, Subdivision C."

Singh's mouth fell open. "I'd have to check that."

"She's right," Hartigan said from the back of the room.

"Thank you, Agent Hartigan." Singh scowled. "How long have activists been making threats?"

"Since before my time. It got worse when Titan started searching for oil. I imagine it will be non-stop now that Titan is about to start drilling."

"Have you had other threats? What about the *Organizatsiya?*"

"What's that?"

"If you've read about Volkov, then you've heard of them."

Robinson shrugged. "Have I?"

Singh heard Hartigan's phone buzz. "Hartigan," she said. He heard her leave the hotel room, the door squealing shut behind her. He drummed his fingers on his thigh and Robinson watched him patiently. "I'm going to keep you in protective custody for a little while longer, Miss Robinson."

"I understand."

"Is there anything else you want to talk about?"

"Yes," Robinson replied. "If you're going to take my laptop, then I would appreciate internet access. I also need some new notepads and a whiteboard."

"I'll look into that for you."

"I would be grateful." She smiled and Singh immediately wanted to collect everything she had asked for just to see her smile again.

That's what he despised most.

"You should smile more often," he said. "It would make you seem more of a person."

She didn't flinch. "I've found that people who accuse others of acting inhuman are at risk of becoming the worst animals of all."

He tapped his finger against his lips. "Is that the ugliness you dismissed so readily before?"

"Agent Singh, a rainbow is many things to many people. It is refracted light, a poet's palette, a child's daydream, or even a sign of God's grace. But, no matter what, it always means rain." She finally reached for her glass of water. "I feel sorry for any man who believes that destroying all those things for all those people will stop a thunderstorm."

***

"What the hell is going on, Lee?" Hartigan demanded, charging along the corridor. "Why didn't you tell me you were interviewing Robinson?"

Singh threw his hands in the air and turned away from the elevator, pushing through the door to the stairs.

Hartigan trailed behind him, taking the stairs two at a time. "Hey!" she called out. "Don't walk away from me."

"I thought you might need some time to recover after last night," Singh said, rapping his knuckles on the banister as he trotted down the stairs.

"Don't bullshit me, Lee," Hartigan snapped. "Trust, remember?"

"Let's talk about that." Singh nimbly climbed down another flight of stairs. "Did you discharge against medical advice?"

"I'm glad I did too," Hartigan puffed, trying to keep up with him. "Andrei Sorokin's computer finally showed up at headquarters this morning. It took the techs less than ten minutes to find some pretty incriminating emails."

"I'll make a note."

"The emails show that Sorokin was having an affair with Giselle Geldenhuys," Hartigan said, wiping her brow.

"Who?"

"The wife of Titan's CEO," she huffed in exasperation. "She administers Lime, the charity. Don't play dumb."

"So what? She was cheating on her husband. Not a crime."

Hartigan raced past him, leaping to the ground floor and blocking the exit to the lobby. "Giselle Geldenhuys started an affair with Sorokin while he was working security for Titan. After he left the company, she kept the affair going, right up until she paid Sorokin to kill Natalie Robinson, using money from Lime's accounts. Giselle believed her husband was having an affair with Robinson and decided to end it, violently."

Singh grunted, pushing her out of the way and opening the door.

Hartigan slammed it shut, using her body weight to keep it closed. "If Sorokin had succeeded, we would've been all over the *Organizatsiya'* s operations in Australia. That's why Volkov was sent here to kill him."

"Enough, Emily."

"Robinson's testimony and the emails from Giselle on her laptop establish a motive for attempted murder and conspiracy."

He tried to open the door again but Hartigan wouldn't budge.

"Take Giselle's fingerprints and I bet you they match those on the bullets in the weapon we found on Sorokin."

Singh shook his head. "We're not taking her fingerprints," he said, "because she's not under investigation. None of them are. Not Lime, or Titan, or anyone else associated with them. Get out of the way before I shoot you."

Hartigan's mouth opened, her protest catching in her throat. She stood aside and Singh pushed through the door.

"You're covering up a murder," she bellowed across the lobby.

The guests and staff looked up, staring at Singh.

He turned back to Hartigan and ran his thumb and forefinger down his cheeks, his mouth open. "*Attempted* murder," he said, nearing her. "I'm covering up attempted murder. If you're going to shout accusations in public places, at least get them right."

"Oh, I got it right," she countered. "Giselle Geldenhuys is nothing compared to her husband. He had motive to commit murder and the means to hire a killer to do it for him."

"That's news to me."

"Geoffrey Geldenhuys could've hired Stepan Volkov through the *Organizatsiya.* For all we know, he had Dr Marco Belo killed in Jakarta to preserve Titan's business interests in the Timor Sea."

"That's wild speculation."

"It's a valid hypothesis."

"Based on nothing," he spat. "What if the *Organizatsiya* killed Belo to make Titan look dirty? What if Sorokin was planted to manipulate Giselle Geldenhuys? What if Sorokin's hit on Robinson was a setup?"

"That's..."

"All of it arranged, and we end up distracted by an investigation that conveniently diverts our attention from figuring out what the *Organizatsiya* is up to."

"We'll never know if we don't fucking investigate," she said.

"Jesus. Do you even listen to the stuff that comes out of your mouth?"

"The deputy director can decide. He needs to be informed."

"Okay, let's go brief him," he said mockingly. "And let's talk about how our trap worked last night and you let the bait bite you while the Wolf ran away."

"I did my best."

"Your best isn't enough!" Singh stepped closer, glaring down at her, stabbing her chest with his finger. "You need to understand what you're supposed to be doing here."

"Our job is to enforce the law," Hartigan cried.

"No, we enforce *our* law. The law is a tool, a weapon that we use to protect our interests."

"Bullshit."

"Titan Energy is working to further our interests," Singh pointed out. "The *Organizatsiya,* on the other hand."

"All equal before the law, Lee. Do you remember that one?"

"Oh, cut it out," he snorted. "I don't think you even believe your own crap." He stepped back. "Titan is not the bad guy."

"But you don't even—"

"Enough," he said, cutting her off. "Before you say another word, think about the guests staying in that hotel last night, all of those terrified people. How many of them want to ensure that Elliot and Murphy are subject to due process? How many of them would want to ensure the Wolf's human rights were protected?"

Hartigan's eyelids flickered. "I'd like to think—"

Singh laughed derisively. "Yes, you're good at that. It's what you *believe* that lets you down. The taxpayers want these animals gone."

"They're not animals," she protested.

"Oh, no, you're right, of course. Take Murphy, for example. The country turned its back on him, the war hero, and threw him in jail without a trial, so we should forgive him."

"That's not what I'm talking about."

"And her." He shook his head sadly. "Jesus. A traumatic childhood, rumours of sexual abuse and neglect. We let her down, didn't we? Of course she was going to become a thief. It's all *our* fault."

"Is that what you really think I believe?"

"You think a simple guy like me couldn't make sense of your academic gibberish? The world isn't black and white like your essays, Emily. It's grey."

"That's why we *have* due process."

"Laws are for people who don't break them or feel guilty when they do," he said. "Next time you want to test a person's faith in the legal system, ask them if they're happy to have an acquitted paedophile living next door."

"Right, much better to have Geoffrey Geldenhuys as a neighbour."

"Yeah, it is."

Hartigan blinked. "You don't feel any shame at all, do you?"

"Geldenhuys is about to drill for oil," Singh said. "Lots of oil. That means hundreds of drillers, drivers, mechanics, engineers, geologists, and that's just the start."

"You can't be serious."

"Ports, roads, schools, hospitals, factories, universities," he said. "Life, food, shelter, security and prosperity. That's what we're talking about here."

"That doesn't give him the right to have others killed."

"Then go kick down his door," Singh said. "Accuse him. Arrest him. Fuck economic development. Who gives a shit, right? You think he broke the law."

"Jesus. I don't..." Hartigan clutched her forehead and turned away. The concierge glanced at her but his gaze fell to the desk. The guests all feigned disinterest, awkwardly clutching brochures and pointing at paintings in the lobby.

"Are you listening to me?"

"I think I'm going to be sick," she muttered.

"That would smell better than your bullshit."

She whirled around and raised a finger. "I can go higher. I can take this to the minister."

"You'll never make it through his front door."

"But—"

"Every country protects their interests in the same way. Korolev is the threat, Murphy is his instrument, and Elliot is our means to get at both of them. They are our targets and we'll use them and then kill them."

"You're as bad as these 'animals' you hunt," she said. "We're supposed to be better than them."

"We *are* better than them, Emily," Singh said. "Do you honestly believe that the *Organizatsiya* uses their oil profits to buy teddy bears for orphans? Everything comes down to interest, to want, to desire. Everybody has theirs, even you."

"This is *not* what we do."

"Yeah, it is, and you need to come to the party," he said. "Forget about Titan. I want Murphy."

She folded her arms across her chest. "What's your interest, huh?"

"That's enough." He placed his hands on his hips. "You fucked up last night, Hartigan. We had an opportunity to gain the upper hand and you blew it. If you still want to be a part of this investigation, then find me some answers. We have less than four hours left until the Sino-Russian deadline and we still have no idea if the *Organizatsiya* plans to force us out of the oil market. You either find a way to learn what Korolev is up to, or find me a way to Murphy so we can ask him." He pointed at the ceiling. "Because that sex kitten knows less than nothing and doesn't even make good bait."

"Sex kitten?" Hartigan shook her head. "You're a pig."

"Trust me," he said, "guys pay good money to download girls like her from the internet."

"Just because she's pretty and young doesn't make her..." Her voice trailed off and she stared at the floor. "A porn star." Her mind started racing.

Singh's phone rang and he turned away.

Hartigan's eyes searched for an emergency exit sign.

"Sorry, who's this?" Singh asked. His eyes widened and he stared at his reflection in the lobby's glass doors. "Yeah, do you have anything?" He listened for a few moments and checked his watch. "How about right now?" He paused. "Yeah, I know it. I'll see you there."

Hartigan was gone before he hung up.

31

CANBERRA, AUSTRALIA

FRIDAY 16 SEPTEMBER

10:02AM AEST

The park was older than most of the buildings, beginning life as five acres of trimmed grass dotted with shady trees. A playground came next and then a winding path, now sheltered by an arch of flowering creepers.

Statues of the gods of Ancient Greece had been erected along the path: justice, wisdom, beauty, love, and health. The statues had glistened brightly when the park had first opened, each deity a pure white stone beacon that lured people to walk the path.

Soon, the planners and developers and trucks and lawyers arrived. Buildings sprang up around the park and the green grass was darkened by the shadows of skyscrapers. Hotels and restaurants had been built on the lakeside while a mall was built at the city end. The park was crisscrossed with dirt paths, pioneered by pedestrians who wanted to get to the bank, the shopping centre, or the taxi rank. The statues had been blackened by the city, vines clinging to their stone skin, their limbs now perches for the birds. Nevertheless, justice, wisdom, beauty, love, and health were still there for anybody who wanted to remember what they looked like.

Emily Hartigan chose a park bench opposite one of the statues. The bench was shaded by a vast tree that sprawled across the sky, its boughs creaking as they swayed back and forth.

Hartigan's hair whipped around her face and she brushed it out of her eyes in frustration. She watched the leaves swirl around the stone goddess before her. It was Themis, goddess of divine justice. Beneath the creeping vines and soot, she clutched a double-edged sword and a set of scales, her eyes hidden by a blindfold. Hartigan looked away, squinting as dust and debris whirled past her. She was forced to turn back to Themis, and shrivelled under her blind glare. Hartigan hoped she wouldn't have to wait long.

Natalie Robinson rounded the corner and stopped, her shoulders slumping when Hartigan moved to block the path. Robinson cast her eyes around but saw that the park was deserted. "Hello, Agent Hartigan," she said.

"How do you know who I am?"

"Your partner used your name while he was interviewing me." She pushed her hair out of her eyes. "Then you volunteered the information when you answered your phone."

Hartigan nodded and gestured for Robinson to sit down. "He's not my partner."

"I'm sorry. Boyfriend." Robinson plunged her hands into the pockets of her coat and sat down. "Or is the correct term 'de facto'?"

Hartigan curled her lip. "I called your professor. He told me you liked to go for a mid-morning walk." She gestured towards the grass. "This was the closest park."

"Did my professor praise you for your work?"

"I'm sorry?"

"I knew your name before we met but not your face," Robinson confessed, crossing her legs. "Like so many others, I read your thesis some time ago."

"I see."

"I couldn't share their opinions, however. It was typical idealistic nonsense written by a person who prefers to base theories on feelings rather than empirical data."

Hartigan felt heat creep into her face. "Is that so?"

"And you were very selective when presenting evidence."

"It's funny you mention that," Hartigan said, pacing in front of the park bench. "I was thinking about that this morning. You see, I did some research on people trafficking but I didn't include it in the final draft, mostly because it turned my stomach. Do you know anything about people trafficking?"

Robinson shrugged.

"Girls were sometimes snatched from the streets, or even their homes. Most were lured to nightclubs and promised modelling careers. They were drugged and sold at auctions, and their parents were killed so nobody would search for them."

Robinson didn't react.

"Those girls went on to become strippers, prostitutes," Hartigan said, plucking her phone from her pocket. "In some cases, even internet porn stars." She pushed a button and showed Robinson the screen.

Robinson watched a video play on the small screen. A naked girl moaned theatrically for the fat man standing behind her, thrusting his hips. Robinson's eyes darkened.

"Naughty Nataliya," Hartigan said. "That's what they called you, wasn't it?"

"The resemblance is uncanny," Robinson said calmly.

Hartigan pocketed her phone. "You're in a lot of films produced by Nikolay Korolev's company. I even found a photograph of you dancing in his club."

"It's not me, Agent Hartigan." Robinson uncrossed her legs and stood up. "I don't know what you're trying to do but I don't appreciate being compared to an adult film star." She turned to leave.

"I know who you are, Natalie," Hartigan cried over a gust of wind.

Robinson stopped and turned around. "Who am I?"

"A girl who was trapped," Hartigan said, "until someone set you free. You must be important because he took a huge risk coming here. Private jets stand out and he had to burn a passport to evade detection."

"Who are you talking about?"

"He didn't take the risk to kill Andrei Sorokin; this was all about saving you."

Robinson raised her eyebrows. "Are you talking about Volkov?"

Hartigan ignored the question. "After I found your films, I decided to poke around your hotel to see how you were spending your time. The staff told me you had an argument with Simone Elliot in the bar the day you checked in."

"I don't know who that is," Robinson said. "The woman I saw was Leanne Waters, the constable."

"The staff heard you call her Simone," Hartigan shot back. "'I hate you, Simone,' you said. 'And I wish he did too.'"

"Why on earth would I say that?"

"They heard the name 'Stepan'," Hartigan said. She clenched and unclenched her fists. "You were talking about Stepan Volkov."

"Perhaps. I can't recall what Waters and I discussed." She turned to leave again.

Hartigan grabbed her wrist. "I don't care what you've done or where you've been. I just need to know what you know."

Robinson laughed but her grin faded when she caught Hartigan's gaze. She shrugged off the agent's grasp and tugged at her sleeve, glancing up at the statue of Themis.

Hartigan stepped back.

"Don't you find it curious, Agent Hartigan?" Robinson asked. "You have so many gods in your history, tangled up in old poems and novels." She swept her arm across the park. "But you left them behind and now they're all crumbling to dust." She dipped her head towards Themis. "Except for this one."

Hartigan peered at the blindfolded statue.

"The god of war was dethroned by video games, and Demeter sold her land to a fracking company. There's an app for wisdom, and beauty and love are available over the internet." She ran her fingers along the statue's arm. "But you need this one. You need to see her, to touch her. You put her in your courthouses and your town halls while all the others are left to die. Why her above all the others? Why are you afraid of losing *her?*"

Hartigan reached out her hand. "I don't know." The stone was cold to touch.

"You're not like Agent Singh," Robinson noted, shoving her hands into her pockets again. "He has animal instincts, like the rest of them. Even the name 'Singh' comes from the Sanskrit word for Lion. They're symbols of courage in India."

"He's not courageous," Hartigan said, letting her hand fall. "At least, I don't think so."

"At least it's easy to tell where he stands." Robinson raised a finger. "You, however, are much harder to figure out. What are you hoping to get out of this?"

Hartigan looked down at her shoes. "I don't know anymore," she mumbled. "It's all lies, all of it." She shook her head. "Everyone."

"So you search for truth," Robinson said. "You believe you will find answers at the end of this winding path and everything will be better." She pushed the hair away from her face. "You must be a fan of fairy tales, Agent Hartigan."

"Maybe I am."

"Okay: once upon a time," Robinson began, "there was a young woman with golden hair who spent her time in an ivory tower, looking down upon the woods."

Hartigan bit her tongue.

"She wrote pages and pages about what it must be like for the animals in the woods but she never dared go in. Yet she believed that she could survive those woods and wanted to prove it badly."

"You've made your point," Hartigan said firmly.

"But the woman didn't know how bad it was in there," Robinson said, circling Hartigan. "You see, while the empire was ruled by Queen Nevzorova, the forest was ruled by the king of the animals, an ogre called Nikolay."

Hartigan's head snapped around and she stared at Robinson. "Go on."

"Nikolay used the beasts of the forest to fight a war against the queen." Robinson leaned against the statue and folded her arms across her chest. "One such animal is a fire-breathing dragon called Maxim."

Hartigan's heart was pounding.

"But his best and most feared warrior was the Wolf," Robinson said. "Even Nikolay was afraid of him."

"Were there other animals?" Hartigan asked.

"There is one other that you should know about." Robinson paused. "The Bear. The Bear from Chechnya."

"The Bear," Hartigan repeated.

"He makes bombs, a craft that cost him some fingers when he was an apprentice, but he became very good at what he does. The ogre needs him. You might even say the Bear was chosen." Robinson tilted her head. "The Wolf was chosen, too."

"Why?"

Robinson shrugged. "The ogre has plans."

"What does he want?"

"He wants to wear the crown," she said. "He wants the kingdom."

Hartigan's mind started racing.

"But the ogre can't control all of the animals," Robinson said. "One such animal is the Serpent, a thief."

"Elliot?"

"The Serpent is an intruder," Robinson continued. "The ogre wants her dead and the Wolf wants her to live." Her face fell. "The Wolf loves her." She paused and then she shook her head. "Last night was an attempt on the Serpent's life."

"Korolev tried to kill her?"

"The Wolf will be angry, Agent Hartigan. People will die." She gestured towards the city. "Meanwhile, the lion believes he can save the kingdom, but he's in chains and can't stray from the path. He stalks the edges of the forest and believes he has control over the animals, but he's wrong. Only vermin like Andrei Sorokin hang around the paths."

"Not wolves or serpents."

"Or bears, Agent Hartigan," Robinson said. "Especially bears." She frowned. "It's much, much darker than you know, deep in those woods."

"Then we have to go in."

Robinson's eyes softened. "Take my advice. Go back to the ivory tower where it's safe."

"I can't do that."

Robinson sighed wearily. "I hope you can, Agent Hartigan." She removed the pencil from her hair and pulled her hood over her straw-coloured locks. "Or else you're going to die in those woods."

Robinson dipped her head, ducking into the wind and walking towards the park's exit. Hartigan watched after her, clenching a fist in her pocket. She felt something crumble in her grasp and pulled out her hand, unrolling her fingers. It was a paper poppy.

This isn't just about oil.

She tilted her head and stared at the wilting paper petals. "Maybe this was *never* just about oil," she murmured.

She peered up at Themis one last time before turning her back on the statue and leaving the path.

Less than two hours to go.

32

MELBOURNE, AUSTRALIA

FRIDAY 16 SEPTEMBER

11:04AM AEST

Simone Elliot shifted on a park bench and lowered her magazine, her eyes scanning the front of the restaurant across the street. The building was two storeys high and three of its walls were rendered brick. The fourth wall, the façade, consisted of over 200 glass panels fused together in a steel lattice that climbed dizzily to the roof. The diners wore buttoned shirts and summer dresses and sat on the ground floor in booths or at long tables, flanked by artificial foliage. In the bar, young men with popped collars sprawled out on sofas or perched on stools, and girls in short denim skirts sat sipping sweetened coffee.

The restaurant's neighbour was an art gallery, its roof held aloft by ornate columns. Flags jutted out of the sandstone walls, snapping in the breeze above the visitors lining up to see a new exhibition. The queue spilled out on to the pavement, stretching past the restaurant's entrance.

Both buildings fronted the road but were otherwise bound by a cobblestone one-way street that was flooded with people, forcing cars to navigate cautiously through the crowd. The sky was blue, the sun bright, and dazed parents led giggling children past convenience stores, cafés, takeaway chains, and independent bookshops. There were people everywhere.

Elliot glanced to her right, frowning at the twelve-year-old boy beside her. He was pale with freckles, and an inferno of orange hair was squashed flat on his head under an oversized baseball cap. His small hands were swimming in the sleeves of his jacket, barely able to hold the ice-cream that he licked hungrily.

"You're not going to see it from here," the boy said, barely looking up from his ice-cream.

She raised her magazine again. "Then tell me."

"The place is crawling with Russians, Simone," he said. "They're pale with lots of tattoos and they speak funny. You can't miss it."

"And you're sure the guy I'm looking for is here?"

"You bet," Rusty said, nodding vigorously. "He's a big guy and some of his fingers are gone, just like you said."

"I think you're telling me what I want to hear," Elliot said, turning the page of her magazine.

The boy glared at her. "Hey, you put the call out. I wouldn't waste your time, you know that."

"Uh-huh."

"Look," Rusty said. "The guy works out of a room behind the nightclub under the restaurant. The stairs inside are roped off but there's a door they prop open with a brick so they can sneak out for a smoke."

"A door?"

"Yeah, an emergency exit. You've got to climb down some steps to get to it, but it's there."

"How do you know that?"

He hesitated. "I snuck in once to steal some booze."

"Rusty!" Elliot smacked the peak of his cap with her magazine. "Jesus Christ! Do you want to end up like your dad?"

Rusty looked away. "It was a dare, that's all."

Elliot shook her head and sighed. "Okay, what's the layout?"

He described the nightclub to her. "I've never heard my sister talk about the club, so I think it's just 'invitation only', you know? A stranger would stand out."

"And you got in through the emergency exit, huh?" She popped her tongue on the roof of her mouth. "These guys are sloppy."

"Maybe, but the workshop your guy hides in is a little trickier." He gobbled up the last of his ice-cream cone and studied his sticky fingers.

"Where is it?" Elliot handed him a napkin.

"Behind the stage," he said, clumsily wiping his hands. "There's a bench with lots of yellow plasticine bricks on it and some cable and stuff. There's even a box full of mobile phones."

Her eyes widened. "Are you fu—?" She cleared her throat. "For real?"

Rusty rolled his eyes. "You can say fuck around me."

Elliot smacked the peak of his cap with her magazine again. "Another dare, Rusty?"

He shrugged. "I heard people talking while I was in there. I had to check it out. The door had a keypad lock on it with numbers and stuff but a guy was standing in the doorway. He was talking to someone inside and I could see past him." He stuffed the napkin into his pocket. "I got my bottle of booze and left before they came out."

"Okay, I've heard enough." She showed Rusty two hundred-dollar bills.

Rusty's hand darted out to take the money but Elliot snatched it away, so his small fist grabbed only air.

"This is for your mum," Elliot said. "Not for you. Now, what are you going to do?"

He peered up at her from under his cap. "I'm going to stay in school and get a job."

"Good."

"And I'm going to read lots and learn about art, too."

"I never said that."

Rusty pointed to the art gallery with a sticky finger. "Dad told me that has some good stuff in it."

Elliot rubbed her nose.

"That's why you robbed it, right?" Rusty asked.

"Your dad talks too much."

"That's what my mum says."

"How is your dad, anyway?"

"He got a new lawyer," Rusty said excitedly. "He's going to appeal."

"Right, well, give him my best." Elliot handed him the cash. "Go straight home, Rusty. And stay out of trouble."

"I will, Simone." He banked the cash under his cap and pushed himself off the park bench. He picked up his BMX bike and hopped on, hesitating briefly.

"Is there something else?" Elliot asked.

"Are you really going to go in there?"

"Of course not. I was just curious."

Rusty nodded slowly. "Be careful, Simone. Everyone on the street knows to stay away, open doors or not."

She raised an eyebrow.

"The man with the mangled hands might be too much to handle, even for you." He pulled his cap down tight and pedalled away.

33

CANBERRA, AUSTRALIA

FRIDAY 16 SEPTEMBER

11:23AM AEST

Emily Hartigan pinched her mobile phone between her ear and her shoulder. She scooped up an armful of files and held them to her chest.

"The Russians provided the passport details," Hartigan said into her phone. "They're legitimate imprints."

She listened intently, careening between the cubicles and past the wall of televisions, walking hurriedly towards the door.

"No, don't give me that shit!" she seethed. "I don't need to make a formal request for this."

Hartigan stopped at the door. She turned around and grunted as she pushed the door open with her back.

"No, stop, shut up," she said impatiently. "Add them and interrogate the database. Do it!"

She rolled away from the closing door and plunged into the hallway. She stepped sideways to dodge other agents that marched past.

"No, I don't need to talk to your supervisor," she said. A passing agent bumped into her and she stumbled.

He mumbled an apology over his shoulder. "Don't you dare put me on hold." She groaned, rounding the corner. The elevator doors were open and people were filing out. She trotted towards them but a jogging agent bumped into her, sending her files spilling across the floor.

Hartigan ground her teeth and fell to her knees. She held her phone to her ear with one hand while using the other to gather the pages that covered the floor.

The elevator doors closed.

"Yes, I'm here," Hartigan said into her phone. The agents walked around her, treading on the paper spread across the floor and leaving footprints on the typed pages. She reached out, placing her hand on a stack of photographs and a passing agent stood on her hand. She yelped, yanking her hand away, and received another mumbled apology. "What did you say?" she asked her phone, holding it between her ear and shoulder again.

The elevator doors opened and she quickly crammed the wrinkled and torn pages into a pile.

"You got a hit?" Hartigan asked.

An agent stepped over her and into the elevator. He turned around and watched the doors close.

"Hold that elevator or I'll rip your fucking arms off!" Hartigan roared.

The people in the hallway froze and the agent reacted immediately, reaching out and sheepishly holding the elevator doors open.

Hartigan stood up, holding her files against her stomach. "You're sure?" she said into her phone. "No, I'm not questioning your—"

She glanced up at the clock on the elevator's display.

11:25AM.

"Did you just say the Bear is in Melbourne?"

34

MELBOURNE, AUSTRALIA

FRIDAY 16 SEPTEMBER

11:33AM AEST

The Bear sauntered down the stairs into the private nightclub, his thick arms reaching into the air as he stretched and yawned. He sniffed and surveyed the room. The nightclub had been carved out of rock, the solid stone now adorned with oil paintings and photographs. It was furnished with red velvet armchairs and Persian rugs that were scattered around a large pool table. The armchairs were grouped together in semicircles around low coffee tables and lit with floor-lamps, the chairs facing the stage. A long bar ran the length of the room.

A woman stood behind the counter slicing limes. She used the knife with skill, her hands steady and her shoulders relaxed. The Bear stared, his eyebrows knitting together. She finished slicing and picked up the cutting board, using the knife to scrape the limes into a steel bowl. Satisfied, she turned on the tap and rinsed the cutting board then towelled her hands dry.

"Have you been following the news?" She gestured to the large flat-screen fixed to the wall opposite the bar. The Bear glanced at the television and saw that a news program was on, the sound down.

The woman picked up a remote control and turned up the volume.

"...Kremlin is holding its breath, waiting for China's official announcement regarding Russia's oil trade proposal," a journalist reported. "Some experts believe Beijing is sure to reject the deal due to the Kremlin's high prices. Others believe that China has no choice but to accept Russia's offer. While Australia could be in a position to supply oil soon, their operations are still immature and analysts aren't certain if China can afford to wait. Beijing's announcement is due in less than thirty minutes and—"

"Interesting times," the woman behind the bar said, muting the television again and tossing the remote control away.

The Bear turned to face the bar, smiling broadly. "Is this why you're here, Miss Elliot?" he asked. "You wish to talk about current affairs?"

"I see we've heard of each other," she noted, pouring a glass of vodka and sweeping her hair out of her eyes. "I guess you're the one they call the Bear." She stood the bottle of vodka on the bar. "Tell me, did you get your name because you're a good hugger?"

"I've been hoping to meet you," he smirked, taking off his jacket. "How did you find me?"

Elliot dropped a slice of lime into the glass. "I made a name for myself in this town when I was young. I also made some friends and they help out when they can." She swirled the drink. "I heard about the oil deadline so, on a hunch, I asked around to find out if there were any fresh faces in town. Your name came up."

"So you thought you'd pay a visit." The Bear tossed his jacket on to an armchair and rolled up the sleeves of his shirt, revealing long pink scars lining his forearms. "How did you get in?"

"I walked straight through the door," she said, jabbing her thumb over her shoulder towards the emergency exit.

"There were two men—"

"They're dead. Your security is sloppy." She clicked her tongue.

"Nikolay Korolev will be very disappointed."

The Bear straightened his back and squared his shoulders, his barrel chest heaving. "You're a stupid girl and you're playing a dangerous game."

"I don't see it that way," she said. "The guys upstairs seem to give you a lot of privacy. I've been here for a while."

The Bear's cheek twitched. "How long?"

"Long enough to see the blueprints, the plans, the disguises, and all the stuff in the workshop you've got behind the stage." She raised a finger. "Didn't anyone teach you not to store fuses with explosives? It's pretty dangerous."

"What have you done?" he growled, stepping towards her.

"I found the two dead Timorese guys in your freezer, too," she continued, contemplating the vodka in her glass. "Caught in their own blast, the headlines will say, and I suppose a motel key will be found in a pocket. The cops will find lots of stuff in their room. Passports, plans, travel documents, and evidence that they were pissed off about the murder of Dr Marco Belo." She looked up. "Pissed off enough to flatten Titan's oil refinery and headquarters."

"You think you're quite clever, don't you?"

"Wait, I haven't got to the best bit," she said. "The media attention will trigger an inquiry into the maritime border dispute with East Timor. Titan will be caught up in red tape but they still hold the rights to the oil, so nobody else can drill until they get their due process. Titan will no longer have the money or the means to drill themselves. And that means China can't depend on Australian supply, so guess who they'll turn back to."

"This is not your business."

Elliot placed her pistol on the bar. "I'm making it my business."

The Bear shook his head. "You won't leave here alive."

"I get it, you know," she said. "You guys need to get Australia out of the energy market. But it makes you terrorists, and nations like dropping bombs on terrorists."

"They won't know it was us."

"The cops won't buy it," she said. "It's neat but too dramatic. They'll come for you."

The Bear grunted, eyeing the pistol. "You fear a war?"

"I fear for one of the soldiers."

"Is that so?"

"You're going to tell me everything."

He snorted and burst out laughing. "Everything? Bah." He dismissed her with a flick of his wrist and neared the bar. "Why should I?"

He heard a click.

He looked down at his leading foot.

"I know what you're thinking," Elliot said casually. "This isn't the movies, right? In the real world, landmines go off as soon as you stand on them. There's no dramatic pause, there's no chance to jump out of the way." She held up a finger. "But you've been around. You know how easy it is to come up with something new."

His eyes followed the path of an electrical cable clearly outlined under the rug.

"It's a custom job," Elliot continued, running her finger along the rim of her glass. "The trigger is from one of your floor-lamps. You know, with those switches you stand on? I'm not sure if you've noticed, but the light doesn't turn on or off until you actually lift your foot off the switch."

The cable ran under an overstuffed armchair that stood beside him, and he felt the blood drain from his face.

"It's not a huge explosive charge under the armchair," Elliot said, picking up the bowl of limes. "*I* should be fine behind this big bar. You, however, will give the nightclub a new organic paintjob." She swept her arms across the room, gesturing to the oil paintings on the walls and the pool table. "And that would be a shame."

Sweat beaded on his forehead.

"I can disarm it." Elliot turned and opened the glass door of the refrigerator. She placed the bowl inside and closed the door. "I just need a reason to."

He could feel his shirt clinging to his back and eyed the armchair beside him.

"Go ahead," Elliot dared. "You can try to disarm it yourself, but I've met blind carpenters with more fingers than you, so you should probably just try to relax instead."

He stretched out an arm but the chair was beyond his reach. His hands fell to his sides and he licked his dry lips. "Disarm it," he said. "Disarm it now."

Elliot placed her glass on the bar. "You've seen people stand on landmines before," she said. "The Russian army left them everywhere in your hometown." She shook her head. "Things like that stay with you. They keep you up at night."

"I said disarm it!" the Bear yelled, his voice cracking.

"You're thinking about it right now. Maybe you're seeing someone's face disappear behind a column of mud."

He wiped his brow with the back of his hand.

"Maybe you're remembering what was left behind after the smoke cleared."

He squeezed his eyes shut.

"Whose face do you see? Is it a friend? A stranger?" Her face hardened. "A child?"

"Enough!" the Bear cried out. "Enough," he whispered.

"Pistol," she said. "Two fingers. Slowly."

The Bear reached behind him and retrieved a pistol from the small of his back, holding it with his thumb and forefinger.

"Throw it away."

He obeyed, tossing it towards the stage.

Elliot gulped down her drink and slammed the tumbler down on the counter. "Talk and we both walk away. Don't talk and you don't walk, ever again."

The Bear wiped the sweat from his face with a clammy hand and contemplated the cable, the armchair, and the switch held down by his shoe. He eyed Elliot steadily. "I don't trust you."

"You don't have a choice."

His shoulders fell. "You expect me to take the word of a woman who left her lover rotting in a jail cell."

"Watch your mouth," she hissed. "You're no stranger to betrayal."

"You don't know what you're talking about."

"You turned on the Chechens to work with the Russians."

"How dare you?" the Bear seethed. "You know nothing! I joined Nikolay Korolev because he offers what we always wanted. He is our best chance."

"Independence?" Elliot snorted. "Bullshit. This is about money. Nikolay doesn't have the clout to give

Chechnya independence," she said. "He'd have to be..." Her face fell.

"Yes, now you see, don't you?" the Bear said. "Nikolay Korolev is going to be the next president of Russia." He slapped an open hand with his fist. "Destroying Titan is just one move in his game of chess."

"How many more moves are there?"

"None in this country," the Bear said, staring steadily at Elliot. "The battlefield is in Russia: Nikolay is playing against the Kremlin." He wiped his sweaty hands on his shirt. "President Nevzorova tried her best move already, attempting to force the failure of the trade deal and starve Nikolay of funds."

"She's almost succeeded," Elliot noted, gesturing towards the television.

"But she doesn't know that Nikolay armed the militants who are now bombing Moscow."

She shifted on her feet. "He's going to destabilise the Kremlin. He's going to use the failed oil deal against the president."

"Exactly." The Bear could feel his calves tightening. "He will strike when she is at her weakest and he will have the Kremlin. On that day, we will push Australia out of the market. Beijing will have to do a deal with Russia, and Nikolay will be the president who saves the country." He massaged his thigh and winced.

Elliot waggled her finger. "Uh-uh, no cramping up yet," she said, walking around the bar. "We're not done."

He grunted. "You want to know about Stepan."

Elliot nodded and flicked the hair from her eyes.

The Bear showed his teeth. "I'll tell you about him for free."

"That's generous of you."

"Your old boyfriend is the most important piece on the board. Nikolay needed to create 'Stepan Volkov': a monster that everyone would fear. A 'Wolf'." He wiped his sweaty lips with his forearm.

"He's been planning this for that long?" Elliot let out a low whistle.

"This deadline was not just about oil. It's the opportunity Nikolay has been waiting for. He's in the perfect position to seize power."

"How does Stephen fit in? Is he a part of this coup?"

"Nikolay has a much bigger role for him," he said. "Stepan is the future, Miss Elliot, but his past has to go."

"Everything?"

"Including you."

Elliot took a step back.

"We've wanted you dead for so many years," he said, his eyes cold. "But Stepan only gave his loyalty to Nikolay in exchange for your safety. He promised he would never set foot in Australia, never talk to you, never see you."

Elliot reached up for her forehead. "When?" she said softly. "When did he make the deal?"

"Soon after he was taken to Russia."

"Seven years," she mumbled.

"But you couldn't stay out of it, could you? You couldn't stay away."

Elliot lurched towards the bar, her eyes darting around the windowless room.

"What do you hope to gain, huh?" the Bear asked.

She leaned against the bar, her hands outstretched.

"You think you can stop this?" He snorted. "It's only a matter of time before someone finds you and cuts your throat. Stepan won't be able to save you. Perhaps he won't even want to."

She closed her eyes.

"They're coming for you," the Bear growled. "An army of them. There's nothing you can do about it."

Her eyes snapped open and she snatched her pistol from the bar. "You're wrong," she said.

"You think you can save yourself?" He laughed, his chuckle scratching his throat. "You think you can save *him?"*

"You're going to tell me where he is, where I can find him," Elliot said. "You're going to tell me everything."

"Not until you disarm this and get me out of here."

"That's not the deal."

"I'm not saying another word."

She aimed her pistol. "I'm warning you."

"Disarm it."

Elliot fired at the Bear's kneecap, the crack echoing through the basement. He stumbled, clutching his knee, his leg collapsing beneath him.

The switch clicked and he held his breath. "No!" he cried, squeezing his eyes shut.

A light blinked on underneath the armchair.

Elliot peeled back the rug and picked up a glowing light bulb. She stood up, clicked the switch, and the light went out. "Do not underestimate me," she warned.

"You really *are* a stupid girl playing a dangerous game."

Footsteps pounded down the stairs to the basement, Russian shouts echoing off the stone walls.

"Gunshots are loud, Miss Elliot." The Bear spat on the floor. "And you just woke the sleeping animals."

***

Elliot sprinted across the rug and vaulted the bar, sliding over the countertop as three *boyevik* s opened fire with assault rifles. She crashed on to the floor, the air whooshing out of her lungs as she collided with a dishwasher. The bullets smashed the bottles on the shelves, showering her in glass as she covered her head with her arms.

The guns fell silent.

A grenade clattered over the bar, bouncing on the tiled floor. Elliot quickly scooped it up and dumped it in the dishwasher, slamming the door shut and slithering to the end of the bar. The grenade went off with a thump, the door of the dishwasher cartwheeling into the bar and black foam spilling across the tiles. Smoke curled up to the ceiling and set off the fire alarms, the loud bell pealing throughout the building.

Elliot adjusted her grip on her pistol and peered around the corner of the bar. The *boyevik* s opened fire again. The rounds pounded into the counter, splintering wood and shattering tiles. Ducking behind cover, her hand swept across the floor and found the knife she'd used to slice limes.

The firing stopped and she heard thudding footsteps. Elliot picked up the knife and crouched. A *boyevik* rounded the end of the bar and she quickly stabbed him in the foot. He doubled over, his mouth opening wide as he screamed. Elliot shoved her pistol into his mouth and pulled the trigger.

She turned around and fired three shots at another *boyevik* at the other end of the bar. He staggered backwards, falling to the ground. Boots shuffled behind her and she stood up, pivoting on the ball of her foot and lashing out with her leg, kicking the third *boyevik'* s weapon from his hand.

He fell back and drew a knife, slashing the back of her hand, and her gun fell to the floor. The *boyevik'* s knife whipped through the air again and Elliot ducked. She flung open the refrigerator door, smacking him in the face. The *boyevik* lurched backwards for a moment but then jumped forward, stabbing wildly. Elliot opened the refrigerator door again and the knife glanced off the glass, then she seized the *boyevik'* s wrist, locking it behind his back, and drove his knife into his kidney.

He cried out, throwing her on top of the counter. Elliot's hand found a vodka bottle and she smashed it across his face before rolling off the bar and springing to her feet.

The *boyevik* shook it off and pulled the knife from his back. He jumped the counter and adjusted the grip on his knife, baring his bloodied teeth and wiping his nose with his forearm.

Elliot walked backwards into the pool table and saw that the Bear wasn't where she'd left him. The *boyevik* lunged forward and she looked up, stepping sideways. She whipped a pool cue through the air, slapping the knife from his grasp, and then kicked him in the crotch.

The *boyevik* howled, his legs trembling, the knife landing on the edge of the table and out of his reach. Elliot snapped the cue into two jagged pieces, dodging the *boyevik'* s fist as he attacked again. She drove one half of the cue under his chin and crouched, using the other half of the cue to snatch his leg. He fell forward towards the floor and Elliot stomped on the back of his neck, the cue bursting through the top of his head.

She caught movement out of the corner of her eye and slipped the remains of the pool cue under the blade of the knife. She whacked the pool cue with her palm and the blade whirled upwards in an arc. The Bear threw himself on top of a dead *boyevik,* picking up a dropped assault rifle and rolling on to his back. He chambered a round as Elliot snatched the knife from the air and threw it. The knife struck the Bear in the chest. He grunted, dropping the rifle.

Elliot crossed the floor, wiping a bloodied hand across her face. She wrenched the knife from the Bear's chest and knelt beside him, holding the blade to his throat. "Tell me where to find him," she hissed. "A hotel? A house? A fucking cave?" She slapped his face. "Tell me!"

The Bear grinned, red foam bubbling from his lips. "Capture—" he wheezed, eyes closing, "—Protocol."

Sirens started wailing weakly over the clanging fire alarm.

Elliot held her breath, yanking the Bear's shirt from his belt. There were no bandages on his abdomen. Her eyes darted around the room. "Where is it?"

He didn't answer.

A mobile phone was lying on the carpet next to his hip pocket. She picked it up and saw a timer ticking down on the glowing screen.

One minute and fifty-eight seconds.

The sirens were deafening. Tyres screeched and doors slammed. Male voices shouted over each other.

Elliot crawled behind the bar, collecting her pistol and shoving it into the back of her jeans. She grabbed a tea towel and a bottle of spirits, soaking the towel with alcohol and cramming it into the neck of the bottle.

Boots pounded on the pavement outside and the restaurant's front entrance crashed open. "Police! Police!" someone shouted.

Elliot grabbed the light bulb and smashed it against the counter. She held the light bulb to the rag and pressed the lamp switch, the filament flaring brightly before blowing out, the towel catching alight.

"Clear! Clear!" the police bellowed, their clomping boots nearing the staircase.

Elliot heaved the bottle at the ceiling near the stairs. The glass burst on the rafter. A pool of fire splashed on the carpeted floor, the flames spreading quickly.

A team of police stampeded down the stairs, their weapons raised. They stopped when they reached the roaring flames. "Go back!" she yelled. "Get out of here!"

The police fired and Elliot threw herself behind the bar, diving through the doorway to the emergency exit, the bullets whistling over her head. She gritted her teeth and lurched towards the exit.

The street is full of people.

She bounded up the stairs, emerging onto the street and squinting into the sunlight.

There were no people in the street.

A police cruiser was parked on the cobblestone street, lights flashing and all four of its doors open. A constable was propped against the car, his back to her, his elbow resting on the roof, his eyes scanning the street as the last shoppers fled the square.

Elliot glanced towards the main road and saw barriers, marked vans, and constables wearing blue fatigues and body armour. She snatched the gun from her jeans and pistol-whipped the constable across the back of the head. He collapsed and Elliot pushed him into the back seat of the car, folding his legs behind him. She shut the door and climbed into the driver's seat, slamming the gearstick into reverse.

The tyres screeched and the engine whined as Elliot steered the car towards a narrow alley, ducking her head beneath the dashboard. Assault rifles chattered, the bullets smashing through the windshield and thudding into the bonnet.

There was a thunderous boom and the ground rumbled beneath her. The car lurched over on two wheels, leaping over the gutter and crashing through the window of a bookshop.

The glass façade of the restaurant shattered and the brickwork cracked, the building shuddering briefly before it started to collapse. A blanket of stone fell over the street, drowning the road in a thick cloud of grey powder.

Elliot sat up and noticed that the gunfire had stopped. She climbed out of the upturned car and felt a dull pain in her arm. A bullet had grazed her tricep. Her skin was covered in blood and it glistened in the sunshine.

You think you can save yourself, the Bear had said.

You think you can save him?

She dragged the constable from the wreckage and laid him down on the floor, checking his pulse while holding her cheek near his mouth to check his breathing. "Sorry," she said, "but better a sore head than dead." She stared at the dust and smoke swirling across the square. "A lot of flags are going to be draped over a lot of coffins in the next few days," she said to the unconscious constable. "And I'm tired of it."

I'm coming for you, Nikolay.

She dusted herself off and walked to the back of the shop, pushing through the exit.

And I'm going to burn it all down.

35

CANBERRA, AUSTRALIA

FRIDAY 16 SEPTEMBER

11:56AM AEST

Lee Singh shoved his way through the entrance of Agency Headquarters, unbuttoning his jacket as he marched towards the security gate. He opened his jacket for the security guards, showing the badge clipped to his belt and his holstered pistol, and walked through without breaking stride.

Singh elbowed his way through a bustling column of agents and walked towards the bank of elevators. The doors opened and a flood of suited agents poured out. Emily Hartigan was standing at the back of the lift, her hand on the rail.

She cleared her throat, walking towards the door.

Singh slapped his hand against the side of the elevator, blocking her path. "Where do you think you're going?"

"Get out of my way, Lee."

He pushed her back into the elevator and pressed the button to close the doors. "Did you or did you not release a Be-On-the-Look-Out today?" He poked the button for Hartigan's floor.

"You know, I *believe* I did." She shrugged. "But you only care about what I know, not what I believe."

His jowls tightened. "Tell me what you *know* about this person of interest."

"Jesus, Lee," Hartigan groaned. "I got a lead on a guy called the Bear. He's Chechen and fought in the war for independence back in the day," she said. "He joined the *Organizatsiya* and Nikolay Korolev made good use of his skills."

The elevator doors opened, revealing a young trainee agent waiting to get on.

"Take the next one," Singh snapped, closing the doors. He turned back to Hartigan. "You found this guy on file?"

"No, we don't have one." Hartigan leaned against the handrail. "But Russian intelligence was more than happy to give me everything they had on the guy, and I mean everything. It turns out they don't consider the Bear a citizen because he fought on the wrong side during the Chechen wars." She smoothed out a wrinkle in her blouse. "One of the things I found in their file was a list of known aliases and associated passport imprints."

Singh put his hands into his pockets and jingled his keys.

"I contacted our guys at Immigration to get the Bear's passport numbers on the database. It took some effort, but I got them added and they immediately scored a hit." She paused to take a breath. "The Bear entered the country through Melbourne three weeks ago. That's when I had the boys release a BOLO."

Singh started pacing the elevator's small floor space. "You know airports have been digitally archiving their CCTV footage since the war, right?"

She held up a hand. "Stand-alone servers, yes. We checked it out to see if we could discover where he went after he arrived. They got a few frames of him climbing into a taxi and they managed to get a fleet number. I called the dispatcher and it turns out the cab company keeps digital archives for employment performance reviews. I got the drop-off address."

"Where?" The elevator doors opened and Singh placed his hand on Hartigan's back, pushing her in front of him.

"A restaurant in an inner-city suburb of Melbourne. I contacted state police and ordered them to activate their tactical response unit." She untied her hair and smoothed it out, pulling it tight behind her head. "They said they'd contact me when they had the Bear in custody." She retied her hair, frowning when she saw a group of analysts crowded around the wall of televisions.

"Where have you been the last twenty minutes?" Singh asked, guiding her towards her cubicle.

“I went for a walk to clear my head.” She sat down on her chair. “Why?”

Singh gestured towards the bank of screens.

Hartigan turned and the blood drained from her face. The news channel had a helicopter in the air above Melbourne and the footage showed the remains of a building, though only one wall was still standing. Bricks were strewn across the street and all of the windows in the area had been shattered. A fountain of fire spouted from a gas main, a row of police vehicles had been crushed on the esplanade, and paramedics were desperately sifting through the dust and stones to find survivors. A crowd of people were gathered in the park across from the restaurant. Nearby, empty body bags had been placed in a neat line on the grass.

“See what happens when you keep me out of the loop,” Singh said.

Hartigan doubled over, vomiting into her rubbish bin.

“Emily!” Singh said, his hands on his hips. “I need you to focus.”

She raised her head and wiped her eyes with the palm of her hand. “But I did everything right,” she said. “This was good police work.”

“And you thought that was enough?” Singh scoffed. “You should’ve told me what you had and we could’ve prevented this.”

She ran her hand over her hair, her eyes searching for something to drink. "I did everything..." She found a mug of cold coffee on her desk and gulped it down.

"Emily!" Singh swivelled her chair around and snapped his fingers in front of her face. "Snap out of it. It's time to move forward."

"Move..."

"I need you to get all the files together. We have to go and we have to move quickly."

Her gaze fell to the floor. "They died because of me," she rasped.

"I put them there. I ordered them to..."

"Hey! Emily!"

"...dead because of me."

Singh stood up. "Clean yourself up. We have to go."

"I can't..."

"Get your shit together, Emily," he said firmly, checking his watch. "Be ready in forty-five minutes."

Hartigan nodded and stood up, dropping her empty mug on the carpet. "Clean myself," she mumbled, staggering towards the bathroom.

Singh crouched to collect Hartigan's coffee mug and stopped to find space for it on her desk. The workspace was piled with reams of paper, thick files, and stacks of books. Sachets of sugar, a jar of coffee, a box of instant soup, and a half-empty bag of jellybeans crowded the computer monitor. Post-it notes bordered the screen, reminders to collect dry-cleaning, buy milk, and pay bills, mixed up with notes about persons of interest, websites, and article references.

He placed the mug on the mousepad, noticing a slip of paper sticking out from under the keyboard. It was a lengthy note scrawled in pen and he unfolded it, smoothing it out on the desk.

Singh read and reread the note before filing it in his jacket pocket. The computer monitor burst into life, and he realised he must have roused it by moving the mouse. He grabbed the mouse, hovering over the shutdown button, but he noticed that a program was open on the task bar: a media player. He clicked on the tab and the program filled the screen. A DVD was cued so he pressed play.

It was footage of Simone Elliot in a jail cell. She had been stripped naked, her hands and ankles cuffed, and she was hanging from a rafter. Her body was a sweaty wreck, her skin mottled with bruises, blood and urine dripping from her toes. Her mouth was covered with tape and she was breathing deeply through her nose, her chest rising and falling quickly, her shouted curses muffled as she fought against the restraints.

Two police constables were pounding her with telephone directories, their uniforms soaked from the exertion. Elliot shouted through her gag, the veins bulging in her neck. Singh skipped forward. They used coaxial cables next; then ice-water; then capsicum spray. He paused the video. There was a face in the foreground, red with rage, and demanding a confession.

Emily Hartigan's father.

And she was watching this shit at work.

"You fucking idiot, Hartigan." Singh ejected the disc and placed it in a case before pocketing it inside his jacket. He straightened his tie and looked up at the news bulletin playing on the television.

The story had changed, the newsreader telling the viewers about something more hopeful. Singh tilted his head.

"...that China has officially announced they will be ceasing trade with Russia due to what they characterise as exorbitant transit tariffs. While Beijing hasn't ruled out revisiting the energy partnership in the future, sources say that Titan Energy CEO Geoffrey Geldenhuys is already scheduled to visit China on Monday to sign a ten-year deal."

"Shit," Singh muttered. He turned away from the wall of screens and marched towards the elevator.

***

The office door opened and Singh leaned forward in the leather chair, pushing a button on the phone and placing the receiver down. He propped his elbows on the deputy director's desk.

The deputy director entered cautiously. "I don't remember arranging a meeting with you, Lee."

"I need to talk to you," Singh said.

"Did you need to do it while sitting behind my desk?"

Singh steepled his fingers in front of his chin. "I need to ask a favour."

"Okay," the deputy director said slowly. "But I'm unlikely to grant you any favours until you bring me up to speed. I distinctly remember telling you to be discreet, and that attack on the hotel was anything but."

"I'll come to that."

The deputy director frowned. "Keep it brief, Lee."

"I need to use the agency's charter jet." Singh folded his arms on the desk. "I need to go to Moscow."

The deputy director snorted. "The charter is booked," he said. "It's going to Melbourne."

"I know. I'm going with it. Then I'm going to Moscow."

The fish tank gurgled and the deputy director stopped in front of the glowing glass. "No, you're not."

"You should reconsider your answer."

"Or what?" The deputy director inspected the fish in his aquarium.

"Or I'll inform the National Security Committee that you told them what they wanted to hear because you were too embarrassed to tell them you had no reliable information."

A large fish drifted in clumsy circles inside the aquarium, its mouth opening and closing slowly, its empty eyes surveying its empire. "I don't know what you're talking about."

"You called her personally."

"What?"

"Emily told me that when I first met her," Singh continued, "but she's just a junior analyst, so why would you do that? Then you asked her that question during the brief about the potential threat to our oil trade, and she had no idea what you were talking about."

Other tiny fish darted around the tank in all directions, swimming circles around the big fish. The deputy director reached for a bottle of fish food.

"I got curious so I asked around." Singh reclined in the chair and laced his fingers together behind his head. "You gave the prime minister a report authored by Emily Hartigan. I got a copy of it and it's full of excerpts from her thesis. It concludes that the

Organizatsiya is made up of men who had rough childhoods and would whine if they lost their money, but they ultimately pose no threat to our national security."

The deputy director used his thumb to pop the cap on the bottle.

Singh swivelled on the chair and placed his feet on the desk. "Then Volkov came to town," he continued. "And you phoned Hartigan personally because the NSC told you to get her back on the case. Her name was all over the report and she was being called in to reassess the threat." He shrugged. "But she didn't know that."

The deputy director sprinkled food into the aquarium and watched the fish chase the crumbs around the tank.

"You arranged the brief so you could ask her that question, hoping she'd put her name to your bad analysis right in front of everyone. Meanwhile, you called me in to operate in the background, hoping I'd clean up if your mistake put us at risk." Singh straightened his tie and stood up. "You must've been praying that we'd catch Volkov. If he had told us there was no threat, you could stand by your analysis, even if he lied. And if he *had* warned us about impending danger, you could blame Hartigan for bad analysis and still have time to save the day, taking all the credit."

The deputy director studied Singh cautiously, his tongue pushing against the inside of his cheek.

"Tell me, do you feel a little bad for being this fucking stupid?" Singh asked.

"You have no evidence that I—"

"I have her thesis, a copy of the report, and a contact in the prime minister's office." Singh walked around the desk and tugged at the cuffs of his jacket. "I want my flight to Moscow."

"Fine." The deputy director tossed the bottle on the table and raised a finger. "But on one condition."

"I wonder what that could be."

"If there's an inquiry—"

"When," Singh said. "*When* there's an inquiry."

The deputy director frowned. "I need you to provide a statement that supports my position."

"Why should I?"

"Because the agency is dead if you don't," the deputy director said, pointing at the ground. "They've been throwing money at us since the war, but our focus has been narrow. This question came out of nowhere, and the Russian desk is staffed by two analysts who have worked there since the fucking nineties, and one kid who believes in unicorns." He rubbed his throat. "But Hartigan knows her stuff and said all the right things in her paper. It was the best analysis I had.

And then Volkov had to kill that bastard in that fucking pub." He threw his hands in the air. "I thought it would be nothing, but I needed you around if it spiralled out of control."

"So you were going to throw your mistake in my lap."

"This is what you were hired to do and I told you to do it quietly." He waved towards the window. "And now we've got bombs going off."

Singh shook his head and ran his hand down his face. "You're a real piece of work, you know that?"

"I'll take that as a compliment, coming from you," the deputy director said. "What's your angle? Why Moscow now?" He stuck out his chin. "You're up to something."

Singh folded his arms across his chest.

"I need some kind of status report, Lee." He shrugged. "How else am I supposed to explain your excursion to the NSC?"

"The embassy in Moscow is pushing for talks with President Nevzorova." Singh glanced at his watch. "If the embassy succeeds, I can be there to explain what the agency has learned so far, and maybe do some work behind the scenes."

"Wow, that's actually..." The deputy director clapped his hands together and grinned. "That's perfect! How did you find out about that?"

Singh walked to the door. "The NSC told me about it when they ordered me to go to Moscow."

The deputy director's mouth opened and closed quickly. "What?" he choked.

Singh placed his hand on the doorknob. "You can ask them if you like." He dipped his head towards the desk. "Your speaker phone's on. The NSC is on line one."

He slammed the door behind him.

36

MELBOURNE, AUSTRALIA

FRIDAY 16 SEPTEMBER

6:04PM AEST

A crisis centre had been set up in the art gallery near the restaurant. Sculptures and glass cabinets were shoved against the walls. A triage centre had been set up in the main hall and the art house cinema was being used for nursing the injured. The gallery's lobby had been commandeered for use by the authorities.

Singh unbuttoned his jacket and cast his eyes over the entourage of agents that had followed him into the lobby. All around them dishevelled intelligence personnel and police officers were darting between the desks and pinning things to maps. Photographs were stuck to a whiteboard decorated with scribbled names and question marks. Telephones rang, ashtrays overflowed, and sheets of paper and empty coffee cups littered the floor.

"Wait outside while I sort this out," Singh said.

Hartigan stared at him numbly and nodded in surrender, pulling her coat tighter around her shoulders and leaving the lobby. She slowly descended the steps to the pavement and studied the scene before her.

The restaurant was now a pile of rubble and rescue workers were trying to clear it away. Earth-moving equipment thundered around the wreckage, shifting debris to waiting trucks, while small front-end loaders whined over the mounds of brick and twisted metal, clearing space for men to search for remaining survivors. A crane was parked on the cobblestones, its long arm reaching up into the sky while the steel cable tugged at girders and beams, lifting them from the ground. Meanwhile, a chain of workers passed pieces of shattered furniture and brickwork away from the pile to a waiting skip bin.

Hartigan ran her hands through her hair and glanced around. Diesel light-sets rumbled at each corner of the block, carving a dome of artificial daylight in the dusk. Lights were flashing everywhere: the orange lights of the earth-movers; the red and blue lights of emergency vehicles, paramedics, and police officers; the pale yellow beam of the rescue workers' torches, shimmering above the wreckage as their operators listened over the din for any calls for help beneath their feet; and the white bulbs of camera flashes as journalists took photographs for the news agencies.

A young boy was sitting on the kerb. He looked to be about twelve and was wearing an oversized jacket and a baseball cap pulled down tight over his shock of orange hair. He was tugging on the sleeves of his jacket, his back straight, his unblinking eyes watching the rescue workers as they rummaged through the rubble. A broad-shouldered police constable stood guard over the boy, his arms crossed.

Hartigan approached the constable, flashing her badge. “Agent Hartigan,” she said. “What’s going on here?”

The constable pointed at the boy. “We caught him in the triage centre,” he explained. “His name’s Rusty and he has form, shoplifting and pick-pocketing mostly. We found 200 dollars on him when we nabbed him.”

“Where did he get it?” she asked, peering down at Rusty.

The constable shrugged. “He said a friend gave it to him.”

“That’s not a crime.”

“He’s obviously lying.”

“It’s also obvious that there are more important matters to attend to, constable. Why don’t you leave Rusty to me?”

“But—”

“You’re dismissed, constable.”

The constable stared at her for a moment, then shook his head and walked away.

She looked down at Rusty. “Hey,” she said, trying to get his attention. “You can go now, Rusty.”

Rusty's eyes remained focused on the ruins in the middle of the square. "I want to stay."

Hartigan sat on the gutter beside him. "Why?"

He waved a hand towards the bomb site. "I think my friend was in the restaurant when it blew up."

"Are you sure? Did you try calling him?"

"*She* isn't answering."

"Oh. Maybe she's busy."

"Maybe." He hunched over and tugged at the shoelaces on his Volleys.

"Do you like this girl?"

He blushed. "She's just a friend."

"Don't be embarrassed, Rusty." Hartigan smiled.

"I should've given her a hug, or something," he said. "Before I left. I was too scared, though."

"You can give her a hug when you see her again."

Rusty shook his head. "It doesn't matter," he said. "She doesn't like to be touched anyway."

Hartigan's thoughts came into sharp focus, her mind racing. She cleared her throat and stood up, studying the wreckage again. The neighbouring shops were all intact, other than their shattered windows, and the art gallery didn't have a single scorch mark on its structure, despite being less than twenty metres away from the bomb site. She cast her eyes around and saw a police sedan burrowed in a bookshop's window. The cruiser's bonnet was peppered with bullet holes, the windscreen shattered. Forensic officers had cordoned off the shop with police tape and were examining the car.

"Do you want to come for a walk with me, Rusty?"

The boy looked up at her with wide eyes. "I want to stay here."

"We won't go far," she said. "I just want to take a walk around the site. Maybe we'll find your friend."

He frowned and scratched the side of his head, deliberating carefully before standing up.

"This friend of yours," she began, staring at her feet as they walked along the esplanade. "Why do you think she was in the restaurant?"

He hesitated. "She asked me lots of questions about it. I think she wanted to see for herself."

"Did she ask you about a big Russian guy with missing fingers?"

Rusty stopped walking and glanced back towards the art gallery.

Hartigan crouched in front of him. "You're not in trouble, Rusty." She nodded towards the command centre. "I'm not like them."

He wiped his hands on his jacket.

Hartigan combed through the debris at her feet, brushing small rocks and smashed bricks aside until she found a shiny brass shell. She picked up the casing and held it up for Rusty to see. "Do you know what this is?"

He didn't say anything.

"This is a shell from an assault rifle," Hartigan explained. "The same calibre used by the police tactical response team. How many do you see around here?"

Rusty looked down, his eyes darting left and right. "Lots," he said.

Hartigan pointed down the street towards the bullet-riddled police cruiser inside the bookshop. "They were shooting at that."

"Why would they shoot at their own car?"

"Good question," Hartigan said. "You know, a lot of people think my job is about finding answers. Most of the time, it's about asking the right questions." She stood up. "Why would the Russians blow up their own restaurant?" She juggled the shell in her hand. "If it was a terrorist attack, why would they destroy their building but leave the others intact? And why isn't there a constable-shaped chalk outline on the pavement? Whoever escaped stole the car, so why leave any of the cops alive?" She turned to Rusty. "Does that sound like the Russians to you?"

Rusty looked away quickly. He closed his eyes. "She said she needed to find out about her friend," he said reluctantly. "She said the Russians knew where he was." His bottom lip quivered. "She sent out a message asking who was new in town, what they were up to, and where they were. I told her I could help."

"Help?"

"I've been inside the Russian place before." He shook his head. "I told her I'd seen a workshop out the back. They were making something out of yellow bricks and mobile phones and cable."

"Jesus, Rusty."

"She promised me she wouldn't go inside." He sniffed, his voice cracking. "I just need to know that she's okay."

"Simone Elliot is still alive, kid," Singh said, walking up behind Rusty. "You know how I know?"

"How?" Rusty asked.

"Because Agent Hartigan hasn't killed her yet." He grabbed Rusty's arm and heaved him towards another agent. "Take his statement when his mum gets here. I want to know what he knows."

The agent nodded.

"I don't know anything," Rusty protested.

"Don't bullshit a bullshitter, kid," Singh said, nodding to the agent.

The agent dragged Rusty away and Singh turned back to Hartigan.

"I hope you rot in hell, Lee," she snapped.

"Shut up so I can brief you," he said.

She scowled.

"The building had already been evacuated by the time tactical response showed up."

"Fire alarm."

"Yeah, it went off." He crammed his hands into his pockets. "Nobody was really around to hear it. The diners took the hint when three guys ran through the restaurant with assault rifles. They all panicked and ran away, clearing the street too."

"So the whole area was empty when the cops turned up?"

"Almost. Some uniforms were shooing away the last of the tourists. One cop was butt-whipped from behind and tossed into the back seat of his car." Singh pointed to the bookshop. "He woke up on the floor in there."

"But if tactical response was breaching the building, how did anyone—"

"They didn't set up the play very well," Singh said, "and only went through the front entrance instead of flanking the Russians. Someone escaped through the emergency exit and used the car to get away from the building."

"Elliot."

"They didn't know that until about an hour ago. All the cops who witnessed the gunfight are dead, the bookshop was empty when the car drove through it, and the evacuees were too far away to see anything. Elliot bled all over the car's upholstery, so they figured it out that way. We're going to keep her name out of the papers for now, at least until we figure out what she was doing here."

"And the Bear?"

"We're keeping his name away from the media too. We're building a story now."

She shook her head. "All of these fucking lies. Is he in there or not?"

"He's in there," Singh said, nodding towards the ruins, "along with some friends of his. A couple of charred bodies were in the freezer, which is weird, and another guy has a pool cue through his head, which is pretty fucked up."

"Freezer?"

"That's a puzzle for another investigator."

Hartigan's tongue searched the inside of her cheek, her arms folded across her chest. "Okay, fine. What do you know that I don't?"

"We've been ordered to go to Moscow."

Her mouth fell open, her eyes wide. "Are you fucking nuts? We don't have jurisdiction in Moscow."

"The National Security Committee has ordered us—"

"Enough with your bullshit. Tell me why."

He shook his head and muttered a curse.

Hartigan rolled her eyes and pointed a finger across the street. "Under that pile of rock is a Chechen bomb-maker who could've destroyed our oil trade but we can't even confirm that because the only witness is a twelve-year-old boy who *thinks* he saw something."

"This isn't a court of law, Emily," Singh said impatiently. "We don't need proof beyond reasonable doubt. If there is even the possibility of a threat, we—"

"The threat is now contained," Hartigan interrupted. "And we are aware of the source. We can tighten our borders and set up a task force. Our investigation is over." She held out her hands. "What more is there?"

"The guy who sent the Bear is still alive. You think he's just going to give up?"

She poked him in the chest. "I'm not going." She turned to leave.

"Nikolay Korolev has been giving arms to militants," he called after her.

Hartigan paused.

"Those militants have been blowing up bits of Moscow, as well as that pipeline you were talking about."

Hartigan closed her eyes.

"An American operative died earlier this week because he knew too much. A friend of mine told me about it today, and he told me what he'd learned."

"I, um," she stammered.

"For the sake of argument, let's say Andrei Sorokin accepted a freelance contract from Giselle Geldenhuys to kill Natalie Robinson. If he had succeeded, he would've brought unwanted attention to the *Organizatsiya.* That's why he was killed." Singh stepped towards her. "But any actions against Australian oil interests perpetrated by the *Organizatsiya* would also bring negative attention to their operations. Any attempt to fight would only narrowly advance *Organizatsiya* interests. So why would Korolev attack? It would have to be pure self-interest."

Hartigan turned to face him.

Singh reached into his pocket, taking out a wrinkled slip of paper. "I got that last bit from a note hidden under your keyboard."

She took the note from him, rereading her own words.

"You were reading an article about Nevzorova when you wrote that."

She nodded. "Yeah. I had this idea but it..."

"Look, Korolev might be using proxies to do his dirty work, but he's still taking a big risk. Bombing Moscow brings a lot of unwanted attention," he pointed out. "So does sending a Chechen bomber to Australia. So what is Korolev's goal? Why is he willing to risk his comfortable life in the *Organizatsiya?*"

Hartigan smoothed out her hair. "I'd, um, I mean..."

"Tell me in the car," Singh said, turning to leave.

Hartigan watched him walk away and took a deep breath.

Why would Simone risk her life to come here?

She tossed the shell in the air and caught it as it tumbled towards the ground.

Physics, she thought. For a woman of Elliot's height and build to force a pool cue through a man's head, she would have to exhibit the kind of strength caused by surges of pure rage.

"The Serpent is angry." Hartigan gazed at the brass shell in her hand, turning it around so it flashed under the floodlights. "She's taking the fight to them."

Hartigan pitched the shell into the rubble and tugged at the sleeves of her coat, following Singh to the car.

37

MOSCOW, RUSSIA

SATURDAY 17 SEPTEMBER

7:06AM MSK

Grigoriy frowned, looking through the windshield. A blanket of grey clouds stretched across the sky, a monochromatic membrane trapping the colours it sucked out of the city. Even the people lurching in and out of the airport seemed pale and bland.

He heard the first raindrop thud against the roof of the car. More followed, slapping into the windshield, and the shower turned into a downpour. The glass blurred. He toggled the wipers and they swished across the glass. His view of the grey world improved, but only for a moment. He went to toggle the wipers again but paused, sighing heavily, his hand falling back into his lap.

Grigoriy jumped when the passenger door opened. "Hi, Boss. How was your trip?" He shifted in his seat and turned the wipers on. "I heard there was a bad dust storm in Dubai. Did you get caught in it?"

Murphy climbed into the car and slammed the door. "Just drive, Grigoriy," he said gruffly. He ran his hand through his short hair, flicking drops of water on the dashboard.

He looked exhausted, Grigoriy thought, putting the car in gear and pulling away from the kerb. His eyes were bloodshot, his face stubbled, and his skin waxy. Murphy slouched in his seat and stared vacantly through the window.

"Did you see Simone?"

Murphy grunted and lit a cigarette, cracking the window slightly. He placed a newspaper in his lap and smoothed it out, studying the front page.

"Okay, then." Grigoriy popped his lips. "Oh, Anna finished her exams on Thursday," he said, his grip tight on the steering wheel. "We went out for chocolate cake to celebrate."

Murphy blew smoke through the gap in the window and turned the page.

"I changed hotels too. I moved Anna last night." He kneaded the steering wheel in his hands. "It's just a precaution."

Murphy flicked the cigarette through the window and closed the newspaper, folding it and tossing it on the floor.

Grigoriy stomped on the accelerator and weaved across two lanes of traffic, ignoring the honks from the other drivers. The car shot into an alleyway, lurching as it screeched to a stop, and Grigoriy yanked on the handbrake.

"Jesus Christ, Grigoriy," Murphy said.

"Fuck you, Stepan!" Grigoriy shouted.

Murphy held up his hands. "Grigoriy, what the—"

"What did you expect?" Grigoriy fumed. "Did you think she'd throw herself at you? Did you really think she was waiting for you all these years?"

Murphy bared his teeth. "I don't need this shit." He opened the car door.

"Hey! Don't you..."

The door slammed shut.

Grigoriy stepped out of the car and into a puddle, the muddy water splashing his trousers. He ran after Murphy. "I'm talking to you," he said.

Murphy ignored him, turning up the collar of his coat and plunging his hands into his pockets.

Grigoriy grabbed Murphy's shoulder and turned him around. Murphy smacked his hand away.

"Watch it, Grigoriy," Murphy growled. "I've had a bad fucking week and—"

"Shut up and listen to me," Grigoriy insisted, shoving him towards the alley's wall. "I'm all you've got." He waved his hand towards the end of the alley. "That world doesn't care about you. *She* doesn't care about you. All of that is in the past. What matters is now."

Murphy turned away, his jaw clenched. He started walking again, hunched against the rain.

"You've lost focus, Stepan," Grigoriy said, walking beside him. "The people in this city are scared. The president is scared." He exhaled. "Anna is scared."

"*You're* scared." Murphy glared at Grigoriy. "You just want to save yourself."

"Yes, because you taught me to think that way," he said.

"Then save yourself," he said. "Why do you need me to do it for you?"

Grigoriy leapt in front of Murphy and held up his hand. "I hacked Maxim's tablet and I found his map." He ran his hand through his wet hair and flicked his wrist, flinging water at the ground. "He's marked all of the targets, including those that are yet to be hit." He stepped back. "Nikolay has persuaded militants to bomb Moscow and I can't figure out why, and, yes, that scares the shit out of me."

"Nikolay is going to war against Valentina," Murphy said. "That's why."

Grigoriy's jaw fell open. "But that's..." He placed his hand over his mouth. "Jesus, we'll all be killed." He looked up at Murphy. "What do we do?"

"We do our job," Murphy said. "We play our part."

"But Valentina will send the army after us," Grigoriy pointed out. "We can't just—"

“What do you want from me, Grigoriy?” Murphy said. “Do you want me to fight? Who should I fight? Should I take on Valentina or Nikolay? And what if I win, what’s left for me then, huh? Where do I go? Who will have me?”

Grigoriy shook his head slowly. “So that’s it,” he said quietly. “You’re a fucking coward.”

Murphy seized Grigoriy’s lapels and shoved him against the bricks. “Don’t you dare lecture me about cowardice. You’re too scared to ask a girl on a date.” He released Grigoriy and stepped back, taking his phone from his pocket. “Here, one last job for you and then you can run away with your tail between your legs.”

“That’s not what I—”

“I bugged Maxim at one of Korolev’s restaurants before I left.” He waved his phone in the air. “I listened to it while I was waiting for the dust storm to pass through Dubai, but I want to get the file off the phone.”

“Why?”

“Because it gives me leverage against Nikolay.” He dangled the phone in front of Grigoriy. “Put the file on a thumb drive and you can leave Moscow.”

Grigoriy took the phone and dropped it in his pocket. “But I don’t want to leave,” he said. “Is this because of Simone? Why don’t you just—”

Murphy's hand darted out, seizing Grigoriy's throat. "Don't say her name," he snarled.

Grigoriy's eyes went wide and he tried to inhale, desperate for breath. He blinked, his vision blurring, and he slapped his open palm against Murphy's arm.

"Delete that name from your brain," Murphy said, "because I'll skin you alive if you say it aloud again." He let go.

Grigoriy clutched his knees and coughed, spitting phlegm on the ground. He took a deep breath, the air rasping through his throat. "She will always hate you, Stepan," he wheezed. "Take a look at yourself right now and you'll see why."

Murphy lit another cigarette and climbed into the driver's seat.

Grigoriy straightened up and fell back against the brick wall. He looked up, the brick walls towering above him, the rain swirling from the sky.

People always die when Volkov is in town, he thought.

But I'm not going to be one of them.

38

MOSCOW, RUSSIA

SATURDAY 17 SEPTEMBER

7:52AM MSK

Murphy closed the door and took a deep breath.

I shouldn't have kissed her.

The thought had been looping through his mind since leaving Simone Elliot in the hotel hallway. Drink couldn't drown it, the movie on the plane had only muffled it, and sleep seemed to make it louder. His temples throbbed and he massaged his forehead.

I shouldn't have kissed her.

He knew that hope was dangerous and could lure a man into traps. A starving man could always be baited with food, the lonely lured by sex, the greedy by money. Entertaining fantasies could be deadly and he'd put his own life at risk for a rejection he'd known to be inevitable.

The rational part of his mind had nagged him since he'd left Moscow to see her again. It had started as an insistent whisper but he'd ignored it until he kissed her and felt his knife at his throat. Suddenly, the whisper became a chorus line of girls, kicking their legs to the lyrics: "I told you so! I told you so! I told you so..."

Murphy dropped his duffel bag by the door and tossed his coat over the back of a chair. The overstuffed sofa wheezed when he collapsed on the cushions. He placed his pistol beside him and let his head fall back, closing his eyes and grasping his forehead.

Seven years: always flying, always driving, and always planning the next mission. Each time he'd glance at glassy-eyed customs agents, knowing that the exit stamp represented another murder, but he'd had purpose, direction. At least, it had seemed that way. All this time, he thought he'd been running away from her but instead he'd run in a complete circle. He'd ended up in the same place, standing in front of her again, unsure of what to say, afraid that she would leave.

I just want her to smile at me.

He picked up his pistol and stared at it, running his fingers along the barrel. He shook his head and let his arm hang over the edge of the couch, the weapon heavy in his hand.

The past was a better place, he thought. When her brother had been alive and nobody needed anything from anybody. She had been a woman with a dimpled smile and bare feet, giggling as the summer grass tickled her. Murphy had been the awkward man who couldn't look her in the eye, feeling like an idiot as he offered to buy her an ice-cream. Things had changed. Everything had changed. It stopped here. It had to stop here.

He let his head fall back and closed his eyes. Darkness swirled through his mind.

But I don't want to let her go.

The pistol thudded on the floor.

Colours turned into shapes and his mind summoned words and images.

"Why do you keep calling Darren 'China'?" Elliot asked, rolling on to her back to look up at the clouds.

Murphy lay down beside her and watched the fluffy formations drift through the sky. "China plate," he said. "It's rhyming slang for mate."

She plucked a flower and started to chew on the stem. "You'll have to teach me some other words."

"One of my favourites comes from England."

"Mmm?" She tickled the palm of his hand with her fingertips.

"I'm afraid to say it in the company of a lady."

"Whisper it to me."

He lowered his head and whispered, her perfumed hair tickling his nose, his heart beating faster.

Elliot rose to her knees and smacked him in the arm. "That's horrible!"

"I promise you I won't use that one." Murphy reached up and cupped her cheek in his hands.

"Good. I hope I won't need to remind a dumb James Blunt like you."

"Lady, huh."

"Don't ever forget," Elliot said with a smile, and then she sneezed.

Murphy woke when he heard a second sneeze. Elliot was gone. He grimaced and rubbed his eyes. "Anna?"

Anna emerged from the bedroom, padding into the room barefoot. She was swaddled in a large woollen jumper and her hands were swallowed by the sleeves. "Did I wake you?" She laced her fingers in front of her.

Murphy ran his hand down his face. "I wasn't really asleep."

"I'm sorry," she said. "I was trying to be quiet."

"Why?"

She looked down at her toes. "Grigoriy texted me. He warned me that you were in a ... mood," she said slowly, carefully choosing her final word.

He frowned. "I paid a lot of money for your private tuition. I didn't think I was paying by the word."

Anna leaned against the doorjamb and hugged herself. "I was concerned that indulging in verbose expressions would fail to adequately articulate your state of *ennui.*" She pirouetted into the room and threw her arms out. "While you indulge in the proclivity of maintaining a solemn countenance, I understand that your current lugubrious disposition is unique. Consequently, I can infer that your mood has been influenced by unique circumstances, and I would not dare risk accusations of conceit by endeavouring to postulate a potential cause." She bowed.

"Dear God," he muttered.

"I finished my last exam on Thursday," she said, tumbling on to the sofa.

"Grigoriy told me. Now you can speak bad English like the rest of us." He groaned as he rose from the sofa, and walked stiffly to the counter to pour a scotch.

"How was your trip?" Anna asked, lying on her stomach.

He glanced over his shoulder.

"Your eyes locked," she said, "the orchestra burst into life, she leapt into your arms, and you kissed passionately?"

"Don't you start," Murphy mumbled. "I've already been lectured by Grigoriy." He lit a cigarette.

"I was actually hoping I was right."

"This is not a movie." Murphy gulped down his scotch and poured another. "Otherwise, I'd be slightly better looking." He turned around and rested against the counter.

Anna smiled but her expression faded. She ran her thumb over the stamped metal of the dog tags draped around her neck. "I've heard stories about the bombings."

"Stories aren't always true." Murphy swirled the scotch around in his glass and puffed on his cigarette.

"Even stories about Simone Elliot?" she asked.

Murphy's eyes narrowed. "I never told you her last name."

"You never told me she was a thief, either."

He gulped down his drink and turned away, crushing his cigarette in an ashtray and placing his empty glass on the counter. "It was none of your business."

Anna sat up on the sofa. "You told me that she was afraid of what people thought of her. It wasn't until I googled her that I understood why. Everyone judged her, but you didn't. You cared about all of her."

Murphy wrapped his fingers around the edges of the countertop, his knuckles white.

"Me, Natalie, and all those other girls were about her," Anna said. "You never judged me. You gave me a second chance. You gave me everything and expected nothing back. You gave Elliot a second chance too, and she rejected you."

His grip tightened and the countertop creaked.

"She doesn't deserve you, Stepan. She's a hypocrite, seeing you for what you are and what you did instead of who you are and how you feel about her."

The edges of the counter shrieked and the timber splintered with a crack.

Anna jumped and then crept back into the embrace of the sofa. He was breathing heavily, his broad shoulders rising and falling.

"It was never about that," he murmured. "I wanted to be *her* second chance."

She stood up and neared him cautiously. "Why now? After all this time, after avoiding Australia for all these years, why go to her again?"

"Because I'd forgotten what it felt like," he mumbled. "It's been so long that I think I forgot how to feel anything."

Her face fell, her brow knitted.

"I don't care if the whole world hates me, just not her," he said. "Not her."

Anna leaned against the counter and stared at him. He refused to look at her, contemplating the bottle of scotch on the splintered countertop instead. "Only she can decide whether she hates you. You can't control that." Anna tilted her head and gazed at him thoughtfully. "That's what you love about her most, isn't it?"

Murphy turned away and dragged his feet along the carpet.

"Stepan?"

He stopped behind the chair and picked up his coat.

"You want her to choose you but you don't want to make her."

"Damn it!" Murphy spat. "The fucking photos are gone." He pitched his coat across the room and ran his hands through his hair. "Of all the things to lose."

"Where did you lose them?"

"I don't know," he said impatiently. "I've barely worn the coat since I left Australia."

"Maybe she stole them," Anna suggested absently, pouring a drink. "She steals everything else."

He kicked the chair, muttering a curse.

"She cares for nobody else," she continued, "only herself. The Melbourne Cup, that gold, Nikolay's art, jewellery from movie stars."

Murphy froze, his eyes hard.

"She leaves a trail of human wreckage behind, including you." Anna sipped from her glass. "Why bother with a woman like that?"

"What did you just say?"

"Don't defend her," Anna said. "She's a user."

Murphy seized her wrist and she stared at him with wide eyes. "What did you say about Nikolay's art?"

Anna's mouth fell open. "I, uh, I said that, um." She trembled, splashing scotch on her hand.

"She stole art from Nikolay?" His eyes were on fire.

Anna nodded quickly, the blood draining from her face.

"How do you—"

"Don't make me say," she pleaded, her voice quivering. "I promised him. He's been keeping the secret to protect you, to protect all of us."

"What secret?" he snarled.

"Simone stole some paintings from Nikolay three years ago," she said quickly. "Nikolay sent people to kill her but she disappeared. They only realised where she'd gone when you ran into her at that pub."

Murphy let go of her wrist. "I'm going to kill Grigoriy," he said. "Where's my gun?" He spotted his pistol on the floor.

"No!" Anna cried. She stepped in front of him and pushed against his chest. "Please, Grigoriy thought he was helping. He thought you would kill Nikolay if you found out."

Murphy glared at her hand on his chest.

"Please don't hurt him, Stepan," Anna begged. He arched his fingers and balled his hands into fists, his chest heaving. Anna touched his cheek with her hand. "Please, Stepan," she soothed. "Please."

"I'm the last person to know about this, aren't I?"

Anna pressed her lips together.

His breathing slowed down, his eyes closed, and his muscles relaxed. He reached up and held her hand against his cheek. "I think I'm going mad, Anna."

"You're not mad, you're just in love."

"Really? Is there a difference between passion and obsession?"

A long pause, then, quietly: "Yes."

"You still haven't told him, have you?" Murphy asked.

Anna handed him the glass. "You haven't exactly inspired me," she said. "Besides, there are things that he's said..." She grasped her dog tags. "What if I disgust him? What if I tell him and he feels nothing?"

Murphy emptied the glass in one gulp. "You have to decide between your fantasy and the truth."

"I don't want to decide." She pouted.

"Then the decision will be made for you," Murphy said. "That's how the world works."

The door opened and Grigoriy walked in, marching towards Murphy.

"Grigoriy," Anna said. "What happened to your neck?" She pointed to the red welt on his throat.

"Go get changed and pack a bag, Anna," Grigoriy said. "You're leaving."

"What?" She frowned. "Why?"

Grigoriy looked down at Murphy. "I just got a warning call from one of the girls. Nikolay is on his way and he's pissed off."

"Do as he says, Anna," Murphy said.

Anna looked at Murphy and Grigoriy in turn. "I guess I'll go pack," she said, leaving the room.

Grigoriy didn't take his eyes off Murphy. "Eight men, Stepan," he said.

"They had it coming."

Grigoriy reached into his back pocket and pulled out a media player wrapped with a set of headphones.

"I thought I told you I wanted a thumb drive," Murphy said.

"This is all I had in my laptop bag," Grigoriy said. "If you find porn on it, it's not mine."

Murphy arched an eyebrow.

"Some of the guys don't know how to use computers," Grigoriy explained. "I do them favours. You know how it works." He shrugged. "Or maybe you don't."

Grigoriy handed him the media player and Murphy grabbed his wrist. "Are there any other secrets I should know about?"

"Now you want to talk?"

"Yeah, let's talk about Nikolay's missing art, Grigoriy."

Grigoriy snatched his hand away.

"This isn't the first time Nikolay has put out a contract on *her,* is it?" Murphy asked. "Is this why she disappeared for three years?"

Grigoriy straightened his back, his chest out. "I did what I had to do, Stepan."

"Jesus," Murphy spat.

"See, this is what's wrong with you," Grigoriy said. "You think you know best, but the world would've crashed down on you and everyone around you." He clicked his tongue. "Look at you now: eight men dead and Nikolay's coming for you."

"I killed five the other night."

"This is different. You defied him."

"Do you think that matters to me?"

Grigoriy's eyes fell to the media player.

"Did you listen to this?" Murphy asked.

Grigoriy nodded. "I never imagined..." His voice trailed off. "He can't do it."

"Do you still want to stay and fight?"

"Not for you." Grigoriy rubbed his throat. "Not anymore."

"What are you talking about, Grigoriy?" Anna asked.

Grigoriy glanced towards the doorway. She was clutching a gym bag, her face twisted in confusion. "It's time to go, Anna. Say goodbye to Stepan."

"But I—"

"Do it," Grigoriy ordered.

"Why?" she asked. "Where are we going? Why isn't Stepan coming?"

"We're going someplace safe and Stepan is going to stay here and do what he's always done." He glared at Murphy. "Wait for permission to die."

39

MOSCOW, RUSSIA

SATURDAY 17 SEPTEMBER

8:22AM MSK

Stephen Murphy dropped the magazine from his pistol and put it on the bench. He worked the slide, catching the ejected round and placing it next to the magazine. He handed over the pistol.

"And the knife," Nikolay Korolev said.

Murphy unsheathed his knife from its scabbard and flipped it over, holding the blade.

"Take all of it," Korolev ordered, nodding to his bodyguards who collected the weapons. "Leave us," he demanded, gesturing to the door of the hotel suite. The bodyguards left, closing the door gently behind them. "Sit down," he said to Murphy.

"I'd rather stand."

"Sit!" he commanded, pointing down with his finger.

Murphy muttered a curse and sat down on the sofa.

Korolev paced in front of him, rolling his coin across his hand. "I told you to remember your place."

"We had a deal."

"Eight men!" Korolev snarled. "Do you think you're worth eight men, Stepan?"

"Is she?"

Korolev turned, stabbing his chest with his thumb. "She stole from me."

"She steals from everyone."

"Not from me," he hissed.

Murphy sprang to his feet. "We had a fucking deal."

"Don't you dare yap at me like some junkyard dog," Korolev said. "Don't pretend that this matters to you anymore."

"There was only one person on this entire planet you weren't allowed to touch and you couldn't help yourself."

Korolev threw a left hook and Murphy blocked, but he missed the right uppercut that followed. Murphy swayed and felt blood pool in his mouth. "And you promised you would stay away from her." Korolev seized Murphy's jaw in his hand and squeezed. "So, tell me, was it worth it?"

Murphy didn't speak.

"She kicked you out like a stray dog, didn't she?" Korolev said. "I treat you like a prince and you betray me by chasing after this woman, a woman who robbed me, and for what?" He shoved Murphy back on to the sofa. "You're nothing to her."

Murphy spat a mouthful of blood on to the floor. "How would you know?"

"Because you came back."

The veins bulged in Murphy's neck. "So I should give up, right?"

Korolev shook his head impatiently, shoving his coin into his pocket. "You already have, Stepan. I know you have."

"I have to let go, so why can't you? Why are you still holding on to Valentina?"

"Enough, Stepan."

"Her grandfather's coin was just the start, wasn't it? Valentina took everything from you, so you had to—"

"You don't want to do this," Korolev said.

"She turned you away," Murphy said. "You disgusted her."

"You don't know what you're talking about."

"She became leader of Russian intelligence, so you became leader of a criminal syndicate," Murphy shouted. "She went into politics, so you bought the politicians. She became mayor, so you stole the city." Murphy shook his head. "Now she's president. What's next, Nikolay?"

"This country will die if I don't do something."

"This isn't about the country."

"Yes, it is." Korolev began pacing across the living room. "And I'll be the one to save it because I know what has to be done."

"Valentina will destroy you."

"She can't. There are hundreds of syndicates in this country and their leaders will move in to take my place. There will be blood on the streets without me. I keep them in line, I control them."

"You won't be able to control them once they find out what you're up to. They'll lose their status, money, property. They won't give it all up for you. They'll fight you."

"They're too afraid to fight me."

Murphy chuckled humourlessly. "You think they're *that* scared of you?"

"No, they're that scared of *you,* and that's why you will stand in my place after I move into the Kremlin."

Murphy held his breath. The whole world seemed to grow around him, as if he were shrinking.

Korolev smiled broadly. "Take a good look at me, Stepan. I'm your future." He crouched down in front of Murphy. "From the moment I saw you in that cell, I knew it would be you."

"What are you talking about?" Murphy stammered.

"I built your myth, gave you the space to grow, and look what you've become. Seven years and the whole world trembles when they hear your name. You're my protégé, my successor, my apprentice."

"No," Murphy said weakly.

Korolev laughed. "I was worried about sending men for Simone, but it worked out perfectly. For seven years, I used her to keep you here, gambling on your guarantee. Now, you've learned the most important lesson of all." He jabbed Murphy in the chest. "You don't need her. You achieved all of this without her."

"It's not what I want." Murphy felt his blood pounding through his body.

"Yes, it is." Korolev's pupils were wide, his lips flecked with spit. "Deep down, you know how good it will feel to take everything she cares about and burn it all right before her eyes. Then, from the ashes, you build it into something that she could only dream about but can never have because you are in control, you decide, you have the power." He jabbed Murphy in the chest again. "They want us to be pitiful wrecks, to long for them, but that's not what a man does. A man rules, a man is king." Korolev stood tall, his back straight. "And they will beg for a second chance."

"I'm not you," Murphy said through clenched teeth.

"You feel it burning inside you, don't you?" Korolev said. "You *hate* her. You know that you are stronger without her, a better man. You know that she should kiss the ground you walk on just for knowing her name."

"You're wrong."

"Then leave, go to her. What has that world ever given you? Your family neglected you. Your army threw you in jail. Your lover hates you and blames you for something that wasn't your fault. Now, they all fear you."

Murphy felt like a heavy weight was pushing down on his chest.

"They took everything from you, and you've only just realised that nothing they took actually matters." Korolev stabbed the air with his finger. "Everything you have here, now, is yours, you've earned it, and no one can take it from you."

Murphy ran his hand down his face and peered through the window.

"You were made for this, Stepan," Korolev said. "Fight this war. Take my crown and rule this place."

Murphy glared at Nikolay Korolev, his nostrils flaring.

"You should take some time to think," Korolev said, checking his watch. "I have business to attend to, but I'm leaving two sentries on your door and some men on the street."

"You'll need more than that."

Korolev snorted. “Their task is to stop unwanted visitors,” he said. “I know you won’t run.”

“You’re sure?”

“You have nowhere left to go.”

Murphy closed his eyes.

“Behave yourself,” Korolev said, “get some rest, and I’ll send for you when I need you.” He marched to the door.

“What if she had said yes?” Murphy asked quietly.

Korolev smiled, his hand on the doorknob. “She was never going to say yes, Stepan.”

***

“Satisfied?” Grigoriy looked up. “Can we go now?”

“I told you, I’m not leaving him.” Anna closed the door behind her.

“He’s already abandoned us,” he pointed out. “It’s time to go, Anna.”

She ran both hands through her hair and folded her arms across her chest.

He sighed. “Fine. What happened?”

“They let me have five minutes.”

“And?” He placed his pistol on the coffee table.

"And he was just sitting there, eating peanuts out of a jar from the minibar and smoking cigarettes."

"Was he dipping the peanuts in mayonnaise?" Grigoriy screwed up his nose. "He does that sometimes."

"Grigoriy!" Anna yelled in frustration.

"Right, I'm sorry," he mumbled, collapsing on the sofa.

"He was watching the news," Anna said. "He hardly said a word, and then he just fell asleep."

Grigoriy stared down at his hands. "Did he tell you what Nikolay said?"

"No." She shook her head. "Like I said, he barely spoke. I think you were right. It's like he's given up."

"It's worse than that."

"It's Simone," she cried. "It's because of her." She wrung her hands.

"I told you, without her, he'll become what Korolev needs to win his war, and I don't want to be around when the first shot is fired."

"Shut up, Grigoriy," she yelled.

He frowned.

"Can't you see? They're scared," she said, waving vigorously towards Murphy's room. "They're afraid of Nikolay, and that's why they stand guard, but they're also afraid of Stepan, and that's why they stay outside."

"They're standing in the hall?"

"And they're calling him 'sir'," Anna panted. "They don't even call Nikolay 'sir'."

"Anna, calm down," Grigoriy pleaded, holding his hands in the air.

"He could fight this, if he wanted to. Why doesn't he want to fight? So many people are dying and he can stop it." She paced in front of the sofa. "I'm scared, Grigoriy," she said, wrapping her arms around her body. She sat down beside him and nestled her head underneath his arm. "Why can't he see it? Why doesn't he fight?"

Grigoriy held her awkwardly and cleared his throat.

"Why couldn't she love him?" she asked, placing her hand on his chest. "Why did she have to leave him with nothing?"

"I don't know," he said. "I don't know anything about these things."

"She only needs to know one thing," she whispered. "Being in love shows a man how he ought to be."

"What does being hated show him?" Grigoriy asked.

Anna squeezed her eyes shut. "Promise me you'll stay with me today, Grigoriy."

"I promise." He said it without thinking. "But we have to leave. We have to get far away from here."

"Wait until tonight," she pleaded. "Just give him a chance. Maybe he'll change his mind. Maybe he'll find a reason."

Grigoriy took a deep breath.

Oh, God. Please give me the courage to keep her safe.

40

MOSCOW, RUSSIA

SATURDAY 17 SEPTEMBER

10:31PM MSK

Grigoriy rested his lips against the top of Anna's head and sighed. Her arms were folded against her stomach, her fingers curled against her face, and her hair tickled his nose and tumbled down his chest. He'd started to stroke her back but he didn't know why. She could sleep peacefully without him.

I'm not strong enough for you.

Murphy had abandoned them and now Grigoriy had to keep her safe, but he wasn't a warrior or guardian: he was an IT graduate.

I wish I could be more like Volkov.

Anna was almost right. Murphy wasn't a machine but he wasn't quite a man either. Grigoriy had been trying to decide if Murphy were human at all.

Of course he is, because a man is the worst of all monsters. That's what people say, isn't it?

Volkov was a wild animal, killing out of necessity, amorally, sweeping aside all compassion and sentiment, the burdens of civilisation. The man,

Murphy, however, still shared the same body, weighed down by chains and fast asleep. Nikolay Korolev had prodded and poked before stirring a pot of emotions and memories right under Murphy's nose. Murphy was waking, his nostrils flaring, straining against his shackles.

But Murphy is tired.

Grigoriy brushed the hair from Anna's eyes and felt his heart sink. He knew he needed to be like Volkov to keep Anna safe, but to be loved he had to be a man. He had to be like Murphy.

Could I be both?

He remembered Anna comparing Murphy to a painting: alive but dead, material but forever. He'd immediately thought of the wolf, a murderous shadow that stalks the living, teetering on the edge of darkness and light.

Is it possible to balance on that edge?

Grigoriy knew the Chechens had named Stepan Volkov and it was easy to see why. The wolf was a legendary animal to those men. It was not afraid to fight, even when outnumbered and overwhelmed. The wolf knew it was smarter, faster, stronger, and it had courage.

God, it was brave.

And if the wolf were beaten, its chest heaving, fur matted with sweat and torn with wounds, it would lie down and face its opponent, its eyes still shimmering, ready to die. That's what the wolf would do, but not what a man would do. A man was never ready to die.

Murphy can't be ready to die.

Grigoriy's phone started to vibrate, shuddering across the coffee table. He gently pried Anna's arms loose and lowered her to the sofa.

"Da?" he said curtly, answering his phone. His eyes narrowed and then widened. "Did Nikolay tell you not to call me?" He paused, smiling thinly. "No, of course I won't tell him. I'm happy to help. I'll even let you take the credit for the idea." He stood up. "Yes, Yuri. Use the meat locker, just like the American. I'll come along to help. I'll be there in..." He glanced at his watch. "Just wait for me, okay?"

Grigoriy slid his phone into his pocket and grabbed the pistol from the coffee table.

It's not over yet, not until I say so.

***

"Wait, Grigoriy," the *boyevik* at Murphy's door said. "You can't see him."

There were two of them, heavy men with big biceps, buzz cuts and bulging stomachs. The spokesman wore a combat vest over a tight t-shirt and grenades slung from his chest pockets. His fingerless gloves hovered over a pistol tucked into the waistband of his jeans. The other man wore a long coat that remained unbuttoned and his jewelled hands hung loosely by his sides.

"It's important," Grigoriy said. His heart was beating furiously and his shirt was clinging to his back.

"I'm sorry, Grigoriy," the *boyevik* said. "We have our orders."

Grigoriy ran his hand through his hair before letting it fall behind him. He snatched the pistol from the small of his back and fired once. The *boyevik* flopped to the ground while his friend drew his weapon. Grigoriy ducked, shifted his aim, and fired again. The second man fell before he could shoot back.

Grigoriy gasped for breath and wiped his forehead with his sleeve. He pushed through Murphy's door. All of the lights were off, the room was dark, and he couldn't see Murphy anywhere. "It's me," Grigoriy rasped.

"Jesus, Grigoriy," Murphy said, emerging from the shadows. "How much caffeine have you had?"

Grigoriy marched up to his boss and punched him in the jaw.

Murphy stepped back, stunned, and reached for his chin.

"Damn it, Stepan, even I could do it. Why couldn't you?"

"What's the point?" Murphy said wearily. "Where are you going to go now, Grigoriy?" He nodded towards the balcony. "There are more of them out there."

Grigoriy took another swing. Murphy blocked and Grigoriy countered by shoving the pistol into the Wolf's chest. "Stop being a fucking coward," he hissed.

"Put it down, Grigoriy," Murphy said softly.

"Do you know what Anna told me?" Grigoriy's voice was quaking. "She told me that being in love shows a man how he ought to be." He lowered the pistol. "I get that now, because when you feel that, everything becomes clearer, and you know what the right thing to do is."

Murphy threw his hands in the air. "It's not that simple."

"It's not meant to be simple. It's hard and it's hard for a reason."

Murphy glanced at his assistant and put his hands on his hips.

"Look, Stepan, she might reject you again if you run away from this life, but I guarantee she will reject you if you stay."

"Damn it, Grigoriy." Murphy folded his arms. "She nearly cut my throat."

"Why? Because of her brother? Did you tell her why you were there? Or did she think you were there for another reason?"

Murphy's mouth fell open and he closed it again slowly, his forehead wrinkling.

"You can never give up," Grigoriy said. "Not when you're fighting for something this important."

Murphy ran his hands through his hair and stared at the floor.

"So what's stopping you?"

He took a deep breath. "I'm afraid," he whispered.

Grigoriy nodded. "It's not the fighting that gets you, is it?" He stepped nearer. "It's the fighting alone." He waved a mobile phone in the air. "But you don't have to."

"What are you talking about?"

"She's coming for you."

Murphy rubbed his forehead.

"Yuri called," Grigoriy said, pointing at the phone. "Nikolay told him not to, but he didn't know who else could help him. Yuri was personally assigned the job and doesn't want to mess it up so he called someone he could trust."

"Job? What job?"

"Simone's about to land in Moscow and he wanted to know if he should use the meat locker."

"What?" Murphy growled.

"She came for you," Grigoriy said again. "Now can you see?"

Murphy started to smile but it faded quickly. He peered past Grigoriy and studied the two dead *boyeviks* in his doorway. He looked back at the dining room table and saw three empty jars of peanuts. "Grigoriy, does your watch glow in the dark?"

Grigoriy took a step back. "Uh, yes. Why?"

41

ON APPROACH INTO MOSCOW, RUSSIA

SATURDAY 17 SEPTEMBER

10:50PM MSK

Elliot was standing on a dining room chair in Darren Harper's apartment when she heard the front door open. She looked down at her bare feet before closing her eyes. Murphy's combat boots clomped into the dining room. She looked up.

"Hi." She waved.

"Hi." He took off his beret and tossed it on the table. "Is Darren home?"

"He'll be a few hours." She folded her arms across her chest.

Murphy cleared his throat. "Are you feeling insecure about your height today?"

"What?" She looked down again. "Oh, the chair." She frowned and curled her toes. "Do you promise not to laugh?"

"I'd hate to lie to you."

Elliot took a deep breath. "There's a spider in the bathroom."

"You're in the dining room." He shoved his hands into the pockets of his fatigues. "And you're standing on a chair."

"The spider is pretty big," she said. "Now that you're here, you can kill it." She shivered and wrapped her arms around her body. "Spiders freak me out."

"They freak me out, too. Did you know some have enough venom to kill a cow four times over?"

"Are you going to get it or not? You're the man."

"Don't be sexist," he scolded.

"C'mon, knight in shining armour," she said. "Don't you guys love swinging to the rescue on a vine?"

"Knights don't swing on vines."

"I don't care if they brandish balloons and ride in on pandas. I want that spider dead."

He groaned. "Okay, but you can't leave me to fight alone."

She raised her hands. "That's not the deal."

"You're coming with me."

"You're going first, though, right?"

He found a newspaper and rolled it up. Then he reached out for her arm and towed her along behind him. She laughed, trying to drag her feet, but he was too strong. They reached the bathroom and she took shelter behind him when she saw the spider. It was crouched in the middle of the floor, staring at them. She spurred Murphy on, poking him in the ribs. He turned and smiled at her, raising his weapon above his head.

There was a loud slap and Elliot woke up. The woman sitting next to her had accidentally unfastened her tray table and it had fallen down on to her thighs. "I didn't mean to wake you," she cooed in French.

"It's okay." Elliot couldn't believe she had fallen asleep. She hated falling asleep on planes. Sleep was a state of vulnerability and strangers could gawk at you while you mumbled your way through an imagined orgasm or drooled on your shirt. She stretched and watched the woman reset her tray table. Meanwhile, the captain announced their descent into Moscow. Elliot's heart sank with the plane and she grasped her armrests, staring through the window at the blinking lights on the wing.

Maybe I'll be dead before I have a chance to leave the airport.

A part of her wanted to die, the part of her that she'd buried deep inside since her brother had been killed. As soon as his coffin had returned, Elliot had set to work building up the lies, rationalisations, and self-deceptions needed to cope. In her mind, she saw it as a castle. It looked impressive, with its towering battlements and wide moat, and it seemed so permanent. But then the ocean would creep towards her castle and sweep it all away, and she would realise that her fortress had been built with sand.

A psychologist had once accused her of indulging in "dissociation". Elliot created identities to complete her cons, building whole histories and eccentricities that defined her adopted persona, pushing her true self aside. She always came back though, and everything was waiting for her when she returned, which just prompted her to find another con and another identity. It had gotten worse, lately. She had run away when Darren Harper died. Then again with Angela James, and Elliot had started wondering if she could ever be herself again.

She'd felt safe as Leanne Waters until she'd met Murphy again. He was like a one-man ocean, sweeping away her carefully crafted castles. Sometimes, it was as if he had the power to steal away all the sand on the beach, leaving her unable to hide at all. So this was her, diving into the ocean instead of waiting for it to come; knowing that she had no control over the tides and the waves, knowing that she could be dragged under.

I can't leave him to fight alone.

The voice inside her was weak but it was enough. She reached into her pocket and salvaged her caduceus necklace. She wanted to leave the airport alive.

The aircraft thudded to earth and Elliot jumped, her chest heaving. The cabin lurched, the tyres squealed, and the engines roared to slow the plane down. She draped the chain around her neck, tucking the medallion inside her shirt, and collected her carry-on bag, joining the queue to leave the aeroplane.

The airport was bare and tired, the brightly lit bookshops and wood-panelled cafés shuttered and closed. The walls were cracked and the windows frosted over with oil and dust. Elliot staggered into the arrivals lounge and fought her way through the groaning crowd. Her skin crawled, as if someone was watching her, but a quick survey of the airport revealed nothing. Still, the feeling was there. She could hear the people grumbling around her, speaking a language that she hadn't used in a long time.

Elliot felt a sharp pain in her thigh, her vision blurring as she turned around. All she saw was a man's shadow in front of her as she flopped into somebody's arms.

42

MOSCOW, RUSSIA

SATURDAY 17 SEPTEMBER

10:58PM MSK

The concierge's head snapped back and he crumpled to the floor. Murphy turned off the lights in the lobby and holstered his pistol. He placed three jars on the concierge's desk and jogged to the glass doors, peering into the darkness.

A van was parked in front of the hotel and four *boyeviks* were leaning against it, smoking cigarettes and talking loudly. Murphy knew there would be more men in the back of the van, playing cards and drinking. They would be tired after a long day.

He returned to the desk and removed a grenade from his pocket. He pulled the pin on the grenade and eased it into one of the empty jars, letting the lever push against the glass. The jar held the pressure and he tossed the pin to the ground. He repeated the process two more times.

Murphy studied the entrance and saw two arcs traced out on the tiled floor where the doors had opened and closed repeatedly. He placed a jar in the middle of each arc and placed the third jar on the concierge's desk, perching Grigoriy's glowing watch on top. Finally, he returned to the entrance, his face close to the glass.

One of the *boyeviks* looked up and smacked the shoulder of his friend with the back of his hand. They froze and Murphy faded back into the darkness, listening to their shouts. A *boyevik* slapped the side of the van and the back doors were thrown open, five men filing out. They moved quickly, tossing away their cigarettes and grabbing their weapons.

Murphy walked to the back of the lobby and turned into the hallway, taking cover. The glass entrance shattered and bullets raked through the lobby, smashing paintings and chipping plaster.

The firing paused and Murphy heard shouting as boots crunched on broken glass. He stood up straight, took a deep breath, aimed at Grigoriy's glowing watch, and fired.

The jar shattered and the lever leapt into the air before clattering to the floor. The grenade twirled on the concierge's desk. The doors flew open, and Murphy heard the other jars shatter as the men swept through the lobby. A *boyevik* paused at the counter and his jaw fell open.

The blast smashed windows and set off car alarms, the mouth of the hotel belching dust and debris. The roar reverberated down the darkened street and a dog started to bark as metal clanged on the pavement.

Murphy stepped through the lobby with his pistol drawn. A man grabbed his leg, holding on desperately. Murphy looked down.

"Volkov, please," the *boyevik* begged.

Murphy shook him off and held his foot on the man's throat, aiming at his head. "That's not my name."

Murphy fired.

***

"So, where do we go?" Anna asked, rubbing her eyes.

"A place that doesn't exist anymore," Grigoriy replied. He picked up Anna's gym bag and reached for her hand, leading her into the hall. A bald man in striped pyjamas was standing in the hallway, shouting at a member of the hotel staff. A woman wearing a nightgown and a mud-mask stood behind the bald man, her arms crossed. An entourage of bleary-eyed guests were standing against the wall, and the uniformed man was trying to calm them down. Two security guards entered the hall, hitching their trousers.

Anna and Grigoriy elbowed through the scrum unnoticed. They rode the freight elevator to the ground floor and she watched Grigoriy disarm the alarm in the loading dock. He led her outside and through a maze of alleys until they reached a row of garage doors.

Grigoriy unlocked one of the doors and then turned to her. "I need to know that you trust me."

She blinked. "Of course I trust you, Grigoriy. I wouldn't be standing here in the freezing cold if I had any doubt."

"Good. Some people don't like my method of emergency transportation." He lifted the garage door, cringing when it shrieked in protest. He paused and glanced around. Car alarms were still wailing from the blast at the hotel and a dog started to howl but there were no other sounds.

"Hang on, Grigoriy," she said, catching a glimpse of his vehicle. "You never mentioned this."

"I need to get you safe," he said tenderly. "Let me do that."

Anna reluctantly agreed and Grigoriy reefed the tarpaulin off the motorcycle. He tossed her a helmet and helped her put the gym bag on her back before mounting the bike and starting it up. He eased it out of the garage before screeching along the alley and launching into the street. The motorcycle bawled along the dark roads as Grigoriy sped through intersections and leaned into corners, opening up the throttle on the straights, the glowing needles flickering on the bike's dials.

I have to be that man.

***

Elliot woke up in what she thought was a musty dungeon. Eventually, her eyes adjusted to the light of the dim bulb dangling from the ceiling. Meat hooks hung from rails and there was a damp stench of rotting flesh. She staggered to her feet and leaned against the wall, taking a deep breath.

The door clanged and a large man with no neck stepped into the room. The most colourful thing about him appeared to be his tattoos. A small man with jewelled teeth followed after him, pushing a trolley laden with tools.

"Watch her, Vlad," the little man said. He spoke in Russian, thinking Elliot couldn't understand him.

"Yes, Yuri." Vlad, the big one, approached her and she shrank against the wall.

Yuri picked up his drill and loosened the chuck, fitting a spade bit. He pulled the trigger to test the battery's charge, and the drill whirred in his hands.

"I thought we were waiting for Grigoriy," Vlad said.

"We have our orders," Yuri said, placing the drill on the trolley.

"Remember what happened with the American?"

"She's not American," Yuri hissed. "She can't give us information."

"How do you know?" Vlad asked.

Yuri glared at Vlad.

"You could ask her," Vlad suggested with a shrug.

Yuri narrowed his eyes. "Just make sure you keep her focused."

He turned to Elliot. "Welcome to Moscow, Miss Elliot," Yuri said in English.

"It's good to be here," she said sarcastically.

Vlad backhanded Elliot across the face. She fell to the floor, her head reeling.

"I have not told you to speak yet," Yuri said.

Elliot placed her hands on the floor and tried to get up. "Nobody ever does."

Vlad kicked at her ribs. Elliot saw it coming and rolled with the blow but there was too much force to absorb. The air rushed out of her lungs and her chest heaved, fighting to breathe again.

Yuri crouched in front of her. "I'll talk and you'll listen." He stood and returned to his trolley. "Our organisation likes information. We thrive on it. What remains of your life will be much less painful if you can offer us something that we would consider valuable."

"What do you want to know?" Elliot rasped.

Yuri ran a finger along the handle of a claw hammer. "Everything."

"I have a better idea," Elliot said. She sat up against the wall and waved Vlad down. He took half a step back.

"You're not in a position to bargain, Miss Elliot," Yuri pointed out.

"Oh, I'm done bargaining." Elliot rolled over and kicked Vlad's kneecap with the heel of her boot. The bone crumbled and his leg collapsed. He cried out and crashed to the floor. Elliot jumped to her feet and vaulted over Vlad's back as Yuri pulled a pistol. She kicked the pistol out of Yuri's hand and punched him in the throat. He staggered back, struggling to breathe. She yanked a meat hook off a rail and drove the hook into Yuri's stomach. He screamed, his abdomen torn open.

Elliot let him flop to the ground and bent over to retrieve the pistol. Her feet were pulled out from under her and she threw out her hands, grabbing the trolley of tools as she was dragged to the floor. The tools crashed to the ground and she rolled over. Vlad let go of her foot and crawled towards her holding a knife in the air.

He brought the knife down.

Elliot rolled, the blade striking the floor, and she kicked Vlad in the face. Spitting blood, his hand climbed up her leg, and Elliot tried to reach for the pistol, her finger touching the butt.

The blade whooshed and Elliot parted her legs, the knife stabbing into the floor between her knees. Her hand out, she found a wooden handle and looked up. A claw hammer. Vlad grasped at her leg, pulling her towards him.

He raised his knife. She grabbed the hammer.

Elliot sat up and drove the claw of the hammer into the top of his skull. He collapsed on the floor like a ragdoll and Elliot slithered away. She struggled to her feet and used the wall to stand up straight, her head dizzy.

She retrieved Yuri's pistol, smacked herself in the cheek, and stepped through the door. Outside was a busy loading dock and about thirty faces looked up at her. Guns emerged from various hiding places and she dropped the pistol.

"Ne strelyai!" she heard a familiar voice shout. They all obeyed and put their weapons down. Stephen Murphy emerged from the crowd and marched towards the freezer, stopping in front of her. "Still underestimated, aren't you, Slim?"

She swayed on her feet and pointed at him. "Your organisation is terrible at welcoming visitors."

Murphy caught her as she collapsed. "I'll be sure to bring that up at our next AGM."

43

MOSCOW, RUSSIA

SATURDAY 17 SEPTEMBER

11:32PM MSK

Anna couldn't see at all. "What is this place?" she asked in wonder, running her hands along the stone wall to keep her balance. Grigoriy reached for her hand and she gratefully laid her fingers on his palm.

"This is where I live," Grigoriy said. "And work."

He had ridden the motorcycle through the outskirts of Moscow to the end of a disused road that carved its way through thick woods. The road looked like it had been built in the 1960s and not used since. Trees and bushes had overgrown the asphalt, cracking the road's edges and littering it with debris. Grigoriy rode slowly and carefully until he reached a sign commanding trespassers to turn around or face execution. They kept on for another kilometre, eventually reaching an overgrown railway line that disappeared into a tunnel.

"How do you know about this?" Anna asked.

"Stepan recruited me because I can find out people's secrets," Grigoriy explained. "This is Moscow's secret."

He turned and wrapped his arm around her waist. "Bear with me."

She heard a click and a buzz and squinted as fluorescent lights blinked to life.

They were standing in a large man-made shelter that had been carved into the rock. She looked behind her and saw the long narrow tunnel stretch into darkness. Grigoriy closed a set of blackout curtains, masking them from the outside world.

One wall was cluttered with bookshelves holding volumes of computer manuals, textbooks, and comic books. In the corner were three computer monitors on a large desk. Bunches of wires and cables had been neatly bound together and snaked along the floor to a power outlet. There was a small kitchenette, a sofa, a dining table, and a thick rug on the floor. Another room branched off, a bedroom with a small bathroom nestled in the corner. There was heating, running water, and even a refrigerator.

"This is an underground nuclear shelter," Anna said.

"That's right," Grigoriy said. "There are about thirty kilometres of tunnel under Moscow that were excavated by political prisoners. Shelters like this were designed and built after America dropped the bomb in World War II. The tunnels were supposed to allow the *Politburo* to escape the Kremlin in the event of nuclear or chemical warfare." He rifled through one of the bookshelves and pulled out a copy of Dante's

Divine Comedy. A frayed piece of folded paper was hidden between the pages. It was a map and Anna helped him unfold it and smooth it out on the table.

"See here," he said, pointing at the faded map. "The main tunnel has a train line that leads to Vnukovo Airport. The most important people in Moscow could be transported by subway to the airport and evacuated. Meanwhile other people, maybe thousands of them, could live through a nuclear attack in shelters all over the city. Or at least the rich people could." He tapped his finger on a mark on the map. "We're here. The shelter is joined to the railway line by the tunnel. We came in by following the railway line."

"Are all the shelters like this one?"

"This is one of the smaller ones. It could support two families," he said. "They're largely forgotten now. The underground trains use a lot of the tunnels and many of the others have been sealed off or filled in."

Anna turned on her toes. "This is amazing, Grigoriy."

"It took me a few months to set up. I had to reconnect to the city's power supply, water, and telecommunications without them noticing, and then I had to get everything down here without drawing too much attention."

"How many people know about this place?"

He cleared his throat. "After me, you're the first."

"Not even Stepan?"

"If he does, he hasn't told me."

Anna smiled at him and he looked at his feet.

"Oh, I have a surprise for you, too." Grigoriy waved for her to follow him to his computer desk. He logged on and all three of the screens came to life. "I hope you don't mind that I did this. I just got curious."

Anna squinted at the screen. "They're exam results." She leaned in closer. "They're *my* exam results."

"I hacked the database this morning, but I wasn't sure if I should say anything."

Anna shrieked excitedly and threw her arms around Grigoriy's neck. "I passed!" she cried. "I passed, I passed!"

Grigoriy felt his face grow hot. "I always knew you would," he said. "I wish I had something to give you but I don't have much. I should have bought some champagne."

She kissed him on the cheek. "You've given me more than enough, Grigoriy."

He blushed but finally found the courage to look up, her eyes swallowing him whole. She placed her hand on his chest. "Now, can we wait in this place until the storm passes?"

"Um." Grigoriy's mobile phone beeped loudly and Anna stepped back. He reached into his pocket and read the text message, turning away and retreating into his bedroom.

"Grigoriy?"

He returned with a bundle of documents and a small box. He placed them on the dining table. "Your new life," Grigoriy said.

"And the box?"

"We can't just wait out the storm." Grigoriy opened the box and reached inside. He placed a pistol on the table. "That's your raincoat." He placed a grenade beside the pistol. "And that's your umbrella."

Anna wrapped her arms around her shoulders. "Oh."

44

MOSCOW, RUSSIA

SATURDAY 17 SEPTEMBER

11:34PM MSK

Elliot inhaled sharply as she woke up, which immediately sent a throbbing pain through her head. She groaned and rubbed her forehead with her palm, slowly realising that she was lying on a soft bed in a room bathed in warm light. Everything beyond that was a blur. She could hear sounds nearby: metallic sounds and running water, cupboards opening and closing, zippers undoing and lights being switched on and off. She didn't want to roll over in case the pain got worse.

The bed creaked and she felt someone sit beside her.

Stephen.

She could hear his steady breathing: "You know, I thought you were unconscious until you started to snore."

"You used to like my snoring," she said. "You said it was sweet, like a purring kitten."

"A purring kitten drowning in a bucket of honey."

"Right," she mumbled. "I always forget that second bit."

"Are you going to sit up? I've got things to do, you know."

"I'm just waiting for the room to come into focus." She felt his hand on her shoulder and wrapped her arm around his to pull herself upright.

Her face wrinkled as a wave of pain broke over her.

"Vlad is a bit of a truck," Murphy remarked, rolling up the sleeves of his shirt. "Or was."

"Trucks have more give in them." She groaned. "Do I have you to thank for that welcome?"

"Nope. That's not my area. I found out at the last minute."

"Well, it's lucky you showed up when you did. Otherwise I would've had to kill all of those people. I'm too much of a lady for that."

"Oh, yeah, you're a delicate little flower." He raised his hands. "I'm going to look you over."

"Are you asking for my permission?"

"Warning you. I'm not keen on giving you more reasons to belt me."

"'Fraidy cat."

"Let me know when it hurts."

"Oh, *you'll* know."

Murphy cupped her face in his hands, gently massaging his fingers into her skin. She tried to stop her eyes watering as he checked her cheekbone for breaks. "Don't be a hero," he said.

"It aches," she confessed, rolling her eyes towards the ceiling.

"Okay, it doesn't seem broken. You're lucky." He picked up a washcloth and wrung it into a bowl before gently washing her face.

"How bad is the bleeding?" she asked.

"He split your lip but it'll be okay." She gazed back at him as he dabbed at her lips. He cleared his throat and looked away, tossing the cloth back in the bowl. She winced as he stripped her coat off her shoulders. He saw the bandage on her arm before she could hide it. The dressing was weeping blood.

"Where did you get that?"

She held up her hand, showing him a bandaged cut. "Same place I got this."

He studied her sceptically. "Uh-huh."

"I was trying to get a chocolate bar out of a vending machine and—"

"And it shot you?"

She pushed out her bottom lip and shrugged.

He shook his head and grabbed a stethoscope. "This could be a little cold," he warned.

She yelped when it touched her chest. "You did that deliberately." She hit him on the arm.

He breathed on the stethoscope to warm it. She inhaled and exhaled and he moved the stethoscope around her chest and her back. "Is it hard to breathe?"

"No more than usual," she replied.

"Okay," he said. "Your lungs sound like they're fine. No crackling or wheezing. Which means no holes or anything." He eyed her briefly. "Your heart rate is a little high."

She looked down at her lap and he ran his hands along her ribs. His hands were warm, she thought.

His hands have always been warm.

"How badly does it hurt?" he asked.

"It aches a little."

He pushed on her breastbone. "What about that?"

Elliot grimaced. "It's not that bad." She felt his hand stop between her breasts and saw him frown.

He flicked the medallion out of her shirt. It was the caduceus medallion he'd bought her before leaving to fight in the war. He stared at it and grunted, picking up a digital thermometer.

Elliot opened her mouth to explain but he placed the thermometer on her tongue.

"Close," he ordered.

She obeyed and he busied himself packing away the equipment. The thermometer beeped. "Normal," he said, reading the temperature. He tossed the thermometer on to the bedside table. "You're fine." He stood up and retreated to the living room.

Elliot heard glasses clink and a cork squeak. She swung her legs off the bed and warily climbed to her feet. She was in a hotel.

"What's with the accommodation?" she asked, entering the living room.

"Shell game." He poured two glasses of scotch. "Nikolay owns three hotels in Moscow and I stay in them, moving every few weeks. He doesn't own this one, though."

"Are we here because of me?"

He shrugged and handed her a glass.

"He's pissed off at you too, isn't he?"

"Shut up and drink your supper." Murphy walked outside to the balcony.

He never smokes inside. He knows I hate it.

He leaned against the balcony railing, watching the rain clouds pour in and swallow the city. She walked out slowly and stood beside him. He offered her a cigarette and she took it, dragging deeply as he lit it for her. They stood there silently, watching the lights burn in Moscow, and she heard a siren cry out from deep in the labyrinth.

Elliot waited until half an inch of ash hung from the end of her cigarette and gulped down her drink. "You're upset," she said.

Murphy looked down at the street and sipped from his glass.

Her voice was cold: "You know, if you want me to leave—"

"I do," he said, flicking away his cigarette. "I'll even drive you to the airport." He gripped the balcony rail, his knuckles white.

"Still playing the cold soldier, huh? You can't pretend that you don't care. You can't fool me."

"You fooled me with that blue uniform."

"I'm *not* a real cop," she said. "I was only trying to..." She groaned and reached for her forehead.

"At the hotel—"

"I was being chased and people were trying to kill me and then you came and you kissed me and I was angry about Darren and I hadn't seen you for so long."

"Stop babbling, Slim." He clenched his jaw. "You're lying to me."

And he always knew when I was lying.

"You thought I was there to kill you," he said.

"No!" she sighed. "Maybe. Briefly, for a second—less than a second."

"And now you're here because you stole some paintings and need me to bail you out of trouble."

She choked. "Is that what you think?"

"Are you going to prove me wrong?"

"What about you?" she said, plucking two photographs from her pocket. "Do you expect me to believe you flew across the world just to give me these?"

"You picked my pocket?" His face turned red, the veins bulging in his neck.

"You promised you would never think of me as just a thief."

"But I'm just a killer to you, right?" He snatched the photographs and jammed them into his pocket. "Is that how this works?"

Elliot shook her head.

"It's just like you," he said. "Any excuse to push people away."

"I am not—"

"I got too close so you forced me into making a promise you knew I couldn't keep. If Darren lived, fine. If not, you had your way out, another excuse not to trust people."

Rain started to patter on the roof and the lights of the city shimmered through the sleet. She ran her hand through her hair. "Don't do this, okay? Not now."

"You didn't even have the guts to come and find out what happened."

"And you didn't have the stones to come and tell me yourself!" she screamed. "You hid in your fucking cell."

"*You* ran away," he yelled. "*I* was locked up."

"What about the seven years after that?" she cried. "You just traded me away. Just admit that you wanted to forget about me, to forget we even met."

He heaved his scotch glass at the building across the street. It shattered against the concrete and the glass tinkled to the pavement. He reached for the balcony rail and hunched over it. "I was trying to protect you," he said, and his shoulders sagged.

Elliot looked away, her eyes stinging. She ran her hand down her face. "I'm sorry, I..." She shook her head.

The rain was heavy now, a barrage of water that pounded the city.

"C'mon, Stephen," she pleaded softly. "We're like two cage fighters circling each other in the ring."

"I know."

"I don't want to fight with you. I never did."

"But you're not ready to drop your guard either."

Elliot peered down at her cigarette and saw that it had burned down to the filter. She flicked it off the balcony and watched it tumble into the darkness. "This has nothing to do with stolen art," she said. "Nothing at all."

Murphy nodded slowly. "And I didn't fly across the world to kill you."

The rain grew heavier, a white noise that threatened to drown out their voices. He looked at her and her chest ached. She was breathing heavily, her mouth dry, and she placed her hand on his. "What are you afraid of?"

"It's funny," he said. "I was going to ask you the same question."

Elliot held her breath, her fingernails running along his bare arm. Murphy turned to face her. He held his hand out, his palm up, and she traced lazy circles on his skin. He cupped her cheek and she tilted her head, her eyes closed. He folded his fingers, pushing her hair away from her eyes.

Elliot stood on her toes, folded her arms around his neck, and kissed him softly on the lips. His breath trembled as she fumbled with the buttons of his shirt. She kissed him again, hungrily, pulling the shirt from his shoulders and throwing it away. He tore her shirt off over her head.

They stumbled inside, rolling across the walls and staggering into the furniture. A lamp toppled over. A glass crashed on the tabletop. She ripped his belt from his trousers and he threw her on to the bed. He yanked on her waistband and she wriggled out of her jeans.

Murphy fell on top of her and she immediately threw him on to his back, her hair tumbling down on to his bare chest, her lips quivering as she kissed him. She pulled his trousers off, straddling him as he sat up. He wrapped his arms around her waist and pulled her close.

Elliot exposed her neck as he sank his teeth into her skin, her body writhing above his. She sank her fingernails into his back and moaned.

Murphy stopped, seizing her hands and staring at her.

"Too soon?" she asked.

"No," he said, gesturing towards the door. "Do you hear that?"

***

Armed men crashed through the door and ran into the bedroom, fanning out and covering them with assault rifles. There were twelve of them. Murphy looked up at Elliot.

"Didn't you think to put out the 'Do Not Disturb' sign?" she asked, climbing off the bed.

"I was busy carrying your big unconscious head through the door," he replied, standing up.

"Why is it men can only do one thing at a time?" Elliot grumbled.

The men formed a semicircle around the bed. Maxim marched through the doorway popping his knuckles, his bald head shining brightly.

"Can you come back later?" Murphy asked. "We're in the middle of something."

"Check their clothes," Maxim commanded. One *boyevik* slung his weapon and collected Murphy's clothes, retrieving a pistol and a full magazine before dumping the clothes on the floor. He tossed the weapon across the room and turned to Elliot, a grin spreading across his face.

"She doesn't like to be touched," Murphy warned him. "That includes her clothes."

The *boyevik* hesitated, looking to Maxim.

"I'll take care of it," Maxim said, waving the *boyevik* away. He snatched Elliot's clothes from the floor and scrunched them in his hands. Satisfied, he tossed them on to the bed. He studied Elliot approvingly, head to toe. "Mmm-hmm," he hummed.

Maxim circled behind Elliot and scooped up some of her hair, inhaling her scent. She squirmed and balled her hand into a fist but stopped moving when Maxim pushed his pistol into the small of her back.

"That feels even smaller than I expected," she hissed.

He smirked at Murphy. "So this is the woman you would throw away your life for?"

Murphy's jaw tensed as Maxim slowly ran his fingertip down the length of her arm. Elliot gritted her teeth and squeezed her eyes shut.

"Personally, I prefer the money, the status, and the respect." Maxim twirled Elliot's hair around his finger and walked around her, looking her up and down again. "But, I suppose nothing beats waking up to a surprise blowjob in the morning."

Elliot glared at Maxim. "You should sleep with your mouth closed."

Maxim whipped his pistol through the air but Murphy caught his wrist.

"Touch her again and I'll kill you," Murphy said, pushing Maxim away. The butt of a rifle struck Murphy in the back and he grunted, falling to his knees.

Maxim crouched down in front of him. "I'm going to enjoy playing with her, Stepan." He grinned. "I'm going to make you watch."

"You're going to beg me to let you live," Murphy said as Elliot helped him to his feet.

"Am I?" Maxim held his pistol against Elliot's temple. "I think you will be the one doing the begging."

Elliot blinked and raised her hands again. Murphy was unsteady but she saw him step closer, the veins bulging in his neck. She heard the nervous shuffle of feet as the *boyeviks* adjusted their hands on their weapons. Sweat beaded on their foreheads and tongues darted out to lick dry lips.

"You have a job to do, Stepan," Maxim said, "a role to play. Nikolay will keep her alive as long as you remember that."

"I promise you," Murphy said calmly. "I'm going to tear your fucking head off."

"Get dressed. You have an appointment to keep." Maxim tossed Elliot aside and glared into Murphy's shimmering eyes. "You're just a man, Stepan." He punched Murphy in the stomach. Murphy doubled over, groaning. "I'm not afraid of you."

Murphy breathed deeply and straightened up. "Then why didn't you come alone?"

45

MOSCOW, RUSSIA

SUNDAY 18 SEPTEMBER

12:19AM MSK

Murphy and Elliot sat beside each other in the back of a limousine, their hands cuffed behind them. Maxim was in the seat opposite, staring through the window, two of Korolev's bodyguards huddled beside him. Murphy slouched in the leather seat and glanced at Elliot. She was staring through the window too, doing her best to ignore him.

No, that's not it. She's trying to look innocent.

She's picking her cuffs.

"I heard about Angela," Murphy said. "I read about it in the paper a few years ago. I'm sorry."

"So am I," Elliot whispered.

"I heard she was murdered. Did you hunt the guy down?"

She shook her head. "It's complicated."

"Angela," he muttered, turning away. He looked back suddenly, his eyes focused. "Didn't she always order that disgusting drink everywhere we went?"

Elliot cocked her head.

"You know," Murphy said in frustration. "The one with icecream. It was always green." His face wrinkled. "Spiders. Always lime."

"I can't believe you remember that," she said.

"It's amazing what you remember, sometimes," he said, glancing towards Maxim. The Russian was pawing at his computer tablet, his eyes focused on the screen.

"Remember how you used to race home so you could see me before Darren arrived?" Elliot asked.

"We're still talking about spiders, aren't we?"

"Their venom can kill a cow four times over, you said. I looked it up."

"It's not right, is it?"

"Nope, I couldn't find it anywhere."

He groaned.

"You were right about one thing, though." He heard her cuffs click as they opened. "I can't leave you to fight alone."

Murphy took a deep breath and tried to look at something other than her green eyes.

"I'm here as Simone, Stephen. No tricks, no lies." She rattled her cuffs behind her back, her eyes earnest. "I promise."

He finally looked her in the eye. "Are you sure about this, Slim?" he asked softly. "I mean, we'll probably just end up killing each other."

"Better than them doing it," she said, nodding towards Maxim. She winked and turned her back towards Murphy, dropping her handcuff keys into his cupped hands.

Murphy eyed Maxim. He was stabbing at the screen of his tablet, his chin resting on his hand, his shoulders hunched. The bodyguards were studying their hands, occasionally scrutinising their captives. Murphy felt his handcuffs click open and held the key in his fist.

"You know what else I remember?" he asked, turning back to Elliot. "China plates and James Blunt."

"I remember that," she said.

"Good, because we're in a bit of froth," he said, testing her out.

Froth and bubble: trouble.

Elliot took a moment to translate. "You have a Jackie?" she asked.

Jackie Chan: plan.

"What the hell are you two talking about?" Maxim asked, looking up from his tablet.

"Well, I know your Germans are still up for dipping," Murphy said.

German bands were hands. Dipping was pick-pocketing.

"You can't conspire your way out of this," Maxim snarled. "This nonsense won't save you."

Murphy ignored him and nodded towards a bodyguard. "In the sky of his billy, he has a bucket."

The guard had something in the sky rocket—pocket—of his billy goat: coat.

"Bucket?" Elliot asked, confused.

"The club is locked down, Stepan," Maxim cried. "You'll be shot on sight if you try to escape."

"Bucket and spade," Murphy said.

Elliot paused for a moment, her eyes growing wide when she realised what he meant.

"I'm ordering you to shut your mouth!" Maxim's face glowed red.

"You're going to need a hot cross," Elliot said. "Or we're brown bread."

"Shut up, right now," Maxim hissed, "or I'll have you both gagged."

Elliot was right, Murphy thought. A hot cross bun was a gun and they were dead without one.

The limousine pulled off the street and came to a stop. Murphy and Elliot hobbled out, led by one of the bodyguards. The other guard fell into line behind them, while four other men emerged from the alleyway with assault rifles in their hands.

The street outside the King's Castle was different tonight. Luxury sedans still lined the kerb but every man on the avenue was holding a gun. There were no girls, no drug pushers, and no lost tourists, although the smugglers still had a truck parked in the alleyway, Murphy noticed. Three men were arguing in the dim glow of the truck's parking lights. A bodyguard spurred Murphy forward and he turned away from the alley.

Elliot and Murphy kept their hands behind their backs, cuffs loose around their wrists and hidden by the sleeves of their coats. They hunched into the rain and were hustled up the stairs of the nightclub, the lead bodyguard holding the door open.

Murphy tripped and stumbled into Elliot. She reached out with her hands as she fell, staggering into the chest of the first bodyguard.

"Your cuffs," he said slowly. She kneed him in the groin and he collapsed on the floor.

Murphy whipped his handcuffs into the face of the bodyguard behind him, and snatched the pistol from the man's waistband. He fired twice and the man staggered backwards into the armed entourage. Murphy slammed the door and locked it before turning and grabbing Elliot. They dived over to the other side of the stage, the door shattering behind them under a barrage of automatic fire. Armed men flooded the room and poured rounds at the stage.

The men watching the show pulled their weapons, believing they were being attacked, and the nightclub erupted into a gunfight. The strippers shrieked and retreated behind the curtains while men tipped over tables for cover.

"Do you have it?" Murphy shouted over the noise, crouching against the stage.

Elliot held out her hand and he saw the concussion grenade. "And you can stick it up your Khyber," she yelled.

He opened the door under the stage and reached inside, pulling out a large bucket.

"What's that?" Elliot asked.

"Glitter for the girls." He checked the pistol and fired three rounds at the window in front of them. The bullets thudded into the glass. A spider web of fissures cracked across the surface.

"Is that supposed to happen?" Elliot shouted.

"Do you trust me?" he asked.

"Can I think about it?"

He pulled the pin, tossing the grenade into the glitter and heaving the bucket at the ceiling.

"Get down!" somebody shouted. There was a loud boom before the nightclub was showered in a thick rain of sparkling paper.

Murphy grabbed Elliot and they ran. He leapt backwards through the window, clutching her to his chest. Elliot gasped, the cold air swallowing them as they fell. They landed with a crash, shattering glass and setting off a car alarm. Murphy groaned, turning his head, and saw they had landed on the roof of a BMW sedan.

"They moved the truck," Murphy breathed, lying flat on his back.

"Get up!" Elliot ordered, rolling off his chest and grabbing his pistol. She fired four rounds at the window before surveying the street at the end of the alley. Nobody was coming for them yet.

Murphy seized her hand and tumbled off the crumpled car.

"Are you okay?" she asked.

He nodded. "Let's go." And they disappeared into the dark alleys of the city.

***

Nikolay Korolev stood in the rubble of his club, the music pounding through his feet. Fluorescent lights flickered and swung from the ceiling. He could hear whimpering from backstage and saw one of the girls clutching her wounded leg. Lucky, he thought. Everyone else was dead. The light from the disco ball reflected off the pools of blood and alcohol that matted the carpet, while bullet-casings, glitter, and glass sparkled throughout the room.

"Turn off the music," Korolev ordered with a wave of his hand.

A *boyevik* obeyed and the pounding stopped. The girl's whimpering got louder.

Korolev whipped his pistol from his jacket and fired. The dancer clutched her chest and fell. "Now you have something to cry about," he said, putting his pistol away.

Maxim entered the club, slinging his rifle, and shook his head: "Gone."

Korolev grunted and turned on his heels, marching towards the VIP room. Maxim caught up with him at the door to his office.

"You have to cut your losses, Nikolay," Maxim insisted.

Korolev went straight to the bar in his office and poured a double vodka. He gulped it down and wiped his chin with the back of his hand.

"He'll destroy everything," Maxim said. "You have to let me end him."

"I need him alive!" Korolev roared.

"They're not like us, Nikolay," Maxim said. "These two don't want money or power. They want their freedom. They want their lives back. As long as they feel our breath on their necks, they will do all they can to kill us."

Korolev took a deep breath, tossing his glass on the counter and running his hand through his hair. He retrieved the coin from his pocket.

"You need to stop thinking like a criminal," Maxim said. "You should be thinking like a king. You'll have an army at your disposal. You don't need him."

Korolev snorted and smiled, rolling his coin across his hand.

Like a king.

He looked towards his television and frowned. He turned up the volume and stepped back.

"...reports that the bomber was known as the Bear, and was an associate of Russian organised crime figure Nikolay Korolev."

A photograph appeared on the screen and Korolev held the coin in his fist.

"The Bear took his own life and those of eighteen police officers on Friday, but new information released today reveals that the Bear was planning to attack Australia's energy infrastructure. The Prime Minister of Australia has announced that negotiations are due to commence with Russian President Valentina

Nevzorova on Sunday night, and that Australia will seek to establish a combined law-enforcement task force to crack down on the criminal threat."

Korolev muted the television.

"How do they know we did this?" Maxim cried. "The Bear was to destroy everything if captured. This." He pointed to the television. "This could ruin—"

"Shut up, Maxim!" Korolev growled. "It doesn't matter."

"But Nikolay—"

"I said shut up," Korolev said, slicing the air with his hand. "It just means we have to move our schedule forward."

Maxim opened his mouth to speak but stopped, holding his hands behind his back.

Korolev paced back and forth furiously, the coin a blur as it tumbled across his hand. He glanced at the television each time he passed by, his forehead deeply lined, his cheek twitching. He stopped pacing, glaring at the television, his coin rolling back and forth over and over again. It suddenly fell off his hand and he cried out in frustration, drawing his pistol and firing repeatedly at the television.

Maxim held his hands over his ears. The pistol clicked empty and Maxim gazed at the smoking television, the screen now a cavernous hole with jagged edges.

He lowered his hands, watching Korolev holster his pistol.

"You get your wish, Maxim," Korolev said bitterly, rubbing the scar on his jaw. He glared at his subordinate. "Don't take all day."

"Yes, Nikolay. I know where they'll go." Maxim bared his teeth. "He'll be dead in a matter of hours."

46

MOSCOW, RUSSIA

SUNDAY 18 SEPTEMBER

1:08AM MSK

"Stop being a baby," Elliot scowled.

"I'm not," Murphy said defensively. "Just give me a second." He emptied his pockets, handing everything to Elliot. A passport, cash, a phone, and a media player.

"What's this?" Elliot said, holding up the media player. "Is this yours?"

"Yeah." He paused. "The porn on it isn't, though."

She arched an eyebrow. "Uh-huh."

"I bugged Maxim to find out what Nikolay was up to," he explained, watching her place his belongings on the bedside table. "The audio is on the player."

"Do you want to keep it?" she asked, squirting hand sanitiser into her palm.

"I'm not sure if there's much point."

"You're right," she said, scrubbing her hands. "You can stream porn pretty easily these days." She reached up and yanked off his coat.

He yelped. "Careful."

"Oh, shush."

"Getting a little passive-aggressive, there."

"Shut up." The coat was torn and his shirt was soaked in blood. "On the bed, now," Elliot said sternly, pointing with her finger.

Murphy sighed and fell on the bed, lying on his stomach.

Elliot straddled him, ripping his shirt from his body and tossing it away. His coat had taken the brunt of the impact but his back was still cut to shreds, the skin purple, bruised, and tender. She puffed her hair out of her eyes and reached for the washcloth, wringing it out in the bowl and dabbing at his wounds.

"Ah!" He cringed.

"I've barely touched you." She squinted, pulling the lamp closer. The bulb was dim but it was better than nothing. "Your friend needs a new interior decorator."

"Grigoriy just vacated the property so I don't think he cares anymore." He paused. "You don't like his digs?"

She rinsed out the washcloth and continued soaking up the blood on Murphy's back. "Bomb-shelter chic?"

"It does have a zombie-apocalypse ambience, doesn't it?"

Elliot tossed the washcloth into the bowl, reaching for a bottle of disinfectant and a gauze pad.

"I thought you might like it," Murphy said. "A hole in the earth you can hide in, away from everybody else. Ow, shit!" He turned his head and saw Elliot holding the bottle of disinfectant in her hand. The cap was off.

"Oops," she said drily.

He muttered a curse and dropped his head on the bed. "You haven't changed."

"You know, you don't know me as well as you think you do," she pointed out, using the gauze to clean his cuts.

"Tell me about Angela," Murphy said.

Her breath froze in her chest. Elliot's mouth fell open but no words would come out.

"It's complicated, right?" Murphy peered over the edge of the bed and started tracing circles on the carpet with his finger. "You would've hunted the murderer down, killed him, and then kicked down the doors of Hell to kill him again. You'd probably tell the Devil to call you when the guy got up again."

Elliot sniffed and wiped her cheek with the back of her bloodied hand. "It *is* complicated." Her voice trembled. She couldn't hide it.

He cleared his throat. "How bad is it back there?" he asked softly, attempting to change the subject.

"You're going to need stitches," she murmured, tossing the gauze away. Elliot tore some sutures out of a packet and rummaged through Grigoriy's abandoned first-aid kit, eventually finding a needle holder. She huddled under the lamp, trying to grip the suture needle with the needle holder. Her hand was shaking. She tried again, but slipped. "Fuck!" She swiped at the bottle of disinfectant and it smashed against the cement wall.

Murphy rolled over. Elliot was pacing the room erratically with her hands on her hips. He sat up and swung his legs off the bed.

She stopped pacing. "How do you do that?" she cried. "I can convince everyone that I'm anyone, but not you, never you." She turned a tight circle.

"Simone, we don't have to—"

"I killed her," she declared.

Murphy's shoulders fell and he slouched forward, his elbows on his knees, his face in his hands.

"I'm still wanted for her murder."

He looked up at her and she set her eyes on the ceiling, tears rolling down her cheeks.

"It's a—" Elliot held her palm to her forehead. "She suffered from chronic pain after she was in an accident." She turned to face him but couldn't bear to look into his eyes. "She started on basic painkillers, moved on to morphine, and then she found heroin." Elliot flopped on to a chair next to the bed. "Her family kicked her out, she lost her job, her husband, everything."

He clasped his hands in front of him.

"I came back from a job overseas and found her homeless. I set her up, bought her a place, and got her cleaned up. She had good days and bad days but we started to get through it." She absently wiped her hands on her jeans, leaving smears of blood on her thighs. "She tried to make amends with her adoptive family but her dad didn't want to know her anymore. He said he was ashamed of her. She took it hard."

Murphy stared at the floor.

"I didn't know she had a stash in the toilet cistern," she whispered.

He closed his eyes.

"I, uh." Elliot cleared her throat. "I found her naked in the tub, a needle hanging out of her arm. I tried to wake her up. I tried naloxone, I tried to resuscitate her, I tried everything, but she was dead. I didn't want anyone else to see her like that, so I dried her and dressed her, wiped the house and took the body to an empty paddock and cremated her." She finally looked at him. "I sprinkled her ashes in the sea."

Murphy rubbed the back of his neck.

"I found her dealer and lost it. I beat him to death with a bar stool and got knocked out in a brawl with his friends. The cops picked me up and tried to book me for Angela's murder but I broke out." She stared at her blood-stained hands. "I'm still wanted for that too."

"Simone, you didn't—"

"No!" she cried, rising to her feet. "Don't say it. Not you. Don't say it." She started pacing again, turning tight circles. "Don't you see? If Darren's death wasn't your fault, then maybe Angela..." She cleared her throat again. "But if it *was* your fault." She shook her head. "I've been trying to find you just to ask you."

He stood up, his hand raised. "Wait a minute. You stole art from Nikolay hoping that he'd send me to kill you just so you could..."

"And then I had to go into hiding," Elliot said. "Being a cop gave me a chance to shake down some of the Russians." She sniffed. "That's when I found out about your girls and arranged a posting near Natalie."

"And then you found me." He hesitated. "I don't remember you asking me anything."

She shrugged.

"But you already knew the answer."

She stopped pacing and folded her arms, staring at the floor and nodding. "I already knew the answer," she whispered. "Earlier, you asked me what I was afraid of. I was afraid that I was right, that Darren's death was your fault." She looked up. "What were you afraid of?"

"That you would never believe me," he said sadly. "I found it easier to think you blamed me." He shook his head. "But I always hoped you didn't. If I didn't see you, I wouldn't know if it was true."

She glanced into his grey eyes, chewing the inside of her cheek. "Is that why you made your deal with Nikolay?"

Murphy looked away. "Look, you have to understand that you were always the strong one, Simone, stronger than me. You always did what you wanted. It was one of the best parts of you but I knew you were still the porcelain doll too. You were still so easy to break and I did that. I gave you a reason to leave."

"No."

"When Darren died—"

"No!" she yelled. "He'd still be dead, even if we'd never met."

"But we *did* meet," he said. "I only gave you up because I believed..." He cleared his throat. "I missed you, but I couldn't make myself believe that you missed me too. At least I could tell myself that you were safe." He finally found the courage to raise his head and look at her.

"Like I said, you don't know me as well as you think," Elliot said, a smile flickering across her face.

Murphy smiled weakly. "I guess you're right."

"And now." She scuffed her shoe on the carpet. "Look, I don't know if you're thinking about running away, or about fighting them." She ran her hand through her hair. "I just want to say that I'm not leaving this time, like I left her, like I left you in that cell."

"You can't stay here because you feel guilty." Murphy stood in front of her. "Or because of some strange obligation you've conjured from the past."

"That's not what this is," she said. "All I've been able to think about since Monday night is the way it was before." She held out her hands, showing her palms. "Before all the guilt, all the second-guessing, all the doubt, and everything else."

"We can't get that back." He scratched his stubbled jaw. "And if we fight, if we're lucky enough to win, there is *nothing* stopping you from running away again, and I wouldn't blame you if you did. You're only staying in this hole with me now because we need to stick together."

Elliot compressed her lips and grasped her necklace. "This isn't about absolution. This isn't about saving myself. I didn't come to Moscow just to run away again."

He frowned and stared into her green eyes. "So what the hell is it all about?"

She let her necklace fall back to her chest and stared at the floor. "Ask me," she breathed.

The words caught in his throat. "I *can't* ask you."

"Then tell me." She neared him, staring at her hand as she placed it on his chest. "Say it."

"I..." His lips touched her head, her hair tickling his nose, her scent summoning his blood, his skin burning.

"Say it," she whispered, feeling for his heartbeat under her hand.

He raised his hand and caressed her cheek. She closed her eyes, tilting her head into his hand to feel his touch.

"Please say it." She raised her mouth to his and he felt her breath on his skin.

He kissed her on the lips, softly, his hand cupping her cheek, her hands moving up his chest. Their mouths parted for a moment, his hands falling to the small of her back. He lifted her shirt, pulling it over her head, and she wrapped her arms around his neck. She pulled him closer, kissing him deeply, his hands searching her soft skin.

He cupped her breast in his hand, kneading her nipple between his fingers and she gasped, biting his lower lip. He tore open the buttons on her jeans and lifted her up, her legs entwined around his waist. They fell on to the bed and she pushed him on to his back. He groaned in pain and she shushed him with her finger, her fingernails searching his scarred chest, wandering lower until she found his belt. She unbuckled it and unbuttoned his trousers. He sat up, her hair tumbling over his arm.

She exhaled. "Say it."

He wrapped his arms around her. "Stay."

"Okay." She held his face in her hands and kissed him. "I will."

***

Maxim moved quickly and quietly, his knees slightly bent, his assault rifle raised. The six *boyeviks* trailing behind him barely rustled the trees as they neared the tunnel that led to Grigoriy's shelter.

They reached the tunnel's entrance and Maxim crouched, placing his weapon on the ground and shrugging off his backpack. He took a computer tablet out of the bag and fixed a radio headset over his ears.

The *boyeviks* around him strapped night-vision goggles to their heads. Maxim extended two fingers and pointed to his eyes before pointing into the tunnel.

The men stood up, the first pair entering the tunnel and lowering their NVGs. The other men followed.

Maxim studied the screen. Everything the men saw was transmitted to his tablet and he watched as the *boyeviks* leapfrogged through the tunnel, each pair covered by the others as they advanced. They reached Grigoriy's shelter quickly and crouched outside.

Maxim placed the tablet on the ground and turned up the volume of his radio, holding his hands over the earpieces. There were noises, loud ones. A woman's moans of pleasure, and there was a man, too.

Again? Perfect.

He smiled to himself, watching his men slowly enter the bedroom. Maxim's cheek twitched, a bed materialising on his screen.

His breath froze in his chest.

The bed was empty.

The radio crackled. "Negative contact," a *boyevik* said.

Maxim squinted at the live pictures and stroked his bald head. "What's all the noise?"

"There's a media player," the *boyevik* reported. "It's on the bed." A ghostly hand extended a finger on the screen. "It's playing a porn movie."

Maxim could just make out the small screen on his tablet.

"Whoa, wait," the radio hissed.

"What's that?" another *boyevik* chimed in.

"I stood on something."

The image blurred as the *boyevik* whirled around to investigate.

"It's nothing," the radio crackled. "It's just one of those foot switches for a floor lamp."

Maxim saw a man's boot on a switch and the *boyevik* lifted his foot.

"Stop!" Maxim shouted into the radio.

The earth shook beneath his feet and he lost his balance, toppling to the ground. The hill seemed to split open above him, the soil and rock caving in, a column of dust mushrooming into the sky. Smoke wafted out of the tunnel's entrance before the stone ceiling collapsed.

The woods fell silent and Maxim staggered to his feet, tearing off the headset and throwing his radio to the ground. He stomped it into the dust and kicked it away before clutching his knees and panting heavily.

His mobile phone vibrated in his pocket and he grabbed it, peering at the screen. His heart started pounding in his chest, his blood ice-cold.

It was Korolev.

He gazed up at the collapsed hill and shivered.

47

ST PETERSBURG, RUSSIA

SUNDAY 18 SEPTEMBER

11:08AM MSK

Grigoriy pushed the empty plates to the end of the table and stood up. He unzipped his backpack and checked its contents. His laptop was still there. Anna's new identity was also there, along with plane tickets to Sydney via London, departing Helsinki on Monday afternoon. There were also two loaded pistols, two grenades, and a dog-eared paperback that Anna had insisted on keeping. Grigoriy had compromised, telling her that he'd bring the book, but she had to leave her gym bag behind. Essentials only.

Grigoriy looked up to see Anna walking along the aisles of the service station's shop. She moved gracefully, her eyes bright, and ran her fingers along the shelves of chocolates, potato chips, tourist maps, propane bottles, and motor oil. She paused in front of a rack of hats and smiled through the corner of her mouth.

His brow furrowed.

Being in love shows a man how he ought to be.

Stephen Murphy had flown halfway across the world to see Simone Elliot because he had hope. He'd known it could mean his death, and he'd known that he could be left with nothing if she rejected him. And then she came for him and he fought back, and Grigoriy found himself hoping that they were both okay, that they were happy.

Happy.

Grigoriy grunted. He'd never thought of his boss happy before. Anna picked up a bright green trucker's cap and put it on, studying it in the mirror. Grigoriy's back straightened.

I'm not like Volkov—I'm like Murphy.

Grigoriy had killed two *boyeviks,* threatened the world's most dangerous killer with a pistol before punching him in the face, and had taken Anna—Volkov's girl, he remembered with a thin smile—from Korolev's hotel, driving her across the city to hide her.

I always was.

Anna was now wearing a hat with flaps. She looked at him, sticking her tongue out between her teeth and crossing her eyes. She laughed.

Grigoriy grinned but his smile faded. So did hers. He crossed the room but he didn't feel his feet touch the ground. Then he was in front of her. He cupped her cheek in his hand, lifted her chin, and kissed her lips.

She kissed him back, her hands climbing his chest until her arms were around his neck, and he placed his hand on the small of her back. He pulled away, breathless, and her lips quivered, her eyes opening slowly.

"Come to Australia with me," she whispered.

"Okay," he said. "But only if you let me buy you that hat."

"Deal." She smiled again and Grigoriy laughed.

He wrapped his arms around her and held her close, his chin resting on her shoulder. He peered through the window at his motorcycle. A BMW was coasting past and eased to a stop next to it.

"Anna," Grigoriy said, unable to keep the stress out of his voice.

"What is it?" Anna pulled away and turned her head. A *boyevik* had climbed out of the BMW and was examining the motorcycle. "How did they know we were here?" she asked.

"They didn't, otherwise there would be more." Grigoriy dragged her back to the table and grabbed the backpack, thrusting it into her hand. "Take this. Go through the back entrance."

"No, Grigoriy," she cried. "Please, I can't."

He held her face in his hands. "Thirty feet away through the back door is a gully that goes all the way around the service station. That's your first stop. It's another thirty feet to the woods. Hide in the trees, circle back to the highway. I'll be right behind you."

She shook her head, her eyes welling with tears. "No, please."

Grigoriy looked over his shoulder. There were four men examining his bike and a Mercedes had driven into the service station, stopping next to a fuel bowser. Four more *boyeviks* were inside. "You have to, Anna." He reached into the backpack and took out the pistols and a grenade. He tucked a pistol into the back of her jeans and gave her the grenade. "Please."

She wiped her cheeks and nodded, turning away and running towards the rear of the building.

Grigoriy shoved his pistol into the pocket of his coat and walked along one of the aisles, scooping up an armful of propane tanks and carrying them to a counter where two microwaves sat side by side. He glanced towards the attendant, but the man was busy with a customer. Grigoriy put his back to him and placed a full propane tank in one of the microwaves, sitting five more on the counter and popping the top off each can. Gas started hissing out of the cans and the air shimmered around him. Grigoriy held his breath and smashed the second microwave's window before tossing a set of keys inside. He turned his head.

The *boyeviks* from the Mercedes were walking towards the shop. The four *boyeviks* from the BMW were circling around the building to cover the rear.

Grigoriy set the timer on the microwave and took a deep breath.

***

Anna took off her hoodie and pulled the pin on the grenade, holding the lever tight. She bundled the hoodie around the grenade and hung the backpack over her shoulder, pushing through the door. She walked quickly, her eyes fixed on the grassy gully ahead and the trees beyond. She heard gunshots behind her.

"Hey, you!" a man yelled.

She dropped the bundle and ran the last twenty feet. Footsteps pounded behind her but they stopped suddenly, and she knew they were about to shoot. She dived to the ground, rolling into the gully.

There was a loud explosion and she stared at the grass in confusion. She raised her head, peeking over the edge of the gully, and saw three men dead on the ground, her hoodie in tatters. Behind them, the service station was on fire. Grigoriy fell through the back door and ejected an empty magazine from his pistol. He rolled to his feet and ran towards her, his empty pistol in his hand.

"Look out!" he warned.

Anna turned around. A *boyevik* had crawled along the length of the gully and leapt on her. She raised her knee into his groin and he groaned, collapsing on top of her. Grabbing fistfuls of earth, she dragged herself out from under him, but he grasped the cuff of her jeans. She lashed out with her foot, kicking him in the nose, and he let go.

Anna tried to draw her pistol but it was caught in her jeans. The *boyevik* climbed to his feet and raised his weapon. She closed her eyes.

There was a shot but she didn't feel anything. She opened her eyes. Grigoriy collapsed to his knees in front of her.

"No!" Anna cried, her pistol finally coming free. She raised it and fired instinctively, shooting the *boyevik* between the eyes. He crumpled, collapsing on the grass.

"No, no, no." Anna crawled towards Grigoriy, helping him sit up in the gully. He'd been shot in the chest and she held his hand on the wound. "It's not so bad, Grigoriy. It'll be okay. We'll go to the hospital."

He blinked slowly, studying her earnestly. "Why? Are you hurt?"

She shook her head. "I'm fine. I'm okay."

"Good, because we have to go to Australia."

Her eyes were stinging and the world blurred. She gritted her teeth, pushing down harder on the wound.

Blood was everywhere, his eyes dull, his skin grey. "You can't do this, you have to come too."

Grigoriy blinked again and gazed at her with his pale eyes. "You've got something..." He reached out for her face and wiped away a tear, leaving a streak of blood on her cheek. "It's gone now," he whispered.

She sobbed, grabbing his other hand. "Grigoriy, I—" His hand felt heavy. "Grigoriy!" she shouted, but he didn't answer. Anna sat back on her heels and sirens wailed in the distance. The tree line was only thirty feet away. She sniffed and leaned forward, touching Grigoriy's cheek and kissing him softly on the lips. "Bye, Grigoriy."

48

MOSCOW, RUSSIA

SUNDAY 18 SEPTEMBER

4:52PM MSK

Maxim paused at the door to Korolev's private study, his shoulders stooped. He closed his eyes and took a deep breath, straightening his back and puffing out his chest. He knocked on the door.

"Come in," a gruff voice said.

Maxim wiped the sweat from his forehead with the back of his hand and slowly opened the door.

Nikolay Korolev's study was the untidiest room in his house. It was lit by a solitary lamp and an oily window that lured only the coldest rays of sunlight, though the blinds were always closed. An old wooden bookcase stretched across the rear wall, its creaking shelves struggling to carry dusty volumes and stacks of typewritten pages. The towering shelves cast a long shadow over a wide desk that was strewn with maps and newspapers, torn envelopes and bulging brown-paper parcels. The desk was the largest island on a sea of green carpet that was stained with coffee and scorched by cigar ash. There were no power cords, extension leads, routers, or laptops. The most advanced technology in the room was the electric pencil sharpener on the windowsill and the transistor radio that hissed beside it.

Korolev's most treasured possession was the chess set on the scarred coffee table in front of a sagging sofa that squatted against the wall.

Maxim entered cautiously. The room was dark, the sunlight banished and repelled by the heavy blinds, and it took a moment for Maxim's eyes to focus. A match was struck, the flame casting severe shadows across Korolev's face as he lit a cigar.

Korolev shook his hand and the flame went out. He puffed on his cigar and slouched on the edge of the sofa, staring at his darkened chess board, his hand hovering over the wooden battlefield.

"You've been ignoring my calls, Maxim," he said, without looking up.

Maxim swallowed, his mouth dry. There was a shoebox on the sofa cushion next to Korolev. It was full of photographs. Maxim knew there were many more shoeboxes just like it, all of them filled with photographs of Valentina Nevzorova.

But there was one photograph that wasn't kept in a box.

His second most treasured possession.

Maxim had seen it once, under the mounds of papers on Korolev's desk, hidden but close to hand. Now the photograph was on Korolev's lap.

“I wasn’t in a position to answer my phone,” Maxim croaked. “I’ve been tracking Stepan.”

Korolev dragged on his cigar and rolled his coin across his hand. “Tracking?” A cloud of blue smoke rose to the ceiling. “I thought you knew where he was.”

Valentina Nevzorova looked young in the framed photograph, Maxim remembered. She was wearing a light summer dress and she was standing on the beach in Marseilles. And then there was her smile. Maxim didn’t know the circumstances but he suspected that the photograph was special. It was perhaps the only photograph she had given to Korolev, whereas he had taken all the others for himself.

“I heard that we got Grigoriy,” Maxim said, shifting on his feet.

“That’s not all that happened today.” Korolev placed his cigar on the edge of an ashtray. “Valentina had some of our men arrested. They were conducting surveillance in preparation for the Tverskaya Street bombing.”

“But we know people who can sign off their release,” Maxim pointed out.

“Valentina.” Korolev paused, holding his coin in the tips of his fingers. “The president has already stepped in. The men were all executed.” He held his hand over the chess board, his finger touching the queen’s crown. “It was made to look like they died during the arrest.”

Maxim wiped his palms on his trousers. "Nikolay, we have to change our plans. It's too risky to move now."

Korolev set his jaw and turned his head. "Tell me," he demanded.

"I tried," Maxim squeaked, a bead of sweat trickling down the side of his face.

Korolev cried out, flipping over his coffee table. It cartwheeled into the wall and the chess set scattered across the floor. He stared at the wreckage on his carpet, his chest heaving. "Where is he?"

"I've been searching all day," Maxim stammered. "Grigoriy is dead so he can't meet up with him and..." He didn't know what else to say.

Korolev started to pace the floor, the coin rolling back and forth across his hand.

"We can't move while he's still out there," Maxim said with a quivering voice.

Korolev seized his coin in his fist, his face hardening.

"It's just that the timing is—" Maxim yelped when Korolev grabbed a handful of his shirt and dragged him closer.

"She taught me two lessons, Maxim," Korolev growled. "Two."

"She?" Maxim's eyes widened.

"Lesson one, from her grandfather, is trust your friends the least."

Maxim panted. All he could smell was vodka and cigar smoke, and it made him dizzy.

"And lesson two, from Lasker the chess master," Korolev continued, speaking through his teeth, "is that the laws of chess do not permit a free choice." He released Maxim, pushing him to the ground. "You have to move whether you like it or not."

Maxim stared up at Korolev, his mouth open.

"Rally the men," Korolev ordered. "We move tonight."

Maxim jumped when the door slammed. It bounced open, the hinges creaking, and a sliver of light stretched across the carpet and over his hand. The chess board lay face down under his palm. There was an inscription engraved on the wooden surface and he traced the letters with his finger.

"To my princess: one day we will live in the palace of your dreams—Nikolay."

Someone had written underneath it.

"Men like you don't live like kings—they die like dogs."

It was signed with a woman's name. Maxim whispered the name aloud:

"Valentina."

49

MOSCOW, RUSSIA

SUNDAY 18 SEPTEMBER

4:56PM MSK

"What would you like?" She was a young Russian girl wearing a t-shirt and jeans, and her curly hair was tied in bunches.

"I'll have the salad," Elliot said.

Murphy eyed her suspiciously.

"And cram it into a hamburger with lots of bacon," Elliot added.

"You had me worried for a second," Murphy said.

"And a hot chocolate."

Murphy cast his eyes around the diner as the girl scrawled Elliot's order on her notepad. The room was half-empty, but it was still a little early for dinner, and Murphy found himself staring at a young couple entertaining their infant. The child was in a high chair, his chin smeared with baby food, watching as his mother hid behind a menu. She showed her face and said *"ku-ku".* The boy squealed with delight, slapping the high chair with his small hands, and she hid her face again.

"And you?" the girl asked, smiling at Murphy.

Murphy cleared his throat. "Sausage, bacon, eggs—"

"It's dinner time, you sicko," Elliot said, wrinkling her nose.

"Also toast, a bowl of fries, and a cup of coffee."

"Hungry, huh?" the girl said. "Anything else?"

"Yes, actually," Murphy said.

"Oh, no," Elliot said, her face crumbling. "Please, no. Don't do it."

The girl's face twisted in confusion.

"Mayonnaise," Murphy said. "Bring the bottle."

"You're disgusting," Elliot said. "Haven't you outgrown this habit?"

"Don't listen to her," Murphy said to the girl. "She has no taste buds."

The girl grabbed their menus and returned to the counter.

"I almost forgot how revolting you can be," Elliot said.

"I blame your cooking," Murphy said, placing his phone on the table. "How do you burn lettuce, anyway?"

She crossed her arms. "Bacteria thrive on foods that contain protein. And, in case you don't know, mayonnaise contains eggs which are—"

"How stupid do you think I am?" he asked with arms outstretched.

"Is this where I grade you between one and ten?"

"It was a rhetorical question."

"You did jump backwards through a window and land on a car, so that will cost you some points."

"Don't you know what a rhetorical question is?"

"I don't think I could put a number on it, anyway," Elliot continued, tapping her finger against her chin. "If I had to, I'd compare you to a gorilla that can play tunes on the glockenspiel."

Murphy wrinkled his forehead. "Glockenspiel?"

"It's cute and pretty clever, but you're still a gorilla."

"Here you go," the young waitress said, placing a cup of coffee and a mug of hot chocolate on the table. "Your food will be ready in a few minutes."

Murphy's mobile phone started to flash, rumbling in a circle on the table.

"You should get that." Elliot stirred her hot chocolate with her finger. "It'll give you time to think of a comeback."

He shook his head and answered his phone. "Anna? Where are you? You can't be in Helsinki already."

Elliot raised her mug to her lips, blowing on her drink to cool it.

Murphy felt the veins bulging in his neck. "It wasn't your fault, Anna," he said calmly. "You get on the first plane you find and get out of there. Destroy that phone, okay?"

Elliot lowered her mug, her face lined with concern.

"No, it's not your fault. I need you to understand that."

Elliot looked down at the table and scratched the veneer surface with her fingernail.

"Okay. Be safe." Murphy ended the call and immediately stood up. He leaned against an empty table, breathing deeply, his palms flat and his head down. He roared, flipping the table and sending it tumbling into a jukebox. Pictures fell off the wall, smashing on the tiles.

"Stephen!" Elliot climbed to her feet and neared him cautiously.

"I'm going to rip Nikolay's spine out through his fucking mouth," he seethed, drawing his pistol.

"Stephen, calm down," Elliot soothed.

"When I start on him," Murphy continued, pacing a tight circle, "his soul is going to try clawing its way out of his arsehole."

"Stephen!" Elliot shouted. "Please, stop."

Murphy stopped pacing and turned to face her, his chest heaving.

"You're scaring these people," Elliot said.

He cast his eyes around the diner. The young waitress was nearby, her hand on her chest, her eyes wide and staring at the pistol in his hand. All of the diners had dropped their cutlery and had stopped talking. They were open-mouthed, some with their hands raised while others made the sign of the cross. The boy in the high chair started to cry, his mother scooping him up and cradling him close to her chest. The boy's father rose from his seat, putting himself between Murphy and his family.

Murphy looked down at his pistol and saw that his knuckles were white. Elliot placed her hand on his arm. "There's no going back, is there?"

Her face fell as she realised what he meant. The infant was howling, his mother shushing and rocking on her seat. Elliot glanced towards the young family. "No," she said finally. "But you can try, if you like."

"Do you think it will work?"

She dipped her head towards the door. "There's the exit," she said. "Turn left, and you can be a beer-drinking baker living in a flat in Footscray."

"And right?"

Elliot dipped her head again. "Turn right, and you go back to Moscow. You stop these people."

"And then what happens? There will always be someone who wants a piece of me." He looked at her. "Of us."

Elliot nodded slightly.

Murphy took a deep breath and holstered his pistol.

"You don't have to do this alone," she said. "No matter what you choose."

He peered at the door. "You and I had a lot of years stolen from us, didn't we?"

"Yes, we did."

He reached into his pocket and retrieved a roll of cash, peeling off some bills and placing them on the table. "Let's get them back," he said, snatching up his coat.

50

MOSCOW, RUSSIA

SUNDAY 18 SEPTEMBER

4:58PM MSK

Emily Hartigan walked along a corridor in the Australian embassy, her hand on her hip, her phone held against her ear. "Yes, I know," she said. "We figured that one out."

She swept the hair from her eyes, glancing at the doors to the committee room. Voices murmured behind them and she wondered what they could be talking about.

"You were there too?" She frowned, sitting in an armchair and grabbing a glass of water from a neighbouring coffee table. She placed her glass down and froze, holding her breath. "Whoa, I'm sorry," she said into her phone. "Could you go back a little bit? What did you say the officer's name was?"

She stood up again, pacing in front of the doors, her muscles coiled, her heart racing. Heat crept into her face.

"Yes, I *would* like your details." She scrambled for her organiser, taking out her ballpoint and opening her notebook to a blank page. "Okay, Professor Sharon

Little with two tees." She dutifully scrawled Little's phone number and address. "No, thank *you.* I'm sorry you had so much trouble reaching us. We can be hard to pin down."

Hartigan said goodbye and hung up, bellowing in fury.

"That lying, manipulative coward," she said.

She stomped around the corridor, zigging and zagging and arching her fingers.

"Agent Hartigan?"

"What?" she snarled.

The young man cleared his throat. "The ambassador will see you now."

Hartigan watched as a line of suited men and women walked through the door, parading down the hallway. She waited until they were all gone and gingerly entered the room.

The ambassador stood behind the chair at the head of the table. He was slouching, his hand sunk in his suit pocket, a folder tucked under his arm. "Perhaps you should take a seat, Agent Hartigan." He sat down at the head of the table, placing his folder before him. He took a gold-plated pen from inside his jacket, clicking it three times.

Hartigan sat down at the other end of the table, placing her organiser next to her phone.

The ambassador propped his elbows on the table, pen poised in his hand. "I've received your report, Agent Hartigan," he began. "Agent Singh briefed me on the events that have transpired over the preceding week and he tells me that your report was the product of a substantial amount of reading you did on the flight over. Is that true?"

Agent Singh is a liar who killed a little girl during the war...

Hartigan shut her eyes and shook her head to clear her mind.

"Is that a no?"

"No, I'm just..." She sighed. "The report is incomplete."

"I see." He cleared his throat. "Well, I have to confess I haven't had a chance to read it yet, anyway." The ambassador clicked his pen three times. "I can tell you, however, that our prime minister is concerned about the *Organizatsiya'* s failed attempt to force us out of the energy market. He believes it will inevitably lead to another attempt in the very near future," the ambassador explained. "Switchboards are melting at talkback stations and people are demanding action so Australia is poised to petition the UN on Monday. Russia is technically in violation of a United Nations Security Council resolution by harbouring those who can now be considered terrorists." The ambassador swivelled back and forth in his chair, drumming his pen on the edge of the table. "President Nevzorova has seized the initiative and invited us to the Kremlin tonight for informal talks. We're hoping to perhaps gain some concessions in this initial meeting, especially after the events in Canberra and Melbourne."

Silence settled on the room. The ambassador shifted in his seat, clicking his pen again.

"I would like your insight, Agent Hartigan," he added.

Hartigan smoothed out a wrinkle in her blouse. "To be blunt," she began, "I don't think Valentina Nevzorova gives a shit about us, talkback radio, or the UN."

The ambassador narrowed his eyes. "I beg to differ."

"Were you here when they rolled Ukraine?" Hartigan asked. "How many strongly worded statements did you issue? Did it stop them?"

"To be fair, that was Nevzorova's predecessor, not—"

"That's why she gave the territory back, right?" she asked, cutting him off. She clicked her fingers. "Oh, wait. She didn't."

The ambassador smiled crookedly. "She's not the topic of discussion today."

"She features in my report."

"Your *incomplete* report." The ambassador frowned and tossed his pen on the table. "Okay, I'll bite. Why?"

"Nevzorova has a large stake in this," Hartigan said. "She has a long history with Nikolay Korolev and it's in her interests to crush the *Organizatsiya,* which she can do now that the oil trade has shut down. Korolev's source of funds has been cut off."

"And it's in Korolev's interests to revive that trade," the ambassador said, reclining in his chair. "The collapsed trade deal compels him to act, pushing us out of the market and giving the Chinese no choice but to turn back to Russia."

"But why would Korolev also fund the bombings in Moscow?" Hartigan asked. "Beijing's rejection may make Nevzorova look inept, but the bombings make her look weak. It plays into the hands of the traditionalists who opposed a female president, the same men who are in Korolev's pocket."

The ambassador laced his fingers together behind his head. "So you believe that Korolev's ultimate aim is to destabilise her government, securing the existence of the *Organizatsiya* and re-establishing trade with China."

"Exactly. Eliminating our trade capacity is just a small part of his scheme."

"But he has to put a puppet in the Kremlin, someone who accepts his existence or is paid to live with it." The ambassador stroked his chin. "And that could be anyone. There are many in Moscow who would like to see Nevzorova fail."

Hartigan fluttered her lips.

The ambassador frowned. “Is there something else?”

She stood up. “Something doesn’t fit,” she muttered. “It’s not grounds for Simone Elliot to pursue Stephen Murphy. Something changed, something that forced her to act.”

The ambassador held out his hands and shrugged. “Is that really relevant?”

“And then there are the militants,” Hartigan added, pacing towards the ambassador. “These guys are very choosy about who they work for. They wouldn’t be participating in Korolev’s campaign unless he’d sweetened the deal. And the pipeline bombing.”

“The Eastern Siberia–Pacific Ocean oil pipeline?”

“It’s out of character. They must be getting something out of it.”

“The militants have a history with Korolev,” the ambassador noted. “Perhaps even a relationship that promotes loyalty.”

“It’s been years since Korolev sold weapons to militants,” Hartigan said with a wave of her hand. “Times changed. Giving them weapons can only reignite a war, which is bad for the energy business in the...” Her voice trailed off and she stared at the table. “Pipeline,” she whispered.

"I'm sorry?" the ambassador asked, grabbing his pen from the table.

"This is not just about oil." She sighed in exasperation. "Korolev *paid* the militants to bomb targets, including the pipeline. That means he *wanted* the deal to fail. China might have paid the high price but only if Russia could secure its infrastructure." She paced furiously, her hands rolling over each other in front of her. "If Korolev positions himself correctly, he can sign an export deal with Beijing, crush the militants in Chechnya, and control the spread of organised crime. The people would worship him. But he can't do that through a proxy. In order to have any control over the outcome, in order to get the Chinese back to the table while ensuring they save face, he would..." She stopped pacing and reluctantly looked up at the ambassador. "And he can turn on the militants and seize territory. He can rebuild the pipeline. He can use the *Organizatsiya* as his own personal army." Her arms fell by her sides. "He can control everything."

The ambassador clicked his pen.

"And we'd be too busy squabbling over maritime borders, arguing over drilling rights, and investigating Titan Energy."

"What are you talking about, Agent Hartigan?"

"Nikolay Korolev is going to stage a coup," Hartigan concluded.

The ambassador snorted, stretching his mouth in a small smile. "You're wasting my time." He rose from his chair, collecting his folder from the table.

"It makes sense," Hartigan protested. "It fits."

"You're over-analysing this, Agent Hartigan." The ambassador hugged his folder to his chest. "Early this morning, local time, Stephen Murphy tore up a hotel that was a front for the *Organizatsiya.* Then, there was a shoot-out at Korolev's nightclub and an explosion at an old underground nuclear shelter just outside the city limits."

"Murphy escaped," Hartigan summarised.

"Some *boyeviks* were caught by the police today, and it led to the arrest of a group of militants who were on their way to Moscow to carry out another attack, a big one on Tverskaya Street. It's the busiest street in Moscow so it's a huge win."

"I see."

"Nevzorova had the *boyevik* s executed, though the official statement claims they were killed during the arrest," the ambassador said. "The militants may meet a similar fate."

"She's hitting back."

"And hard," he added. "Hopefully, her actions will strengthen her presidency. I'd say Murphy saw the writing on the wall and got out while he could."

"Then why petition the UN?"

"It's no secret the Kremlin is marred by corruption. We need to ensure that Nevzorova continues to dismantle the *Organizatsiya* without making exceptions." He clicked his pen and smiled with satisfaction. "If you're right about her desire to starve Korolev of funds, it should be easy to ensure her cooperation."

"All of that information still fits my analysis."

The ambassador frowned. "Korolev's bombing campaign has been stopped in its tracks and his best man has run away with a thief," he said. "It's unlikely any puppet president will challenge Nevzorova." He shrugged. "She has the means to strengthen her position, and having her in the Kremlin is in our national interest, especially if she's cutting back on oil exports."

There was a knock on the door and Lee Singh stuck his head into the conference room. "Sir, sorry to interrupt, but you're needed in the communications centre."

Hartigan cast a withering glare towards Singh.

"Of course." The ambassador tucked his pen inside his jacket and stuck his folder under his arm. "You have a lot to learn, Agent Hartigan, so I'm going to give you an opportunity. I'd like you and Agent Singh to join me at the Kremlin tonight to participate in our negotiations. Perhaps a real-world education will complement your academic qualifications, and make you better at your job."

Her mouth fell open and she stared at the floor as the ambassador left the room. Singh closed the door behind him and walked towards her, his hands deep in his pockets.

Hartigan turned to face him, her chest rising and falling, her eyes flashing.

"What's wrong with you?" Singh said.

Hartigan struck, smashing Singh's nose with the heel of her hand. He staggered back into the table, blood running down his chin. "You give me one good fucking reason why I shouldn't arrest you right now," she seethed.

Singh found a handkerchief in the pocket of his jacket and wiped his nose and chin. "Try it and I'll kill you." He sniffed. "Is that good enough?"

"Shut your damn mouth," she hissed. A bell jingled and Hartigan glanced at her phone on the table. "That will be the Americans."

He dabbed at his nose with his handkerchief. "What are you talking about?"

She scooped up her phone and peered at the screen. "Apparently," she said, "the Americans had never heard of you before an operative met you for brunch the other day."

Singh's face hardened and he crammed his handkerchief into his pocket.

Hartigan raised an eyebrow. "You gave them some information and they told you about Greg Lambert."

"Greg Lambert was executed," Singh said. "His coffin was left outside the US consulate with a stone wolf sitting on the lid."

She slid her phone across the table. "Do you happen to remember the American telling you that the Bear had fallen off the grid?"

Singh held up his hand. "He only told me about Murphy."

"Because that's all you cared about," she said through her teeth. "You were looking for reasons to justify killing him. You don't really need any but those who review the case might like one or two. And that's why you brought me here, isn't it?"

He stalked towards her. "Enough," he growled. "You have no fucking idea—"

"Sharon Little," she bellowed. "Remember her?"

"I'm warning you, Emily."

"Little told me what happened during the war."

"Witness accounts are unreliable."

"You killed that girl, Lee!" Hartigan cried. "And Murphy went to prison for it."

"You weren't there. This is all just academic to you."

"Jesus Christ." She breathed out, clutching her head. "You've got a huge conflict of interest that compromises our—"

"Again," he interrupted loudly. "Academic."

"Tell me you're not here to kill him."

"He is a clear and present threat to our national security."

"No, he's a threat to *you.* Kill him and you can avoid prison time. Sharon Little tried to testify against you but no one believed her. But Murphy and her together..." She poked him in the chest. "You're afraid of him, afraid that the truth might finally come out."

"I *will* bury you out here, Emily."

"Or maybe you're afraid he's a better soldier than you." She held up her little finger. "Or a better man."

"Fuck you, Emily," he roared. "You're no better than any one of us. We're all neck deep in the swampy moats we call souls and people like you think you can climb out and look down on everyone else." He jabbed her in the shoulder, shoving her backwards. "You sit on top of a tower of books and hide between the words thinking you're safe. But no matter how high you build your tower, it will always sink. We always end up back in the swamp because you can't escape who you are."

"You don't know me!"

"Oh, I know you. I know what you need, and I know what you want." His eyes were wide, his lips flecked with spit. "Whether it's your stupid crosswords or the latest lead in a case, you need a puzzle, a riddle, a question." He stepped closer, forcing Hartigan to step back. "You'll crawl through broken glass to get the answers. You need to solve it. You need to get your fix."

She stopped walking, her back flat against the wall.

"You came here because I threw you a clue," Singh said, reaching into his jacket. "You came here hoping to find Elliot so that you can solve another puzzle." He held up a DVD.

"Where did you get that?" she asked, her voice trembling.

"I know you want a piece of her, Emily."

"You're wrong."

"She killed all of them except your dad. She crippled him for life instead. You want answers. And then you want her dead."

Hartigan threw her hands in the air. "It's against the law," she cried.

"Stop pretending the rules matter to you." Singh tucked the DVD back into his jacket. "You've been disobeying orders and following lines of inquiry that were not sanctioned—"

"I was doing my job!"

"*You* broke the rules," Singh said.

"You covered up a crime!"

"You're a self-centred hypocrite, a fucking self-righteous—"

She threw a punch and Singh blocked it with his forearm, shoving her into the wall and drawing his pistol. He pushed the weapon into the nape of her neck.

"Get that thing away from me," she spat, her palms flat against the wall.

"Enough of this academic bullshit, Emily." He pushed the pistol deeper and she groaned. "There is no right or wrong here," he said, "no good guys or bad guys."

Hartigan shook her head. "You think you know me, Lee?"

Singh raised the pistol, holding it against Hartigan's forehead. "You get on board now, or you *will* get killed."

Her eyes opened. "I know all about you. You were a burnout, kicked out of the army and left to rot in the gutter."

"I'm warning you."

"The agency hired you when no one else would. You're worse than him, worse than Murphy."

"Last chance."

"You're a killer. Prove me right. Kill me."

"Give me a reason!" he roared.

Hartigan cried out, slapping the pistol away and grabbing a handful of Singh's lapel. She heaved with all her strength and threw him on his back. He tried to raise the pistol but Hartigan stomped on his wrist and dropped her knee on his neck.

She pried the pistol from his fingers and sprang to her feet, falling back against the wall. Her hands trembled and she panted heavily, raising the pistol until it was pointing at his head. He climbed to his knees and grinned.

Hartigan gasped, dropping the pistol as if it had burned her hands.

Singh stood up and retrieved his weapon. "There's an animal in you, Emily," he said, holstering his gun. "Be sure to bring it."

51

MOSCOW, RUSSIA

SUNDAY 18 SEPTEMBER

10:02PM MSK

Emily Hartigan excused herself from the conference room at the Kremlin but none of the men paid her any attention. Both delegations, Australian and Russian, were busy with their words, too many words that didn't seem to mean anything. She closed the door behind her and trudged away, her footfalls echoing behind her as she walked along the empty hall. She paused when she felt a cool breeze through a doorway. A breath of wind touched her face and she closed her eyes.

It looked like a study, she thought, stepping slowly into the room. An ornate writing desk was nestled among towering shelves, and the ledges were neatly stacked with leather-bound volumes. Heavy curtains billowed beside an open door that led to a darkened terrace, and the fluttering cloth flagged a bottle of vodka on the sideboard.

Hartigan poured herself a drink and found her eyes drawn to a television that was hidden away in the corner cabinet by the entrance. A news presenter murmured quietly on the screen and Hartigan leaned against the chair in front of the fireplace, staring vacantly at the stern anchorman.

Pictures appeared showing four men on their knees with their hands behind their heads and policemen casually pacing behind them. One policeman was beaming with pride, surveying his prisoners as they eyed the water-stained wall in front of them.

"Animals," a woman said in Russian.

Hartigan started and turned to see a woman in the shadows of the terrace, a cigarette smouldering between her fingers. "Who are they?" she asked, pointing at the television.

"Militants from Chechnya. A policeman caught them on the train to Moscow earlier today."

Hartigan pulled her jacket tight around her shoulders, collecting her glass of vodka and stepping into the darkness. "They don't look like animals." Her eyes adjusted to the light.

Valentina Nevzorova stepped forward, the white streaks in her hair iridescent in the moonlight. Her lips wrinkled around her cigarette as she inhaled. "You are seeing what you want to see."

"And what is that, Madam President?"

"Men with a noble cause."

"My understanding is they just want independence." Hartigan immediately regretted her remark when she saw Nevzorova's face harden. Perhaps her Russian was worse than she thought.

"Your understanding is flawed," Nevzorova said icily. "Who are you?"

"I'm with the Australian delegation," Hartigan replied nervously.

"Your Russian is passable." Her eyes wandered, focusing on the badge clipped to Hartigan's belt.

"I've had practice."

The cigarette flared again as she inhaled. "What is your name?"

"Emily Hartigan, Madam President."

"Why are you out here?" Nevzorova asked.

"I don't understand what they're talking about in there." Hartigan took a deep breath. "Nikolay Korolev is threatening our country and yours, but not one word has been said about it in that meeting."

"Let me guess, they're talking about trade tariffs and infrastructure development instead of extradition orders and military intervention."

"Shouldn't we be questioning people, rounding up suspects, studying files?"

"That's useful when you're looking for a purse-snatcher or a man who killed his adulterous wife."

"The only difference with these men is the scale."

"Perhaps." Nevzorova grunted and waved at the television. "I see men who want power and an opportunity to seize it. A cause is always a means to gain what they want. They think they will win because they believe we will not fight on their terms." She gazed at Hartigan. "They believe the same about you."

"About us? I don't understand."

"You, we, all of us, have signed treaties and negotiated international oversight to prevent new wars from occurring. Belligerents are punished when they invade another country. They are isolated economically, politically and militarily."

"It's worked."

"No, it hasn't," she snorted. "These men have no state and no regard for our rules because they were not designed with them in mind. They believe we turned our backs on them so they turn their backs on us: mocking our institutions; bombing our airliners, department stores, and subways."

"Out of desperation."

"So we should forgive them? We should allow them what they want?"

"Well—"

"Do you believe we should lower ourselves to accommodate them rather than expect them to honour the rules that you praised only seconds ago?"

"It's more complicated than that."

"Why should their interests be more important than ours?"

Hartigan felt her blouse cling to her back despite the cold night air. "But their motives—"

Nevzorova laughed humourlessly. "You police and your motives. If a man breaks into *your* house, do you consider his motives?"

"The rule of law—"

"Is an ideal," Nevzorova interrupted. "When I call the police, I'm not calling them to see that the thief has a fair trial and his interests are taken into consideration. I am telling them to do what I'm unable to do, and that is to confront the thief, to punish him for invading my house." She crushed her cigarette in an ashtray.

"But we correct that behaviour and control it." Hartigan knew her words sounded hollow.

"Your rule of law is ignored by these people." Nevzorova pointed to the television again, which was now showing a story about polar bear cubs born in captivity. "Just like the international regulations the West thought would preserve their way of life."

"It works in most cases," Hartigan said. "People and governments don't violate the rules because they fear them."

"If that were true, Korolev would be afraid of the police instead of Volkov."

Hartigan stared down at the drink in her hands and realised her fingers were numb.

"They don't fear your laws. They fear power they don't have." Nevzorova offered Hartigan a cigarette and the agent thanked her as she took it.

Hartigan lit her cigarette and dizziness overcame her, the nicotine swimming through her blood. "I didn't know that he was afraid of Volkov." She coughed.

"Everybody is afraid of Volkov because he's afraid of nothing, least of all you and your badges and uniforms."

"He's an animal," Hartigan murmured, glancing at the television.

"And the only way to kill animals is to unchain that part of us we convinced ourselves is no longer there."

"But what if that part of us *isn't* there?" Hartigan asked, contemplating the cigarette in her hand.

"It's in every one of us, Emily. We built processes and treaties and rules around it and convinced ourselves that we were better but we never changed.

That's why when restaurants are bombed, you can hear a growl inside of you."

Hartigan shook her head and closed her eyes.

"You disagree?"

"I don't know anymore," Hartigan whispered. The smoke from her cigarette seemed to swirl all around her, swallowing her in a toxic fog.

"Think about it, Emily, or find another job."

Hartigan sucked on her cigarette.

Nevzorova looked at her watch and arched an eyebrow. "It was a pleasure to meet you," she said, "but I must go. I have to meet your delegation and ensure the negotiations are meeting our needs."

"It was a pleasure to meet you, too."

Hartigan listened to the fading footsteps of Valentina Nevzorova and butted out her cigarette. She gulped her drink down in one mouthful, grateful for the numb warmth it gave her. Darkness swallowed the balcony and Hartigan looked up to see the moon flee behind thick clouds.

There was a loud chattering noise in the darkness and Hartigan peered over the balcony. There was another loud chatter and she saw something explode.

A grenade? Small arms?

She heard shouting and more gunfire.

Oh, God. What do I do?

52

MOSCOW, RUSSIA

SUNDAY 18 SEPTEMBER

10:10PM MSK

President Valentina Nevzorova's protection detail swirled around her, howling orders and smashing open doors. The Australian ambassador and his entourage were swept up in the rush, blown along the halls and down the staircases by blustering bodyguards. Nevzorova was in the middle of the tempest, her face serene and her pace measured. It looked to Singh as though she were slightly late for a board meeting rather than fleeing an attack on her palace.

"Mobilise the army," Nevzorova said calmly to her assistant. "I want infantry with armoured support, and get in touch with the *Spetsnaz* commander. I want a squad on standby and ready to move within the hour." Another door was thrown open and she didn't break stride. "I want law enforcement patrolling the Moscow River, both the water and the bank. Tell them to set up a cordon and to restrict traffic for a five kilometre radius." A bodyguard waved her down a stone staircase lit by halogen lamps. "Contact state radio and television. I need to tell the people what's going on and assert control before we have panic."

She wasn't his president, but Singh would've been happy if she was. They were ushered down the staircase into a cavernous parking garage. The armoured limousines were already idling and soldiers had been deployed to cover her escape.

"Also," Nevzorova continued, "contact the air force and tell them to have their jets ready to scramble at a moment's notice."

"But, ma'am," her assistant protested.

"I don't care if I have to burn this city down," she said firmly, "Nikolay will not live through the night."

Her assistant shook his head. "But we don't know that it's—"

"Of course it's him," Nevzorova barked. "He had the most to lose." A bodyguard opened the limousine's door and Nevzorova paused, eyeing the Australian ambassador. "And contact the Prime Minister of Australia," she said to her assistant.

"Madam President," the ambassador interjected. "I can take care of that."

She glared at him. "It's already done, Mr Ambassador."

He nodded submissively.

An aide neared Nevzorova, a mobile phone in his hand. "Madam President, we have reports that Stepan Volkov has been sighted in the city. It appears he's heading towards the palace."

Nevzorova grunted. "He'll be *in* the palace soon. Keep me informed." She turned to Singh, and he felt like she was looking straight through him. "Your partner was in my study," she said. "That's the last time I saw her. If you wish to find her, that's where you should start." She climbed into the limousine.

Singh stared at his reflection in the tinted window.

Stepan Volkov has been sighted.

Singh felt for the keys in his pocket, holding them in his fist.

He'll be in *the palace soon.*

Nevzorova's car screeched out of the garage, driving up a steep slope towards the streets of Moscow.

"Lee!" Singh looked up to see the ambassador waving his arms. "Lee, get over here," the ambassador called out, pointing to a waiting limousine. "You're supposed to be on detail."

"I'm going to stay," Singh said.

"Stay? Why?"

Singh unbuttoned his jacket and loosened his tie. "I'll see you back at the embassy," he said, climbing to the top of the staircase.

"Lee, you get in this car right now and do your job," the ambassador bellowed, pointing at his toes with a trembling finger. "Don't you close that fucking—"

The door closed with a boom and Singh peered down an empty hallway. He threw away his tie and exhaled.

***

"Could you shut up for a minute?" Elliot asked sternly, fidgeting with the volume of the radio.

The taxi driver ignored her and took another breath to continue his rant about the evils of organised crime. He pounded the steering wheel and described how the *Organizatsiya* had snatched his friend's sister and turned her into a prostitute. He spat as he told of the police finding her body in the river, claiming she had died of a drug overdose. "She'd never touched it, man, never. It was those bastards, those same bastards who have been paying guys to bomb Moscow."

The car lurched over a pothole and fishtailed, bouncing as the driver fought to keep control. Murphy gently laid his hand on Elliot's shoulder. "Don't kill him," he whispered.

"Why not? I can drive," she said, turning around.

"You can't drive while he's bleeding to death in that seat and we're hurtling into oncoming traffic."

Elliot scowled and crossed her arms. "Fine." She slouched into the passenger seat and stared at the radio. She had heard enough between mouthfuls of the taxi driver's tirade to understand what was happening, anyway.

Nikolay Korolev had seized the Kremlin with an army of *boyeviks,* containing himself inside the Presidential Palace. Nevzorova had been evacuated safely but many others had been killed in the attack. The president had given a speech from Red Square and state radio was playing it on a loop. She informed her people about the coup and assured them that the army was being deployed to overcome the *Organizatsiya.*

"Korolev's crazy for even trying this."

"He's not known for giving up easily," Murphy said.

"How are we supposed to get into the Kremlin?" Elliot asked. "The place is literally a fortress."

"Just drop us off here," Murphy said to the driver, pointing at the stairs to the underground subway. The taxi driver obliged, mounting the kerb and screeching to a stop. Murphy grabbed some cash from his pocket but the driver had already left the car.

"What's he doing?" Elliot asked.

The taxi driver went to the back of the car and pulled out a tyre iron. "I'm going to Red Square," the driver said. "I'm going to help stop these dogs." He jogged towards the Kremlin, leaving his taxi parked over the pavement.

"Every vote counts, I guess," Murphy remarked, grabbing their duffel bag from the back seat.

“Democracy doesn’t get any better than this.” Elliot pointed to the columns of people heading towards Red Square, rivers of humanity rushing into an ocean.

“We better make a move before this turns into a bloodbath.”

Elliot nodded and followed Murphy, descending into the Moscow underground.

53

MOSCOW, RUSSIA

SUNDAY 18 SEPTEMBER

10:48PM MSK

Nevzorova climbed on to the roof of her limousine to look across the sea of bobbing heads that poured through the palace gates. The swelling tide foamed with rage and rolled towards the Presidential Palace, the roar shaking the ground beneath her feet. She reached down and the flow of Russians lapped at her hand, smiling proudly and reminding her that she was still their president. Nevzorova straightened her back and waved her people towards the palace walls. The *boyeviks* guarding the courtyard shrank back when the crowd surged towards them.

"Ma'am, we may have to get you out of here soon," one of her bodyguards said.

Nevzorova turned to the square and saw that Korolev had ordered his men to form a defensive perimeter around the palace. Some stood with their weapons ready while others had started to force the crowd back, bashing the people with the butts of their rifles. They were making room to lay mines.

Nevzorova leapt off the roof of the car and grabbed her assistant's sleeve. "Where's the infantry?"

"The tanks are waiting on the other side of the fortress walls, ma'am," her assistant replied. "All you have to do is give the order."

***

Murphy grunted, leaning into the door with his shoulder. The hinges shrieked and the door opened slowly.

Elliot walked into the room and cast her eyes around. "Presidential bomb-shelter chic," she said, unslinging her assault rifle. "It has more of an apocalyptic feel than Grigoriy's place," she conceded, shivering in the unstirred air.

"The threat of nuclear winter will do that to a room," Murphy remarked. "Every interior decorator knows that."

The railway track terminated at the bottom of a sheer concrete wall that climbed fifty feet to the ceiling. Streams of icy water cascaded down the wall, the cracked concrete straining to hold back the Moscow River. Elliot could hear the drains gurgling, returning the water to the river.

There was a raised platform that stretched along the wall and several rooms branched off from the shelter. An iron cage was recessed into the earth—an elevator, Elliot realised—and its cables ran vertically to the palace above their heads. A rusted ladder climbed up to a catwalk that crisscrossed the shelter, held by support struts bolted into the stone ceiling.

"Is there only one way out?" Elliot asked, turning on the spot. She studied the small door in the blast wall behind them. The wall was the height of the tunnel and could be opened to allow trains in and out.

Murphy pointed to the top of the dam wall. "At the end of that catwalk, there's a concrete ledge and a ventilation shaft that goes all the way up to the bank of the river. You can fit two people side by side on the ladder."

"I like the way we came in," she said, staring up at the rickety catwalk.

"Me too," Murphy said. They climbed the stairs to the platform and he opened the elevator.

"How do you know this still works?" Elliot asked.

"I used it a few days ago. Valentina had me over for a chat."

She arched an eyebrow. "Just for a chat, huh?"

"I was scared even asking for that."

Elliot stepped into the elevator and turned around, facing Murphy. "You *do* have a plan, right?"

"Trust me," Murphy said, following her into the cage. "This gorilla knows what he's doing."

"I trust you." Elliot clapped him on the shoulder and he winced in pain. "Oh, that's right. You jumped through a window and landed on a car."

"We'll be fine."

"You sound unnaturally confident." She clicked her fingers. "You're lying to me, aren't you?"

"Honestly?" He closed the cage, unslinging his assault rifle.

"Sure."

"I'm scared shitless," he said calmly, chambering a round. "You?"

"Same." She peered into the elevator shaft above them and cocked her rifle. "I hope we're as good as everyone thinks we are."

He slapped the lever and the elevator groaned. "How hard could it be, right?" The cable heaved the rattling cage upwards into the palace.

***

Nikolay Korolev stared through the window and gritted his teeth. He clutched his radio close to his mouth, holding it tight. "I want the bulk of the men deployed to the forecourt. I want the other exits in the palace secured by sentries. I want roving patrols through the palace. Do you understand what I'm saying?"

"Yes, sir," the radio crackled.

"Tell the men in the forecourt to stand guard and keep the crowd back. Do not open fire unless you hear the order from me."

"Yes, sir. Confirm hold fast and don't fire until you give the order."

"The ammunition cache has been set up on the ground floor," Maxim said, entering the committee room. "We can hold them off until dawn, if they attack."

Korolev grunted, glaring through the window.

"I've deployed men with RPGs to the windows above the forecourt," Maxim continued. "They'll be set up in a matter of minutes."

"Good."

"Where do you want me?" Maxim asked.

"Here, Maxim," Korolev replied, pointing at the floor. "By my side where you belong." He toggled the transmit button on his radio and held it to his mouth. "Disperse the crowd. Fire at will."

***

"I'm sorry, ma'am, but I need another hour," the radio crackled.

"One hour?" Nevzorova growled. "You're in charge of the *Spetsnaz.* You're supposed to be ready to move within thirty minutes."

"Ma'am, we're doing the best we can. We've been caught flatfooted," the *Spetsnaz* commander replied.

Nevzorova dropped the radio when she heard the gunfire. The burst prompted bodyguards to reach for the president but she slapped their hands away, looking towards the palace.

Boyeviks were pouring rounds into the crowd and volleys of automatic fire rattled through the compound. The people screamed and moaned but they stood their ground and the rage boiled over. They lobbed Molotov cocktails and started to fire their own guns at the *Organizatsiya.*

"Mobilise the tanks," Nevzorova ordered. A grenade exploded in the crowd and her breath caught in her throat. Her assistant was frozen, his mouth gaping open. She grabbed his jacket by the lapels. "Deploy the fucking tanks!" she roared. "Take down the fortress walls and get them into the fight."

***

"Status report," Korolev demanded, spluttering into his radio. "Answer me!"

The radio squealed back at him and he could hear distant shouts and the screams of dying men.

"What the fuck is going on?" he yelled, staring through the window. The fortress walls suddenly fell in a cough of dust and tanks rumbled through the dark cloud. They rolled up the grassed embankment, knocking down trees and shuddering over shrubs, plunging towards the forecourt.

Korolev stepped back from the window, his eyes darting around the room. Six of his generals stood guard on the other side of the long oak table, holding their weapons tight.

"Somebody answer me!" he shouted into his radio. His broken voice echoed back through the hissing static. He rushed to the window and looked down at his men. They were firing at the crowd and tossing grenades. The people were surging forward, triggering mines on the ground before ebbing back and leaving the dead behind. The crowd parted to let the tanks into the square. A soldier sat atop the turret of each tank embracing mounted machine guns, and the people regrouped behind them.

The people climbed over the tanks and crashed into Korolev's men, swarming over the compound. They snatched the *boyeviks'* guns and fired. If they didn't have weapons, they scrounged for anything they could find, stabbing the *boyeviks* with bottles and pounding them with bats and bricks. Then they used their hands, pummelling the men with fists and ripping limbs from sockets.

No. She can't win.

Maxim snatched the radio out of Korolev's hands and changed to an alternate frequency. "This is Maxim. Rockets?"

"We're still getting into position," the radio crackled.

"Hurry up!" Maxim shouted. "Get those tanks!"

***

Murphy dropped a dead body at his feet and lowered his knife. Elliot ejected her empty magazine and slapped a new one into her weapon.

They crept to the end of the hall and Murphy peeked around the corner. Two men were sprinting towards them. He held up two fingers before pointing to her and waving to the far side of the hall.

Elliot nodded and raised her weapon to her shoulder.

Murphy stuck out his arm and caught the first *boyevik* around the neck. The man tumbled backwards, flipping on to his face. Murphy ducked, plunging his knife into the base of the man's skull, and Elliot leaned around the corner, firing a three-round burst. The bullets struck the other *boyevik* in the chest and he fell, sliding on the marble floor.

"Is it just me, or does it feel a little lonely in here?" Elliot asked.

"I think Nikolay deployed all his guys into the square." They could hear the crowd outside, the roar pounding against the walls and shaking the palace. "We'd better find him before he runs."

"We're going to have to split up to find him," Elliot said, stealing a pistol from a dead *boyevik.*

"I don't think that's a good idea," Murphy said slowly.

She shoved the pistol into the back of her jeans and hefted her assault rifle. "I can take care of myself, you know."

"I know."

"Then what's wrong?"

"I, uh—" He sighed.

She kissed him. "They're not getting rid of me that easily," she said. "Twenty minutes."

"Twenty minutes," he repeated.

Elliot checked her watch. "Or whenever the palace starts burning down."

"Take care of yourself, okay, Slim?" he said, brushing her hair from her eyes.

She winked and ran down the hallway.

54

MOSCOW, RUSSIA

SUNDAY 18 SEPTEMBER

11:12PM MSK

After an hour of evading the *boyeviks* patrolling the Kremlin, Singh had managed to reach one of the palace's kitchens. He had hoped to find a weapon, but he was forced to hide when two hungry *boyeviks* arrived behind him. When they placed their shotguns on the stainless-steel counter, Singh grabbed a butcher's knife from a wooden block and stalked silently along the tiled floor. The blade whirled through the air and caught one of the men in the throat, blood washing over his hands. Singh pounced on the other *boyevik,* swiping at the man's face with a frying pan. The *boyevik* blocked and punched Singh in the ribs before reaching for his shotgun. The gun boomed as Singh kicked it away, buckshot smashing plates on the shelves. He grabbed the barrel of the gun, pushed the *boyevik* against the wall, and headbutted him until the *boyevik'* s nose burst. He wrestled the shotgun barrel under the man's chin and pumped the handle. The Russian's eyes widened.

Singh pulled the trigger.

***

Stephen Murphy could hear Nikolay Korolev yelling through the window of the committee room. A smashed mirror was on the floor nearby and he grabbed a shard of glass before creeping to the doorway. He held the glass in front of him to study the room's reflection.

Six men stood to the rear of the committee room, eyeing each other nervously. Korolev was standing in the corner clutching his head, flanked by Maxim who was shouting into the radio. Murphy checked his weapon. He was running out of ammunition. He rifled through his duffel, finding some detcord, and cut off three feet with his knife before taping a wireless detonator to the end.

It's not enough, he thought, glancing back towards the committee room.

I need something bigger.

***

"Fire!" Maxim spat into the radio. The missiles streaked down to the square and a tank exploded. The people nearby were swallowed by fire and ripped apart by shrapnel. Splinters of metal rained down upon the forecourt. Three more missiles lanced through the sky and burst. Blood splashed on to the stone ground.

The tanks were trapped, hemmed in by swarms of people. One of the machine gunners started to pour rounds at the palace, pocking the brickwork and shattering the windows. Another tank started elevating its gun, lurching and spitting fire.

Maxim dived away from the window, the incoming shell whistling through the air.

***

Emily Hartigan peeped out from behind the curtain and saw that the study was empty. The roar of the crowd was punctuated by gunshots and the palace shuddered violently under her feet, but that was all outside. In the study, the only sound was a ticking clock.

Twenty minutes earlier, a man had come in to check the room but he hadn't looked behind the heavy curtains. He'd simply turned off the television and left. Hartigan had held her breath until he'd walked out but her relief had only lasted until she'd thrown up on the floor. Now, she made a choice.

I'm not waiting here to die.

She wiped her palms on her pants and stepped warily from behind the curtain, stripping her jacket off and dropping it on the floor. She opened the door.

"Hey!"

A *boyevik* stood in front of her, his assault rifle pointed at her face. She slapped the weapon away and kicked him in the groin, his rifle spilling from his hands as he fell to his knees. Hartigan picked up the assault rifle and crashed the butt of the weapon into his face. She tossed the weapon away and stole a pistol from his unconscious body.

***

Maxim stood up gingerly, his ears ringing. The shell had pierced the window at the other end of the room and had crashed into the ceiling behind the sentries. He was covered in plaster and glass and brushed himself off. There was no blood.

"Nikolay?" he called out.

The room was thick with dust and the lights flickered above him. He staggered towards the table, reaching for something to hold him upright. He froze when he heard two gunshots and a groan deep within the cloud of dust.

"Nikolay?" His own voice sounded muffled, drowned out by the squealing in his ears. He drew his pistol and fired three rounds into the murk.

The cloud gasped and blood sprayed across Maxim's face. He heard someone gurgle before they thudded to the floor.

Stepan?

"Stepan?" He fired three more rounds and tried to wipe the blood from his face. "I know that's you. Come out and fight me," he stammered.

There was a grunt and a yell before a dead body tumbled out of the dust and rolled across the table, flopping to the floor at Maxim's feet. He fired again and again until the magazine was empty.

"Come out and face me!" Maxim demanded, his voice breaking. He hurled his pistol into the cloud. It banged harmlessly against the wall and he shrank into the corner, his heart pounding.

Maxim felt his skin tighten under his chin and he tried to suck in air but nothing happened. He was being strangled. Something cold and hard was forced into his mouth and he was pushed to the ground.

The noose was tight and he couldn't breathe. He pulled the obstruction from his mouth: a wolf, carved out of onyx.

Murphy appeared before him and crouched, holding a detonator taped to detcord. Murphy dropped the detonator down the back of Maxim's shirt and retrieved a garage door opener from his pocket.

Maxim peered into Murphy's eyes. "No," he rasped, his hands scrambling behind him to find the detonator.

"I warned you that I'd rip your fucking head off," Murphy said, his eyes shimmering.

"Please, no!" Maxim choked. Bright dots flashed in front of his eyes, his hands finally finding the loose strand of detcord. He fished the detonator out of his shirt and tried to tear it off the cord with his fingernails but it wouldn't budge. He looked up, seeing Murphy's silhouette melt away, and he closed his eyes.

Maxim heard a buzz and a click, and his headless body toppled over.

***

Hartigan ran around a corner and stopped in the middle of the hallway. Two men turned and raised their weapons, but her pistol dangled uselessly by her side.

A figure darted towards her and speared into her ribs, tackling her.

Elliot.

They crashed through a door on the other side of the hall while automatic fire ripped across the bricks and smashed into the plaster. The two women rolled across the tiled floor of a laundry room.

Hartigan picked herself up and levelled her pistol at Elliot's chest.

"So it's like that, huh?" Elliot said. Her rifle was on the floor, out of reach.

"Yeah," Hartigan said, wiping her face with her hand. "It is."

"Don't do it, Emily," Elliot warned.

"Why did you let him live?"

Elliot's face contorted with confusion.

"You killed all the cops that hurt you, but not Dad." She cocked the pistol. "Tell me why."

Elliot jerked her thumb towards the doorway. "This isn't the time."

Hartigan sprang towards her. "Tell me!" she shrieked.

Elliot slapped the pistol away and seized Hartigan's arm, heaving her on to the ground. Hartigan kicked Elliot in the stomach and forced her back into the wall.

Bullets pounded through the wall and both women ducked. Bottles of bleach shattered on the shelves and cartons of powder burst into blue clouds. The palace rumbled around them and Hartigan glanced up to see a crystal chandelier swaying from the ceiling in the hallway.

Men shouted to each other in the corridor.

Hartigan got up and steadied herself, circling Elliot. There was more gunfire and a fire extinguisher ruptured, spilling dry powder. Hartigan saw the fire cabinet on the far wall, a crash axe fixed to its mount. She pounced on the axe and ripped it from the cabinet, swinging at Elliot.

Elliot ducked under the axe and drove up at Hartigan, grabbing the axe handle, holding it against Hartigan's throat, driving her into the wall.

Boots pounded along the hallway.

Hartigan managed to push the handle away from her neck and throw Elliot on to the floor. She wrenched the axe free, raising it above her head. Elliot rolled away and the axe crashed into the tiles.

Elliot rolled towards her rifle, snatching it up just as a *boyevik* appeared in the doorway. She fired and the man staggered back into the hall, collapsing on the floor. The axe was falling again and Elliot rolled over, blocking the blade with her rifle.

Hartigan wrenched the rifle away with the blade of the axe and Elliot stabbed her boot into the back of Hartigan's thigh then tackled her into the wall. She punched Hartigan in the jaw before snatching the axe away, whirling around and driving the handle into the analyst's stomach.

Hartigan cried out and doubled over, noticing another *boyevik* in the doorway, a cigar clenched between his teeth. She quickly straightened up and Elliot pirouetted, swinging the axe towards Hartigan's throat.

The *boyevik* aimed his weapon.

Hartigan raised her hands in front of her but the axe crashed into the wall next to her head. A winch cable snapped with a twang and whipped through a recess, zipping up into the ceiling. The chandelier in the hallway shuddered and rushed towards the ground, crushing the *boyevik* into the tiled floor. Blood splashed into the room and Hartigan squeezed her eyes shut.

Elliot wriggled the axe free and tossed it on the floor. She held her forearm against Hartigan's throat and drew her pistol, pushing the barrel into the hollow of the agent's cheek.

Hartigan clawed at the arm on her throat, but she had no strength left. She was suffocating.

Elliot was breathing heavily, her jaw set, but her face slowly softened and she lowered the pistol. "I didn't want to make you an orphan, Emily." She stepped back and released Hartigan. "I didn't want to take your dad from you."

Hartigan slid down the wall and sucked in air, her throat burning. "You're lying!" she croaked. She coughed violently and crawled forward on all fours, her hands sweeping across the stone floor, searching for her pistol. "Come back and fight me."

"Go home, Emily," Elliot said. "If you stay, then you become one of them, one of us."

"Fuck you!" Hartigan found her pistol and flipped on to her back, aiming at the doorway. She fired until the pistol clicked empty but it didn't matter.

Elliot was gone.

55

MOSCOW, RUSSIA

SUNDAY 18 SEPTEMBER

11:30PM MSK

Singh paused and peered into the room. It was stacked with ammunition crates and assault rifles, grenades and jerry cans of water. He stuffed his pistol into his pocket and glanced around warily before opening one of the boxes. It was full of landmines. He armed one and placed it on the ground behind a stack of crates, gently placing an empty bucket on top of it. He grabbed one of the jerry cans and stabbed the bottom with a knife, standing it on a neighbouring crate so the water could pour into the bucket.

Singh stepped slowly out of the room, doing the calculations in his head. He knew that the landmine would detonate with nine kilograms of weight applied to the trigger, or nine litres of water.

I've got about three minutes before that bucket is heavy enough.

"Lee!"

He turned around. "Emily?"

She staggered along the hallway and collapsed against the wall beside him.

"Where the hell have you been?" he asked.

"Around. Are you going to tell me why you're still here?"

Singh checked over his shoulder.

"They're here," Hartigan said. "I had her and she ran away."

Singh's head snapped around and he looked into her eyes.

Hartigan swapped the pistol between her hands and wiped her palm on her blouse. "We can split up, okay?"

"Are you sure you're up to this, Emily?"

"Let's find out." She dipped her head towards the stairs. "I'm going up." Hartigan set off and climbed the stairs, loading a fresh magazine into her pistol.

Singh ran his hand down his face and eyed the ammunition cache.

Two minutes.

He pulled his pistol from his pocket and ran after her.

***

Murphy stopped at the end of the hall and peeked around the corner. A sharp pain shot through his thigh and he cried out, looking down to see a knife jutting from the back of his leg. He whirled around and Korolev's fist crashed into his jaw. Murphy tumbled to the floor, his assault rifle sliding away.

Korolev followed up with a kick to the stomach but Murphy blocked the blow, catching Korolev's leg and twisting his ankle, the Russian falling back into the wall. They wrestled, and Murphy tried to throw Korolev to the ground, but the Russian grabbed the knife, twisting it in Murphy's thigh. He screamed and headbutted Korolev.

Blood streamed from the Russian's nose as he lunged for the assault rifle on the floor. He took aim but Murphy ripped the rifle from his grasp and looped the sling around Korolev's neck, yanking tight. Korolev yanked the knife from Murphy's thigh and cut the sling.

Murphy chambered a round in the rifle and pulled the trigger but Korolev leapt around the corner. The bullets peeled a painting from the wall and crashed into a china cabinet, shattering plates and wine glasses.

"I'm not done with you, Nikolay," Murphy growled, limping to the corner. He leaned against the bricks, trying to catch his breath.

Murphy poked his head around the corner and saw Korolev snatch a pistol from a dead *boyevik* before seeking cover. A shot ricocheted off the wall and Murphy ducked.

"What do you think happens now, Stepan?" Korolev yelled, his voice booming down the corridor. He fired another shot and it smashed into the bricks. "What happens when you're outside of this palace? Do you think you'll be free?"

There were three more shots, the bricks crumbling on the far wall.

"You will be trapped by the words they use to define you," Korolev said. "You will be caged by their accusations. You will be chained to the very thing you're trying to kill me for."

He fired three more shots and Murphy turned his head away from the corridor.

"Not even death will set you free, Stepan," Korolev said. "Their fear is your only freedom."

"Maybe you're right," Murphy said. "But it's my choice."

"You're a foolish man," Korolev said. Murphy heard a yelp and looked around the corner. Korolev had his arm around Emily Hartigan's chest and was holding his pistol to her temple.

"Let me go!" Hartigan said, squirming in his arms.

"So come make your choice, Stepan." Korolev held Hartigan tighter. "See if they think you're any less an animal."

Hartigan cried out: "Let me go!"

Murphy ejected the rifle's magazine and his shoulders slumped. It was empty. There was one round left in the chamber.

"C'mon, Stepan," Korolev said. "Come set yourself free."

There was a loud crump and the palace shook violently. Murphy reached for the wall and peered around the corner in time to see Korolev and Hartigan fall through the floor.

Murphy stepped out of the shadows.

"Stop right there, Murphy!" a voice bellowed.

***

Hartigan was lying flat on a pile of rubble. Sparks spat across the ceiling and she could see the reflection of flames dancing on the far wall. She sat up and saw that she'd impaled her thigh on a metal spike that jutted from shattered stone. It was a barbed length of steel reinforcing from the floor that had collapsed beneath her. Blood gushed from the wound but she couldn't feel a thing.

Something shuffled nearby and she looked up. Korolev punched her in the face and Hartigan lurched backwards, shaking her head as he raised a knife.

No!

She blocked him and drove her fist into his throat. The blade fell into the rubble. He toppled on to his back, coughing for breath and searching for his knife.

Her pulse quickened and she grasped the spike in her leg, gripping it tight. She took a deep breath and yanked on the barbed steel. Korolev lurched to his knees, holding the knife. Hartigan cried out, pulling on the spike. It came free just as Korolev pounced. She blocked his attack with the spike, kneed him in the groin, and headbutted his bloodied nose. Dazed, she heaved with all her strength and pushed him away. He rolled on to his stomach and she raised the spike above her head, yelling as she drove it into his back.

Korolev screamed and exploded to his knees. Hartigan staggered back on to the rubble. He snarled, his eyes gleaming and his bared teeth dripping with foaming blood. He lunged at her, his hands outstretched, and she felt his tight grip around her throat.

No!

Hartigan reached out her hand, fumbling through the rubble for something, anything, that would save her life. She felt dizzy, her brain screaming at her to find air, and her heart pounded in her ears. Her hand fell on a rock, a brick, and she smashed it into Korolev's face. He collapsed, his grip falling away, and Hartigan swallowed a lungful of air, her eyes blurry, her breath rasping through her burning throat. Korolev tried to lift himself up.

No!

She raised the rock above her, holding it with both hands, and pounded the back of his head. She smashed his skull over and over, screaming for him to die, until the stone in her hands was slick with blood.

She stopped, the rock heavy in her hands. The stone slipped out of her grasp and she trembled.

Hartigan crawled backwards, her chest heaving, and stared at the man she had killed. She picked up a coin, holding it in quivering fingers, blood dripping from her hands.

"Lee!" she cried out.

Nobody came. She sobbed, her body shaking, and ran her bloodied hand through her hair.

"Lee! Help!"

***

Murphy raised his assault rifle, peering over the sights at Lee Singh, his fingers tightening around his weapon.

"I said stop!" Singh growled, his pistol aimed at Murphy.

Murphy clicked his tongue. "Well, well, Lee Singh," he said, his finger hovering over the trigger. "I was wondering if I'd run into you."

"Miss me?"

"It *has* been a while," Murphy said. "I spent a lot of time fantasising about what I was going to do to you when I found you again," he said, limping around Singh. "And then a couple of other things came up and you suddenly didn't matter anymore. I almost forgot all about it."

Singh tilted his head, turning with Murphy. "Aw, I'm hurt," he said drily.

Murphy felt his insides burning, the blood pounding through his veins. "It's all coming back to me, now."

"So what are you waiting for?" Singh asked, licking his lips and taking another step closer. "Are you out of bullets, or something?"

"Are you?"

"Lee!" Hartigan's cries echoed along the hallway.

Singh glanced over his shoulder but looked back to Murphy quickly. He adjusted his grip on the pistol.

"This rings a bell," Murphy said.

Singh took another step. "Shut up."

"Lee! Help!" Hartigan wailed.

"We've been here before, remember?" Murphy said. "The job or the girl?"

"I did the right thing!" Singh said. "I did the *right* thing."

"And he died anyway."

Singh shook his head. "Take your shot." He cocked his pistol. "Let's see who the best soldier really is. C'mon, teach me something."

"Okay, lesson one: don't shoot innocent girls in the face."

Singh slapped Murphy's weapon away and fired but Murphy had ducked, dropping his rifle and lunging forward. Singh sprawled across the floor, the pistol spilling out of his hands.

Singh sprang to his feet but Murphy punched him in the jaw and Singh fell into the shattered china cabinet, the broken glasses shuddering. He reached behind him and grabbed a broken wine bottle, jabbing at Murphy who stepped aside, feeling the skin tear open on his back. He gritted his teeth, his movements slow, and Singh sliced Murphy's arm. Singh slashed again but Murphy turned inside the attack, flinging Singh into the wall. Murphy grabbed the stem of a broken wine glass and stabbed Singh in the stomach. He pulled the glass stem out quickly and whirled around, stabbing it into Singh's forearm and driving it in with his palm. Singh cried out and dropped the wine bottle. He threw a haymaker at Murphy but Murphy blocked the blow, punching Singh in the stomach and giving him an uppercut to the chin. Singh staggered back and fell to the ground, tumbling over and leaping on to Murphy's discarded rifle.

Murphy grabbed Singh's pistol and rolled over, firing.

The pistol clicked. It was empty.

Singh stood up and wiped his mouth with the back of his hand, the rifle in his grasp. "Look who just took you to school." He sniffed, grabbing the base of the wine stem in his forearm and dragging it out of his flesh. The glass tinkled on the floor and Singh raised the rifle, aiming at Murphy. "Lesson number two: you always get what's coming to you."

A shot rang out, the crack echoing along the hallway. Singh whirled around, toppling on to his back, the weapon falling from his hands. A dark stain spread across his chest. A shoe pressed down on his throat and he wanted to push it away, but he couldn't raise his arms. He peered up through blurry eyes. A pistol was pointing at his head.

"School's out, sweetie-pie," Simone Elliot said.

She fired.

56

MOSCOW, RUSSIA

SUNDAY 18 SEPTEMBER

11:38PM MSK

A missile rocketed out of one of the windows, spearing into the square below. A tank raised its gun and fired, the shell thumping into the stone wall. The remaining tanks launched their own shells, and the walls of the palace started to crumble.

The infantry were fighting the *boyeviks* in a swamp of blood and dust. Volleys of bullets whistled across the square. Wounded soldiers and civilians were carried to safety, their clothes tattered and their bodies torn. Some staggered on the lawns with glassy eyes, while others curled up in balls and clutched their ears. An explosion had blown out the windows on the ground floor and flames licked from the building through yawning cracks in the walls.

A neglected cigarette burned between Nevzorova's fingers, her mind racing.

An army general approached hurriedly, his trousers swishing as he marched. "Ma'am, I have the latest," he said anxiously. "The commander says that he can storm the palace when reinforcements arrive but that could take another hour."

Nevzorova shook her head and tossed her cigarette to the ground. "Tell the army to pull back," she ordered. "I want them to evacuate."

"But, ma'am," her assistant protested.

She glared at him, her eyes clear. "Deploy the air force. I want them to scramble bombers and destroy the palace."

"Madam President," the general interjected. "I have to—"

Nevzorova grabbed a handful of his jacket and yanked him away from her car, forcing him to stare at the palace square. "Take a look at that," she demanded. "They are our people and they are dying. Korolev did that and he will escape before the infantry break through. I will not let that happen." She let him go and turned to her assistant. "Burn it down."

"Yes, ma'am," her assistant said, and he picked up the radio with a quivering hand.

***

Nobody is coming for me.

Emily Hartigan crept towards the wall and used her fingertips to climb to her feet. She leaned against the wall, her legs like rubber, and staggered forward. She wailed painfully and threw out her hand, falling to the floor.

The fires were spreading hungrily and Hartigan gritted her teeth, lurching to her knees. She stood up shakily, stumbling between piles of rubble and roaring flames, her head dizzy. A glowing sign hovered in the haze and she walked towards it, coughing violently and crashing into a door. She pushed the door open, a gust of cold wind swirling past her.

Hartigan staggered into the square outside the palace. She could hear popping sounds, like gunfire, and she could hear cries of pain. She ignored all of it, her eyes focused on a tank parked nearby, its rumbling engine luring her.

Bullets plinked off the tank's armour as the tracked vehicle retreated towards Red Square, the soldiers still firing at the *boyeviks* huddled against the palace walls.

Hartigan was suddenly lifted off her feet and looked up to see a soldier cradling her in his arms. He ran alongside the tank, flanked by soldiers who returned fire as they moved towards the fortress walls. The soldier yelled orders, shouting at his men to evacuate.

Hartigan let her head fall back, lolling numbly against the soldier's shoulder. Jet planes shrieked overhead and banked over the river, forming an attack column and turning towards the palace. Hartigan blinked, trying to make out the small triangular shapes against the velvet sky, and then the whole world went black.

***

Murphy inhaled sharply and rolled on to his stomach. "What took you so long?" he wheezed.

Elliot helped him to his feet. "Yeah, you're welcome."

"Oh, shut up," he grumbled.

"Our time's up," she said, letting Murphy prop himself against the wall.

"No," he said. "We have to stop Nikolay."

"But the elevator's just there," Elliot protested, jabbing the air with her thumb.

"Relax. I know where he is." He started limping along the hallway, turning back to see Elliot clutching her wrist and panting heavily. "You should quit smoking."

She opened her mouth to speak but the words caught in her throat. Something through the window caught her eye. It was moving low and fast.

She was ten feet away from him. There was nothing she could do.

The first aeroplane dropped its bomb short and it crashed into the square in front of the palace. The explosion shattered the windows on the second floor and threw shards of rock at the walls. The shrapnel crashed into the chandelier behind Murphy, showering him in hot metal, plaster, and crystal.

Elliot was bowled over by the shockwave. Her ears rang and she felt dizzy but she got up and dusted herself off. Murphy was lying on the marble floor. He wasn't moving.

"Stephen!" She ran over, sliding on her knees and stopping by his side. "Stephen!" she shouted. His eyes were closed and blood was pouring from his scalp. She ran her hands over his body to check for other wounds. "Oh, God, oh, God, be okay. Please be okay." She held her hands in front of her face: they were covered with his blood. "Stephen, wake up," she ordered, pinching his ear. She could feel her eyes stinging. "Oh, Stephen, please wake up," she breathed.

Elliot stood up and reached under his arms, the heels of her boots squeaking on the tiles as she dragged him towards the elevator. Her ribs tightened as if someone were standing on her chest. The tendons in her wrist went taut and she cried out in pain. They fell backwards into the elevator and she wriggled out from underneath him. She slammed the gate and slapped the lever, the cage lurching down towards the shelter.

Murphy's eyes were still closed. "Stephen!" She slapped him in the face. "Please, Stephen," she whimpered. "Stay."

The earth rumbled above them and the lights flickered. The elevator shuddered to a stop and Elliot staggered against the cage. She cursed and ripped open the elevator gate. It was dark and she couldn't see a thing.

The emergency lights blinked and warmed up, the cavernous shelter glowing dimly beneath her feet. They were level with the catwalk. It was only three metres away. Murphy groaned.

"Stephen, wake up," she said urgently. "Please." She heard the thud of bombs above them and the palace trembled.

"I'm all right, I'm here," he murmured.

"Get up, you sissy. We have to jump."

He sat up, wearily studying the catwalk. She helped him stand up, her body quivering with pain. The bombs thundered above them and dust rained from the ceiling. "You go first," she shouted over the barrage.

Murphy nodded and blinked, reaching out for the wall to keep his balance. He leaned back before leaping for the catwalk, and he landed feet first on the edge. He threw his leg over the railing and toppled on to the metallic walkway. Elliot jumped, her chest smashing into the handrail. Air rushed from her lungs. She slipped and threw her arms out in desperation.

Murphy grabbed her by the hand and she grasped on to his arm. She cried out, her muscles aching, her fingers numb, but Murphy pulled her on to the catwalk where she collapsed breathlessly beside him.

The jets screamed above them and the roof shuddered. More bombs pounded the earth and the elevator crashed to the floor of the shelter, shattering to pieces. The dam wall started to crack and the small streams of water turned into a torrent.

Murphy climbed to his knees and wiped blood from his forehead while Elliot tried to steady him. They limped towards the wall, the catwalk rattling beneath them, the support struts screeching under their weight. Murphy stumbled and fell, clattering on to the walkway and taking Elliot down with him.

"No!" Elliot cried. She reached under his arms and heaved with all she had left, gritting her teeth and straining her muscles. The water roared beneath them, pouring into the shelter, and stones rained down from the ceiling. She felt waves of pain roll through her body but she heaved one last time, yanking Murphy off the catwalk and on to the ledge. Boulders broke loose from the roof and crashed into the catwalk, the metal shrieking under the barrage as the walkway surrendered and plunged into the raging water.

Elliot straddled Murphy on the concrete ledge. His eyelids were heavy. "Stephen," she shouted. "We have to get out." She pointed to the vent shaft above them. "You have to climb."

He nodded weakly.

She knelt under his arm and wheezed, helping him up. They staggered forward and fell against the ladder. She felt the water lapping at her shins and held his hands against the rungs.

"You've got to climb, Stephen," she yelled, the water rushing around them.

They clung to the ladder and tried to reach for the next step but the water rose quickly, swallowing them up. The cold stole the air from their lungs and Murphy started drifting away. Elliot held on to him and clutched the ladder.

She started to shiver and pulled him close. His arms were around her waist but his grip was weak. The water foamed around them and washed over their heads. Elliot kicked desperately to keep Murphy's head above the surface, tugging on his clothes. She gulped down air and then felt the icy water drag them under. She kicked again and broke the surface, gasping and holding Murphy's mouth out of the water. The night sky seemed to be getting bigger and bigger above them but she could feel the life draining from her body, the pain numbing her, the air rasping in and out of her lungs. They were dragged underwater again and she struggled to keep her eyes open.

Then she felt weightless.

They crashed into the river and Elliot's eyes snapped open. She reached out for Murphy and held on to him tight, lashing out with her feet and fighting the pain and the cold, pulling on him to get him to the surface. She thrashed until she felt the cool night on her face and she gulped in a lungful of air.

57

MOSCOW, RUSSIA

MONDAY 19 SEPTEMBER

12:05AM MSK

Valentina Nevzorova studied Hartigan's bruised face and sighed heavily, stepping towards the head of the stretcher as the paramedics tended to the agent's wounds. Hartigan's clothes were torn and bloodied, her hands stained red, and blood dripped down her leg. Nevzorova gently stroked Hartigan's matted blonde hair, stopping when she saw something shining in the analyst's hands.

Nevzorova unfolded Hartigan's fingers and picked up the coin. "Korolev's dead," the president declared.

"That's his?" her assistant asked.

Nevzorova nodded, absently wiping it on her skirt.

He raised his eyebrows. "He was a coin collector?"

Nevzorova swept her hair away from her face and rolled the coin across the top of her hand. "Twenty years ago," she said, "Korolev was a small-time nightclub owner in Moscow who liked pop music and had contacts in the US entertainment industry. He also liked smoking marijuana. The state couldn't prove that he was a spy for the US, but they imprisoned him anyway as a part of their promise to rid the city of crime." She reached over Hartigan and pushed the coin back into the analyst's hand, folding her fingers gently. "It was a new regime with old habits."

Hartigan's eyelids flickered, her eyes slowly coming into focus, and she peered up at Nevzorova.

The President of Russia stroked the analyst's cheek. "Emily, how are you feeling?" she asked softly.

"I..." She blinked slowly. "I thought about what you said," Hartigan choked, "and I'm not sure if it's the right thing to do."

"Emily," Nevzorova murmured, "the difference between right and wrong is how much everyone is willing to live with." She brushed the hair from the agent's eyes. "Can *you* live with it?"

"But, what I did—"

"Was heroic," Nevzorova finished. "Korolev is dead. You helped save my country, and perhaps yours."

Hartigan's eyes fell.

"Rest, now, Emily," Nevzorova said. "I'll come and visit you in the hospital."

Hartigan opened her mouth to speak but changed her mind, nodding and looking away. Her eyes became heavy.

Nevzorova nodded to the paramedics and they pushed Hartigan's trolley into the back of the ambulance. The president went to leave.

"Madam President," her assistant called out. "The coin?"

Nevzorova paused, folding her arms across her chest. "It was a gift from a woman that loved him very much," she said, her eyes cold. "Of course, that was a long time ago, when he was a very different man." She turned away. "And she was a very different woman."

***

Elliot pressed down on Murphy's chest before blowing air into his mouth. "I need a doctor!" she yelled at the crowd.

The tenants from nearby apartment buildings had gathered on the street to watch the bombing of the Presidential Palace. When the dust had cleared, they had been confronted by Elliot struggling out of the Moscow River, dragging Murphy behind her. Two men had helped her pull him on to the pavement and she'd started CPR. Her lungs were still on fire and each breath rasped through her throat. "A doctor!" she wheezed hoarsely. "Please!"

"I'm a doctor," an elderly man said, stepping out of the crowd and kneeling beside Murphy.

Elliot continued pushing down on Murphy's chest, each compression sending a shot of pain up her arm. She couldn't stop. She refused to stop.

Don't go, Stephen. Stay. Stay.

"Please, Stephen, wake up," she begged, her voice cracking.

He coughed and spluttered, rolling on to his side and releasing a lungful of water on the pavement. He lay back gasping and Elliot collapsed on top of him, groaning in pain.

"Why don't you come inside?" the doctor said.

Elliot nodded and patted Murphy on the chest. He moaned and looked at her. "You scared the hell out of me," she said, smiling.

"Where am I?"

"With me," she said, touching his cheek.

He ran his hand through her hair and smiled before letting his head fall back to the pavement. Two men helped him to his feet and another grabbed Elliot, her legs wobbling beneath her. They helped them up the stairs and through the door of the apartment building.

58

MOSCOW, RUSSIA

MONDAY 19 SEPTEMBER

12:55AM MSK

Murphy's eyes opened and he stared at the mouldy ceiling above him. He was lying on a single bed that creaked on old springs. Elliot hunched forward in a wooden chair.

"Hey," he said.

"Hey." She reached out and touched his cheek. "How are you feeling?"

"Like I was hit by a train."

"You took a nasty hit to the head and split your scalp open. You bled everywhere but there's no concussion."

"Why can I taste strawberries?"

"That's my lip gloss."

"What did you do, give me a makeover?"

"You're lucky I did anything."

"Hey, I caught a bomb in my back."

"Now you're exaggerating."

"And my back was already cut and bruised, which—"

"Was your own fault. I remember, I was there."

"I'm just telling you what it feels like."

"You shouldn't feel anything. The doc pulled all the fragments out and numbed you up."

"Well, my leg hurts," he grumbled. "I got stabbed, you know."

Elliot gently squeezed his thigh with her hand and he groaned. "What about that? Does that hurt?"

"I don't think I did anything to deserve that."

"Oh, really? Let me give you a list." She started counting on her fingers. "I nearly drowned, I was attacked with an axe, shot at, took a shower in broken glass, got bombed by aeroplanes, and I nearly fell off the catwalk."

"An axe? Was I there for all of that?"

"You slept through a lot of it."

"It was a bit close, wasn't it?"

"Tell me about it. The water forced us through the vent shaft and we landed in the river. I dragged you to shore and we were lucky enough to land in a place where a doctor lived."

"All according to my brilliant plan."

"Nobody plays those odds."

"Not alone, they don't." He reached for her hand, weaving their fingers together. Her face softened. "Thanks, Slim."

She shrugged. "Hey, you saved me a couple of times. I think we're square."

"I never would've made it without you."

"Don't forget it, either," she said, smiling. "And you might want to send a thank-you card to Canberra, too."

"Why's that?"

"Nikolay's dead." She brushed the hair from her eyes. "He was killed by an Australian agent, a woman."

Murphy grunted and glanced away.

"The television won't shut up about it," Elliot continued, gesturing towards the living room behind the door. "I think she's going to get a medal from the president."

His eyes glazed over.

"Hey." She poked him in the ribs. "Did you hear me?"

Murphy shifted on the pillow and sighed heavily. "I need to tell you something," he murmured.

"No, you need to rest."

"It's important, Simone. I lied to you."

Her face crumbled but she tried to smile again. "Look, let's not do this—"

"No, please," he said. "I have to tell you. It's eating me up."

"What is it?" she croaked.

He lifted her chin so she was looking into his eyes. "I've always really liked your cooking."

Elliot grinned.

"You always score points off me and I just needed some ammunition so I chose that," he said. "I'm sorry."

"You owe me so big."

"I thought you said we were square?"

"A holiday. Somewhere warm."

"How am I going to afford that? I'm unemployed."

"Get some rest." She kissed him on the forehead and stood up. "I'm going to give the doctor more money so we don't end up in jail."

59

160 KILOMETRES SOUTHWEST OF BRISBANE, AUSTRALIA

SATURDAY 4 MARCH

4:06PM AEST

Stephen Murphy leaned against the bonnet of the car and closed his eyes briefly. The sun tickled his face and he smiled. The magpies squawked in the eucalypts and swooped to the ground to peck at the earth. Cows lumbered through the swaying grass, flicking their tails to shoo away the flies, and a dog yelped at them through a crooked barbed wire fence. The dog trotted up to Murphy, its tongue hanging out as it panted. Murphy patted its head and its tail wagged.

He sighed and looked at the clouds on the horizon. The closest had bulging grey stomachs and were topped with fuzzy white fronds. Behind them, he could see the gloom of an approaching storm. The sky flashed over the mountains and the thunder rumbled across the earth, rattling the windshield of the car.

The dog dropped a soggy tennis ball at his feet and stared at him longingly. Murphy crouched to pick up the ball and the dog's tail wagged, its eyes twinkling.

"Run, fella," he said, tossing the ball. The dog barked and yelped, skidding through the gravel and kicking up dust. "You're free," he murmured.

"Talking to the animals, huh," Simone Elliot said from behind him.

He turned and smirked. "They don't talk back."

She stuck her tongue out.

"How much was the fuel?" he asked.

"We're doing okay," she said. "Stop worrying about the money."

"If we had nothing to worry about, you'd have an armful of chocolate bars."

"Relax. I found us a job."

He glanced at the service station. "Please tell me you're not going into customer service, because that would be—"

"Shut up." She pouted and smacked him on the shoulder. "It's a contract job. I checked my email while I was waiting in line."

Murphy looked down when he realised the dog was at his feet again. "Where?"

"Romania."

He squatted, the dog dropped the ball and nudged it towards him with its nose. "You think the world's ready for us?"

"We've been hiding long enough," she said. "Sooner or later they're going to work out we're still alive. But if you don't want to do it..."

"Hey, I didn't say that. A man's got to eat."

Murphy picked up the ball and scratched the dog behind the ear.

You're not free at all, are you, fella.

Murphy gazed at the tennis ball.

This is all you know.

Elliot frowned. "Something on your mind?"

He threw the ball again and watched the dog chase after it. "Is the job a good one?"

"Challenging."

"As in, we could die?"

Elliot kissed him on the cheek and turned on her heels, marching towards the driver's-side door.

"You're not going to get very far without..." His voice trailed off as he patted his pockets.

Elliot held the keys in the air, jingling them vigorously.

"So it's like that, huh."

"Oh, I almost forgot." Elliot lobbed his wallet over the roof of the car. "You probably want that back." She climbed in, turning the key in the ignition.

Murphy stuffed his wallet into his pocket and grinned, looking down at the dog waiting patiently at his feet. He picked up the ball, tossing it in the air and catching it again. "We are what we are, aren't we, fella?" He hurled the ball far away, the dog barking excitedly as he ran after it. "And we do what we do." Murphy shook his head in surrender and climbed into the car.

She mashed the buttons on the GPS. "How does this thing work, anyway?"

"Just shout 'Romania' at it," he suggested. "The car will figure it out."

Elliot threw the GPS over her shoulder. "How hard could it be, right?" She put the car in gear and drove on to the highway, heading towards the thundering clouds.

ACKNOWLEDGEMENTS

To Mum and Dad: thank you for filling our home with books and stories and laughter; thank you for letting me own my successes as well as my mistakes. To Dad: thanks for reading so many drafts and answering the phone when I wanted to talk about them. To Mum: thanks for stubbornly resisting the urge to read my story until it was in the shops—it's one of the things that kept me going.

To John Acutt: to me, you're a Promethean figure, a great teacher who opened up a world of words and ideas. Dedicating this book to you is the least I can do—you started this, after all.

To Sarah Gleeson-White: I'm grateful that you made time for me. Thank you for your advice, your support, and for pointing me in the right direction. I'd also like to thank Bruce Bennett for taking the time to read my earliest manuscript and give his feedback.

Thank you to those who have read drafts of my story and shared their thoughts at various stages: Ian Gibson, Amye Petersen, Rob Hack, Angela Jennison, Shaun Jennison, and Julie Greenwood. To Sarah and Gary Donaldson, and Lisa and Zac Cummins: thank you for reading my stories, and a big thank you for opening up your homes, sharing your thoughts and ideas, your scotch and cigarettes, and feeding me delicious home-cooked meals. Thank you all.

To Deonie Fiford: thank you for your sharp editing—you raised great points, made brilliant suggestions, and it has made me a better writer.

To the superheroes at Pantera Press, Alison, Marty, and John M. Green: thank you for believing in me and this story. I'm grateful for your patience, your professionalism, your passion, your humour, your encouragement, your ideas, and your understanding. To Lucy Bell and James Read: I'm grateful for your sharp eyes and fearless questions. And to the rest of the team at Pantera Press: thanks for all you've done to make this story a book, and this mechanic an author.

To the reader: to you, most of all, thank you.

GRAHAM POTTS

War defines the first decade of Graham Potts' adult life. Always on the move, he has lived in almost every state in Australia. After challenging assignments with the Royal Australian Air Force, his inner strategist acknowledged the truth: writing is his true passion. His action-packed style throws you into international conflicts closer to home than you think. Graham has a fondness for literature and an appetite for intrigue. He tells stories that captivate, thrill and touch on the truth. And if you buy him a scotch, he might tell you a tall one or two.

Printed in Great Britain
by Amazon